WINDS OF DECEPTION

ENIGMA SERIES VOL. II

Tierney James

Paperback-Press
an imprint of A & S Publishing
A & S Holmes, Inc.

ISBN -10: 0692447784
ISBN-13: 978-0692447789

DEDICATION

Dedicated to the brave men who served on the
USS Liberty on June 8, 1967

For More Information
The History Channel: Cover-up: Attack on the USS Liberty
Dead In The Water – Visit www.usslibertyveterans.org

CONTENTS

ACKNOWLEDGMENTS

Bryce Lockwood – Thank you for your service on the USS Liberty and for bringing this fantastic story to my attention. I am deeply appreciative of your kindness and patience with all of my questions.

Mary Pat Kelley Tierney – You are one awesome ER/Nurse Practitioner. Without your help I couldn't have stopped the bleeding or saved important lives.

Dr. Candace Detchon – Not only can you be my eyes in D.C. but help me get in the heads of my characters. Dr. Wu of Enigma appreciates the assistance as do I.

Kelly Rear – Your technical support and advice helped me out of many tight spots.

Meghan Fanning – Without your editing skills I'd still be stuck on trying to figure out what went wrong. Your first round edits were painful and necessary. I'm glad you know the characters almost as well as me.

Shirley McCann – By the time you got Winds of Deception for last round edits I had begun to wonder if I'd ever see the manuscript completed. With your keen eye and encouragement I forged ahead. Thank you for your continued support, kindness and love of all things Captain Chase Hunter.

Patricia Wilkerson – I think every author needs a cheerleader. You are always there for me when I need a Beta reader or someone to bounce an idea around. Promoting me and my work has almost become a full time job for you. Thank you for your love and support over the years.

Sharon Kizziah-Holmes – Thank you for not booting me out the door with all my questions. In spite of being my publisher on this project you've become a dear friend. I so appreciate your patience and ideas concerning bringing this project to completion.

CHARACTERS IN THE ENIGMA SERIES

1. Tessa Scott – Begins her adventures with Enigma after coming in contact with Libyan terrorists in An Unlikely Hero. Continues to stumble into trouble with Enigma.

2. Captain Chase Hunter – Former Delta Force Captain. Team leader for Enigma. Works for the military and the President of the United States when called upon to serve.

3. Director Benjamin Clark – Head of Enigma

4. Carter Johnson – Former astronaut turned Enigma agent

5. Samantha Cordova – Professor of Economics and agent at Enigma

6. Vernon Kemp – Works as tech support at Enigma

7. Nicholas Zoric – Former Serbian assassin who specializes in interrogation for Enigma

8. Dr. Wu – Psychiatrist for Enigma teams

9. President Buck Austin – President of the United States

10. Vice President Warren McCall – Vice President of the United States

11. Tobias Stewart – Secretary of Homeland Security

12. First Sergeant Tom Cooper – A Marine that is called upon to assist Enigma

13. Sergeant Ken Montgomery – Army Ranger that is called upon to assist Enigma

14. Gilad Levi – Prime Minister of Israel

15. Dov Kemper – Director of Mossad

16. Jake Wakefield – Tessa's uncle

17. Jim Gault – Speaker of the House

18. Amon – Egyptian

19. Dr. Francis Ervin – Biblical archeologist for Enigma

20. Martha Francis – Married to Dr. Francis Ervin – Freelancer for Enigma

21. Robert Scott – Married to Tessa Scott

22. Sean Patrick, Daniel, Heather – Children of Tessa Scott

23. John Elliott – Secret Service Agent

24. Dr. M.P. Kelley – Personal physician to the president

25. Peggy McCall – Wife of the Vice President

26. Micah & Ari – Bodyguards for the Prime Minister of Israel

27. Carman – Special friend of the Speaker of the House

28. Daniel – Secretary to the Prime Minister of Israel

29. Four Liberty crew members captured:
    a. Mel Stark
    b. Carl Robbins
    c. Johnny Simon
    d. Mike Strafford

30. Shelly & Kate – Best friends of Tessa Scott

PROLOGUE

June 8, 1967

The Mediterranean Sea grew choppy the morning the USS Liberty sailed eastward, like an innocent child walking toward a predator lying in wait for its next victim. Because it failed to receive at least five warning messages crew and officers dressed casually in tropical or dungarees attire expecting a non-eventful day. In spite of a war raging between Israel and Egypt a little more than a dozen miles away, a few enlisted men planned to do some sunbathing before they took up their posts. The jovial mood among the men came from arguing over who would be first at the soda fountain that evening when it opened at 6:00 P.M.

Duty Officer Mel Stark admired the sunrise when an Israeli plane came out of nowhere. It circled the ship several times before heading in the direction of Tel Aviv. The USS Liberty was an American General Technical Research Vessel, but those down below, where the listeners of secrets worked diligently, identified the plane as an ally.

After looking up, Mel turned to Jake Wakefield, a Russian language interpreter brought on board in Spain. "What the heck is he doing here?"

"Making sure the Russkies aren't helping out the Rabs, I guess." Jake frowned lifting his hand to wave to the pilot. "Don't like it. Can't trust those guys."

"Ahh!" Mel waved him off. "The commander worried we

were too close to shore. That on board NSA officer wouldn't hear of moving farther out to sea. Convinced the commander it would compromise their mission."

Jake nodded. "We wouldn't be able to get an ultra-high-frequency range. Guess that's why we've been doing a back-and-forth patrol of the Sinai coast. This is pretty shallow water."

Mel chuckled. "You spies don't trust anyone. Israel is our friend. We've got nothing to hide."

Johnny Simon rushed up and handed the duty officer and Jake a slip of paper. Catching the last few words of their conversation, he chimed in then turned his eyes skyward. "No. But the Israelis sure do." He watched Jake's frown deepen as his eyes scanned the contents.

"Says here the Israelis are killing Egyptians by the hundreds. Their orders are to bury them in the sand dunes near El Arish." Jake reread the information, shocked at the brutality.

Inhaling the fresh sea air, the duty office looked upward at the American flag waving in the twelve knot breeze. The deceptive calm of the morning failed to prepare them for the assault coming to cripple and nearly sink an American vessel.

Jake hurried to his station below deck to listen in on Israeli secrets. Not only could he speak fluent Russian, his Arabic wasn't bad either. He listened in horror at the reports coming in from Egyptian transmissions.

"Holy Mother of God." Jake jumped to his feet.

The commander stopped as he navigated the close quarters. "What is it? You look like you've seen a ghost."

Jake touched the headphones as if continuing to listen before addressing the senior officer. "The Israelis just gut shot a bunch of soldiers that surrendered. They had been hiding in the desert. Came in because of thirst. The Israelis poured water into the sand then let'em have it."

"You heard wrong." The commander spoke forcefully, afraid of the alternative.

Jake yanked off the headphones. "Has there been any other Israeli planes fly over, sir?"

The commander chewed the inside of his lip. "Little while ago a plane circled the Liberty. The crew waved and the pilot returned the gesture. He flew so low I thought he might clip the masts of the

ship. Star of David was clearly visible."

"Commander?" Another crewman shouted. "Heard some chatter. Can't understand it though. Let Jake have a crack at it."

The commander nodded toward Jake.

"It's some Israeli officials, I don't know who, discussing that an American spy ship is just off shore." Jake listened more intently. "I think they want to sink us."

The commander dropped his hands as his fists started to open and close. "What the hell for? We're no threat to Israel?"

"Couldn't get it all, sir, but it sounds like the Israelis started this war, not the Egyptians like we first thought. If that's true President Johnson won't be throwing any tax dollars their way, not with the Russians itching for a fight. They'd throw in with the Egyptians and bang! Nukes would start raining down everywhere. Israel wants to look like the victim so the United Nations won't condemn their actions. We've got it on tape."

"Meaning?" The commander already started to move toward the ladder that led to the deck.

"They're planning to sink us and destroy the evidence."

The American president liked a good fight but only if he could bet on the winner. His Jewish background, unknown to most Americans, had him squarely in their court. Jake realized nothing must change the president's high opinion of Israel.

The explosion jarred him right down to his very core. They were under attack from the very nation that claimed to be an ally. His skin burned as fire swept through the room. Water gushed in when the USS Liberty began to list. Several men already floated face down in the murky water. In spite of his burns, Jake grabbed his buddy, lifting him over his shoulder to carry him up on deck.

Another trip down in the bowels of the ship exposed more dead. The man who had first brought Jake information of Israeli treachery, screamed as he clutched his shattered arm. Just as Jake reached him another explosion rocked the ship. Without a thought for his own life, he lifted the seaman in his arms. Struggling to reach the ladder, he heard the hatch slam shut. As he reached the top step, Jake yelled for help. The water rose higher. Jake laid his friend in the rising water, careful to keep his hand on the man's chest.

After banging his fist on the hatch for several minutes, the creak of rescue opened a path for escape. Men pulled Jake and another from what threatened to be a watery grave.

The attack continued for over an hour. Just as quickly as they appeared, the Israelis vanished. The USS Liberty learned later the Israelis intercepted a message from the Destroyer Squadron 12. The USS Davis and USS Massey arrived the following day near sunrise. A Russian destroyer appeared around midnight, standing by in case assistance was required.

Even after Jake stood on the deck of the Liberty, surveying the damage, he realized if they had been in deeper water the Israelis would have sunk them. Every man on board suffered some kind of injury.

Thirty-four dead.

In the days that followed, a cover-up of monumental proportions erased the atrocities Israel committed against the United States of America.

Israel failed to take into consideration one man might survive to take revenge.

That man was Jake Wakefield.

CHAPTER 1

Glass shattered when a bullet penetrated the mountain cabin window where Tessa tried to hide the last two days. A gust of fifteen degree wind followed by puffs of icy snow, burst into the room as if needing more space to pile its merciless whisper of a cold death. When she tried to find cover, the wet snow matted to her boots, and sent her sprawling into her partner's bleeding body on the floor.

He'd taken the bullet as he pushed her out of harm's way. Frantic, Tessa covered his body with hers when more rounds of an automatic weapon pulverized the upper wall over the fireplace, sending debris into the flames, flickering light into the otherwise dark room. Knowing the moment of payback had arrived, she slid her hand down to the SIG rifle. Her partner, Chase Hunter, taught her how to use it the day before. She felt his firm grip on her wrist. Because she wasn't an agent like him and the others on his team, fear caused her hand to shake. After all the times Chase had rescued her, she couldn't let him down because of a lack of training.

"Tess, I want to tell you something." He started to cough. His camouflaged shirt now covered in blood warned of no tomorrows. "About you. The way I feel."

Just then the door of the cabin exploded inward. Tessa lifted the SIG and rolled to a sitting position as three men in goggles and white down suits rushed in. Without hesitation her finger met the trigger, knowing the weapon would deliver the accuracy she needed to end this nightmare. Men gasping for a last breath and landing like bombs against unsteady furniture sounded like music to Tessa's ears, with the realization this nightmare had concluded one more time.

Like the other times, she would lower her weapon, before kneeling down next to him. Looking into his dark eyes, she watched as he stared at something in another time, another place.

It always ended this way. "Chase, don't leave me. I need you."

"Come closer."

Lowering her ear to his lips, now blue with the coming of death, the words never varied. "I'm here."

"You need to buckle your seatbelt."

"What?" she said incredulously as her head jerked upward.

A hand touched her shoulder. "Mrs. Scott, we are about to land. You need to buckle your seatbelt." A soft, comforting voice of a mature flight attendant caused her to startle awake.

Tessa shot a worried glance at the other passengers. Had she talked in her sleep? No one seemed to be giving her a second look when she buckled up, then ran her fingers through tangled curls. Aware of sleep drool on the corner of her mouth, she licked her lips then swiped away the moisture.

Embarrassment at the dream forced the march of red up her neck and onto her face just as the flight attendant came by once more for a final check. The dream sequence occurred often over the last year.

The attendant's concern added a layer of discomfort. "Are you alright, Mrs. Scott? You look a little feverish."

She scooted lower into her seat.

The bulky man sitting next to her started to rub his face and neck, as if he were preparing for a big race. He prevented her efforts at becoming invisible by stretching his arms forward then up over his head. She recognized the California congressman when he yawned. With exaggeration he flipped his tray into place before dropping his plastic Bloody Mary cup into the trash bag offered him by a second flight attendant. This one, much younger than the first, leaned over Tessa.

She paused a little too long, bestowing a brilliant smile down at the lawmaker. The trash bag dangled against Tessa's knees. She tried to move the bag from touching her to no avail. Continuing to lean in toward the congressman, the attendant flirted a moment longer.

The pilot's voice began to inform the passengers of weather conditions in D.C. A chill started up her spine as the voice continued with a litany of information. No one paid much attention to the announcements except for her.

The voice, familiar in a disturbing way, did more than catch her undivided attention. "Excuse me." Tessa caught hold of the trash bag, drawing the attendant's eyes to meet hers. "Did we stop along the way?"

"St. Louis. You were asleep." The attendant shifted her eyes back to the congressman then offered a playful wink.

Sheepishly, Tessa leaned out over her arm rest to look down toward the locked door of the cabin where the pilot resided. The flight attendants busied themselves with stowing the last bit of clutter away before buckling themselves in for landing. She twisted her body to look down the aisle toward the back of the plane.

Her eyes glanced off the passengers to reassure herself friends of the voice on the overhead speakers were not hiding in plain sight amongst innocent travelers. Had she been so asleep when they stopped in St. Louis that she might have missed a familiar face board the plane?

Tessa straightened back into her seat with a loud sigh when a large hand patted her arm.

She frowned at the congressman and withdrew her arm from his touch. "Worried about landing?" His breath reeked of alcohol. He didn't appear to notice her contempt. "I take this flight all the time. Never a problem." He rolled his eyes upward then made an effort to straighten his suit coat. "Of course, I usually fly first class. This has been a little trying." He extended his legs out further, enjoying the extra space behind the first class section.

The concern for her anxiety was misplaced; the truth being she loved flying. In spite of having a fear of heights, the feeling of flight enhanced her senses; the roar of engines, the lifting of the landing gear and even the occasional bump during wind turbulence. The rapid exhilaration of speed, sending her back against the seat usually filled her with euphoria.

After hearing the captain's voice a deep concern materialized.

The voice of the pilot sounded enough like Carter Johnson,

one of the agents she'd met a year earlier, to cause paranoia. Could hearing the intercom voice when she slept activate memories of her past with a secret organization called Enigma?

Against her will, Tessa had been forced into a national security emergency. She used her skills as a geographer to thwart an impending attack in northern California. Shrouded in mystery and funded by unknown benefactors, Enigma did the work other government agencies felt might get their hands dirty.

Closing her eyes she felt the landing gear lower.

The probability of Carter flying this plane bordered on impossible. Even though he must have better things to do, she imagined the ex-astronaut flying the plane. Yet there could be no mistake in recognizing the voice. If he flew the plane chances were he'd had sex with one of the flight attendants somewhere over the Ohio River Valley. In spite of herself, she smiled.

The notorious playboy had been one of Captain Chase Hunter's team members in their mission to save an isotope plant. A former astronaut would not be flying a passenger plane to D.C., she reasoned. He had access to faster toys at an unmarked hangar at Sacramento International Airport. An overactive imagination must be out of control. Again.

Fighting the compulsion, to once again dwell on thoughts of Captain Hunter, Tessa realized he'd haunted her dreams since the week he'd burst into her home and saved her; the first of many times over the days that followed. What would have become of her if Enigma hadn't sent him to intervene? The mysterious agents vanished from her life as quickly as they'd crashed into it.

Sometimes she wondered if it had all been a dream; like the one she conjured up several nights a week. A bomb nearly forced her death along with the capture and torture of her neighbor. The events catapulted her into the secret battle against terrorism. Caught in a forest fire, Tessa died for a full three minutes before the captain revived her. There were other events during those days; an assassin tracking her family, assisting a hostage who went into labor at a most inconvenient time and her own capture by a terrorist named Essid.

None of those moments woke her in the middle of the night with guilt and uncertainty. The memory of waking up in the captain's arms in total bliss now consumed her each night. That scene played over and over, sweaty bodies tangled as one, large hands pulling through her hair and the strength of something wild and wonderful saving her every night.

Just like the dream where the captain died in her arms, the romantic interlude never occurred. She suffered from a guilty conscience for something she'd never experienced. There had been no love making resembling wild abandonment. The captain, tired of sleeping on the floor, slipped into the king size bed after she'd fallen asleep. Somewhere between darkness and dawn, Tessa found herself wrapped in his warm arms against the freezing temperature of the air conditioner he'd cranked on high.

Not very romantic, she reasoned.

Captain Hunter, a gentleman to the end, remained aloof and protective as his mission pulled her into unknown danger. Only when they'd said their goodbyes did she sense their emotional connection. He strode out of her life like a ghostly aberration, never to be heard from again.

"You are the bravest woman I've ever known." His words, strong and sincere, haunted her even today.

People began to rise from their seats. Overhead bins snapped open and the sound of bags being dragged out with an occasional "excuse me" reached her ears. Clicks of laptop covers, shuffle of feet and grunts of maneuvering out of narrow seats filled the cabin. Before she could stand, the congressman pushed up and over her, reaching for the carryon bag the flirty flight attendant extended to him.

She stood to block the other passengers for him. He put his hand on her hip with a smile. A whisper and a nod spoke of something later between the two. A business card palmed into her long, slim fingers appeared to close the deal as the congressman moved away toward first class and off the plane. Grumbling accelerated the throng of travelers forward.

The urgency to exit evaporated when Tessa decided to hang back to catch a glimpse of the pilot. What if it really were the unapologetic playboy from NASA? Carter would be shocked to see her, maybe even a little pleased. The man was a romantic scoundrel drawn to any pretty face and a few curves. She'd idolized the accomplishments of his work at NASA for years, nothing more.

The thought of Chase also being on board heightened her awareness of those exiting. She stole another look back down the aisle. Imagining him in a camo jacket, he might hold a copy of *Anna Karina.* The ear buds of his IPod funneled music of Chris Botti into his ears. She liked to envision him with longer hair, ebony and thick, even though he usually wore it short. His head would be bowed over the words as he occasionally let his hand slip inside his jacket to reassure himself the nine millimeter weapon was secure and ready for action.

Disgusted at fantasizing about a man who took great delight in giving orders, the memories returned of how he saved her life numerous times. He deserved a little respect, she reasoned as she edged out into the aisle with her backpack. Wouldn't a man like that have better things to do than fly commercial? Wouldn't he be actively saving the world from itself or something?

Finally she could stand straight feeling the weight of her backpack. A slight twinge in her shoulder caused Tessa to wrinkle her nose. The flight attendant by the door glanced at her watch hinting at impatience. It was the woman who had taken the congressman's card. Tessa wondered if they were meeting sooner rather than later.

Their eyes met only for a moment before Tessa diverted her attention to an older gentleman having difficulties with his carry-on bag in front of her. An exasperated sigh escaped as if some great tragedy had occurred. Tessa grinned. She helped him shift it to move smoothly toward the exit.

The gentleman tipped his old fashioned tweed hat then offered a smile which looked too small for his chubby face. He stopped then straightened his tie. "Thank you, young lady. I'm afraid my wife packed more in this carry-on than I realized. It doesn't seem to want to roll very well. Sorry I'm holding you up."

Tessa's eyes left the cockpit door as it swung open. "It's all right. Here, let me square it up a bit. There." Tessa reached down and adjusted it again. "The wheels may need a little W-D 40 when you have time. Looks like you've put a few miles on it." Tessa now followed him taking baby steps.

The gentleman chuckled then continued in a Bostonian accent. "Oh my, yes. I should just have Martha buy a new one but I'm rather attached to this old thing. Martha's my wife." He pulled at ears that reminded her of Dumbo. He bowed toward her with an extended hand. "I'm Dr. Francis Ervin. I'm in D.C. for the World Geographic Conference."

The backpack began to slip off her shoulder as she reached for his hand. The weight made her grimace, but managed to raise her shoulder suddenly to keep the bag from falling across her extended arm. He quickly reached out to assist with the shove of her backpack onto her shoulder. "Sorry," she said grasping his hand, noting that it was calloused and tan, unlike most professors she'd known. "I'm Tessa Scott. I'm here for the conference too." She nodded toward the front which brought his attention back to exiting.

"Oh," he said moving clumsily forward once more. "Are you a presenter?" His bushy gray eyebrows lifted in curiosity.

Tessa laughed at the thought. "No. I'm an attendee. My two colleagues should have landed an hour ago. We couldn't all get on the same flight. Our grant didn't cover all the expenses. We took whatever was cheaper." Another passenger in front of the plane now complained about something that occurred during the flight drawing her eyes to the cockpit then back to the professor.

"What is your presentation? Maybe I can drop by." Tessa didn't want to promise in case the session might involve a new textbook promotion or something like *"Isotherms and the Classroom."* She felt drowsy just thinking about it.

The professor cleared his throat. "I'm a Biblical Archeologist. I'll be helping teachers set up an archeological dig for their classroom. I also offer trips to the Holy Land for graduate credit in another session. There are grants available if that is something you'd be interested in. Are you a geographer?" He stopped moving even though no one was ahead of him.

Tessa's heart leaped. "Yes, I'm interested and I am a geographer. This is amazing. Count on me attending both your sessions."

Traveling to the Holy Land someday where her Christian faith sprouted along with Judaism and Islam, never failed to spark a desire to explore. Meeting this man could only mean that once again God must be stirring up her life. She wouldn't fight fate. An excitement bubbled up inside her.

First the dream of the captain dying in her arms, the voice of

Carter Johnson, and now this man suggesting a trip to the Holy Land might be possible. Was God about to play another cruel joke on her?

The sound of someone clearing their throat drew both passengers' attention to the flight attendant. "Guess we better get going," she whispered. "I think she has a date."

The professor nodded enthusiastically and started forward. "Right." He offered a smile to the young woman. "So sorry, dear." His voice remained pleasant. "Nice flight. Thank you so much." Tessa noticed the plastic smile and nod of unconcern on the attendant's face.

She stopped in front of the flight attendant. "Is the pilot still on board? I thought I knew him."

The woman's smile started to fade a bit. "Sorry. He just left."

Tessa noticed the professor made his way into the exit tunnel. "Maybe I'll catch up with him." Before the flight attendant could respond she slipped out of the plane and easily overtook the professor. "Did you see the pilot by any chance?" she asked looking ahead of her.

"Why no, Ms. Scott. Problem?" His concern showed.

"No. Just thought I..." She didn't finish when he turned his eyes on her in bewilderment. "It's nothing."

She tried to breeze past him when his bag tilted, preventing a quick escape. Entering the airport Dr. Ervin stopped, blocking her way once again. Scanning the throngs of people who arrived or waited for flights dashed hopes of seeing Carter.

Tessa hadn't asked the flight attendant the name of the pilot. Chances were good Carter used an alias. The president might frown on his fair-haired boy letting the general public know what he was up to.

Dr. Ervin touched her arm. "Here's my card, Ms. Scott. I hope to see you at the conference and thank you for your assistance on the plane." He tipped his tan hat revealing a bald head.

"Thank you, Dr. Ervin." She glanced down at the card. It wasn't anything fancy; white with black lettering on heavy cardstock. Without reading the information, Tessa shoved it into the still unzipped top of her backpack. "See you soon." She smiled before pulling a cell phone from the side pocket of her backpack.

~~~

The professor watched Tessa stride off, scanning the crowd for someone she recognized. He heard the theme song of Indiana Jones and the Last Crusade coming from his cell phone. His wife had downloaded the ringtone for him just a few days earlier. The choice made him chuckle.

"Hello." He said drily, having lost the jovial tone in his voice. "Yes. She just left." He could still see Tessa Scott with her cell phone to her ear, stopping occasionally to look into terminal shops for someone. "You didn't tell me Tessa Scott was such an enchanting creature." He listened to the voice on the other end of the phone. "The business card I gave her will jam her phone for the next twenty minutes. That should be plenty of time for you." The call ended before the phone ended up in the pocket of his jacket.

~~~

For the tenth time Tessa looked down at the information her friends, Shelly and Kate, had given her before they departed earlier in the morning. The overhead monitors, full of information concerning arrivals and departures, led her to believe they should be waiting for her. She wasted nearly a half hour searching for them. But they were nowhere to be found and they weren't picking up their phones.

She'd given up on finding Carter. Maybe he had been a figment of her imagination. Dreams conjured up Captain Hunter of Enigma. Now she felt silly thinking the possibility someone like Carter would be flying her to Washington D.C.

Tessa dialed again, wondering why her phone dropped each call. Whatever was keeping her from contacting her friends for the last twenty minutes suddenly disappeared. This time someone picked up. "Shelly. Thank heavens. Where are you?" Spinning around her eyes searched for friends to magically appear. "A bar." Taking a deep breath she rolled her eyes upward to keep from sounding irritated. "Seriously, couldn't you wait until tonight?"

In the end knowing her two friends liked their fancy drinks and a good time forced her to smile. They jumped at the chance to come on this trip with Tessa, even though they knew her 'good girl' image might spoil their fun. The three of them were best friends at work.

"Okay. I'll be right there. Don't wander off." Tessa folded the paper slipping both it and the phone back in the front pocket of the backpack.

Racing down Terminal B, she found The Chamber Bar and Grill in quick order. There, sitting at the bar laughing and sipping on colorful drinks were her friends. Tessa couldn't help but grin as she came up to them, dumping her things on a bar stool.

"Got an early start, I see. What am I going to do with you two? Those drinks are expensive."

Shelly lifted hers up to toast with Kate. "Nope.They were free."

"Free? You expect me to believe they're giving drinks away?" Tessa saw the female bartender approach. "Ice tea?" She nodded and went off to fill Tessa's order.

"Tea. Honestly, Tessa you are as interesting as a bag of cotton balls." Shelly growled with great fanfare.

She laughed, taking the tea from the bartender. Hurling insults was Shelly's way of showing friendship. "Yes these drinks were free. A good looking pilot strolled in and said 'you ladies look thirsty.'"

Kate nodded. "He'll be right back. Said he needed to make a call to an old friend he saw on the plane."

A chill of nervous anticipation forced her hand to tremble. She sat the tea down gingerly when her cell phone chimed. Lifting it to her ear, Tessa felt panic engulf her as the voice spoke on the other end of the line. "Hello, Tessa. Remember me?"

Turning to stare out the glass windows of the bar, Tessa did a quick scan of the travelers moving in the corridor. The voice remained quiet as if he were waiting for her to reassure herself. Some twenty feet from the bar, a pilot stood with his back to her holding a cell phone to his ear. Standing in front of him was a woman. She looked to be wearing a TSA uniform but Tessa couldn't be sure.

He spoke again after the woman's lips moved near his ear. "You've found me. Good. I'm sure you're surprised. You were sleeping like a baby when I boarded in St. Louis."

Words remained paralyzed on the back of her tongue. She

could see the TSA woman lean forward and whisper something as he covered the phone.

"Who is it, Tess? Robert checking up on you?" Shelly turned to Kate. "He must be afraid we'll corrupt her." She laughed loud enough for others to look their way.

A nod followed by an eye roll made her friends moan. "That's right, Robert. I'm here safe and sound."

A chuckle came through on the phone. "You're here, but I'm not sure how safe and sound you're going to be." The pilot remained with his back to her. "The captain wants to see you about a matter."

Tessa faked a laugh. "I'm pretty busy so you're going to have to make other arrangements."

"He'll be in touch. I might add you're looking extremely lovely today."

The pilot shoved his phone in his pants' pocket before nonchalantly walking away toward an exit. His companion remained, staring at Tessa with a smug grin on her face. Raising her hand to form a gun with her index finger and thumb, she proceeded with an imaginary shot toward her. Dropping her hands to her side, the female Enigma agent disappeared into the crowd.

Every nerve ending in her body began setting off alarm bells. She realized the female Enigma agent might be the death of her.

CHAPTER 2

The prime minister of Israel, Gilad Levi disembarked from his private jet. It was only the second time it had been in service since its purchase. The Mossad, his protection detail, had made a compelling case for its purchase after the last prime minister ran into trouble when he'd traveled to the United States.

Two years earlier, after landing at JFK Airport, protocol dictated that weapons be checked through in their luggage and transferred with the prime minister to Washington D.C. Unfortunately the four 9mm semi-automatics and three Glock17s never arrived.

The Pelican cases, which carried the weapons, had been inspected, according to directives established by Homeland Security, in front of the security guards to reassure them. Three days later the empty cases were located at the Los Angeles Airport. Without further inspection they traveled back to Washington D.C. only to end up in O'Hare Airport outside Chicago. The FBI took possession at that time and realized the weapons had been removed. They were never found, forcing the Israeli security detail to let the Secret Service protect their prime minister.

Gilad walked with purpose down the steps of his jet at the urging of his bodyguards. Two of those men, in their mid-thirties, looked as if they should be playing for the NFL. Their bodies, toned and hard from strenuous exercise, tensed as the prime minister disembarked. The third bodyguard walked a breath in front of the prime minister. He towered above the five foot eleven

Israeli Prime Minister by several inches.

Although covered in dark glasses, their eyes moved rapidly to survey their surroundings, looking for dangers that would take the life of Gilad Levi. The Secret Service formed another perimeter outside the plane and they too scanned the area for trouble. No matter that the prime minister wore a Kevlar vest under his bullet proof suit; a sniper could easily make a head shot, eliminating one of the United States most powerful and faithful allies. The president's limousine, known as The Beast, waited conspicuously on the tarmac not far from the plane.

Gilad slowed his pace only a fraction as the door of the limo opened and a tall, familiar man emerged from the backseat. Dressed in a black suit, he looked very much like the other American Secret Service agents that began to back toward the limo. He knew the agent to be a formidable death sentence for anyone who threatened the president or the United States.

This man stood six foot one, maybe two, with closely cropped black hair. The good looks of a man with some undetermined ethnic heritage, made you forget that, at least for part of the year, he taught French literature to students at a small university in Sacramento. It amazed him that this hardened ex-Delta Force officer could be content reading anything by the gutless French. His tanned skin looked darker on such a cloudy day.

The wide mouth showed no expression as his eyes scanned the horizon in anticipation of danger. Dark glasses covered what the prime minister knew to be almond shaped eyes which were often narrowed in observation. Even though they were the color of chocolate, Gilad witnessed them turn black with rage on several occasions.

He trusted the man with his life. Benjamin Clark, Director of Enigma, as well as President Buck Austin considered Captain Chase Hunter the ultimate line drawn in the sand for terrorists.

"Captain." The prime minister spoke matter-of-fact as he slipped into the backseat of the Beast where another man waited in the shadows for him.

"Sir," was the only reply he offered before joining them in the car.

Gilad's largest bodyguard awkwardly pushed into the front seat. The head of state watched the others disappear in several black vehicles on the tarmac. When the man in the front seat spoke into his sleeve, the procession began to move away from the plane.

Prime Minister Levi turned to the other man who sat patiently eyeing his most important passenger. "Ben, you look like hell," he quipped as he pounded his brother on the knee with his fist.

Usually a solemn man and not given to outward expression, a rare smile spread across Benjamin Clark's face as he pushed the prime minister's fist aside and tried to slap him upside the head, only to be deflected with a quick punch to the solar plexus. Ben grunted as he grabbed his chest and began to laugh deep in his throat. Gilad reached out and pulled the director into his arms and gave him a bear hug. "I've missed you, little brother."

The bodyguard in the front seat turned to make sure the prime minister remained secure. His facial expression showed resentment that the American agent protecting Enigma's director sat in the backseat with the prime minister.

"So," Gilad said looking around the limo with interest and running his hand across the seat, "this is the president's Beast. Impressive." He smiled over at the solemn Captain Hunter. "And how are you, captain? You're looking fit and mean as ever."

"Thank you, sir." The captain offered with a cool reserve as his eyes continually drifted outside and out the back of the limo, watching to see if anything suspicious caught his attention.

"I've heard that several pints of the president's blood are carried in the trunk." He smiled. "Just in case."

"I wouldn't know, sir." The captain spoke with the emotion of a sleepy bear.

"Like hell you don't." Gilad laughed. "Any booze for this cruise?" He looked to his brother. Even though his brother wasn't a drinker due in part to his evangelical mother, Gilad knew Ben could hold his own with a good bottle of Jack Daniels.

"You're on your way to see the president. It wouldn't be appropriate for you to arrive smelling like a Tennessee distillery." Ben continued to smile at his famous half-brother.

They shared the same Israeli father by blood. Gilad's mother died when he was but a toddler. The only mother he'd ever known and loved was the American woman his father had married. She showered as much affection and guidance on him as her own son, Benjamin. They didn't even know they were half-brothers until they were in their early teens. Gilad, groomed for the Israeli army from the time he could walk, spent most of his teen years in Israel. Benjamin was expected by his forceful father, to attend the military academy and serve the United States in hopes of aiding Israel if the need should ever arise.

Both boys considered Israel and the United States home. As the boys grew older their loyalties forged differently; Ben wrapped himself in the red, white and blue. Gilad became the power behind the Star of David.

"How is the president?" Gilad said as his face slid into a more serious expression.

"Troubled. There appears to be a glitch with the hearings on the USS Liberty tragedy. Someone doesn't want this to happen. Looks like the Egyptians are involved. We just don't know why or how. These hearings could reveal the truth. Israel is the one who stands to lose face."

Gilad sighed as he looked out the window. "Why can't the world leave us alone? We want peace, not a fight." His pale blue eyes cut to the captain who sat quietly, pretending not to listen. "Is your team in place, Captain?"

Chase nodded. "Yes, sir."

He removed his sunglasses and met the Israeli leader's eyes with a cool, steel determination that in an odd way reassured the prime minister.

Benjamin took a quick breath before proceeding. "Part of the crew of the Liberty was scheduled to arrive yesterday. Four of the five men asked to testify, never reached their hotel."

"And the fifth?"

"Checked in and out within an hour of arrival. Disappeared before we knew anything was amiss." Captain Hunter tightened and released his jaw before continuing. "He did contact his brother, a Billy Wakefield in Franklin, Tennessee."

The prime minister shook his head and pursed his lips impatiently. "Is this important?"

"We contacted the brother saying we were with the Liberty hearings. Didn't really give us any indication of a problem except..." The captain paused as he lifted a finger to rub an area over his heart. The spot had started to throb again, just like a year ago when he'd run a mission for Global Navigation.

The director eyed the captain, ill at ease with the conversation. "The brother told us his daughter was to contact the uncle when she arrived in D.C. He wanted to see her. He knew she was attending a conference."

"Sorry, Ben. I'm not following."

"The niece is Tessa Scott. She worked for us a year ago. It's rather convenient her being here at the same time as the hearings. She's nothing more than a school teacher attending a geographic conference it seems. Eyes have been on her today since St. Louis."

"What do you think is going on? Pick her up. See what she says."

"She'll say it's divine intervention." Ben chuckled remembering the obstinate manner in which the woman liked to explain away the impossible. "We had plans to recruit her, but the captain here," he nodded toward Chase, "has some reservations."

The captain raised his chin slightly as if objecting to him being involved in the decision. "We thought it best to see if he makes contact with her. If she becomes aware we're here and if I know Mrs. Scott, she'll go out of her way to avoid us. In the meantime nothing out of the ordinary has popped up on our radar. Your visit wasn't announced until yesterday. The media is scrambling to find out why you're here."

The prime minister chuckled without smiling as he slapped his brother on the leg. "Your American media loves a fight as much as a disaster killing thousands of people. They fidget when nothing big happens in the world."

Benjamin nodded and patted his brother's arm. "Maybe a celebrity will be arrested while you're here. That usually takes precedent over real life and death drama which could quite possibly change the world. Remember Sharia Palla Como?"

The prime minister nodded and withdrew his hand. "Yes. At the time all hell broke loose in Iraq between the Sunni and Shiites at a mosque. That young reporter." He seemed to pause.

"Someone from NBC," the captain offered in a flat line voice.

The prime minister snapped his fingers. "That's him. He tried to report the horror and warn the military but only got about ninety seconds. Whatever happened to him?"

"He got his head shot off." The captain's bland voice failed to show sympathy.

"Everyone wanted to hear about the blond bombshell." Gilad's voice quieted. "What has this great country come to, Ben?"

Director Benjamin Clark did not answer but stared straight ahead.

~~~

The rain had stopped on the mall, allowing tourists to begin drifting out of the Smithsonian Museums. A hint of sun teased the pudgy clouds that parted in clumps. Heavy humidity began to burden the August heat as children splashed in puddles against the warnings of exhausted parents. The sudden thunder storm drove the city into a quiet state, forcing tourists, lobbyists, government officials and city dwellers indoors for several hours. The sounds of taxis speeding through puddles followed by the blare of horns mingled with voices drifting across the mall. Sirens came and went with little evidence of concern.

The rattle of tourist maps, hot dog vendors and the shrill whistle to attract a cab, floated over the Reflecting Pond at the Washington Monument. It reopened after years of renovations and repairs. A minor earthquake had occurred leaving cracks in places engineers felt needed to be addressed. Long lines waited to enter and glimpse the towering obelisk from within and hear the park ranger's speech about its historical significance. Tessa wanted tickets to the monument but not at the cost of standing in line at 6a.m.

Sleep seemed like a better alternative especially since her two friends insisted on partying until after midnight on the roof top restaurant of the W Hotel. Then the mysterious man with the photograph of her uncle appeared. Sleep eluded her until nearly four. Methodically, Tessa went over every minute of the previous evening.

Shelly won the dinner drawing at the registration table after arriving early for the conference. A roof top dinner at the W Hotel was quite a coup. Other teachers from around the country also found their way to the ambience of a candle light dinner. People were drawn to Tessa's fun loving coworkers. The party grew in spite of Tessa's unease at being in an unfamiliar place. Seeing two Enigma agents at the airport kept her eyes searching everywhere for the one man that managed to invade her dreams each night.

After midnight people began to say goodbye. Shelly's laugh, with Kate's encouragement, started to grate on her nerves. Tessa wasn't sure how much the two drank, but the morning light would certainly make them regret trying to be college students instead of mature women in their late thirties. Mature might be a stretch, Tessa reasoned as she told them to say their final goodbyes.

Strolling to a seat near the edge of the roof, she could gaze at the White House grounds one last time while her friends paid their bar bill.

Lightning flickered in the distant clouds and the smell of rain once more filled the air. A humid breeze began to stir the white tablecloths and toy with the edge of Tessa's black skirt. She absentmindedly laid a hand on the hem to keep it from lifting up over her thighs.

Taking a deep breath, she became aware of someone sitting down in the rattan chair across from her. Trying not to appear startled forced her body to tense. Her eyes examined the man from head to toe in one sweep. She'd learned a year earlier the world and the people in it could be immensely deceiving. Being in Washington D.C. heightened her senses to danger. The dim lights of flickering candles made his features hard to distinguish.

What she could make out was his narrow smile. It reminded her of the cat in Alice in Wonderland. He sat with quiet reserve, dark hands resting on the arms of the chair. With crossed legs, his suit jacket parted ever so slightly. Tessa saw the bump under his jacket and knew in that split second he carried a holstered weapon. She wanted to bolt, but realized it was absurd to even contemplate an escape. Dangerous men always had a backup plan. Was he to be her contact?

By sitting in a shadowy area, Tessa wasn't able to see much of his face. How long had he been watching her? Why didn't she make better notes of her surroundings? This was how women got taken advantage of when they least expected it.

She stared at him for only a moment when he reached inside the left side of his jacket with his right hand and withdrew a small photo. Holding it midair for a few seconds, the man seemed to tease her. Without warning he stood, dropping the mysterious photograph on the glass top table in front of her.

Like a random snowflake it dropped in slow motion. She refocused her eyes on the stranger who now leaned in enough for the flickering candle light to reveal a man in his late thirties. Jet black eyebrows and a thick mustache gave him the look of a diplomat. Large eyes with generous eyelashes created a less menacing figure. He reached down and slid the photo over with one finger before smiling.

"You know this man?" The accent was Middle Eastern with a British slant.

Tessa's eyes dropped to the photo where his finger rested. Gingerly, she lifted the photo then pulled the candle nearer to get a closer look. The photo was of a battered and nearly destroyed ship. A man stood on the dock pointing to the name of what was left of the USS Liberty.

"Do you know him?" This time the voice was deeper and more sinister.

Tessa looked up at him and nodded, afraid to speak.

"If you want to keep your uncle safe, I suggest you convince him to abandon his folly. Tell him to stick to the plan." His eyes ran over her face then slid downward across her body creating a smile. "Be careful, Mrs. Scott."

He started to reach for the photograph when she grabbed it. For a moment she thought he would snatch it out of her hand. Drunken friends wobbled up accusing her of being a wet blanket once again. She tried to smile as the picture got slipped inside her clutch. The man walked away with indifference and disappeared.

After tucking her friends into bed and making sure their room was secure, Tessa reluctantly escaped to her own room two floors above them. Still surprised the hotel provided her with an upgrade as a result of not being able to accommodate all three women together as originally planned now created questions of their generosity. Since the reservations were in her name she would be alone in her own space. Considering her two best friends snored loud enough to wake the dead, she felt relieved knowing she would avoid their foul moods.

Now the thought of being in a Washington D.C. hotel room, all alone, forced her to feel on edge. It was intuitively obvious that someone wanted her to be isolated. Closing the door, Tessa flipped on the light switch then stood statue still. Observing the expansive room with the king size bed, sitting room and office area, she guessed it was nearly twice the size of her friends' room. Blue silk drapes outlined the set of French doors leading onto a narrow balcony with an ornate iron railing. The rich dark floor was covered in a faux leopard rug that started under the bed and reached across the room to the brown leather couch and wing back chairs.

It was more than an upgrade, it was a distraction. This could make her lose focus. Enigma's handy work showed in having her isolated. At least this scenario made more sense than getting reservations mixed up.

The turned down bed, covered in a blue duvet trimmed in a soft leopard, beckoned her exhausted body. She remembered the last time she'd slept in a bed of this size. Because of the incident, she would be forever haunted by a tall Enigma agent.

Tessa pulled the small photograph from her clutch and stared at it with suspicion. Her parents had left a voicemail the day before about a new cell number for her Uncle Jake. He would expect a call when she arrived. Did that have anything to do with Enigma making contact today? Disgusted at herself for feeling a quickened pulse and a little breathless, Tessa forced herself away from the door.

Carelessly, she tossed her purse and the photo on the couch before snapping up the flat screen remote. Without checking the channel, she exited into the bathroom and began running a bath. She felt the caffeine from drinking too much iced tea and knew she needed something to relax.

Striping off her clothes, she tossed them into the other room before sinking down into the churning waters. The weather forecasts on the television sounded in the other room; something about a hurricane. A deep breath followed by a sigh helped her tune out such news. This wasn't so bad. Distraction or not, it wouldn't take much to get used to this kind of life.

After soaking and wrapping in one of the hotel's plush white robes, she decided it was time to address the problem concerning her uncle. Barefoot and refreshed, she padded into the sitting room. She'd shoved the number into her clutch earlier in the evening in hopes of calling him. Time slipped away while she tried to keep her friends from making fools out of themselves. Because of the late hour, she laid it out next to the phone as a reminder for the morning. The dim light of the roof top restaurant prevented her from reading the words written on the back of the photo. Now would be a good time to have another look. Clarity might follow now that she felt relaxed.

Walking into the sitting room, Tessa noticed the clothes she discarded earlier. Folded neatly on the footstool in front of the wing-backed chair, they looked as if she'd just unpacked them. She ran to the door to reassure herself the dead bolt had not been compromised. Could someone have come through the door? She believed the safety lock had been secured, yet it remained open.

She second guessed herself. Did she actually fold the clothes and was too tired to remember? Reaching over the back of the couch to retrieve the photo, her eyes fell on the French doors. Slightly ajar, an evening breeze smelling of a coming rain pushed the white sheers out like a ghost. Dumped on top of her clothes were the contents of her purse. A quick search revealed her money, credit cards and identification still in tack. Only the slip of paper with her uncle's phone number was missing.

Tightening her robe up around her shoulders prevented the sudden chill from overtaking her body as she realized the photograph was gone.

CHAPTER 3

The tall woman dressed as a park ranger, stood near the image of Lincoln at his memorial. Most tourists gave her only a passing glance then hurried children or other annoying relatives away from her. Whether it was her menacing glare if they examined her too long or her sinister, narrowed smile on full lips, most dropped their heads or looked the other way. The long black hair, tied in a ponytail fell to the middle of her back. The recent exposure to too much sun made her olive skin a little darker and rosier than usual. Her ridged posture stood perfect as did everything about a body that practiced hard exercise and a strict diet of protein and fresh vegetables. The slight turn of her head looked robotic.

A couple of college aged men tried to engage her in conversation. Once she moved her long fingers to rest on her holstered weapon and turned her mirrored sunglasses their way, their smirks faded. They backed away, making Amazon women comments, which she committed to memory in case she encountered them again.

Having to monitor Tessa Scott on a hot, humid day ranked up there with having a tooth pulled without the help of a deadening shot. They met over a year ago in California during a mission involving a terrorist attack. Team leader, Captain Hunter, took great pains to protect the woman. The ordinarily solemn and methodical captain tolerated the woman's rebellious disregard for authority on several occasions. He called her "an innocent" and after all wasn't that what they were fighting for in a lawless world?

The woman frowned remembering how the captain had shown Tessa kindness, even admiration, at her assistance in the whole mess in Sacramento. She suspected more than a mutual respect between the two, but in the last year he had made no contact with the Grass Valley woman. It was as if she never existed. In return, Tessa honored her promise to never reveal the seriousness of how close terrorists came to wiping out life-saving isotope production.

Sam watched the three women dust off the seats of their pants after sitting on the steps. They were the same friends from the airport bar from the previous day. Rubbing their necks and foreheads indicated how clueless they were about the danger around them. Only Tessa's eyes scanned the surroundings.

"That's a good girl." The female Enigma agent mumbled. "You'd better be observant."

Maybe she was hoping to see Captain Hunter to fulfill some kind of fantasy. There could be no mistake about the looks that passed between them.

It would be so easy to take a shot from here. The thought of taking Tessa out in broad daylight forced a smile.

"Sam?" A voice in her earwig failed to stop her fingers from twitching over her holster.

A rage started to well up inside her. Knowing that as beautiful and available to the captain as she was, he only showed interest in that pathetic little mouse. How she managed to endear herself to the most respected man at Enigma remained a mystery. Playing second to another woman irked her. Here she was again, watching after the very person who threatened any hope of a relationship with the captain.

"Sam?" This time the voice grew anxious.

"She's still here. No one has tried to contact her. I think her friends are fading fast. They appear to be complaining about something." Samantha Cordova moved forward like a feline to the first step of the memorial. "Their next stop is lunch then the National Gallery. How do you want me to proceed?" She waited patiently, knowing the voice on the other end was trying to get instructions.

"Stay with her until she boards the bus. Carter will pick you up. He'll tail the bus until it stops for lunch. Wait outside until they leave for the National Gallery. If her uncle hasn't made contact by then you can return to headquarters. Once inside the museum Zoric will take over."

Sam could picture the face belonging to the voice on the other end of the phone. The young Vernon Kemp became Enigma's tech support member and continued to be extremely shy around women, especially her. Although smitten, he grew tongue tied in person. Communicating over cyber space made him sound normal.

She found him endearing. Respectful and appreciative of her work, Vernon never made unwanted passes or suggestive remarks concerning her perfect body. She toyed with him mentally, enjoying the stutter he developed in her presence. He remained a great deal calmer on the phone where he didn't have to make eye contact. That too, amused her.

When Tessa walked into Enigma a year earlier, Vernon's tongue couldn't stop wagging. Something about that woman made men slobber like an infant. She'd watched them chat like old friends and even share a few jokes. Vernon commented that Tessa was his hero. The information grated on her volatile temperament. She'd even witnessed Vernon slipping an arm around her shoulders like old combat buddies.

No woman was that innocent and sooner or later she'd miss a step.

Unconsciously snapping the holster band open that secured her weapon, a thought ran through Sam's head on the merits of killing Tessa now. Why prolong the inevitable?

"Sam?" It was Vernon. "Sam? You there?"

Sam snapped the holster in the secure mode. "They're on the move."

"You okay?"

Sam noted that Vernon's voice sounded unsteady as she continued to listen.

~~~

Tessa smiled at her two friends climbing aboard the bus as if they were one hundred years old. The lunch of sandwiches and salads from a popular D.C. restaurant, followed by cheesecake, put the finishing touches on her friends' inability to make nice with other conference goers on the city tour. Their eyes drooped toward a nap after settling down in their seats across from Tessa.

"Put us in a cab," Shelly moaned as Kate laid her head on her friend's shoulder. "My head is killing me. Do you want me to throw up on a Monet?" A wide mouthed yawn followed. "Unless the National Gallery has a live display of Chippendale Dancers, I'll pass." Kate nodded in agreement.

When they all exited from the bus, Tessa hailed a cab for them, relieved to send them on their cranky way.

While the conference goers gathered around their guide for instructions, Tessa shaded her eyes to look at a vehicle parking in a reserved space just past a second bus. It was a black sedan, not the SUV style she'd associate with a government vehicle. A healthy dose of paranoia followed her all morning.

The stranger last night left her with a sense of dread. Why hadn't Enigma made contact? The sedan caught her eye when they left the Lincoln Memorial. A familiar woman got in the passenger side; a woman who resembled Samantha Cordova from Enigma, definitely a frightening turn of events. Black sedans moved like army ants in D.C. so when one parked across the street from the restaurant Tessa let herself get distracted by her whining friends.

"Isn't that the car we saw at the Jefferson Memorial?" She elbowed Shelly.

An eye roll followed by her sticking out a thick tongue with a spit blow "You're in D.C." Tessa tried to shush her without success. "Heavens. You are going to have to get a life."

Now here it was again. She slipped on her sunglasses and shifted her eyes to take in the surroundings. Although she heard the voice of her guide, the words fell flat as Tessa looked for surveillance cameras. Washington D.C. let no secrets wander around aimlessly in their city.

The group now moved up toward the entrance of the National Gallery. She decided to stop imagining conspiracies where none existed. She turned for one final look only to see the car disappear into traffic. Relief washed over her.

The guide answered a few questions about the different wings of the museum and then set the group free to explore. Tessa headed toward the special exhibit seeing that most of the others headed toward the famous works of Monet and Degas. She stopped to look down at the special exhibit brochure on East European artists. One name stood out; Nicholas Zoric. With a kind of reverence she passed into the next gallery.

A gasp slipped out of her mouth, echoing against the expansive gallery. Her hand tried to cover her throat, feeling a hot blush creep up her face. Mouthing an apology at a frowning docent forced her to take a deep breath before turning back to the painting. Seeing oneself hanging in the National Gallery shocked her back to reality.

The large portrait of her resembled a warrior angel. With long curly blond hair and vivid blue eyes, her pale skin revealed a bruised cheek. Some kind of weapon lay on the floor beside her.

The second painting, just as large, was at the back of a transport plane. The same angel stood ready, her hair blowing into a tangled web of beauty as she drew to her side a soldier ready to jump into the abyss for some unknown mission. They stared into each other's eyes with a secret that only they shared. One hand rested around his waist while the other touched his chiseled cheek. Although most of the soldier's face was hidden, Tessa recognized the stance of Chase Hunter.

"This cannot be good." Even as a whisper, her voice carried throughout the gallery.

A hand touched her elbow. She spun around and staggered two steps back, startled at the man dressed in black leather.

"It has been too long." His voice carried an East European accent.

After staggering away from Zoric, Tessa stood almost frozen at his approach. In one swoop, he wrapped his arms around her and lifted her feet off the floor. Tessa heard the docent clear her throat. A nervous chuckle escaped her lips as Zoric sat her feet back down. He kissed both cheeks then took her hands in his grip.

"Ah. We meet again. Do you like it?" He waved at the paintings.

"What on earth were you thinking?" Tessa shook her head and laughed. "It's embarrassing."

He was a wiry five foot ten inches tall. His long, oily hair had been pulled back into a ponytail. The close set eyes were a little bloodshot above a long narrow nose. Below his thin mustache he began to reveal a smoker's yellow smile. "At least you aren't naked."

"Well thanks for that, Zoric. Holy cow. This is the most romantic thing I've ever seen." He looked more like a vampire than an artist, she realized.

As a timid smile began to play at her lips, she flashed back to their first meeting. It had been in a Black Hawk helicopter. He'd tried to intimidate her and made no bones about his plans to entertain himself at her expense. The captain thumped that notion out of his head pretty quick. It took days before she trusted him. In spite of being a hired assassin, Zoric became someone she liked.

Tessa gazed at the paintings once more. "What were you thinking?"

Leaning in as close as he dared, he chuckled. "That if my wife was still alive I would be dealing with a jealous woman. You and Chase gave me a story to paint." He shrugged. "So I painted."

Without thinking, her eyes looked behind her then toward the door.

"He is not here, Tessa Scott." Zoric grinned as his hands squeezed hers. Then like a gentle lover, he kissed her fingers.

"That's a relief." She smiled feeling a warmth surge inside her at seeing an old friend. She felt uncomfortable that Zoric knew she looked for the captain. "How is he? Annoying as ever, I expect." The friendship forged between them was rocky at best. Yet Zoric captured something in his art.

The Serbian intimidated his way through life. He looked into her eyes, causing Tessa to stare at the floor. He pulled at her hand and locked her fingers through his as he tugged. Had the fear shown in her eyes? "I mean you no harm, Tessa Scott." He developed the habit of saying both her names. "We have serious business to discuss."

He didn't look back or release Tessa's hand until they were outside the museum when she dug in her heels and refused to budge. He looked around at her in confusion.

"I'm not going anywhere with you until you tell me what this is all about." Jerking her hand free she tried to move the blond curls from her face, but the wind had taken control.

"I'm hurt, Tessa Scott." Zoric's smile took on a familiar satanic slant.

It was the same expression which frightened her a year ago. Could he be trusted? She'd never been alone with him.

"We both know if harm comes to you I will suffer at the hands of your protector. Now, come with me. I want coffee."

Tessa nodded, hoping deep down he meant her no harm. The image of him slamming her up against bars of a jail before throwing her to the floor, as he'd done the day they met, gave her pause. In spite of those memories, she followed him to a nearby café. They sat in the corner where Zoric could look out the large windows for trouble.

His eyes drifted outside often, even when he spoke, as if waiting for something to happen. Ignoring the "no smoking" sign, Zoric lit a cigarette only to have a waitress ask him to obey the request. With a snarl, Zoric pinched off the lit end with his fingers and shoved the cigarette into the pocket of his black shirt.

"In Serbia this would be…" Zoric noticed Tessa's smile as her eyes looked down into her skinny latte. "But we are in America where the government enjoys telling you everything from not to supersize your beverage to what kind of health insurance you should buy. They are like a Jewish mother, I think." It wasn't until he reached out and grabbed one of Tessa's hands that she looked up in panic. Zoric massaged the tension in her fingers. "You are still fearful of me."

Tessa withdrew her fingers and laid them on top of his scarred, leathery hand. "Surprised to see you is all. I thought you gave up painting."

Zoric suddenly laughed; a strange sound coming from such a violent man. It felt strained, as if he weren't used to doing it. Patting his hand, she smiled, waiting for him to fill in the missing pieces.

"Last year after we worked together…" He paused and pulled away from her touch. Taking a sip of his coffee, Zoric's eyes again went to the street outside. "I wanted to start over, to see things as you see them." His smile widened in a mischievous tease. "Anyone who can make Chase…" He stopped as if thinking better of what he wanted to say. Zoric gulped down the last of his coffee. "The two of you must someday come to terms with your complicated relationship."

"Relationship? He nearly killed me."

"He also saved your life as I remember." Zoric surveyed the others sitting at nearby tables. "He had a job to do. We all did.

Now," he watched with amusement as Tessa's shoulders pulled back and her chin lifted in anticipation. "Now it is time for you to do what you do best for us." Tessa took a deep breath and pushed away from the table. Just as she started to stand Zoric reached across the table and grabbed her arm with such violence, she failed to see a masked man walk up outside the café. "Down!"

Tessa felt Zoric lunge forward, knocking her to the floor. Her breath burst from her lungs as he fell on top of her. Glass shattered inward as screams, mixed with the rapid fire of an automatic weapon, came from outside the café. The splitting of objects hit by gunfire sprayed cups of coffee like rain across the interior. The scent of cappuccino and gunpowder wafted over them.

Zoric managed to pull out his weapon before jumping up during a split second lull. He fired and missed, letting the shooter escape into traffic. Sirens were already drawing near when Zoric reached down for Tessa who cowered against an overturned table. His grip on the back of her collar was anything but gentle as he dragged her up and toward the door like a rag doll.

"We must leave. Are you hurt?" He poked his head out the door with caution then back at Tessa who had begun to tremble. Zoric's eyes narrowed. "Just like old times, huh, Tessa Scott?"

CHAPTER 4

Congressman Gault looked up from his desk before cocking his head as his secretary entered the office. The room, lined with bookshelves, showed a burden of law books and biographies of great men like Lincoln, Kennedy and Roosevelt. Paintings of George Washington and Thomas Jefferson hung prominently on either side of the window. The oversized desk built from recently harvested planks of endangered rainforest mahogany, centered between the two presidents. It held this position to impress anyone who entered his office. The intent was to associate the congressman's face between two great presidents. Heavy dark paneling, shined and polished, hinted at luxury for someone deserving power.

The red Oriental rug from India and the gold silk fabric on the camel backed sofa transformed a dark space into something regal. Blue vases from Russia, pottery from Poland and other mementoes, given to him from heads of states during his many visits abroad, adorned the shelves of his glass-fronted display cases on either side of the door. The display gave him excuses to gaze upon the gifts at his leisure and contemplate his many contributions to world politics. Now that he was Speaker of the House, he wallowed in his own importance.

The congressman watched his secretary, who was well into her forties, lay file folders down on the library table behind the sofa in order to pour him a cup of coffee. He needed it strong. The young flight attendant knew how to please. Too much wine and kinky sex, wore on a man his age. In spite of being fifty, the rich foods and expensive drinks, took a toll on his once trim figure. Graciously, the congressman accepted the coffee, then the files before watching the icy secretary move toward the door. Even now, after conquering the little whore the night before, he looked with admiration at the woman who'd served him for so many years. Classy, reserved and sexy as hell, he thought. Once more he wondered what it would be like to be with her. He'd not made a move. It was important that someone believe him to be pure of heart. When an occasional rumor surfaced about his escapades, it was his secretary who defended him. He sighed as the door closed. Even he must make an occasional sacrifice.

His thoughts ran back to the flight attendant. Leaving her in his townhouse, unsupervised when the car arrived to take him to work wasn't going to work for him. Bringing a tray of blueberry muffins and cranberry juice on a silver tray, he sat down beside the sleeping form and gently rocked her awake by resting his hand on her buttocks. Pleased at his simple gesture, she enticed him into the shower with her where she managed to satisfy him yet again. By the time she'd dressed and nibbled on a muffin, the congressman grew anxious for her to be gone. Her quiet demeanor made him nervous.

The night before, the woman voiced how impressed she was with him. Could it be in the bright light of day she'd noticed his expanding stomach or the receding hairline? Dismissing such an outlandish possibility, the congressman decided the sex, wine and late night partying could take a toll on a twenty something woman too. Putting her in a cab, the congressman promised to call her that evening. At the rate she was going that pretty body of hers wouldn't last long. He decided to take advantage of it as time permitted. Making a mental note to call the doctor for another prescription, the congressman planned to keep up with the young woman who clearly enjoyed trying new delights of the flesh.

Sitting the China cup down, it rattled with a soft tinkle. Gault opened the files his investigator had compiled. Attached to a typed letter was a picture of a woman; a very attractive woman who looked vaguely familiar. Releasing it from the paperclip, he brought it closer to his face. He pushed back his chair to carry it to the light of the window. In that moment, he remembered. Once again he reached for the file folder. Squinting at the information, he shoved a pair of narrow rimmed reading glasses on his nose before scanning the contents. Shifting his tired eyes back to the picture, he remembered the woman from the plane. She hadn't looked so appealing yesterday with her mouth open, emitting an occasional snore and a bobbing head. Turning the picture over the congressman read the name; Tessa Scott.

~~~

Tessa ran only because Zoric half dragged her as they fled down the street, away from the café. The screech of brakes, impatient horns and the distant piercing sound of sirens kept her feet moving faster than she thought possible. The Serbian's savage grip around her wrist felt like handcuffs meant to torture rather than restrain. After a two block escape, he hailed a cab and motioned it on, as well as three others before forcing her inside the fourth. She knew speaking, and certainly protesting, was of no use. The look on Zoric's face had morphed back into that unapologetic killer she knew him to be. He kept glancing behind them and insisted on the cab drive down various streets before letting them out at the National Cathedral.

"I don't understand." Tessa couldn't keep her voice from trembling as Zoric rushed her up to the doors of the church. "Who was that?"

Zoric pushed open the door looking first toward the street then inside with caution before allowing Tessa to slip inside. "You tell me."

His voice demanded rather than questioned. The Serbian accent thickened. She found it appealing until it reminded her of Dracula.

"I don't know." Her voice, although a whisper, echoed with a kind of strange desperation against the walls of worship. "Maybe it was the same person who came in my room last night." Tessa's breathing started to slow as Zoric led her to a corner.

Zoric frowned. "Someone came in your room last night?"

"While I was in the bath." Tessa sighed and felt better by resting her hand on Zoric's bony arm. "I think whoever it was hid on the balcony so I never noticed them when I came in. It was late.

I thought maybe it was someone from Enigma since I talked to that creepy guy at the W Hotel."

"I assure you it was not one of us. Tell me about this man you met."

Zoric led Tessa into the sanctuary and down a few row of seats before indicating she needed to find a spot to sit. She couldn't help but be swallowed up by the beauty of God in such a holy place; another planned distraction, she reasoned. The man she once feared now edged close enough his breath moved a wayward curl that fell across her forehead. The smell of cigarettes and coffee on his breath forced her to look toward the altar. His close proximity raised the question whether this was a safer alternative that being shot at in a coffee shop.

"Last night at the W Hotel my friends and I had dinner. Around midnight a man came over and dropped a picture on the table for me."

"A picture of what?"

"My Uncle Jake. He was standing on the USS Liberty."

"Can you describe this man, Tessa Scott?"

Although a little timid, she slipped her hand onto his and squeezed then withdrew it. Was it possible to disarm him by a feathery touch? She knew Enigma men didn't like to be distracted by such outward shows of affection.

"He stayed in the shadows and I tried not to make eye contact. Dark hair, mustache, and he smiled like a Cheshire cat. Middle Eastern but spoke with a definite British accent. Narrow shoulders, well dressed, and he wore a gun." She realized her words sounded rushed, as if under interrogation at the local police precinct.

"For someone who couldn't see him very well you have a great deal of information. How do you know he carried a gun?" He offered a patient smile as if her imagination might be running away with her.

"I saw the gun bump under his jacket. When he sat down he unbuttoned his jacket and it showed a little."

"Maybe you're mistaken. You said he sat in the shadows."

Tessa rolled her eyes. "You guys showed me enough guns to last me a life time. He wore a gun," she insisted.

Zoric slipped his arm on the back of the pew and let his hand touch her shoulder. She tried not to flinch at his sudden familiarity.

"Okay. He had a gun. Then he left? Did he say anything?"

With a shrug she met his eyes. "Told me to convince my uncle to stick to the plan, abandon his folly. It didn't make any sense to me. He tried to take back the picture, but I slipped it in my purse."

"Do you have the picture with you now?

"I laid it on the couch in my room. I was beat so I went in to take a bath. When I came out the French doors were open and the picture was gone, along with the new cell phone number for my uncle."

Zoric withdrew his arm and faced the front of the sanctuary. "I told the director we should just come out and tell you."

"Tell me what? Do you know how hard it's been this last year for me, dealing with the terrorist attack and losing Mr. Crawley?" The old man had been her neighbor who tried to warn her of danger.

"I was sorry to hear of his passing. He was a good man."

"I've just got where I feel comfortable going to the grocery store without taking a different route every time I leave the house."

This brought a laugh from the Serbian's mouth which drew a grin from Tessa. "I forgot how funny you can be, Tessa Scott. You were the only one that could make our captain laugh. We didn't know he knew how until you came along."

The heat of a blush forced her hands to cover her cheek. Thoughts turned to the captain; dark and foreboding at times, warm and safe at others. The nearness of him turned her into a stuttering imbecile on more than one occasion. Then there were the dreams; passionate, dangerous and forbidden. "Is he well?" As soon as the words were out of her mouth she realized how ridiculous it sounded.

"Sometimes he is tolerable. Other times," he waved his hand in question, "demanding and obsessed with his job. Many times I wanted to call you and have you put him in his place for the sake of our sanity."

"Me? What could I do? He was harder on me than anyone. At one point he would have gladly shot me." She pushed her hair away from her face. "He even threw me off a cliff."

"It was to save you."

"I drowned." The truth hurt.

"He revived you."

That was one of the recurring dreams; Chase bending over her, applying CPR after she'd died. Bringing her back to life changed their relationship; feeling the warmth of his mouth on hers, the breath of life, the realization her world would never be the same. Working with him carried consequences.

A year had passed without seeing him. It was part of the deal; no contact with Enigma. At the time it seemed like a perfectly reasonable idea. No Enigma and no Captain Hunter putting her life at risk. Except the captain restored her desire to live life to the fullest and never sit on the sidelines. There wasn't a day she didn't wonder where he hid and if he was safe from those who terrorized the world. Each morning Tessa breathed a prayer for his safety, knowing he lived in the shadows, protecting the country from the monsters who hated freedom.

"Why have you approached me after all this time?" Tessa turned her face to meet the Serbian's eyes, noticing the whites were not as red as they once were. Maybe they just no longer surprised her. Seeing his yellow smile made her body tense as he laid his lizard-rough hand on her pale one.

"In 1967 the USS Liberty sailed off the coast of Egypt. It was a mission to collect data about the Six Day War against Israel."

A dumbfounded Tessa frowned. "My uncle was on that ship. If it weren't for him several men would have lost their lives. Israel attacked a virtually unarmed ship clearly marked as an American vessel."

"Yes. We know." He watched confusion spread across her face. "Your uncle deserved the Medal of Honor. But that would have meant he had to come to the White House for a photo shoot with the president and the press asking a lot of questions. The administration didn't want Israel to be put on the spot."

"American lives were lost and a twenty million dollar ship crippled almost beyond repair. Israel covered up their soldiers killing Egyptian POWs then burying them in the sand. They decimated the Egyptian Air Force in a matter of hours. Maybe, just maybe, I can understand the way they attacked their enemies after what happened to the Jewish people during World War II, but to attack an American vessel..." her voice trailed off as she tried to compose herself. "But that's not even the worst of it. The

American government virtually turned their backs on those men who suffered the attack. They accepted a pitiful apology that 'it was a case of mistaken identity, a tragic event, a--"

"I take it your uncle has spoken to you about this on several occasions since you seem to be well informed." Zoric tore his eyes away to scan behind him then to his left and right. Tessa waited for him to continue. "When did you speak to him last?"

So this had something to do with her uncle and USS Liberty. "Why?"

Zoric frowned as he cut his small eyes over at her. "Listen to me, Tessa Scott. Your uncle has gotten mixed up with some very bad people. He is missing."

"Missing!" Tessa shook her head as if clearing newly formed cobwebs, then ran her fingers through her tangled locks. "I donno. Maybe a couple of weeks ago. He was at my parents' house for Sunday dinner, like always. I always call home then so I can talk to everyone. He asked to speak to me, which wasn't unusual, but he sounded a little concerned."

"What was he concerned about?"

"About me," she said flatly. "Said he'd be here for some hearings when I came for the conference." Tessa's eyes widened. "Wanted to meet with me to go over his will. I teased him about it and he changed the subject."

Zoric no longer resisted touching Tessa as his hand moved to rest on her leg, just above the knee. She couldn't repress a startled flinch, but she did not pull away.

"A year ago I wondered what touching such a beautiful woman would feel like again. Did you know I watched you, memorizing your facial expressions? The way you manipulated Captain Hunter with those sky blue eyes of yours, caused him discomfort. I liked that." He nodded as if admitting to some kind of sadistic joy. "That's why I painted you the way I did. It was a reminder of good in the world."

Tessa knew Zoric felt no romantic intentions toward her, although he wasn't the kind of man that would rebuff any interest if she offered. His paintings reflected an interest in events that occurred between the captain and herself.

Zoric cleared his throat then patted his jacket, looking for a cigarette. "Has your uncle tried to contact you since you arrived in

D.C.?"

"No."

"You must convince him to come to you for his own protection. We need to talk to him. It isn't too late."

"I don't understand. Why is he missing? Is someone after him? Was it the man who shot at us?"

"I do not have all of the answers. But for now, here, you are safe. Enigma will be watching you." Zoric's knees popped as he stood then edged out into the aisle. "I will make sure everything is as it should be before leaving."

Tessa followed him into the aisle. "You're leaving me?" She couldn't hide the panic in her voice.

"Someone comes for you." Zoric patted her on the cheek. "You are in God's house. I thought you of all people would feel safe here."

"When will I see you again?" Tessa grabbed his arm as he started to leave.

Narrowing his eyes he appeared to contemplate the answer. "It is more important that I stay hidden so my eyes watch out for you. Do as you are told, Tessa Scott. I remember your stubborn streak." This time he grinned. "Go talk to your God. He seems to listen to you."

Tessa withdrew her hand from his arm. "I'll mention you by name."

"I hope He remembers me. Take care."

Turning, she started down the aisle toward the front of the church. She didn't want to watch Zoric disappear. Pretending he remained somewhere nearby, gave a great deal more comfort than thinking she'd been left to her own devices. Her eyes looked around at the grandeur of the church as she found a pew to wait. Leaning forward she folded her hands on the back of the next pew before closing her eyes in prayer and solitude. The act gave her clarity. This would invite peace to wash over any safety concerns.

God always protected her. Always. She wasn't so sure Enigma could promise the same.

~~~

Zoric backed down the aisle until Tessa leaned forward in

prayer. Something about that simple act pleased him. He didn't know many people who prayed and knew no one who prayed for him. Becoming a hollow being with the deaths of many on his black soul felt normal. Closing his eyes after reaching the back of the church, he imagined her pouring her heart out for his well-being and protection against the forces of evil. The smell of her remained on his hands as he lifted them to his nose to inhale. An urge to paint her in this setting momentarily distracted him until he saw a movement to his right.

Slipping around to the side of the sanctuary, he saw a tall man watching Tessa. The figure, muscled and lean, almost stood as one of the statues throughout the church. He stood with his large hands down at his side. The back of his neck looked dark above his Grateful Dead tee shirt. Zoric's stealth-like steps moved to intercept. He noticed the man's short black hair made his neck look thicker than most men. With each light step, Zoric began to make out the profile of the man's face. Even in the shadows, the narrowed eyes the color of dark chocolate displayed danger. So intent on the man's observation of Tessa kneeling in prayer, he failed to notice when Zoric approached like a determined killer. The man clenched his jaw several times. The nostrils flared in some kind of mental control. Not once did he bat his eyes or move a muscle as if by doing so would reveal his imposing presence.

The Serbian slipped his switchblade from his pocket to his hand. With a knowing touch the knife sprung open as he slipped it under the chin of the man who was several inches taller than himself. With surprise on his side, Zoric forced his weight against the watcher, pushing the man against a pillar.

"You should not be staring as such at this woman," Zoric growled in the man's ear. When the man did not respond the Serbian withdrew the knife and placed it back in his pocket.

Captain Hunter turned around and leveled a dangerous glare at his Enigma friend. "Do that again and I'll use that knife to turn you into a eunuch." He let his eyes return to Tessa.

Watching Chase place a thumb on his chest to rub a spot over his heart, Zoric knew this was the first time in over a year his partner felt a familiar stab of lightning pain. It happened the very first time he saw Tessa and several times after when he nearly drowned in the woman's blue eyes. Zoric wondered if Chase welcomed the pain, proving he was alive and capable of emotion. The rumors of him being nothing but a military robot dissipated once he involved Tessa in a terrorist plot.

"I could have killed you. Again you let the woman get to you." Zoric looked at Tessa talking to her God as if there was only good in the world.

"Shut up," was Chase's only mumbled response.

"We need to talk, my friend. She is in danger and doesn't even know it. Someone came into her room last night while she was bathing."

Chase turned narrowed eyes back to Zoric. "Who?"

Zoric shrugged. "She thought it was Enigma, maybe even you. But..." he let his sentence fall.

"Did she see who it was?" Chase didn't like someone prowling around in Tessa's hotel room in the middle of the night. He'd had her watched from a distance until she'd entered the hotel lobby, but after that it was assumed she'd be safe.

Zoric told him what little information Tessa relayed to him. "I did not tell her if it had been you, perhaps you would've stayed to make passionate--"

"Stop it. She's a happily married woman with a family. Your fantasies have nothing to do with me." Chase bit his words off as if they were bitter.

"Then why were you staring at her like a love sick puppy?"

Chase turned from watching her and strode away with Zoric grinning as he followed. "Making sure you behaved yourself. Between you and Carter it's a full time job. We've got work to do."

~~~

Just as the two Enigma men walked away Tessa jerked her head up and looked around, knowing deep down Chase was near. How she knew this remained a mystery since there was nothing to link them together on some metaphysical level. Yet she knew it to be true. The sudden flutter of her heart, the march of heat up her neck and the feeling of being watched engulfed her ability to continue with prayer. Her eyes scanned the area, hoping to see the man who'd saved her life and forced her world in a different direction. The ability to breathe became difficult, knowing his presence meant both danger and safety. Turning her eyes to the crucifix, she asked for forgiveness for her impure thoughts.

"Mrs. Scott?"

A male voice, comforting yet strangely unholy, broke the spell of the transcendental connection she tried desperately to make with a man she'd known for such a short time a year earlier. Tessa looked over to see a priest dressed in black cassock with the typical white collar. He nodded as his hands folded in front of his short body. "Dr. Zoric asked me to see to you. He was called away. If you need more time to pray I'll wait in the back."

Tessa wasn't surprised to see a priest in an Episcopal church. She just couldn't remember ever seeing an Asian American priest. But after all, it was Washington D.C., a multicultural Mecca. He was a little taller than herself, she noticed; five six or seven. His eyes were so narrow they looked almost shut as she edged out into the aisle. He carefully removed his round glasses and wiped them on his sleeve before returning them to his narrow nose. His smile looked artificial but patient. A few strands of gray were visible in his ebony hair. She thought it odd an Episcopal priest would wear his hair long enough to be pushed behind his ears. He even wore a diamond stud earring on his right earlobe.

Must be the youth pastor, Tessa thought. He appeared vaguely familiar when he extended his hand, indicating she should begin walking. "I'm sorry, Father--"

"Wu."

"Father Wu, did Dr. Zoric say where he was going?"

A fake-like smile came to his narrow lips, revealing teeth that appeared to have been bleached. "Dr. Zoric only said for me to escort you to your hotel room." Their steps grew slow, as if prolonging the departure. "I see now why Dr. Zoric painted you. You are quite lovely."

Tessa's eyes widened in surprise. "Thank you, Father Wu."

A soft chuckle escaped his throat as he took her elbow, steering her in an unexpected direction. "Are you surprised I've seen that old Serbian's work or that I find you fetching?"

Tessa resisted pulling away. "A little of both, I guess."

"Confucius say 'just because you're on a diet, doesn't mean you can't look at the menu.'"

"I don't think that was Confucius."

Father Wu shrugged. "Well it wasn't John the Baptist." This drew an unexpected laugh from Tessa. "So this is the magical laugh that toppled the mighty Chase Hunter. I find it infectious for sure; light, spontaneous and happy. I never thought I'd meet the person who could break through that barrier of steel the captain cloaks himself in."

Opening a door, he stood aside to let her pass into a driveway. The car turned out to be a dark and dated limo from the eighties. Chipped paint around the front bumper and a hairline crack across the windshield gave the wide vehicle the appearance of a bygone elegance replaced with forgotten maintenance.

He opened the door with such careful manipulation that Tessa almost missed the creak of rusty hinges that came with a vehicle kept too long. A fleeting thought that this would be a great car for Halloween crossed her mind. She slid into a seat made of faded leather that bore creases resembling spider webs. A little Yankee Candle air freshener danced with the movement of air as the priest joined her.

Visiting with a complete stranger, especially a priest, created a feeling of being trapped with her sins. She remained quiet, forcing a cool stare out the window in hopes of communicating a lack of interest in conversation.

"I'm glad we have this chance to visit, Tessa." The car lumbered out into traffic as Tessa searched for a seatbelt and found none. He pointed out various green spaces along the way, indicating special gardens planted in honor of this person or government agency. "I understand you are a gardener."

Her heavy silence eventually caused Wu to end any attempt at conversation until they entered the elevator at the hotel. "Chase is not the most forthcoming person at Enigma. We aren't exactly on good terms."

Finally her interest peaked at his choice of subjects. Tessa turned to face Wu fully. "Why is that?" Dr. Wu reminded her of a Jedi master; choosing his words carefully, moving with purpose and examining the world around him at each step he took.

"He calls me a mind bender. My job is to help people cope with the stress of saving the world. I'm the psychiatrist for Enigma."

"Not a priest."

"Well not an Episcopal priest." He grinned. "I thought perhaps this outfit would set you at ease for our first meeting. You never came to see me last year after your first encounter with Enigma." He motioned Tessa to hand him her key card then inserted it with ease. Swinging the door open, Dr. Wu walked in first. "Please sit, Mrs. Scott. I'm just going to check things out before I leave."

Reluctantly, Tessa went to the couch, sat on the edge, straight backed and ready to bolt. She waited for Dr. Wu to finish his sweep of the rooms. Her mind raced back now to their first encounter. His appearance and demeanor that day was of a caring physician, encouraging her to seek help for posttraumatic stress in the weeks to come. She never had.

"I don't need a psychiatrist, Dr. Wu."

"You will before this is all over, Mrs. Scott."

Dr. Wu, after making sure there was no danger, bugs or prying eyes, began boiling some water in the coffee pot. "Let's have tea while I explain how we need your help."

"Why?"

"Someone is going to try and kill the president. We think it's your uncle."

CHAPTER 5

Something about the way Zoric ignored how others reacted to the darkness in his eyes, gave him an edge during interrogations. Chase took advantage of that gift whenever a situation needed immediate results. He'd gotten used to people stepping aside for him to pass on elevators, sidewalks and especially narrow hallways. Much to his amusement he realized the hollow cheekbones and close set eyes added to his evil demeanor. Chase suggested wearing something more American to soften his look when not on the clock.

"Would it hurt you to wear jeans and a baseball jersey?"

The Serbian shrugged. "You are cranky, my friend. Thinking of the woman?" Zoric enjoyed baiting him about Tessa.

"More like unloading my Glock into your head." His voice was calm as he poured over a city map lying on the table before him. They headed to the safe house after leaving the cathedral to go over any new information.

Chase's eyes never left the paperwork. "Just wondering if the doc tried to play mind games on Tessa. Being so naïve, she could easily fall for his gibberish." The woman was in his head again.

He could hear the muffled sound of Zoric's voice but his mind drifted back to the year before when he'd tangled with the housewife. Stubborn, innocent and idealistic mixed with tenacity and courage, frustrated his no-nonsense personality. She'd forced him to laugh, something he'd not done in years. The sadness and guilt that plagued his conscience evaporated every time her lips parted. Even now, he could see the shape of her mouth, the blue of her eyes and the few freckles across her nose that makeup couldn't conceal.

In spite of being terrified, Tessa had come through for Enigma, nearly giving her life in the process. He remembered the smell of her hair and the way it curled around his fingers. The press of her body against his…

"Are you listening to me?" It was Zoric. "Chase?"

He blinked to clear the flashback. "I'm listening. What did Wu say after dropping her off at her hotel?"

Zoric frowned. "I just told you."

"Tell me again," he snapped as he turned to face the Serbian with folded arms across his chest. "Give it to me straight without all the romantic crap."

Zoric shrugged, pulling up a bar stool. "When Wu told her about the plot to assassinate the president and her uncle being involved she nearly flipped. She refused to believe it. Remember how that temper of hers could flare up at a drop of a hat?" Chase nodded recalling how it had nearly gotten her killed. "She unloaded on Wu for a good ten minutes, informing him her uncle was a hero and would never do such a thing."

"Did Wu turn all Shaolin Warrior to calm her down?" Chase could envision the doctor becoming aggressive to get her to shut up. The unassuming housewife had once brought Chase to his knees after attacking him. She'd even put one of his men in the hospital using nothing but a broom stick. Later she'd redeemed herself by saving the life of another soldier from a Libyan terrorist using the pepper mace in her purse.

Tessa never failed to surprise him. Maybe that's why he…Chase stopped himself from thinking further.

The Serbian took out his switchblade and started opening and shutting it; a habit that usually annoyed his friend. "I doubt he even flinched. The man has ice water in his veins." When his partner didn't respond, he continued. "He basically laid out the facts. Her Uncle Jake is one of the leaders in the Remember the USS Liberty movement. Some sons and daughters of survivors have gotten involved but nothing serious. It's only been recently that Tessa's uncle started disappearing on trips for days at a time."

"The reason?"

"Dr. Wu asked Tessa about that but she didn't know anything."

"Or she wasn't telling the truth."

"Dr. Wu would've known. Besides she's a terrible liar."

Chase nodded and grinned as well. "Let's hope if she comes to work for us she doesn't get captured."

Zoric's cynical glare met Chase's eyes. "You should tell her we've been evaluating her for the last year."

"She'll over react." Chase folded the maps and papers on the table. "I'm not exactly her favorite person." He rubbed the aching spot on his chest. The pain disappeared a year ago. The doctor checked him out and said he was in perfect health. Men didn't get any more fit than him.

The doctor forced Chase to see Dr. Wu, thinking it was something deeper. The visits resulted in a staring contest, Chase answering questions with questions of his own. When the two sessions concluded, Dr. Wu filed a report saying the captain leaned toward god-like tendencies and felt very little responsibility for actions that may have led to the deaths of others. In the weeks that followed the pain disappeared. Now the pain returned with an image of a bumbling housewife in his head.

Dealing with women and the emotional baggage that came with it wasn't new to Chase. There usually was a willing female waiting back home for him. If she started asking too many questions, complaining about not seeing him enough or wanting him to meet the parents, he moved on. Broken hearts failed to concern him.

This strange sensation he experienced every time the Grass Valley woman's name came up was disquieting, even irritating. At the same time Chase took solace in the fact he was capable of feeling something other than apathy and revenge. She made him want to be a better man.

"When are you going to see her?" Zoric joined Chase at the table and shuffled through the information.

"I'm not-if I can avoid it." He forced his concentration back on his work.

~~~

The Smithsonian decided educators should be treated like royalty by using the Mandarin Pacific Hotel as its launch site for the conference. In partnership with the Smithsonian, government agencies and other university gurus, presented to seduce educators into promoting their platforms.

Normally Tessa would have believed she had finally reached Nirvana if not for Enigma agents sneaking around, making her life miserable. Then there was Robert's news from back home. The new neighbors had started moving in to old Mr. Crawley's house.

She mentally turned over Robert's earlier report. "I only met the lady. Her husband was on some business trip or was it a conference? I forget what she said. No I didn't get her name. She's kind of the grandmotherly type. Kids took to her right off." He paused long enough to reprimand one of the boys for farting.

"Jeeze! What are you feeding these kids, Tessa? Anyway, we're taking over those cookies you have in the freezer. Will they still be good?" She heard Heather singing. "Gotta go, honey. Another dinner at McDonalds. Yay. I wouldn't mind if you left us a few meals in the freezer when you decide to get a wild hair and take a trip with your rowdy girlfriends." He made a kissing sound and hung up.

After walking her friends to their scheduled session Tessa searched until she found the poster outside a room that read: "Can You Dig It? Dr. Francis Ervin." Slipping inside she noticed six others had taken seats at the round tables.

Dr. Ervin looked up and spotted her immediately and waved in recognition. He really was a dear, she thought, and worried the audience might be too small. This first evening of workshops might not be well attended. She smiled, noticing he was having some difficulty with the smart board and computer.

"Can I help you with that? I have the same system in my classroom. They're tricky." She reached for the computer. With his nod of approval, Tessa managed to pull up his power point presentation and showed him a few short cuts. "There. All set. It's nice to see you again, Dr. Ervin. I'm looking forward to hearing you speak."

He chuckled then wiped imaginary perspiration from his forehead. "Whew. I'm glad you came along. I'm not very good with computers. Give me a shovel or a box of shards and I'm a genius."

Tessa laughed glancing at the clock. Time to begin. Another ten educators arrived. She took a seat at the closest table and waited for him to begin.

Within minutes Dr. Ervin began his lesson, which actually turned out to be very useful. She definitely would try this in the coming school year. Two attendees asked lots of questions which were answered with patience and enthusiasm. Copies of the program were passed out as people began to exit.

"Excuse me, Tessa?" Dr. Ervin began trying to set the computer up for the next session. "Could you wait to make sure I do this correctly?"

She came to his side and watched. "Perfect. You're a quick study."

He clapped his hands together once. "Wait 'till I tell Martha I got the hang of it. Martha is my wife."

"Yes. You told me on the plane. Packs too much for you." Tessa felt amused.

"So I did." He chuckled. "Would you mind waiting here with my things for just a few minutes? I need to get some water and stretch my legs. I'll be back in five, plenty of time for you to get to your next class."

"Sure. Go ahead."

It was more like ten minutes. Tessa remained by the computer, leaning against the table where it rested. Yawning, she looked down to see that the screen had gone black. Fearing the power had been compromised; she reached down and touched the refresh pad. A picture popped up on the screen of a badly crippled navy ship. Across the screen in capital letters read, "REMEMBER THE USS LIBERTY."

Sucking in her breath, her eyes lifted to see Dr. Ervin walking into the room chatting with some teachers he invited in from the hall. She hit the escape button and quickly gathered up her things.

The smile she offered the professor felt fake as she tried to exit. He mumbled a "thank you" when his phone began the Indiana Jones theme song.

~~~

Moving to the computer, the professor hit a few buttons and smiled triumphantly before raising the phone to his ear. "Yes. She saw it." He listened a second before answering. "Because she was pale as a ghost, that's how I know. Besides I had the computer programmed to her touch. It let me know when the picture was accessed." Dr. Ervin positioned the phone between his shoulder and ear as he pulled up the next presentation on his computer. "So how is the move going? Meet the neighbors yet?" A smile spread across his face when his wife told him about the stale cookies from the kids next door.

CHAPTER 6

Escaping to the bathroom, Tessa locked herself in a stall and stood frozen in confusion. How could this be happening to her again? After her near brush with death a year ago, she vowed never to put herself or her family in harm's way again. Now here she was in the most powerful city known to man, being sucked into a conspiracy to assassinate the president, and if that wasn't enough, her uncle may be involved.

She listened for the person washing her hands at the sink to leave before slipping out of the stall. Pulling her purse open, Tessa searched for her cell phone. Activating it, she saw there were two messages; one text, one voicemail. The voicemail was her husband, Robert, calling to let her know all was well on the home front and ended with "miss you". Then there was the text message from an unknown number.

"We need to talk. I'll be waiting at the National Geographic booth in one hour."

Knowing it would be futile to redial the number, Tessa slipped the phone back in her purse before glancing at her watch. Was it Zoric checking up on her? There remained a certain amount of mistrust between her and Enigma. No matter if Zoric claimed to be her forever protector, he was a dangerous killer that could easily turn on her.

Then again maybe it was Captain Hunter. He'd pledged no such thing. All he ever managed to do was give her nightmares for the last year. Pushing her into a fight against terrorism she'd not realized existed; he'd barged into her home saving her from Libyans.

Kidnapping her, the captain drove a hard bargain to secure her support a year earlier. Through it all he remained aloof and determined to see the mission completed. Saving her life multiple times resulted in damaging the once clear and focused values she'd carried like a badge of honor. Would there ever be a time when circumstances forced her to step up and return the favor?

Whoever sent the message was of no consequence. She planned to ignore it.

~~~

Jake Wakefield looked around his motel room with disgust. A sluggish roach meandered near the baseboard nearest the bathroom. After stomping on it with a cruelty that shook the Norman Rockwell calendar picture on the wall, he went into the bathroom to tear off some toilet paper to dispose of the creature. Frowning at the smell of mildew due to a poorly operating air conditioner, he turned the weather report up on the television. His hearing started to fail after the bombing on the USS Liberty. Cocking his head, he listened carefully, worried that plans were going to need an adjustment.

The forecast called for a tropical disturbance in the Atlantic then showed all the signs of turning into a full blown hurricane. The Weather Channel displayed several possible tracks of the storm, one coming ashore in Cape Hatteras, North Carolina, another farther north at Virginia Beach, Virginia and the most serious one, Ocean City, Maryland. This one would move inland and hit Washington D.C. almost head on.

He imagined the damage that would occur, not to mention the chaos from being cut off from the world for a few hours. Loss of power, communications and transportation could possibly bring the most powerful government in the world to its knees. Throw in a dead president and the stock market would plummet, militaries around the world would go on high alert and the fear of a terrorist attack would consume the American public. How had he gotten to this point? What would his family say when they found out about his plans?

Jake lifted his canvas suitcase off the floor and gingerly laid it on his bed. With a deliberate slow motion, he unzipped then pulled the flaps back to see his hunting rifle. Reaching inside he let his fingers touch the stock of the weapon, remembering fondly all the times he'd taken his two nephews and niece hunting. Since he didn't have children of his own, they had become his greatest fondness, especially his niece Tessa.

She had been the one to always ask impossible questions, wanted to tag along and hug his neck every time he came and went from their house in Franklin, Tennessee. Smart as a whip and stubborn as the day was long, she'd forged a different path than her brothers. He missed her being so far away in California all these years. Reaching out to her might place her life in jeopardy. Would she come in search for him if he didn't make contact?

For now there was work to be done. The country needed to know the atrocities the Israelis committed to the USS Liberty. He rubbed his shoulder, remembering how he'd gone into the bowels of his ship over and over to bring out men burned and deformed by the attack. Even when he'd been locked in the rising water he never let go of those that needed him most. Sometimes when he closed his eyes he could still hear the screaming, smell the burning flesh, and feel the jarring of a torpedo hitting the hull of the ship.

For decades he'd lived that day over and over, knowing President Johnson did nothing to get justice for him and his mates. The commander of the USS Liberty had been awarded the Congressional Medal of Honor for his role while serving during the attack. However, he was rudely denied receiving the award, as is tradition, at the White House by the president. Instead the commander was presented the medal at an obscure naval yard by the Secretary of the Navy; better to have a presidential snub than insult the Israeli lobby. The citation failed to mention Israel and maintained the lowest possible profile. Jake never understood.

His phone gave off a soft ring. He squinted at the number on the surface before pushing the word "talk". He'd picked up the phone from the desk clerk at his first hotel. Folded inside the envelope revealed minimal instructions on how to use it. Technology wasn't his thing. Basics. That's what worked in his day.

After he left the Marines in 1970, he swore to never leave his home of Franklin, Tennessee again. But the nightmares never vanished. The remaining crew of the USS Liberty shared the atrocities done to them with each other at reunions and book promotions concerning the cover-up. He experienced comfort being with those men. Some suffered more than others. Knowing that the whole dirty little secret wasn't a lie gave each man hope that someday the truth would come out and they would receive a deserved recognition.

He wanted more than that; he wanted Israel to admit what they'd done.

"Hello?" Jake cleared his throat and spoke again. "Hello."

"Tomorrow night. Ballroom of the Mandarin. During the speech." The voice sounded like a computer robot. It reminded him of the television show in the sixties Lost in Space. *Danger, Will Robinson, Danger,* was a famous line that now played around the fringes of his conscience. He shook it off. "Where will you be?"

"Close. You don't need to worry about me. Do as you're told and…"

"I know," Jake snapped. "I know." The line went dead but Jake continued to hold the phone to his ear. Doubts of his sanity started to surface as his mind played over and over again what he was about to do. He probably wouldn't survive.

Those Secret Service boys were dead shots.

Thinking of the Israeli protection detail, forced an involuntary shiver up his spine as he returned the phone to his backpack. The Israelis, rubbed the wrong way, could easily make you wish you were dead. Matter-of-fact you didn't even want to make eye contact with them if the prime minister was within a mile of you. There was Israel, then everyone else. The prime minister might as well be God because his angels of death were not about to let him be exposed to danger. The voice on the phone promised to neutralize that obstacle.

Then there was his niece Tessa. If he'd known in the beginning she'd be in danger he would not have tried to arrange a meeting. Now they knew she was here. It was another means of making sure he followed through on his promise. He lifted two pictures off the bed that someone slipped under the door when he was in the john. One picture was his niece having coffee with a dangerous looking man. They were sitting close, heads together, touching hands.

Was she having an affair? Considering what a rock her husband was and the importance she put on family, the picture only confused him. Someone had written on the back of the photo *your niece is working with a secret government agency. This is Nicholas Zoric, a former Serbian assassin and interrogator. Your niece has a history with him.* Jake shook his head in disbelief as if by doing so would bring clarity.

His eyes shifted to the second photo. Tessa was getting into an old car, maybe a limo, looking over her shoulder with frightened eyes. Although the wind had forced some of her curls across part of her profile, there was no doubt it was her. The man holding the door of the car was a priest, not much taller than her. He looked over his shoulder in the opposite direction. It was obvious he was of Asian descent. It was also obvious this man was no priest. Like the first photo there was information written on the back. *Dr. Wu is a psychological profiler and therapist for the government. The Serbian, the doctor, and your niece have made a pact with the devil.*

~~~

Amon, the Egyptian, knew his voice showed irritation with Jake Wakefield as he hung up the phone. He needed to keep an eye on Tessa Scott. It would be a shame to have to eliminate such a lovely creature. But if she was working with that Serbian, her involvement was far from innocent. Amon knew the man worked for a secret government agency blessed by the president himself. Was it too late to abandon this folly?

~~~

Congressman Jim Gault spotted the figure in the rear of the restaurant sitting in a red leather booth. Lit only by a small candle flickering lazily in an amber colored glass, the booth provided a secluded atmosphere where lovers might linger. Maybe the flight attendant would be available later for a drink or more interesting activities, depending on how this meeting went. As he scooted into the booth he looked at the Egyptian eyeing him with reserved indifference. The waiter came over to take his order.

"Just water with a twist of lemon." The waiter nodded as the congressman turned his eyes back to the Egyptian who leaned back with folded hands in his lap. Jim winked at the man sitting across from him. "No drinking just yet. May need my strength when I meet a certain flight attendant tonight." The water arrived with a menu positioned in front of him as if it might hold important information.

"You disgust me," the Egyptian said straight faced.

"Really? I never figured you Brotherhood types would turn their nose up at a little free sex. Pretty good sex I might add. That girl and I do mean girl, can--"

"I do not wish to hear about your clumsy attempts to mate." The Egyptian leaned closer, never changing the expression on his face.

"Mate is a far cry from what I plan to do."

"Being the dog that you are, that is exactly what you do."

The congressman frowned, not liking that he was losing control of the situation. "I wouldn't get so high and mighty, Pharaoh. We both need each other a little longer." Jim took a sip of his water then stuck his spoon in to fish out the lemon. He sucked on it just a second before making a puckered face. "Did you transfer the money into my Swiss account?"

"Yes." The Egyptian's eyes scanned the recesses of the dimly lit room. "Where are your watch dogs, Mr. Speaker?" He was concerned the Secret Service would notice too much about him.

"At the front ordering dinner. I told them I didn't want to be disturbed." He waved for the waiter to order bourbon then leveled a pompous look at the Egyptian. "And Mr. Wakefield?"

"The shooter is ready. I'm concerned he will change his mind."

Jim remembered the picture of Tessa Scott and let one corner of his mouth lift in a grin. "He won't. I'm going to take a little insurance policy out for that."

"What do you mean?"

"I'm going to take something that belongs to him. Rather you're going to take it with a couple of your very capable people. I'm sure he'll want it back." He chuckled and motioned again with impatience for the waiter. "And when the deed is done I'll collect on the insurance."

The congressman imagined several possibilities for the niece. He felt his body stir at the prospect of her having no option but to submit. "Soon you'll have your revenge and I'll be one step closer to being President of the United States."

"My organization can count on you in the future for support, and the destruction of Israel?"

The congressman lifted his class in a toast. "To success!"

CHAPTER 7

Tessa opened the French doors to her room and leaned against the door facing. Hurricane Candace was pushing bands of rain inland ahead of the storm. Warnings of doom traveled up and down the Atlantic seaboard. News footage showed people in North Carolina buying supplies until store shelves emptied like a looming apocalyptic event. Even Virginia Beach battened down the hatches, but as of yet the D.C. crowd held to the opinion the hurricane wouldn't dare hit anywhere close. Even so, thunder storms rolled across blackened skies, putting on a lightning display that fascinated her.

Never afraid of weather, her father often scolded her as a child for standing too close to windows when watching an approaching storm. The rumble of thunder would reach deep inside her. Pounding rain made her sleep like a baby. From May to October in California was postcard perfect. Then, in November, the rains fell without the lighting she loved to watch dance across the sky back home in Tennessee. She missed that kind of weather. Maybe that's why she was drawn to Enigma, it was an advancing storm she couldn't resist experiencing.

Hugging her arms from the wind pushing against her black nightgown, Tessa felt the first drop of rain. With the lights extinguished behind her, Tessa thought she'd be safe from prying eyes. Besides it was late. Kate and Shelly's partying from the night before finally caught up with them. After only one drink they'd decided to call it a night. Tessa didn't argue with the decision.

Now here she was alone, confused and full of anxiety over the prospect of working with Enigma yet again. This time it would be against her favorite uncle.

A snap of lightning caught her by surprise as she dropped her arms to her side. Her eyes searched the windows of the other rooms while the lightning flickered like a dying light bulb. What she hoped to see in that flash of light was the man who could keep her safe at any cost. Where was he tonight? Was he with the president, a beautiful woman, or watching her from afar as she tried to decide which path her life would take?

Zoric claimed Enigma never entered her room and stole the picture. He had no reason to lie. His body language alone convinced her he spoke the truth. So who was it? How did they get in and out without her knowing? When Tessa thought Enigma had been lurking in her room, her temper flashed like drops of water on burning grease. Now fear replaced anger. A wind gust swirled her already tangled curls around her head, blinding her momentarily. The rain started in a slow rhythmic beat against the balcony. In moments she'd have to retreat from the evening shower.

~~~

Why did she keep standing there when the lightning grew close? Chase lowered the binoculars for only a second to rest his eyes. He leaned his chair back on two legs against a dresser before raising them again to watch Tessa standing in the doorway off her balcony. That lacy black negligée revealed answers to questions he'd thought about for the last year. The image of some Greek goddess came to mind when the wind played recklessly with her hair, then would drop it back down gently to her shoulders. A few strands would fall across her face without fear of being pushed away. Seconds later it would all start again. She stood like a classic statue at the Greek Parthenon. Watching her staring out into the night, Chase imagined where her thoughts wandered.

He refocused the binoculars to zoom in to Tessa's face. Her lower lip pouted ever so slightly, and her eyes were drunk with fatigue, yet she watched the on-coming storm with interest without a hint of fear. Only once did her eyes stray to the other rooms as if searching for something or someone.

Then he saw it. Her lips moved to say, "Chase."

Dropping the binoculars on the bed, he checked his weapon before lifting the back of his shirt and shoving it in his waistband holster. As he moved toward the door, Zoric yawned while pouring himself another cup of coffee.

"Where do you think you're going?"

Chase paused at the door long enough to nod toward the window. Zoric would know he meant Tessa. "Don't wait up."

He walked with purpose to Tessa's room, careful to avoid the surveillance cameras. Before he knocked on the door his fist paused in midair. This went against everything he vowed to believe in. You didn't sleep with co-workers and you never slept with another man's wife. He planned to do both.

The tap on the door seemed quieter than the hammering of his heart against his ribcage. The door opened slowly at first then Tessa stood aside for him to enter as if she'd been waiting for him.

She closed the door before brushing past him to stand at the foot of the bed. The vulnerable look in her eyes locked with his intense stare. The halos of light mounted on the exterior of the building seeped into the suite outlining her body. One strap of the negligee dropped over a pale shoulder. In her bare feet she appeared smaller, more defenseless than she really was. Yet he knew she was capable of fighting her way out of a situation if threatened. The fight wasn't in the blue eyes he could barely make out. He took a step toward her as she slid to the side, raising one hand to stop him.

Without knowing how, he could feel her breathing increase and knew that her eyelashes blinked a little faster, like they did sometimes when she was insecure. The smell of body lotion reached his senses as he removed his weapon in slow motion. His eyes fixed on her, exploring the face and body, shrouded in semi darkness. With one cautious step toward her, he laid his gun on the end table next to the couch. This time she didn't retreat. Traces of raindrops on her collarbone and the lace outlining her bodice forced nervous fingers to touch the skin his eyes caressed with desire.

"Why are you here?" Her voice came out in a whisper. "I don't need saving."

"But I do," he said unashamed as she fell into his arms,

burying her mouth against his neck, then his ear and jaw. Her own desperation met his longing as he swung her up in his arms and carried her to the side of the bed.

"What the hell?" It was Zoric. He kicked the chair of the sleeping agent.

Chase opened one eye as he let all four legs of his chair fall back down on the carpeted floor. It was a dream. Correction. A nightmare. He pinched his nose with thumb and fingers, trying to wake himself up.

"What?" His growl made Zoric turn around.

"Someone is headed toward her room. Looks like room service, but she's been out on that balcony forever." Zoric reached over to retrieve his gun from the dresser with one more glance at the security feed from the hall camera.

Chase pulled his Glock from his holster and together they raced to intercept the waiter pushing the cart toward Tessa's door.

~~~

The waiter struggled against his captors as they dragged him back to their room. With a cloth napkin shoved in his mouth and hands zip-tied behind him, the young man shook his head with panic. A black leather jacket thrown over his head, just as he'd approached a room at the end of the hall, prevented any chance of identification of the two men who now terrorized him.

A door opened and he felt hands pushing him. The sound of a dead bolt caused the waiter to spin around clumsily. A hand on his chest then a shove forced the waiter to cry out in fear as he hit the mattress. Words uttered about an open window, concrete below and smashed brains made the young man quiver. The napkin started to choke him as a gun pressed against his temple.

When his body began to shake violently Zoric leaned in.

"I'm going to remove the jacket." His Serbian accent sounded matter of fact. "Then if you're a good boy I'll remove the gag." The waiter continued to tremble. "I mean you no harm. I just want information." The waiter nodded like an animated cartoon character with a rubber band for a neck. "Very good. Keep your eyes on the ceiling. If you look at me, I will kill you. Do you understand?" Again there was an exaggerated nod of the head.

The waiter stared at the ceiling obediently after freed of the head covering and napkin in his mouth. Covered in complete darkness, he couldn't have seen his tormentor even if he'd wanted. The drawn curtains blocked any dappled light from outside. He could hear another person in the room.

"What do you want?" The waiter sucked air as if there weren't enough.

Zoric took a step back from the bed. "What room were you taking the cart to?"

"Room 1419."

"Why?"

"Because…" He stuttered just as the dark voice moved and touched his crotch with the gun.

The yelp gave the Serbian pleasure. "Let's try again." His voice became a hiss. "What was on the tray?"

"Cheesecake, strawberries, some chocolate covered pecans, maybe some champagne."

The waiter couldn't see that Zoric's eyes lifted to someone else in the room. "Who ordered it?"

"I donno. The person in 1419, I guess," he said feeling the gun again. "I mean…"

Zoric put one knee on the bed and pressed the gun firmly into the waiter's crotch. "The person in that room doesn't drink, so the champagne was a little over the top."

"Okay, okay. Just don't hurt me," he begged. "That tray was for someone on the third floor. A man got on the elevator with me and offered me three hundred dollars to take it to 1419. Said it was a joke. He laughed and everything." The waiter started to look down from the ceiling only to hear a growl from his captor. "I'm telling the truth. I'm sorry. That's all I know."

"What did he look like?"

"Old. Had a southern accent. Who are you? What can I do to make this right?"

Zoric removed the gun. "I'm the hotel hospitality police doing a service check and guess what? You failed. Not only did you take a bribe from one of my plants, but you blabbed to a complete stranger about what you did."

The waiter moaned. "What's going to happen to me?"

He reached in the leather jacket and pulled out a small

canister. "I'm going to release you. You better show improvement or I'll be back."

More tears. "Thank you. I-I promise I'll never do such a stupid thing again."

The contents sprayed from the canister into the waiter's eyes forced him to fall asleep. "That's for sure." He turned on the bedside lamp before searching the waiter. The three hundred dollars found its way into his pocket before turning the light back off. Zoric heard the curtains push back and lightning momentarily flashed into the room, outlining his friend looking out the window toward Tessa's room.

~~~

She was still standing on the balcony, safe and unharmed. Chase exhaled as if he'd been holding his breath under water far longer than wise. Staring at her created that ache in his chest again. He watched her head turn to look back into the room. Tessa's posture changed as her hand smothered a scream. An arm reached out the French doors, grabbing her free hand and jerked her out of his sight. Chase knew before he entered Tessa's room that she was gone. The black nightgown lay on the turned down bed. Her purse had been emptied on the couch. The only thing that remained was the scent of her body he thought he remembered from a dream.

~~~

"What do you mean he left?" The congressman whispered as he turned his head to see the fetching flight attendant step out of the shower. He almost forgot what to say as his eyes explored her wet body. She smiled at him with sidelong glances and motioned for him to join her.

This time he spoke harshly into the phone. "I'm busy. Do you understand? I can't be bothered with these details. What am I paying you for? Find the old coot and remind him the others are depending on him. If he doesn't comply then shoot one of those Liberty seamen you have locked up. That'll get his attention. Better yet, go get that niece of his. That should do the trick. We can't have him rethinking this. Too much at stake."

He slammed the phone down a little harder than he planned. The lovely creature coming out of his bathroom paused to lift the glass of champagne to her narrow lips. He'd brought it to her as she disrobed and turned on the shower. If the phone hadn't interrupted he might be a bit more relaxed by now.

"Problem?" She smiled mischievously as she let the black robe drift open.

Jim Gault didn't return the smile but eyed the woman from top to bottom as if trying to decide what to do next. "Yes. I may have to leave."

The flight attendant pushed out her lips in a pout as she came to him sitting on the edge of the bed. "Let me help you decide what to do, Jimmy. All I've been able to think about today is how you..." She felt his hands enter her robe. "That's right. Now what could be so important that you would want to leave this?"

The offer of her champagne, then another, until the glass was drained encouraged his hands to explore. She moaned as he pulled her closer, tasting the fair skin and drops of water that still clung to her belly. Drizzling the few drops of champagne left in the glass onto her breasts, the evening was finally set into motion.

The congressman felt her push him back on the bed. He decided, as his head began to spin, that third drink earlier in the evening coupled with the champagne had been a mistake. He wasn't sure he'd be able to keep up with this one tonight. He let her take control. Being a powerful congressman certainly had its perks.

Tonight the Egyptian would have to take care of business alone. His eyes grew heavy. It had been a long day, a stressful day. Sleep played on the edges of his consciousness as he felt the woman's hands soothing and coaxing him into submission. He wondered if he were dreaming as strange foreign words whispered against his ear.

~~~

"Director Clark, you're calling awfully late," Dr. Samantha Cordova cooed into her Enigma phone. "It's not like you to distrust me with such an important assignment."

Director Clark sat in the White House with several Secret

Service agents who, like him, were making follow-up calls. "I trust you completely, Sam. Just wanted to make sure everything was okay. This is just a final check on your charge."

Sam looked over her shoulder and smiled at the Prime Minister of Israel propped against pillows in his bed. He wore only a pair of boxer shorts, revealing a hairy chest and a very fit torso. Gilad Levi examined some reports delivered to him moments earlier. He had placed a pair of black glasses on his nose, giving him a distinguished look in spite of being nearly naked.

"Yes, Director. I just tucked him in for the night."

"Very good. And," the director paused, "thought you should know someone has taken Mrs. Scott."

Sam couldn't control the flare of anger welling up inside her. "Was anyone hurt?" She held in her thoughts, *please let that bumbling woman be lying dead somewhere.*

"Chase and Zoric are suffering from bruised egos, but there isn't any word on Mrs. Scott. They think it was her uncle. We're looking into it. Any thoughts?"

"Do you want my thoughts or my suggestion?"

Director Clark was keenly aware of the animosity Sam felt toward Tessa. "Suggestion, Sam."

"If the uncle has her he'll probably bring her back. If it's someone else, she's probably a hostage or dead. Wait."

"Thank you, Sam." The director cleared his throat. "I'm sure my brother is tired of waiting on you to get off the phone. So goodnight." He clicked off.

Sam put down the phone and turned to look at the prime minister who had removed the glasses and was turning out the bedside light.

"No doubt that was Ben checking up on you."

Moving toward the bed Sam dropped her silk robe and crawled in next to Gilad Levi. "On you actually. He knows I can take care of myself," she said rising up on her knees.

Gilad eyed her with appreciation. "Then I think it's high time you took care of me, Dr. Cordova."

"With pleasure, Gilad."

~~~

Shivering under an awning of a dark coffee shop, Tessa waited for her Uncle Jake. She realized he'd gotten in her room because she hadn't thrown the dead bolt again. What if it had been the same person who had stolen the picture instead of a man she'd known and trusted all her life? He'd somehow managed to obtain a secure key card for her door.

Jerking her into the room Jake had handed her a yellow tee shirt, a pair of sweat pants and hoodie. While she quickly pulled them on he'd found her slip-on tennis shoes. Before she could even complete the transformation, he pulled her toward the door. She hopped on one foot, trying to slip into a tennis shoe.

"Let's go," he urged frantically. "I don't have much time. We'll take the stairs first."

"Uncle Jake, why are you here? Are you in trouble?" She already knew the answer to that question. Why else would he be here? Zoric was right. Something sinister was underfoot. She only hoped it didn't involve the president. "Stop."

He stopped on the third floor landing then cracked the door open enough to be spooked by what he saw. "Your friends," he said despairingly. He grabbed her hand as she tried to look over his shoulder. Tugging so hard she had to stumble-run to keep up, brought home the seriousness of the situation.

Tessa knew she had to follow. Of all her relatives this man had been the one to attend every band concert, school play and soccer game. He always sat next to her father, applauding like she was the next best thing since sliced bread. His kindness, slow-to-anger personality and jolly laugh did not fit the man dressed in the long brown hunting jacket. A black ball cap covered his head that she knew was nearly bald. He was wet, but warm as he clung to her arm making sure she didn't try and escape.

When she realized they'd gone down past the first floor door Tessa tried to resist. "We've gone too far, Uncle Jake."

His silence continued as they rushed down toward the basement and an emergency exit. He pulled out a revolver from the inside of his jacket and pushed the door open wide enough to look out into the alley. "Clear. Hurry."

"Jake. No. Talk to me."

But he didn't talk to her. He ran down the dark alley smelling of rain and garbage as flashes of lightning brightened their escape.

She shook him off, but followed dutifully as he came out onto the street and looked in both directions.

He'd left her alone for a few minutes to find a better hiding place. So now, here she stood under some awning waiting for him to return. Watching him cross the street toward her as he dodged cars and puddles splashing up over the curb slowed his walking.

"There's a place around the corner."

Without question, she tightened the hoodie around her throat and followed. The small café appeared to be closed for the night. The doorway was deep and dimly lit so hiding out of sight would not be a problem. A clap of thunder and snap of lightning made Tessa jump into the arms of her uncle. She felt his arm that carried the revolver go around her. A gentle pat on her back made Tessa slowly push away. The good man she'd always known looked like he'd aged ten years since she'd seen him at Christmas.

"Uncle Jake, what kind of trouble are you in? Please tell me."

He moved to look out around their hiding place then slipped back in. "National security kind of trouble. They want me to shoot the president."

"Who is 'they', Uncle Jake?"

He dropped his head, shaking it like a troubled child. "I donno, Tessa. Somebody who doesn't like the president? I just donno. They took my USS Liberty mates and are holding them hostage 'till I do the deed."

Tessa grasped both his arms in panic. "Why them, Uncle Jake? Why you?"

"I might've made a few threats over the years," he said sheepishly, "you know, like 'somebody should take out the president and the two-faced Israeli murderers that they are.'"

"Uncle Jake!" Tessa couldn't believe her ears. "Why now?"

"The president wants talks to begin on what really happened to the USS Liberty. The Prime Minister of Israel is here. I kill the president at some shindig the Geographic folks are havin' this week. Implicate Israel. Relations with them will fall apart and..." He took off his hat and wiped the water from his forehead. "You gotta believe me, I don't wanna do it."

She took her uncle's face in both her hands. "Look at me," she demanded. "All my life I've heard you say how you hate the Israelis for what they did in 1967, how it ruined your life and someday you'd get even."

He choked back a sob. "I know. I know. But not like this. Whatever happens, don't let them kill my mates. They don't deserve to die like this. Tell your dad I'm sorry." His face grew contorted like he wanted to cry. "They sent me a picture of you and some man. It looked like you two were..." He couldn't finish the sentence thinking his favorite niece might be having an affair with a dangerous man. "It was taken today, Tessa. I mean you and Robert..." His words fell as hard as the rain.

"A friend. That's all. We..." she paused wondering how much could be exposed, "work together. He can help you."

A look of confusion spread across his face. He took a step away, his eyes showing alarm. "He's dangerous. Do you know he's working for the government?" He stopped and looked closer at his niece with surprise. The southern accent thickened as he spoke. "You're working with the government. That's why you're here. You've come to set a trap for me." His voice showed signs of being wounded. "Stay away from the speeches tomorrow night, Tessa. You're in danger. They may try to use you against me." He backed toward the escape, looking with caution for signs of danger on the street. "They're here. The Egyptians are looking for me." His eyes turned back to Tessa as he reached up, smashing the light above their head with his gun. "I stopped checking in with them to go it alone."

Shoving her back into the farthest corner of the small doorway, Jake could barely make her out in the black clothing covering her body. Even the yellow tee shirt had become invisible with the way Tessa hugged her jacket tightly together.

"These are dangerous men following me. Stay here until they're gone. I'm sure they'll run after me. Don't move." Jake leaned in and kissed his niece on the top of the head. "I love you, sissy." That's what he'd called her as a little girl when her brothers would get too rough in their horse play.

"Uncle Jake," she yelled as he stepped out into the thunderous rain and turned to level his revolver at something, or someone she couldn't see. The flash of his gun muzzle muffled her scream. With shaking hands she pulled the hoodie tighter and watched him flee in the opposite direction of the gunshot.

In moments two men passed her doorway. One stopped and

looked in, meeting her eyes only briefly before another gunshot made him dodge. He too vanished in a heartbeat, in search of her uncle, she guessed. In spite of her terror, she tried to memorize the features of the killer tracking her uncle. Maybe the information would help Enigma save him.

Tessa's feet slid on the damp tile toward escape. Guardedly, she peered out toward the direction in which her uncle had fled before looking in the opposite direction toward safety. She figured the hotel was only a couple of blocks away. The hair on the back of her neck unexpectedly rose as Tessa saw a large shape emerge from the darkness under a streetlamp.

He moved with speed in her direction. One hand was down at his side as if carrying something and in that split second as lightning flashed, Tessa knew it was a gun. Pushing back in the farthest corner of her hiding place, Tessa hoped this new gunman had not seen her. She held her breath as the rain slowed.

The dripping from awnings and the sudden splash made by boots, drowned out the occasional car horn and the gurgle of rain gutters. Footsteps grew slower and closer until she knew they'd stopped. Even though crouched low, she tried to wrap her dark clothing tighter. Someone watched her. Raising her eyes, a man stood in the doorway of her hiding refuge.

A large gun hung at his side and the extension on the barrel told her it carried a silencer. He stood tall, six foot one or so. His stance, although relaxed, warned of danger and determination. Wearing an army issue coat that looked black from being soaked in the thunderstorm gave the man an ominous aura. Tessa tried to stand, hoping that she could fight him off if he decided to move forward. The man pushed back his rain hood with his free hand as he looked back over his shoulder then back to her.

She jerked herself up as straight and brave as physically possible and shivered.

The man extended his free hand toward her. "Time to go, Tessa." Captain Hunter reached out and grabbed her trembling hand, tugging her gently to his chest. "Ready?"

Nodding like an anxious child, she stepped out into the night with the man who haunted her dreams and could possibly change her life forever.

CHAPTER 8

The sound of their feet wading through deep puddles pooling up over the curb drowned out the ragged breathing coming from Tessa's mouth. Her heart pounded as she clung to Chase's hand that seemed to be dragging her forward. Stumbling twice because she looked back, Tessa felt Chase catch her momentarily, then continue on as if time meant death.

Without warning, Chase pulled Tessa into a wide alley that went between two buildings. Transformed into an urban oasis, a few solar lights flickered on the sides of buildings, revealing flower beds full of hostas and ferns. Small trees planted in terra cotta pots the size of a small piano promised a shady respite on hot D.C. summer days. Round concrete tables were scattered the length of the oasis where hotel employees, tourists or businessmen could stop for a break.

Releasing her hand, he turned to look back down the street from where they escaped. The two men searching for her uncle were back tracking. Did they know who she was? Had they seen her with Jake Wakefield?

Resembling a drowned terrier, she held the hood of her sweatshirt tightly. Her soaked sweats sagged. A strand of hair of underdetermined color fell down the length of her small nose. The unemotional examination from where he stood caused her to shiver.

"Did they see you?" His gruff voice made her nod a "yes".

He took one more look. "The trackers have split up. Looking

in every doorway."

Chase found himself weighing whether or not she was their intended target. He strode over to her, invading her personal space.

"You can get into more trouble than anyone I've ever known."

The skies opened up again, dumping rain hard enough to cover the approaching steps of the trackers. The dead end alley didn't allow escape. He eyed Tessa harshly as he watched her cower under his penetrating stare.

"Those men are looking for you."

"What about my uncle?" She looked up into his wet face smeared with an impending deadly force.

"Must have gotten away." He took a quick look to his right before lifting her onto the table as if she weighed no more than a child. She jumped back down. "I know you're not going to like this, Tessa, but I need to draw those men in to you."

"How?" She appeared to consider his order before speaking. "No. I can't, Chase. I'm scared."

Even before she finished her words, he backed deeper into the shadows. "For once do as you're told, Tessa."

~~~

Tessa swallowed so hard it sounded like a thump in her ears. She stood in the open, shivering. Rain drenched the last bit of confidence in her better judgment as a man started by the alley then halted and turned back. His hesitation forced her to take several steps away from the table. The man followed with caution as he called to someone else. When there was no response, he looked over his shoulder and yelled louder in a foreign language.

She didn't notice where her backward steps took her as the man now approached with more confidence. He looked young, or at least younger than her. Black hair fell into his eyes, dripping rain onto a dark face outlined with a five o'clock shadow and a thick mustache. His large eyes appeared too big for his narrow face and his nose too small. Other than a cold resolve, the man's face didn't indicate his next move.

"What have you done to my uncle?" Tessa fell back against another one of the concrete tables, and then yelped as if surprised by its existence. The words caused a thin smile to move his mustache. He motioned with his gun for her to come with him. Reaching back with her hands to touch the table, Tessa tried to move herself along the edge as if by doing so would create distance.

He lifted the gun with such speed that Tessa screamed before covering her head with forearms she pretended could stop a bullet. A flashback of her children, a distraught husband and a life left in California, almost caused her to forget she wasn't alone. When the man chuckled, she lowered her arms in time to see a large shadow come behind her attacker.

Pulling back her shoulders to look brave she nodded to the stranger. "Okay, just don't shoot. I'll come. Please, just put down your gun."

The man continued to grin as he lowered the weapon just as Chase slammed his pistol into the man's head, causing him to stumble away. He rallied in time to lift his gun. Chase easily squeezed the trigger twice into the man's head. It seemed like only seconds for him to drag the body deeper into the darkness.

Blood had spewed out, speckling both Tessa and Chase. With the rain falling so hard it quickly washed away as if it had never appeared.

"What do you have on under that hoodie?" He sounded a little impatient.

Before she could answer he unzipped her jacket revealing a bright yellow tee shirt. She tried to fumble it shut even as Chase pushed her hands away. Yanking it off her shoulders he then pulled her back to one of the tables. Rain quickly soaked Tessa's body. His eyes lingered driving home the realization she wasn't wearing a bra. Trying to cover her breasts with folded arms, sent the message of how mortified she was at revealing this much information to him.

"I'm going to need you to fight me." The captain had removed the jacket of the dead man and now forced his larger, more muscular body into the sleeves.

"Fight you?"

Later she'd experience confusion as to whether he felt any remorse at taking advantage of her.

~~~

Hiding in the back seat of an unlocked car, Jake pulled a blanket on top of him before locking the doors. He could hear the Egyptians speaking English instead of their native tongue. Taking a risk he raised up to look out the back glass when the voices moved away. They doubled back running. Taking advantage of their confusion, he slipped out of the car and into the darkness. Did his niece make her way back to the hotel where she'd be safe? Luckily a cab waiting for a fare was parked near where Jake exited the car. In moments he was in the cab and moving away from a life he might never return to again.

Once back at the hotel with the flickering vacancy sign, he quickly packed up his things. It was time to move to another location. Smashing his cell phone, he slipped the new one in his coat pocket. He'd purchased it at a kiosk earlier in the day, programing any numbers he might need. The memory wasn't what it used to be. Not that it mattered. Chances were he wasn't going to come out of this alive.

His thoughts turned back to his niece. Was she really working for the government or had he jumped to conclusions? The mysterious man in the photo sitting with his arm around Tessa did not look like her type.

She had always been so squeaky clean and naïve. The few boyfriends she'd brought home were typical southern boys who liked to hunt, fish, and go to church on Sunday. Careful not to get mixed up with a puffed up high school quarterback or self-inflated rich kid, Tessa spent more Friday nights at home than out with a date. He had always been proud she preferred books over boys. When Robert came into the picture he knew this was the one for his Tessa. That young man was going places and he worshipped the ground she walked on.

So what did she mean they worked together? Wasn't she a stay at home mom who only recently went back to teaching? How could that sinister looking man possibly help him out of this mess unless he worked for the government?

The night resonated with cars driving too quickly through standing water as he left the hotel behind. A heavy mist, mixed with sudden downpours, fell with the occasional rumble of distant thunder. Jake looked down at his feet as he walked, passing a pimp and a hooker. Forced laughter and an insult followed him when he turned the corner to wait for a cab. He'd call the voice on the phone later. His body was too tired to tackle that tonight.

~~~

Without warning, Chase laid his gun down next to Tessa then forced her legs apart as he stepped between them. Her eyes grew wide as she looked down at her lap then back up at the man towering over her. When she didn't move he reached up and ripped the sleeve of her tee shirt, causing her to back away.

"Fight, dammit. He knows his partner found you," he growled. It would be just like her to remember their history, not their present situation. She wasn't foresighted enough to realize a gunman wanted her dead. The hero worship in her eyes needed a wake-up call.

With his left hand he jerked her against his chest. For good measure he slipped his hand down into the back of her sweats, feeling the bare skin soaked from the rain. Finding Tessa's mouth, he forced her lips apart, hearing her resist with pain. He knew his unshaven chin scratched. Attempting to twist away, she still didn't fight back until he put his right hand under the back of her shirt.

Terrified, she came alive, thrashing and beating against the Enigma agent's chest. Her legs tried to break free enough to kick just as he removed his hand from her shirt. Grabbing her hair, he pulled her head back. A scream escaped from her throat. Burying his face in her neck, he worked his way back to her mouth. With his peripheral vision, he watched a man enter the oasis.

"Ameen, is that you?" The words were in Arabic. The tracker must have recognized his partner's jacket.

Chase nodded and answered in his Arabic. "Yes. I've found her. Hurry before she draws attention." He raised his head enough to watch the man approach knowing Tessa's struggle would draw his attention. "Who says we can't have a little fun for all our trouble."

Tessa continued to kick and thrash with all her strength seeing the man marked for death step closer. Lust in his eyes sealed his fate. In that split second Chase released his grip on her hair, lifted his weapon and put a bullet in the forehead of the stranger. With urgency, Chase dragged the man into a dark area near a planter before taking a quick look at the contents of his pockets. His face looked middle-eastern like the other dead man. No identification indicated where he was from.

~~~

Returning to Tessa's side he looked her in the eyes with reluctance. He'd destroyed any trust they gained a year earlier. "Tessa, I--"

With all the force she could muster she drew back and slapped him across the face. The next motion was a doubled fist which he caught in midair and pulled down behind her back so she couldn't move.

Pinning her against his chest he put his face in hers. "I'm sorry, Tess. I know I frightened you." He released her hand with caution, hoping it wouldn't meet with his stinging face. "I could never hurt you, Babe. Do you know that? Tessa? Do you know that?"

His breath was warm against her mouth as her eyes searched his. Water dripped from what black hair he had, and down his face as he stared at her unblinking. She recognized the deep pain he carried, usually hidden behind angry eyes. The man who saved her would someday die alone in some undetermined battle against America's enemies.

Tessa nodded half-heartedly. Raising her hand as if to touch his face she stopped when his eyes narrowed, waiting for another one of her deserved reprisals. She let her hand fall back to the concrete table to steady herself.

"I know," she whispered. Not wanting to look in those dark eyes, Tessa hoped she'd be able to control her emotions long enough to stay alive.

There was no expectation of privacy as he pulled out his phone and dialed. "Both targets down. Need clean-up crew ASAP. Do you have my location? Yes, I'm headed back now with the package," he said looking over at her shivering. The two dead men were still visible, even in darkness.

"Going to push them under the back of the table. Make it fast. Not much activity but you never know." He slipped the phone back in his pants pocket. With his finger under her chin, he turned her head toward him. "We need to go, Tess."

"What about them?" Her small voice forced him to lean in closer.

"Taken care of. Not to worry. But we need to question you about this evening." As her eyes drifted back over her shoulder where violence had just occurred, his hands grabbed her shoulders as he gently shook her. Tessa's attention shifted back to him. "They wanted you dead, Tessa. Do you know that? I had to kill them."

Turning away and heading back to the sidewalk, Chase kept her close. Aware that he constantly scanned the area forced her to realize there might be others looking for her uncle. The rain stopped and a shadowy moon appeared to bounce on clouds moving across the sky.

An occasional car drove past. Pulling her into a doorway or dark corner he would lean against her as if they were in a lovers' embrace. The thought of resisting the act evaporated each time his hands circled her waist. Once she involuntarily touched his side with open palms. After that she fought the urge to embrace him by visualizing him killing her trackers.

When they neared the hotel Chase slowed his steps and appeared to watch an approaching black van with shaded windows. It drove past then made a U-turn before heading back their way. Slipping an arm around him as his back pressed against her, Tessa stood on tip toes to peek over his shoulder. Her fingers dug into his jacket as the sound of brakes stopped outside their hiding spot.

The echo of doors sliding back bounced off the concrete canyons of Washington D.C. "Come on," he urged as he stepped toward the van. Taking her hand, she tried to resist. He tugged hard enough to cause her to stumble.

The inside darkness of the van did not shatter with an overhead light. Tessa saw others inside. She looked to her protector in confusion.

"They're Enigma. You need to go with them. I've got to go back and help. Maybe they left something we can use. They'll get you back to the hotel." She offered more resistance as he helped her up into the van. "Thanks," he said to someone sitting in the darkness. The van door slid shut even as it began to pull away from the curb.

A hand guided her into a seat. Someone wrapped a blanket around her shoulders as she looked out the windows to watch Chase storm off toward the crime scene. Her body twisted until he was completely out of site. Turning to face the front she realized they were not stopping at her hotel. A wave of panic washed over her, followed by trembling brought on by fear more than being soaked to the bone.

"We'll be just a few minutes, Tessa." The voice across from her was familiar. "The captain will be fine. You need not worry about him."

Pulling the blanket tighter around her shoulders she shivered a response. "Director Benjamin Clark." Her voice sounded more accusing than relieved.

"Correct." The director was a man of few words unless the situation demanded more.

"I'm not worried about your agent. I'm worried about my uncle."

"That makes two of us."

~~~

It was almost 4a.m. when Tessa entered her hotel room. She half expected someone to be waiting for her. Her nightgown still lay crumbled on the edge of the bed. The French doors were ajar letting in the cooled air. Before removing her clothes she moved to shut them. A hot shower, a couple of Tylenol and half a bottle of water had Tessa yawning. Wrapped in a white terry cloth robe she returned to the bedroom.

She'd been given assurances that someone would be down the hall watching. The director offered to send another agent to stay with her, but Tessa refused. Having someone so near sounded invasive when all you wanted was to be alone. With the dim light of the bedside lamp extinguished, she slipped beneath the sheets. The robe on her naked body remained until she warmed. As her eyelids grew heavy with sleep Tessa tried to force her mind to empty the events of the last few hours. Even as she drifted toward sleep, Tessa kept the image of Enigma's director in her head.

"Director, sir, where are we?" Tessa asked as the director

assisted her out of the van.

Dressed in a suit worn too long, he started removing a crooked tie. The open collar exposed a pale throat above a blue shirt. He looked around as the van moved away. His hand went suspiciously to his hip as if to reassure himself his weapon was ready. The parking lot was well lit next to a brick warehouse.

"We'll talk here after you get into some dry clothes. I promise not to keep you long." He opened a metal door then stepped aside for her to enter.

Nodding acceptance, she didn't wish to prolong the encounter. Even though she wasn't an agent, experience had taught her a year earlier the director respected her and could be trusted.

Upon entering the warehouse, Tessa noticed it had been scrubbed cleaner than the exterior indicated. Several nondescript vehicles sat idle. A workshop area, a few mismatched tables and chairs were about the extent of the lower floor. The metal stairs leading to the second floor echoed with their footsteps as they neared the sterile gray door. Once again Ben stepped aside for her to enter as he opened the door.

Someone fetched dry clothes for a quick change. The director stood with bent head as several young techie types filled him in, on what Tessa guessed, was information concerning the men who came after her. He returned to her soon enough then ordered her back to the van. Soon they were sitting at an all-night diner ordering pancakes and maple coated bacon with lots of hot coffee.

"You've stepped into another mess, Tessa." Ben sat with his back against the wall in the furthest booth from the door. He reached for a mug of steaming coffee the color of crude oil. "Hope you're hungry. This place makes the best pancakes east of the Mississippi River." Motioning toward her plate with his fork, he waited for Tessa to begin eating before he took his first bite. "We have not located your uncle. We found where he'd been staying. It appears he packed up and left before we arrived. But we think we're close."

"The men after him, who were they?" Tessa tried not to like the warm syrup dripping from her fork, but the director had been correct. The pancakes tasted extraordinary.

"Chase said they spoke Egyptian Arabic, a common language in the Middle East due to Egypt's influence in business and the cinema." He took another sip of the black liquid and paused as he met her eyes over the rim of the cup. "There are indications that they may be part of the former secret police."

"I thought after Arab Spring the Muslim Brotherhood disbanded them." She felt confusion at this new information.

Her studies in grad school centered on Middle Eastern geography. It both fascinated and disturbed her at the lack of respect for human life some societies had in these countries. It was no secret that the Egyptian police under President Mubarak used whatever means necessary in order to keep dissidents in line. When President Mubarak's government fell so did his henchmen.

"The Muslim Brotherhood would like for us to believe that. They are still active but go under the name of Homeland Security. It's a mocking gesture toward the United States implying that our Homeland Security is as ruthless as Egypt. Their point is that we corrupt and violate the human rights of our citizens, just as they practice."

"Why would they be after my Uncle Jake?"

"You are aware of the 1967 bombing of the USS Liberty?"

"That keeps coming up."

"Yes. President Johnson dropped the ball in calling out the Israelis on this. He accepted their story of mistaken identity because our ship wasn't flying our flag."

"My uncle says different." Tessa bristled.

"Your uncle is correct. Every survivor on the Liberty swore the flag was raised. Several even waved at the Israeli pilots who flew over. The ship was clearly marked. It was an intel gathering ship."

"They were spying in other words." Tessa spoke as she used her finger to catch a drip of syrup at the corner of her mouth.

"For our purposes let's say they were on a fact finding mission in case the Russians decided to interfere with the war between Israel and Egypt. They promised to stay out of it if we did. We were merely making sure that was the case."

"Thirty-four men lost their lives and our government never honored them because they feared offending Israel." Tessa's voice sounded edgy. She knew Ben's father was an Israeli general and his brother was the prime minister. "I'm sorry, Director. I mean no disrespect."

Ben nodded then a tired smile started to appear on his lips and just as quickly disappeared. "None taken, Tessa. I don't approve of what President Johnson did. He let those men down. As for Israel…" His words seemed to fade as he sat his cup back down then pushed his plate away. "I'm not proud of what they did either. They should have been held accountable. The money they offered in the early eighties for the destruction of the ship hardly covered the cost. A few families received a small compensation but they would have preferred a public recognition of their service and Israel's betrayal."

"Yes. I believe that to be true. Director, my uncle is a kind and gentle man. I know he has complained loudly for the last forty or so years, but…"

Ben held up his hand for her to stop talking. "He's done more than that. Jake Wakefield has sent threatening letters to every sitting president since he returned from his military obligations. The Israeli Embassy receives at least one letter a month expressing his desire for their demise as a nation. His demands of a Palestinian homeland and immediate withdrawal from Gaza, the Golan Heights and the West Bank are pretty much required reading by the Mossad. Were you aware that every year on the June anniversary he comes to Washington D.C. and stands outside the Israeli Embassy carrying a sign that calls them murderers?"

"The truth hurts," Tessa quipped. "And no, I wasn't aware he did that. I'm sure my father doesn't know either. I don't agree with my uncle's methods, believe me. Heaven knows I'm a big supporter of Israel, but even in our own American history we've done despicable things. Look at the Native Americans, slavery and innocent Pakistanis we mistakenly killed several years ago in an air raid. We had to own up to that. There have been many more times when we were called on the carpet for our screw-ups. Why not Israel? You know I'm not even angry at Israel for what they did. It's our government that let those men down." Tessa leaned back against the warm brown leather and took a deep breath. "Those men of the USS Liberty have been made to feel like liars. And now because of my uncle's pro-active agenda he's been targeted by people who want him to do their dirty work."

"What dirty work is that?" The director of Enigma leaned forward and frowned, his eyebrows meeting over his sharp nose giving him the look of a resolute bald eagle.

"Whoever these people are, they've kidnapped some of the USS Liberty crew and are holding them until my uncle kills the president and the Israeli Prime Minister." She laid down her fork before grabbing another napkin to dab at her mouth. "He's terrified. This wasn't the way he wanted attention brought to the USS Liberty. If he succeeds everyone will say, 'see they were all crazy and Jake Wakefield is proof.'" Tessa was too tired and traumatized to cry.

"Tell me what you know, Tessa. We need to get your uncle before he makes a terrible mistake. This president and prime minister are meeting this very week to decide how to resolve the USS Liberty. It was my father's dying wish that Israel not be perceived as the monster Hitler became in slaughtering so many Israelis. I fear that Egypt is trying to derail the talks and diminish what is trying to be done."

"Why would they do that? Considering how many innocent Egyptians died at the hands of the Israelis I would think they would love to gloat over the truth told to the world."

He leaned back against the torn fake leather and sighed so heavily she worried he was tiring of her questions. "We think there are two possibilities. One is that Israel would be vulnerable, thrown into chaos without my brother to lead. They could be invaded, attacked or a number of other scenarios I won't go into right now."

Tessa felt her heart beating rapidly. "And two?"

"Maybe the prime minister would survive. With the president dead, terrorists could implement any plans they have on standby. Now that your uncle is involved, it may be that Israel would again look like they were trying to keep atrocities that happened in the Six Day War quiet. Blame would shift to Israel for a dead American president. Any further support, financially or militarily would be suspended until a thorough investigation was completed. We both know D.C. investigations move at a snail's pace. With a dead president, the stock market could crash; world leaders would feel we were no longer invincible and make deals with the devil. France would be at the head of the line. They have a long history of selling arms to countries we boycott or deem rogue nations. That's just a start."

Tessa covered her face with her hands, forcing back tears. "Uncle Jake, what have you done?" She dropped her hands to the table, rattling the dishes. "Tell me what to do. They've threatened him with me." She told him about the pictures of her and Zoric. "When I told him Zoric could help he got spooked. Thought I worked for the government and was sent to trap him." She noticed a slight change in the director's facial expression.

"I'm glad to hear that, Tessa. Let's hope you prove as valuable as the last time you helped us out."

CHAPTER 9

Frowning, Gilad Levi looked over the front page of The Washington Post. He'd already read most of the highlights when his secretary came in with a security update from Israel. Folding the newspaper as if he were diapering a newborn, the prime minister exchanged it for the report. The male secretary stood silent, waiting for instructions while holding The Washington Post like he'd been handed a piece of used toilet paper. Even his usually impassive face developed a sneer as his unflinching eyes looked straight ahead.

"Thank you, David. Anything else I need to attend before finishing my coffee?" Without waiting, Gilad picked up his cooled cup of coffee with one hand as he passed the report back to the secretary with the other.

"Director Kempler requests you call him before meeting with the president."

Gilad cut his hawk eyes up at his secretary. "Dov doesn't have enough to do at Mossad? He needs me to hold his hand?"

The secretary repressed a rare smile. The Prime Minister appreciated that David kept most of his comments to himself. Displaying intelligence and resourcefulness on numerous occasions, the secretary proved to also be intuitive to the moods of his boss. This was one of those times laughter would be most inappropriate.

"I believe he is concerned about your safety, Sir."

Gilad waved his hand in the air with contempt. David took the prime minister's cup and refilled it before pouring himself one. Sitting it down on The Washington Post, a few drops sloshed out onto a picture of a Hollywood actor being led off to jail in handcuffs.

"How is our guest, David?" Gilad blew gently across the vapor rising from his cup. "Is he still resting? Perhaps he'd like to join me for coffee."

"I believe he has showered and is pacing like an angry..." David seemed to search for a word as he looked up at the ceiling. "What do you call those large cats that roam in American woods?"

"Mountain lions, cougars, pumas; it really depends on what part of the country you're from."

"Pacing like a mountain lion."

"Have Ari bring him down to me." Gilad pushed back from the table and crossed his muscled legs before taking a large swallow of his coffee. "Is this the coffee my brother sent over?"

"Yes. But Prime Minister, I must advise seeing this man is political suicide. If the president should find out or even your brother..."

"Let me worry about the American president. As for my brother, what he doesn't know won't hurt me." He grinned and held out his cup to be refilled. Drinking coffee all day was a habit the prime minister enjoyed. "Coffee. Guest. In that order, David."

David rose quickly from his plush chair and moved to the buffet. "Have you eaten, Sir?"

Gilad grunted as he picked up the newspaper again. David knew a guttural sound meant he hadn't bothered. With coffee delivered, David made the call upstairs.

In moments footsteps approached, stopping outside the large dining room before lightly tapping on the door. David opened the door trying not to reveal too much in case it wasn't Ari, all two hundred and seventy five pounds of him, with the guest. Ari's partner, another Israeli agent, was nearly as big. The guest in the middle looked more like a little hobbit between the two giants. David jerked his nose up in distaste as he stepped aside for them to enter.

The guest began looking around the room as if he might bolt. He was uneasy until his eyes fell on the man sitting at the table reading a paper. Although the guest couldn't see his face, the secretary watched him come to an immediate realization of the importance of the man who sat before him. Everyone remained quiet until the prime minister lowered his paper and stood.

Gilad, dressed in a dark gray suit, white shirt and red tie, looked imposing as he eyed his guest. "Take off the handcuffs, Ari." Gilad stared into the eyes of his guest and recognized he'd locked horns with an equal.

"Sir, I don't think that is wise." Ari pulled out the key and stood rigid.

Gilad frowned, as his booming voice vibrated the pictures hanging on the walls. "I am the Prime Minister of Israel. I'm sick and tired of people telling me what's wise or what's safe or," his eyes went to David, "that my coffee is from my brother when it is not."

David arched an eyebrow in an admission of guilt. He'd seen these tirades before. "I will fix a new pot of coffee, Sir. But this is a good example of why you should drink decaf."

Gilad moved closer to the guest and eyed him from head to toe. He waved David away then pointed at the handcuffs on his guest. Immediately Ari released the guest before slipping both cuffs and key in the pocket of his blazer. The guard went back to standing at attention. The guest looked at Ari before measuring up the second guard.

"What are you feedin' these boys?" The guest rubbed his wrists carefully.

Gilad laughed as he pointed toward the table. "Join me for breakfast, Mr. Wakefield. I believe we have a lot to discuss."

~~~

Congressman Gault looked down at the flight attendant covered only with a wrinkled sheet. Confusion as to whether or not he'd satisfied her last night remained in question. Confused thoughts swirled in a foggy head. He was going to have to take it easy on the booze if these kinds of mornings continued. Pulling the Egyptian cotton sheet back, he saw that she was nude and laying on her stomach. The neck length auburn hair covered her face.

He quickly showered and shaved before going back into the bedroom where he found the bed empty. Before he could wonder where she'd gone, the bedroom door opened and Carmen entered carrying a tray. She had slipped on the white shirt he'd laid out to wear today. No matter. He had others.

"What have you brought me? Aspirin I hope. My head is killing me." He smiled, spreading open the unbuttoned shirt which swallowed her slim figure.

"Umm," she purred as she handed him a Bloody Mary. "No. Drink this." She watched him gulp it down. Then she handed him a small glass of water. "Then this."

"Are you an expert?" he teased as he began to sip the water.

"Yes. You'd be surprised what kinds of things I learned in my training to be a flight attendant." She took the glass from his hand and sat it on the nightstand. "The best thing for a hangover is sex. Did you know that?"

"I don't believe it and my head hurts too bad to try," he whined, yet managed a quick kiss on her lips.

"My head feels just fine, so I will take care of you." Carmen opened his robe and stepped inside. "And tonight don't drink so much. I have plans I think you'll like."

"Can't tonight," he said pushing her at arm's length. "I have to work. This just might be the biggest day of my life."

"Really? Why is that? Introducing a bill or something? And besides what could be better than being the Speaker of the House?"

"Being president," he chuckled then moaned as he rubbed his forehead. He turned her around to admire her backside before swatting her buttocks. "Get dressed and I'll have my driver drop you at the airport. You do have a flight today." It was more of a statement than a question.

Carmen started gathering up her scattered clothes around the room before heading to the bathroom. "To St. Louis, then Chicago then back here if I'm lucky. Since I won't be seeing you I'll try and pick up another route. It might be a few days before I'm back."

The congressman smiled as he looked at himself in the mirror to adjust the collar of his pale blue shirt. "You'd be surprised how things can change in a few days, my sweet Carmen."

~~~

She slipped into the bathroom, turning on the shower.

Extending her hand under the water, she hoped it was hot enough to wash the repulsive smell of the congressman off her body. Stripping off the white shirt, she called over her shoulder. "That sounds pretty cryptic, Jimmy."

"Hurry it up, Carmen. Some of us have important work to do."

As Carmen stepped into the shower, a wicked smile formed on her face. She mumbled under her breath. "That's for sure, Mr. Speaker of the House. Some of us have very important work to do. And you will discover too late that I'm very good at what I do."

~~~

Tessa reached for the alarm clock to check the time. The message light flickered on the phone as she swung her legs over the side of the bed. Still wrapped in the white robe, she retied the belt before gingerly touching the carpet with her toes. Ten o'clock. Pushing her matted curls from her face she retrieved the messages with apprehension.

The first one was from Shelly.

"Hey you. Got your message about heading out early for a behind-the-scenes tour of the Egyptian exhibit at the Smithsonian. I'm off to the Native American Museum and Kate is going to the Air and Space Museum. Several other science teachers got invitations for an escorted tour. Call us and we'll meet for lunch. Have fun today. I know you love that creepy, boring stuff. Hugs."

Realizing Enigma had already taken control of her life, she wasn't all that surprised they'd made arrangements for her friends to be occupied. Hopefully they'd located her uncle and put him under house arrest to keep him from creating a catastrophe of monumental proportions. She'd been warned on the way back to her hotel not to contact her family concerning her uncle. There was no doubt in her mind that all lines of communication were being monitored in case her uncle slipped up.

The next message was unexpected. "Mrs. Scott. This is Dr. Wu. I'll meet you at 10:30 for coffee in the hotel café. We have some things to go over."

Sucking in her breath, as her legs stumbled toward the bathroom; she realized the appointment was in twenty minutes.

~~~

The smell of all things baked, filled the air of the hotel café when Tessa rushed in with her heart pounding in her ears from too much exertion in a short period of time. She knew working out needed to be part of her daily routine since she was seeing forty on the horizon. Donuts and a teacher's lounge thought differently.

The twenty minute deadline forced Tessa to cut corners in her appearance. Sleeping on wet hair caused the long tresses to curl up above her shoulders. She tried to tame the locks by pushing them back with a narrow headband. It wasn't enough to keep a curl from escaping down her forehead. A pair of dress jeans, white shirt and a black sweater carried lopsided over one arm made her wonder if she came too casually. At the last minute she'd slipped on some low heels. Everyone in the café appeared to be dressed for a business meeting except one man sitting in a booth near the back.

Navigating through a room with too many tables and chairs, with hands flying up in expressive condemnation or excitement, forced her to pause several times. Shifting her eyes to the man in the booth made her feel like a baby chick cracking open its shell to enter the world. Once she offered a nod of greeting with a thin smile at him, but the gesture was not returned. A pudgy woman dressed in a leopard skirt and black top suddenly stood up, pushing her chair into Tessa's hip, causing the notebook and purse she carried, to drop to the floor. The leopard clad woman grabbed her latte and headed out, unaware of the accident.

Tessa bent down to gather up her things, causing her head band to fall off. She blew the wayward curls from her forehead as her hand shoved the band back into place. Another pair of hands joined in clearing the chaos as others walked around her.

"Dr. Wu." She tried to stand without looking like an arthritic granny when he took her elbow and assisted with a gentle tug. "Thank you. I'm sorry I'm late, but…"

"Shall we sit?" He spoke with patience then guided her toward the booth. She found a Styrofoam cup of coffee waiting for her. The lazy vapor trails lifted from the hot brew as Tessa inhaled, loving the smell of the possibility of rejuvenation.

"Any news of my uncle?" Her eyes searched his face anxious to hear something positive for a change. "He was so distraught last night."

"Yet he left you to face the Egyptians alone." His shrug hinted at condemnation as he slipped into the seat across from her.The insult made her bristle. "He led them away from me. My uncle would never jeopardize my safety."

His narrow eyes scanned the room, just as Zoric's and Chase's always did; watching for some unknown threat to appear. He nodded at the coffee. "It's just like you prefer: three creams and two sugars. And I'm sorry there is no news of your uncle. We found where he stayed for a short time, but after he left you last night, he moved. I believe you already know this from speaking with the director."

After sipping the brew she continued to hold the cup so the warmth would seep through her fingers, a habit she'd started in college. "How did you know about the coffee?" Then she shook her head. "Never mind. I assume my life is an open book at Enigma."

Dr. Wu smiled revealing straight teeth which made his nostrils flair ever so slightly. Creases formed at the corners of his eyes making the cool expression evaporate. "You are required reading. When you tangle with Enigma, my job is to straighten things out."

"Maybe if I could read some of their files I wouldn't keep getting into so much trouble." Another sip of caffeine started the coming awake process. "Are you here to get me up to speed, Dr. Wu?"

His smile remained as he folded his hands on the table. She wondered about his age. With such flawless skin it was impossible to tell. There was youthfulness about him Tessa found distracting. A few hints of long gray hair showed behind his ears.

"No. I'm sorry. I'm here to evaluate your state of mind."

Taking a deep breath, Tessa sat her cup down and folded her hands before meeting his eyes with steel resolve. After all, what did she have to lose? It wasn't like she had a choice. When she didn't say anything further, he eyed her with appreciation.

"You are stubborn."

"You are correct." She tilted her head like an inquisitive child. Unaware the look gave her a kind of innocent charm, she watched the doctor lift a notebook lying on the seat next to him. "Do I get an ink blot test or something? I'm sure I can fail if given a chance."

"That sounds like something Captain Hunter would say. Did he coach you in the art of taunting me?"

"No. I don't take orders from cavemen. Better write that down, Dr. Wu. I'm sure he'll find it very amusing."

"I have a photographic memory. I don't need to take notes or use electronic recording devices with my—clients. Besides, patient doctor privilege you know."

"Really?" She felt skeptical as she picked up the cup again. "So the notebook is just for show?" Tessa didn't want to like him but she couldn't help herself. "I was really hoping you'd tell Chase I think he's a Neanderthal. Oh well," she sighed lifting the cup to her lips. "Probably more effective coming from me anyway." This brought a quiet chuckle, making his shoulders shake as if he were suppressing a larger belly laugh.

"Please. Let me, Tessa. I so love throwing him off guard."

His smile, although cynical, was infectious. "So do I, Dr. Wu. Go ahead and tell him. I think I've already called him that on occasion."

"Are you in love with the captain?" Dr. Wu was so casual about the question, he could have been asking about the weather.

Tessa choked on her coffee causing a trickle to run down her chin. Grabbing a napkin to dab away the embarrassment, she tried to clear her throat, but her voice still came out sounding like a frog. "Absolutely not. I'm in love with my husband. Why would you ask such a thing?" Her indignation was evident as she gathered up her things to leave. "Is it because of that little diversion Chase orchestrated last night?" The color rose up her neck, giving too much away. She blew a wayward curl up out of her eye. "I should have known."

With the calm of a Black Mamba, Dr. Wu eyed his flustered companion. "What diversion?"

The fidgeting stopped as she shot Dr. Wu a warning look. "Dragging me into that alley and..." Realizing the doctor was unaware of Chase's physical efforts to distract the Egyptians ended her comments. "It doesn't matter."

Her breathing increased just as she felt a vein on her neck begin to pulse. Resisting the urge to touch it was difficult, remembering Chase's mouth pressed against her skin. She only knew that Dr. Wu continued to exhibit a thin smile of amusement at her awkward attempts to show indignation. "My personal life is none of Enigma's or your business."

"I am your therapist…"

"You most certainly are not. I don't even know you. Why would I tell you anything?"

Dr. Wu nodded but remained calm and unreadable. "I meant no disrespect, Tessa. I'm very aware that you and your husband, Robert is it?" She lifted her chin in defiance as he continued. "You and Robert have a remarkable family. He's a good provider, father and husband, by all accounts."

"So why would you ask such a ridiculous question?" She fumed then slid to the edge of the bench.

"Many women find the captain quite charming and…"

"I'm not one of them," she insisted with a hiss.

"Be that as it may, I needed to ask. The two of you went through some dangerous encounters a year ago, where he saved your life on several occasions. He can be ruthless and unforgiving to those who work for him. Demanding, lethal, risk taker and short tempered have all been used to describe him. And I might add, those are the compliments."

"I still don't see why you asked me about my feelings. I've experienced a lot of what you just said first hand. Why on earth would I fall in love with someone who feels comfortable killing for a living?"

"Because he saved you from unspeakable torture and even death."

"And I will be forever grateful. But that doesn't mean I'm carrying a torch for him. Surely I'm not the first damsel in distress he's saved. Do you question them?"

"No. However, you are the first damsel that changed him." Dr. Wu watched her expression soften as her eyes dropped. His expression indicated he believed something occurred between the two; something deep, hidden from their coping mechanisms.

"I'm grateful. Not in love." Tessa whispered. "Someday I'll return the favor if I can." Although, that scenario likened to a mouse saving a charging bull elephant. "Are we done?"

Dr. Wu scooted out then reached for Tessa's coffee. "We're just getting started. Now, since you are supposed to be getting a tour of the Egyptian exhibit I think we should head in that direction."

She felt excitement at getting a behind-the-scene tour at the Smithsonian. Guilt moved in knowing she could be so easily distracted from the plight of her uncle. "And you are my escort?"

She stood just inches from the doctor, aware that even he, like the other Enigma agents, possessed a magnetic charm which could turn into an emotional poison.

He handed her his notebook as he removed the one she pulled to her chest. "What is this?"

"The files on Captain Hunter."

Her eyes widened as she looked down at the closest thing to the Holy Grail she'd ever possess. "Is that even ethical?"

Laying a hand on Tessa's back to gently move her forward Dr. Wu whispered in her ear. "Absolutely not. If that is a problem for you, I will gladly take back the file."

"I just might need a few therapy sessions after all."

Dr. Wu looked smug as he motioned her toward the exit. "I thought in the future we might need each other."

CHAPTER 10

The Prime Minister felt admiration for the Tennessee man sitting across the table. Even though his captive understood the danger surrounding him could end his life without a trace, Jake Wakefield remained relaxed. He funneled a second helping of eggs into his mouth. Gilad respected that not once did he exhibit fear. The old guy might as well have been having breakfast with his hillbilly kinsmen back in Franklin, Tennessee. He knew from experience the man was stalling, trying to connect on a personal level, in hopes of avoiding the death that would eventually occur.

They spoke of hunting, the drought in the Midwest, how he'd built his log home with the help of friends and family. When Gilad inquired about Jake's niece, Jake made a loud swallowing sound and pushed his plate away. He leaned back into the cushioned chair. The old man's eyes narrowed as his tongue moved around his teeth to remove any pieces of food before he tried to speak.

"My niece is none of your business." Jake caught a glimpse of Gilad's secretary flinch at the sour response.

"She is working for a secret government agency. Did you know?" Gilad couldn't help but notice how Jake's body stiffened ever so slightly. "It wasn't her idea, of course."

"Whose idea was it?" he snarled leaning forward. "Yours?"

Gilad motioned for David to come forward with a black file folder he carried precariously in his hand. He handed it to Jake then stepped back. "No. Someone named Captain Hunter thought she possessed a set of unique skills." His smile suggested something tawdry.

"I don't believe you," Jake said with a growl. "She's a school teacher. Not some government whack job."

The Prime Minister chuckled and motioned his guest to open the file folder. "Take a look before you make too many quick judgments, my friend."

One corner of Jake's mouth lifted in a snarl. "I'm not your friend and never will be."

Gilad nodded and stood. "Understood. While you get reacquainted with your niece, would you like David to bring you anything?"

"How about my rifle?" he snapped through gritted teeth. He proceeded to open the folder.

Smothering a chuckle with a cough Gilad proceeded to leave the room. "Perhaps later, Mr. Wakefield. Take your time. You're not going anywhere."

"You're holding an American against their will." Turning his head enough to see the prime minister leave the room, Jake noticed David wore a shoulder harness with a deadly looking weapon.

~~~

Gilad walked briskly into his office before stopping at a window. Ari, his body guard, followed at a safe distance, giving the prime minister plenty of room to breathe. Pretending he was just an ordinary citizen of Israel and didn't need twenty four seven protection helped in times like these. Staring at the grounds outside, his hands clasped behind his back. Chewing on the inside of his lower lip developed the intense concentration required for his job.

The argument David made earlier, about kidnapping an American citizen on American soil, weighed like a ton of bricks. Did it really border on recklessness or just insanity?

The Prime Minister watched a Mossad agent the night before drag Jake's unconscious body out of the trunk of an embassy car. He hadn't been harmed, only disengaged for the ride. Now he sat examining a file on someone he thought he knew. No matter Tessa Scott had been selected as a pawn to find her uncle. His own investigation showed the woman was clueless as to the mess her uncle had stepped into.

By the look on his face, the old hillbilly wouldn't approve of his niece working for the government. Maybe he could use that to Israel's advantage. After all, whatever made Israel safer would be justified in the eyes of God. At least that's what he told himself every time he bent the truth. How much truth should he share with his brother Ben?

Raised in two worlds, America and Israel, Gilad loved both countries, but served the Star of David as his father had for so many years. The father groomed both his boys for the future: one to serve Israel and one to serve Israel's interests if the need ever arose.

In his mind, there was no doubt who Benjamin served. He served America and the president. The Enigma Director meant for both to remain safe on his watch. Gilad frowned knowing the brother he loved so dearly might turn against him when he found out his plans.

A tap at the door, another beefy agent named Micah, stuck his large head inside to break Gilad's concentration. "David says he's ready to talk, sir."

"Do you have his rifle?" Micah nodded as he pushed the door open wider for the prime minister to exit. "Bring it to me." Micah disappeared then returned momentarily with the weapon. Gilad examined it with care, making sure it was unloaded. "I want the Tavor too, Micah."

"Yes, sir. David isn't going to like this." Gilad leveled a dangerous scowl at his bodyguard.

"Right away, Sir."

Strolling back to the dining room, he entered nonchalantly, holding the rifle over his shoulder as if he'd been out squirrel hunting with the man from Tennessee.

"So how old is this thing? I'll have to say it's in remarkable shape."

Jake was pouring himself a cup of coffee from the buffet as David stood to the side, watching with apprehension. He took a sip of the hot brew and nodded at the rifle. "Belonged to my daddy. Still shoots true. Clean it once a week." He swirled his words around like a man chewing tobacco.

Gilad removed the rifle from his shoulder and eyed it carefully as if seeing it for the first time. "I used to squirrel hunt with my grandpa in North Carolina." He extended it to his guest.

Jake couldn't cover his surprise. "Didn't know you were an American."

"Not by birth. My stepmother adopted me so I became an American and an Israeli citizen. In the end I chose Israel as the country to serve. But her father gave me lots of guidance in hunting and surviving."

The old man moved gingerly toward the table, sitting his delicate porcelain cup down on the table. He sensed the prime minister was trying to tell him something. "Guess he didn't teach you how to be an American." He grabbed the rifle a little too eagerly.

Micah entered the room and handed the prime minister the Tavor who cradled it like a baby. A thin, sinister smile appeared on his tan face. "Ever see one of these?"

Jake laid his rifle down across the tablecloth before reaching for his coffee. He shook his head as he leveled curious eyes over the edge of his porcelain cup.

Gilad stepped forward and offered him the weapon. "Have a look."

He eyed him suspiciously before grasping the Tavor. A slow smile appeared as he examined the weapon from every angle then lifted it up to check the sight. He slowly turned it toward Gilad and held it steady.

"Do you know anything about the USS Liberty, Mr. Prime Minister?" Jake's voice sounded raspy from years of smoking.

Micah took a step closer to the prime minister as David nervously sat the cup down on the buffet with one hand and reached inside his jacket with the other.

The old man chuckled as he lowered the weapon and handed it back to Gilad. His eyes went to the two other men in the room. "Relax boys. I might be from Tennessee but I'm no dummy. I know when I'm out gunned."

Gilad smirked and handed off the Tavor to Micah. He nodded to follow him into a light-filled sitting room, where they could sit across from each other in winged back chairs. With a sigh, he crossed his legs and began tapping his index finger on the leather arm of the chair.

"Yes. I'm aware of the mistakes made concerning the USS Liberty, Jake. You have written us so many times about the mindless slaughter of Americans aboard that rust bucket that I can quote most of them by heart." Jake remained quiet. "My father was serving on the Egyptian border at that time." Jake narrowed his eyes in hatred. "He carried out orders that sickened him. Although he did not take part in the attack on the USS Liberty my father did..." Gilad stopped and turned his eyes upward thoughtfully before continuing slowly. "It was my father's wish that someday he would be able to make amends to the Americans who were killed that day."

"Then apologize for killing the thirty four men on that ship. Admit that President Johnson helped hide your murderous deeds." Jake had straightened in his chair and pointed a finger toward the prime minister.

Gilad nodded. "Agreed. There is one little thing I want you do for me first."

"What is that?"

"Continue with your orders from the Egyptians."

"I don't know what you're talking about." Jake pushed out his lower lip as his eyes became hooded.

Gilad smiled cat-like. "You were told to kill the president.

CHAPTER 11

The Museum of Natural History seemed to suck any kind of words from Tessa's mouth as she walked into the grand foyer. Her eyes fell on an African bull elephant posed for confrontation to the world around him. The amusing thought of him coming to life after the last tourist left at night forced her eyes to slide around the upper balconies to wonder at the mysteries awaiting her. She hadn't realized her lips were parted or that she stared in awe at the worlds displayed around her until Dr. Wu touched her elbow and gently moved her toward one of the halls coming off the grand foyer.

A narrow and ominous smile spread across Dr. Wu's closed lips. Extending his hand toward a door that read *Museum Personnel Only,* the doctor nodded for her to move in that direction. With his side long glances, she felt he continued to evaluate her.

"Curious, suspicious and obstinate." He spoke with the same interest a scientist might use looking at a lab rat.

She offered an exaggerated sigh of disgust as her feet turned toward the door and tried to open it without success.

He slipped in behind and reached around her, laying his hand over hers. Tessa became aware his face had touched her hair. For a moment she thought the doctor sniffed at her unruly curls. The attempt at withdrawing her hand forced him to step closer.

Tessa speculated, *maybe Chase doesn't like Dr. Wu because he is a little more than a mind bender. Or maybe he was just another reminder that Enigma agents were one step away from being just like the men they hunted. I would never fit in with this bunch.*

"Allow me, Tessa. It's a bit tricky." The lever pushed down as he pulled, forcing her to step back into him. He quickly stepped aside.

Without a word or a glance back, Tessa passed into the world of knowledge. She took no more than three steps when she halted. It looked like a lab and beyond that she could see shelves of artifacts. Moving forward, she couldn't resist a smile at smelling the age of time that comes with old things. The hum of environmental controls and the quiet voices of people working reached her ears. She turned back to see if Dr. Wu strolled behind her with his smug, evaluating gaze. He imparted a feeling of standing naked before an audience of one, but he had vanished.

With nerves on end, Tessa turned around several times to see where he'd disappeared to. Aware she'd been left alone, behind the scenes of the Museum of Natural History, her imagination kicked into overdrive.

Maybe someone would now force her into submission with a coma inducing drug so that they could turn her into a mummy.

Or perhaps she'd accidently, on purpose, get bitten by some exotic beetle from a tropical rainforest.

Just as she thought about the poisonous bite of a Black Mamba she heard her name.

"Tessa! There you are!" came the jolly yet familiar voice of Dr. Frances Ervin. "Think you were lost?" He chuckled as he rushed up with his lab coat flapping. "I see Dr. Wu has just abandoned you. He likes to think of himself as a ghost, I think." His smile reminded Tessa of a patient father. "I texted you last night but you were a no show, as they say."

She blinked in confusion while eyeing the professor. So the message had come from him?

"You have the USS Liberty as your screen saver. Why?" Her brain tried to sort this new turn of events into place.

He puffed out a sigh but continued to look jolly at her direct approach. "After the conference I'm due to speak at a hearing on the USS Liberty. Quite extraordinary really." He smiled as he swiped a handkerchief across his forehead. "My oldest brother was killed on that ship. My mother was never the same after she got the news. I didn't understand it all at the time because of my age. But in recent years I got curious and did a little digging."

The tension began to ebb away as the professor looked at her with bewilderment. "My uncle was on that ship." She tried to sound nonchalant.

"Yes, of course. He's rather a loose cannon, I hear. Got Enigma and those Secret Service boys all in a twist. You have my card. Have him give me a call. I'm putting a book together for the families. I'd love to take a few pictures and get his story. They tried to get me to visit them at a reunion in Arizona last year, but I was in Jordan doing some work at Petra."

"Dr. Ervin?" Tessa couldn't resist showing surprise as her words spilled out in a stutter. "Why are you here?" She looked around her, wide eyed.

"To give you a behind the scenes tour, of course." He smiled handing her a crisp white lab coat. "You'll need to wear one of these."

No Black Mamba bite, no tropical beetle or sarcophagus to lay her wrapped body? "I don't understand." He took back the coat and held it out for her to slip into, which she did slowly. "You knew I was coming?"

The professor jammed his hands into the pockets of his coat. "Yes, of course. The director set it up last night. Didn't he tell you? I happily agreed to be your escort while things are getting sorted out."

Her head shook in confusion. "Wait a minute. You know the director?" Maybe this was a trap to find out if she withheld information from Enigma. That whole mummy thing could still happen.

"Come this way, Tessa. I'm working on some things I brought back from Petra. I could use a hand. We're a little short staffed. So many people out in the field or helping with the conference this week. Understandable. I don't mind." He started to walk away then stopped when she didn't follow. Walking back, he smiled and lowered his voice. "Yes. Director Clark calls upon me from time to time to assist Enigma. I'm a Biblical Archeologist that can come and go throughout the Middle East without much suspicion. Who would suspect a musty old man, like me, of being a spy? Chase calls it a 'get out of jail free card'." He shook his head and chuckled. "That boy has had me use it for him a time or two. Why just last year…"

Tessa grabbed his arm. "Are you telling me you work for Enigma?" She watched the jolly expression on his face turn cold and hard. "The truth."

"Yes. Not full time. Getting too old for that sort of thing and Martha would put her foot down."

"Does Martha know about your work?"

"Certainly." He began to move down the narrow aisle of tables and shelving units as he motioned for her to follow. "She too, is on the payroll."

Tessa was intrigued that someone actually had a spouse and knew of the secrets kept at Enigma. "What does she do?"

"Whatever is needed." He pulled her forward as the room opened up. "Enough about all that…"

"Did you know who I was on the plane?"

"Yes."

"Did you really need my help with the computer last night?"

"No."

"You wanted me to see the picture of the USS Liberty?"

"Yes. I thought maybe your uncle had contacted you and I would find out."

"So you lied and played me?"

"Yes. I'm afraid so. I'm not nearly as helpless as I appear." He looked sheepishly at her and tried to smile. "I ask your forgiveness. I wanted to see how things played out. The director is a stickler for following his wishes. Now we have a lot to see and even more to do."

Walking beside him, she eyed the surroundings for a hint of trouble. "Your opinion of Dr. Wu?"

"A mind bender, but an excellent therapist. He's helped me on a number of occasions as I'm sure you'll find out."

"I don't need a therapist," she said confidently.

"You will, my dear. You will."

~~~

Their first meeting at the White House the day before had

been in secret. It had lasted less than two hours. The aides did most of the talking and planning. The president and the prime minister chose to stroll the vegetable garden the first lady had planted with their children. A few words about Iran and Syria passed between them only to be interrupted by Secret Service calling them back inside because of weather concerns.

Now on the second day with the luncheon concluded and the photo op with the press behind them, President Austin and Prime Minister Levi strolled back to the Oval Office for a meeting without aides, secretaries or advisors. Each had a security detail nearby, but not inside the walls of the most coveted space in the world. Both men selected a tightly upholstered chair in blue and gold with a small table between them. A coffee service rested on a serving cart near the leaders who sat down heavily.

Earlier they had joked openly with each other for the cameras and the small talk at lunch flowed easily as if all were right with the world. Two of the president's children escaped their Secret Service agents and ran into the dining room to hide underneath the table.

"Children? What children?" Gilad openly lied to the agents about the whereabouts of the children with his own devious smirk. The giggle of small children will always give away a good hiding place and they were soon led from the room.

Now dead silence hung like the August humidity between them. All pretenses evaporated and both men seemed to ponder their agenda carefully before speaking.

With a light tap at the door before it opened, the president's aide announced Director Clark from Enigma had arrived. The president nodded and held up a finger before waving him away.

"Your brother is concerned I'm going to get killed."

Gilad crossed his legs and picked at a piece of lent from his pant leg. "As am I, Mr. President. There is always a risk."

"It's just us, Gilad so 'Buck' will be fine." Gilad nodded and squared his shoulders. "This whole USS Liberty thing is going to be a problem. LBJ should have taken care of it when this whole thing started."

"It was a different world then, Buck. Israel was so young and brash that we often tried to take two steps forward before anyone could knock us four steps back. The Holocaust was still so bitter in our mouths. We'd learned to be ruthless from the best. The Cold War raged between Russia and your country. Even though both countries promised to stay out of the Six Day War we feared the Egyptians would secure help from the Russians. I'm not sure we could have survived that."

Gilad stood and reached for the coffee. He pointed at a second cup and the president declined with a nod. Sitting back down, Gilad took a sip and smiled. "I see my brother has tipped you off to the kind of coffee I enjoy."

The president narrowed his eyes when he tried to smile. "Your brother is very devoted to me and this country."

Gilad took another sip. "But you wonder if it came down to me or you would Benjamin be so loyal?"

The president leaned back in his chair, which he noticed was uncomfortable, and made a mental note to get rid of it. "No, I wonder if you could handle it if he took you to task and spanked your sorry ass for holding an American citizen hostage in your embassy."

Gilad looked dangerously over the rim of his cup at the president. "A hostage, I might add, that has promised to kill both of us in revenge for the attack on the USS Liberty."

"So what are you going to do? Just make him disappear and expect the problem to go away? There are others just as determined to see this issue resolved."

"Compensation was made several years after the fact. We thought that would be enough. Americans are very greedy."

"And Israelis are as ruthless as we are greedy. What made you think this was about money? That pittance you gave the U.S. wouldn't cover the cost of the paint and repairs made to the Liberty."

"LBJ's grandmother was Jewish. Did you know that? He saved many of our people during World War II. He knew our potential and wanted to keep us as allies in the years to come." His tone had become sharp.

"Keep your friends close and your enemies closer," the president quipped.

"Israel is not your enemy, Buck. I love this country and the last administration nearly destroyed any layer of protection you had for the U.S., not to mention for Israel. The Six Day War turned

Israel into a country to be reckoned with in spite of our lies and deception. Do you think Americans would have had any sympathy if they knew it was actually Israel that started that war? No. This country loves an underdog and will stand up and cheer every time someone like us is picked on."

"That doesn't excuse the cover up and dishonoring of those men on the Liberty. They were patriots for heaven's sakes. That Jake fella was whisked away to Germany, sleep deprived and interrogated like an enemy combatant. And for what?" Before Gilad could speak the president continued, "So his recollection of the story would grow fuzzy, disjointed and unbelievable. By the time we got finished with him and the others their story was leaking like the bombed out Liberty." The president took a deep breath. "We need to own up, Gilad. These men, what's left of them, deserve that."

"Agreed." Gilad sat his cup down with a frown. "The Egyptians are in it now. I'm sure the Muslim Brotherhood wants their own kind of revenge in this matter. Israel admits wrong doing and all hell could break loose on our borders. They're waiting for a reason to invade. This time it will be their fault and we'll finish what we started in 1967."

"But if we're both dead, chaos will plunge the world in such darkness that Egypt could easily take matters into their own hands." The president's frown deepened.

"The Egyptians will simply exploit the world's outrage and capture what was once theirs. With me incapacitated…"

"Or dead," the president smiled ruefully.

"Yes. Dead. The Palestinians would take advantage of the chaos and begin a bombardment of missiles into Israel. Since they possess little regard for human life they will ignore the real possibility that Israel holds the ultimate reason to finally wipe their miserable existence from the map. A definite upside to the whole scenario."

Another light tap at the door came followed by the director of Enigma as he pushed into the room, with a hard look etched on his hawkish face. He seemed to unconsciously pull back his shoulders in the dark blue suit he wore when his eyes fell on his brother then the president.

"Mr. President." The director outstretched his hand as Buck

Austin stood. The two men grasped hands in a friendly manner, both aware of the other's strength.

"Has the prime minister been playing the part of the bully again, Mr. President?"

The president looked over his shoulder at his guest with a smirk. "Actually he's been whining like a little girl. Very undignified for someone in his position." He motioned for Ben to take a seat on the sofa across from them. "What have you got, Ben?"

The director opened his black leather notebook to retrieve several typed pages for each man. He waited for them to skim the contents before proceeding. "I've given copies to the FBI director, but held off on anyone else."

The president raised his eyes sternly. "Are you aware your brother is holding Mr. Wakefield against his will at the embassy?" He watched Ben's eyes shift to his brother and narrow with fury. "The question arises why you didn't find him first? All those brains and muscle you claim to have at Enigma couldn't find one hillbilly roaming the streets of Washington?" The president's voice cut through the director's calm.

"I assure you, Mr. President, we were aware of that. My brother's gorillas were allowed to take him."

The prime minister burst into a fake laugh. "Fat chance, little brother. You didn't know until this very moment he was my guest." He examined his finger nails as he spoke. "He's a rather likeable fellow. A bit on the crude side, but I think that is all a ruse. After all he did work for the NSA and can speak fluent Russian. Why the hell would a hillbilly learn Russian? I'll tell you why, because he was one of your decoders. The man likes to put on the 'ah shucks' façade but the eyes never lie. I've looked into those eyes and I see a very clever old man who is determined to get what he wants, even if that means throwing in with the Egyptians."

"Agent Cordova will escort him out immediately." Ben wanted to threaten his brother and would have if the President of the United States hadn't been glaring at him.

With an insulting smirk, Gilad continued. "I meant to inform Samantha, sorry, I mean Agent Cordova last night when you called to check on me." He smiled as if remembering the beautiful Enigma agent that had shared his bed. "I'll have to be more conscious of my responsibilities next time. She can be," his eyes shifted to the president with amusement, "very distracting."

"What are you running at Enigma anyway, Ben? A dating service?" The president wasn't happy. "Gilad doesn't need our resources to protect him."

"If I might add, sir, that with Agent Cordova in the embassy we managed to keep a close eye on Gilad's activities." His eyes locked with his brother's. "We figured he'd try something idiotic like this if given the chance."

Gilad clicked his tongue impatiently. "And here I thought Samantha liked me for my witty conversation." He'd left the beautiful agent with David to go over the plans for the evening events with the Geographic Convention. He planned on attending with Samantha as his escort. If all went well they could return to the embassy together. On the other hand if things went south then he'd probably be dead and it wouldn't matter.

"I'm pulling her from your protection detail. I wouldn't want you to have the burden of undue distraction," Ben offered sarcastically.

He took out his phone to call Samantha. "Sam?" Ben listened for a few seconds then disconnected. "You really are out of your mind, Gilad."

The president's bewildered look forced Ben to continue.

"The prime minister released Jake Wakefield several hours ago."

CHAPTER 12

$$\oplus$$

"Hurricane Candace is now barreling toward the east coast at sustained winds of 110 miles per hour. Rain bands have inundated the D.C. area since around noon." There was a television giving the latest report in a room where security went about preparing for the evening visits of two heads of state.

Chase watched the guests arriving in the ballroom from his position, in a tucked away security command post set up by the Secret Service. They worked for several weeks prior to the conference to make sure the president's visit, providing he didn't have a national emergency, would go without incident. Everyone remained on high alert, given the hurricane and threats against the president. He was the keynote speaker for the convention. His aides encouraged him to go since having educators, corporate kings and science gurus at his disposal translated into votes at the ballot box.

Adding on the visit of the Prime Minister of Israel, who volunteered to speak briefly to what he hoped, would be future support for his country, tacked on another layer of concern and security issues. Gilad's people continued with meticulous preparations, working like a methodical machine with little small talk toward the Secret Service. They volunteered no information and offered no advice unless specifically asked a question. Their presence grated on the Secret Service. The Israelis aired themselves as superior to the Americans.

Taking all of the territorial issues in stride between the two protection details, gave Chase an opportunity to look for her. Sticking a finger between his white collar and neck, he pulled slightly as if doing so would make the black tie more comfortable. Yet his eyes never left the camera scenes. They would go from monitor to monitor searching the halls, then the ballroom, before clicking on other areas of interest. Once a Secret Service agent frowned at him before locking in observation points and remained at his side to make sure they remained fixed.

Chase's silence deepened as his relentless scan continued until he found Tessa Scott.

That hammering pain in his chest caught him by surprise when he dropped his hands to his side. Clenching his fists as if to start his circulation, he watched her enter with her friends. They occasionally stopped and spoke to others. She would wait falling into a kind of measured patience. Smiling after an introduction, she then stepped back to scan the room, with what he knew to be unbelievable blue eyes. Who was she looking for? Her uncle?

Suddenly she locked onto something and moved forward to stare into a small mounted camera the size of a thimble attached to a house plant near where she stood.

"Now that's a fine looking woman," muttered the Secret Service agent. "Think she knows the camera's there or is just into plants?"

"She's one of my people."

The agent looked up at Chase for the first time. "I think I'm going to request a transfer."

"I'll see what I can do. I'd advise you to be careful around that one." He turned to leave.

"Why is that?"

"She could get you killed." Chase checked his weapon in his shoulder holster.

"There are worse ways to die," he smiled as he watched the no nonsense agent exit the room.

~~~

Zen inspired music floated out into the waiting area carpeted with a geometric design in gold and red. Replicas of famous Terra Cotta Soldiers stood guard on each side of all entry doors to the ballroom. The dragon murals along the wall added an ambiance of adventure and romance most educators would never be able to afford.

Authors stood with anticipation at their tables, piled with books concerning everything from how to be a better teacher, to lesson plans on botany. Roaming waiters walked around the shop-talking educators with trays of hors d'oeuvres.

The winding staircase to the mezzanine level made gawking out the windows, toward the lights of Washington D.C. impossible to ignore. The lightning flashes and smashing of horizontal rain, slamming into the panes of glass added a lure of danger Tessa's friends appeared to enjoy. They laughed and waved at people, some of which they didn't really know, hoping to be a part of someone's party after the dinner and speeches.

Through it all, Tessa remained cool and aloof with vigilant attention to finding her uncle. Or at least, that is what she tried to tell herself. Something inside her anticipated Chase would materialize, rescuing her from the evening's mindless parade of people showcasing their fashion sense, when in truth, they had none. Even Shelly made a comment concerning a sixty something woman in a purple sequin dress.

"What was she thinking? Who do you think convinced her that was slimming?"

Both Kate and Tessa burst into laughter and entered the foray of attendees. "That's why you can't go wrong with black," she whispered to her friends. They nodded in agreement having decided to go with black dresses in varying degrees of sparkle. "You girls look fabulous by the way." Tessa eyed her friends with an approving nod.

Shelly sniffed. "Not that anyone will notice with you in that strapless cocktail dress. Your boobs are pushed up so high they'll think you're a Victoria Secret model."

Kate started laughing as Tessa swatted her friend on the butt. "Unfortunately, there's way too much of me to get that impression."

"There's my new best friend." Shelly chirped spotting the bartender. She slipped an arm around both her companions, giving them a tug. "Distract him, Tessa, and maybe we'll get our drinks free."

Removing her friend's arm, Tessa smiled. "Honestly, Shelly,

you're incorrigible."

They stood at the end of one of the lines to the bar. At least ten people waited ahead of them. When the three women stopped at the edge of a corridor, Tessa's eyes drifted back to the flashes of light seen through the large plate glass windows. Shelly and Kate chatted with others in line, knowing no stranger or limit to topics of conversation. Without warning someone in the corridor reached out and slipped a hand in hers.

Jerking her head around, she tried to pull her hand free. Chase leaned against the wall with a grin on his face. He eyed her appreciatively, making her feel almost naked. When his eyes came back to meet hers, he dropped her hand. Shifting his eyes down the corridor, she decided to follow.

"Shelly, I'm going to find the ladies room."

"Want anything?"

"No. I'll get some tea at dinner." She started to move away as her friend made a flippant remark about being a stick-in-the-mud.

Chase had already neared the end of the corridor when she started to follow. He turned right and opened a door which began to close behind him almost immediately. Just as Tessa caught the handle she stole a look back down the corridor to make sure no one had seen her. She slipped into the room. Acutely aware the room was in total darkness except for a small security light hanging over the door, Tessa tensed at the eerie glow. Uneasiness swept over her.

What was I thinking following such a dangerous man into a dark room, Tessa thought as she turned to leave? But the feel of Chase's hands on her waist made her back up so quickly she thumped against the padded wall.

The red glow cast him into the look of the devil himself and made Tessa's heart race with anticipation and fear. She knew what he was capable of; last night reminded her of that. He could make love to you one moment and kill a man in the same instant without so much as elevating his heartbeat.

~~~

Pushing his hands away only brought a breathy laugh so close it moved the strand of hair that had fallen across her face. He wanted to touch it but knew she'd over react.

"You look beautiful, Tessa." His words were laced with sexy warmth meant to unnerve her.

"What are you doing here? Isn't the Secret Service in charge now? Have you seen my uncle? Where are the others?" Tessa's nervous chatter seemed to be edged in guilt for something he couldn't understand.

Chase put his hand on the wall near her ear. When she tried to slide away he cut off the retreat by putting the other hand up. "Questions. You're full of them. I'd forgotten how you chatter when you're nervous."

Her eyelids fluttered, making the corners of his eyes crease in amusement. She liked putting on a brave show, but her body language spoke something completely different.

"I have a right to know anything about my uncle."

"True. After all, it is your crazy uncle that has gotten you into this mess." He managed to make her stiffen at the insult. "I'm here, Tessa, because you are distracting the Secret Service from their watch." His smile glowed in the dark. A large hand came down on her bare shoulder, causing her to bump into his other arm in hopes of escape. "Easy."

"Don't talk to me like I'm some racehorse that needs a rub down."

"Trust me, Tessa; I would never think of rubbing you down like a horse." He continued to smile wolfishly, knowing he was unnerving her.

Putting her hands on his chest she pushed, but only succeeded in making him chuckle deep in his throat. "You should not be following men who carry guns into dark rooms. I see you've a great deal to learn if you're going to keep getting into Enigma business."

"For your information this is the last thing I ever do for your rogue band of sketchy agents. I'm still not convinced you're on the up and up."

She dared lift her eyes to meet his and bit her lip. He wanted to cast common sense to the wind and succumb to the desire welling up inside him. Their eyes embraced, confused and stimulated by something taboo.

"You're a terrible liar, Tessa. You get off on all this cloak and dagger stuff. I can see it in your eyes. Everywhere you go you're looking for something to happen." He slid his hand from her shoulder down her arm slowly. "Following me in here was risky."

"Oh I see," she fumed. "I think that little nod you gave me and the twitch of your fingers was some kind of order to follow so you could fill me in on what the heck I'm supposed to do tonight. But no," she pushed against his chest again and slapped his hand from her forearm, "you're trying to finish what you started last night. Despicable."

"Last night I only wanted to get you out of trouble. Again." His eyes darted to the lip she was biting. "You didn't protest all that much as I remember."

"It's pretty hard to protest when your tongue is half way down my throat," she growled, which only made him laugh deeper and trap her again with his hands on either side of her head.

"Are you angry because I kissed you or because you kissed me back?"

Tessa sucked in her breath with astonishment. "You are so full of yourself. I'm not one of your brainy bimbos that swoon at the mere sight of you."

"That you are not." The temptation to pull her into his arms forced him to take a step back. His clothes were getting uncomfortable and his heart hammered in his ears. "Why don't we go to your suite and discuss strategy?"

"That's the poorest attempt at a come-on I've ever heard." Now that he wasn't so close, Tessa straightened and attempted to pull up the bodice of her dress. She had no idea how much of a target she'd become to Chase's careless visual examination.

"What's gotten into you? You don't like married women and you certainly don't fraternize with other Enigma agents." She gave the bodice another yank. "Seems to me I'm the poster child for double trouble."

"Yeah," he grinned eyeing the woman before him with unabashed approval. "That was before you wore that dress. I'm thinking maybe I was a little hasty."

Tessa jerked her chin up in mock disgust. "Are you really flirting with me, Chase?" Her voice was appalled. With narrowed eyes he appeared to consider the question before speaking. "No. I'm pretty sure I'm hitting on you. It's all the more enjoyable that you don't even realize it. You're such a babe in the woods, Tess. I'll have to make sure no one takes advantage of that. It really is such a temptation to some men."

She took an angry step toward him. "And who will watch you?"

His smile faded to a narrow line as he caressed her face with his dark eyes. "I'm counting on you to do that." He quickly encircled her waist with one arm as she tried to slip away. But when he pulled her tighter against his chest she stopped and glared up at him. With his free hand he reached up and removed the clip from her curls so they fell around her shoulders.

Releasing her, Tessa stumbled back against the wall. He handed her the rhinestone clip which she snatched. "It's hard for me to concentrate with so much skin showing. That dress doesn't leave much to the imagination, I might add."

"Well next time I'll wear my flannel pjs, and Spiderman house shoes. That should cool your jets a bit." Tessa pushed her hair away from her face. He watched the movement like a starving tiger, ready to pounce on his next meal.

"Maybe that works with your husband, but let me be clear," he said with one corner of his mouth turning up, "the thought of you in flannel pjs, and Spiderman house shoes is kind of a turn on."

This broke the frosty attitude Tessa tried so hard to maintain. She started to laugh until a tear squeezed from the corner of her eye. Chase laughed too. "Okay. Stop it." Choking on her laughter caused her to place a hand on her throat before she cut her eyes back up at him.

Chase fought the pull of his needs. "I don't think a woman has ever found my advances so funny."

Tessa cocked her head teasingly. "I bet." The words rushed from her mouth before she could stop them, causing a blush to start up her neck.

"You are a dangerous distraction." He could smell her fragrance, soft and unusual. The low red glow from the security light bounced off her hair leaving it a strange color of copper. "But as of now, we have other matters to deal with." He waited for her to respond, noticing she'd begun to shy away from him again. Resisting the temptation to pull her back, Chase continued. "Your uncle is still at large. We thought we had him this morning but managed to slip away without Sam noticing."

"Sam!" Tessa's blood ran cold. The dark beauty hated her and the reason was standing right in front of her. "How would she know anything about my uncle?"

"It doesn't matter. What we do know is that the Israelis are involved somehow. Sam should be here soon with the prime minister."

"Doesn't he have his own protection detail?" The fact that Chase stood close enough to feel her breasts rise and fall with each breath diminished the seriousness of her uncle's disappearance.

"Sam is escorting him to the banquet." He smiled knowingly. "You needn't be concerned about Sam. Maybe the two of you will learn to get along." He hid his doubts.

"Are you sleeping together?" Tessa asked sarcastically.

"You know better than that. Besides it's none of your business."

"Look, I don't care who you sleep with, I just don't want her to think we are. That could get me killed. Maybe you think national security is nasty business, but finding myself alone with that Amazon could really ruin my day."

"I'm not sleeping or having sex with Sam." He flashbacked to a small motel in the Sierra Nevada Mountains a year earlier where he'd found himself under the sheets with Tessa. Apparently by the expression on her face, she was remembering the same thing. "I promise you're the only Enigma person I'll ever take to my bed." It was impossible to stifle his throaty laugh when she groaned with embarrassment.

"Not a word of that to anyone," she shushed. "That will never happen again."

"Does that mean no flannel pjs and Spiderman house shoes?" he teased looking seductively into her blue eyes.

"No flannel pjs."

"Even better." Again the wolfish show of teeth. "Gives a man something to live for."

"What do you want me to do?" she snapped realizing it was a poor choice of words when he lifted one eyebrow in speculation. "Seriously? The president's life is in danger and you want to play word games? I'm appalled. I see you've been getting some 'pick-up' advice from Carter, the playboy astronaut. I'm making a mental note to buy you both a book called *Pickup Lines for Dummies.*"

He eyed her for a few moments before speaking. It wasn't like him to bait anyone, especially a woman. Foreshadow, strategize, and activate the plan. Chase used that mantra for life in general, including for women. Why change when your blueprint worked with everything? Except Tessa didn't appear to be anywhere close to succumbing to his charm. Obviously his advances were seen as trivial and unsophisticated.

"As I was saying before you started obsessing over Sam." He raised his hand for silence when her mouth opened. "It doesn't hurt to have another layer of protection." He took a breath trying to slow down his heartbeat. "Shortly after both men speak they will be escorted out."

Tessa felt her body relax as Chase returned his hands to his sides and edged slightly away from her body. "Sounds simple and safe."

"Except the president's aides think he should shake a few hands and kiss a few butts. The election is a year and half away. The audience tonight has tremendous power. Think of all the students, then their parents affected by this one night and you've got a pretty powerful voting-block. The president is just cocky enough to think he's invincible."

She smiled and reached up to straighten his tie. The sudden impulse to pull her into his arms rushed through him. Chase wondered if his desire showed in his eyes because she withdrew her hands slowly as if trying to avoid a hungry tiger.

"And me? What do I do? I feel so helpless. My uncle is only doing this because his Liberty buddies are being held against their will." She took a deep breath. "Is it even possible he could get through security?"

He frowned. "Not likely, but clearly the Egyptians have had this in the works for some time. Someone else is involved. We just don't know who. We've found out which Liberty sailors are missing. Their families all thought they were traveling to D.C. for the hearings scheduled in a few days. Someone claiming to be from the Veterans' Administration sent them plane tickets and expense money to come early."

"But that wasn't true?"

"No. The V.A. doesn't have that kind of money to throw around. Every dime is spent before they get it these days. With the Iraq War and the ongoing war in Afghanistan they're not real interested in something that happened in 1967. Besides they're in trouble for all their mishandling of funds as it is."

"Did the men arrive in D.C.?"

Standing so close, impaired his matter of fact voice. His eyes never stopped exploring her face; first her eyes, then a slide to her mouth before lifting to her hair. Just because he preferred single women and civilians didn't mean he wouldn't zero in on what he felt was an irresistible target.

"Chase?"

Chase shook his head. "Out of the five only one made it to the hotel. The others landed at Reagan but never arrived at the hotel. Security cameras showed them getting into cabs but after that they were off the grid."

"What about the one who got to the hotel? Did you talk to him?"

"No. That was your uncle. He has all the information we need to fill in the gaps. Is there anything else you remember from last night that he told you? I realize things were moving a little fast..." He stopped and looked at the door which slowly began to open. Reflex forced his hand inside his jacket to rest on his weapon.

~~~

Tessa held her breath and unconsciously put her hand out that came to rest on Chase's side. As the door groaned a ribbon of light poured into her eyes forcing Tessa to lift one hand as a shade. She felt Chase jerk away from her as he reached through the opening, yanking a man inside. Just as quickly, Chase released him then shoved the body against the closing door.

"You kids in here making out?" Carter Johnson tried to smooth his tux as his eyes went to Tessa. A wolf whistle escaped his lips as he reached out and pulled her forward. Much to her objections, the former astronaut twirled her around, making her a little wobbly on her high heels. "Sweetheart, you are one hot babe. No wonder those Secret Service guys upstairs are scanning the place for you. Should have known," his eyes went to Chase, "our captain would corner the market."

"Are you in junior high?" Tessa pushed his hands from her hips. "I don't appreciate being referred to as a commodity or a horse." Her eyes darted to Chase who still glared at his partner.

Carter grinned. "Tell me you didn't compare her to a horse, Chase. Did I teach you nothing at Monte Carlo last Christmas?" Carter refused to be ignored and placed his arm around her shoulders, making sure he never took his eyes off Chase.

"You're a little early." Chase's tone grew frosty as he pushed Carter's hand off Tessa's shoulder, not realizing he'd dropped it against her buttocks with a squeeze.

Tessa gave Carter a shove and pointed a finger at him. "Excuse me," she quipped.

Carter chuckled. "Come on, Tessa whata ya say we blow this place. Wait a minute. You're my date tonight." He reached for her hand and pulled her to his side, looking triumphantly at his boss. "Bet he forgot to tell you that." He chuckled as he felt Tessa try to free her hand. Lifting it to his lips he kissed the palm of her hand, never taking his eyes from Chase.

Jerking her hand free Tessa turned bewildered eyes back to Chase. "I was about to get to that," he said off handedly. "Since Carter appears to have established himself in the good graces of your friends at the airport he'll be seated at your table. Together the two of you can watch for any signs that your uncle has breached security. Carter will relay any info at that point." He nodded toward Carter. "He knows what to do if the president or the prime minister is in danger."

Tessa frowned. She wasn't so sure fighting off Carter's unwanted attention during the evening would protect the president if he got into trouble. "Where will you be?"

The two men still locked stares as Chase spoke. "Close." It was maddening how he was a man of few words. However, she knew better than to question him. He tired of her inquiries too quickly. "I'll do my best to keep your uncle from getting his fool head shot off."

Raising her chin in defiance, the captain refocused his eyes on her, sternly. Gone was the smoldering examination he bestowed on her moments earlier. All that remained was a cold indifference. Forced to believe he was as ruthless with a woman's heart as he was with a loaded gun terrified her.

Brushing by Carter and opening the door, she looked back coldly, hoping to say something witty and clever to the man in charge, but nothing came out of her parted lips. With recklessness, he allowed his eyes to focus on that area of her mouth. The question arose in her mind; did he feel any guilt at all about taking advantage of her the night before in the alley?

~~~

Grabbing Carter's arm as he started after Tessa, created a look of concern on the captain's face. The former astronaut smiled down at the tight grip.

"She is so deliciously gullible." He saw the concern leap into Chase's eyes. "Don't worry, buddy. I'm all business tonight. Your little Grass Valley commando has nothing to fear from me." Carter jerked his arm free then winked. "And neither do you."

"Be alert. Those two friends of hers are noisy. Don't let them distract you."

"Got it covered, Chase. Relax. I want them out of the way too." He took a step out the door. "After all, if this turns out to be a no brainer, I want those two occupied so Tessa and I..." he realized Tessa had moved a ways down the corridor. "Gotta go."

He let out another soft wolf whistle as he cocked his head to watch Tessa walk away. With a quickened pace, he looked over his shoulder one last time at Chase who'd stepped out of the room. He slipped his hand in hers, tugging her to follow him.

CHAPTER 13

The waiter's jacket felt a little too big when Jake slipped the last button into place. His black pants appeared only slightly different than the other men and women bustling in the kitchen. Their lack of attention worked to his advantage. He entered the walk-in refrigerator to retrieve the cartridges left in the cardboard box of pasta noodles.

Careful to keep his eyes on the door, he jammed his hand inside the box. The crisp noodles knocking against his fingers sounded like thunder to him. Even in a gallon size bag he could feel the cold touch of death when his hand pulled out three stocked magazines, each capable of ten shots. Dumping them into a deep pocket on the side of his pants, he managed to free the note he'd written earlier.

Looking over the words one last time, Jake rolled his eyes up toward Heaven, sniffing a renegade tear back against second thoughts. With shoulders pulled back, he laid the paper down on a shelf near a five gallon plastic container marked potato salad. Prying off the lid, he winced, feeling the arthritis in his hand activated by the incoming hurricane. The only thing inside was a rifle scope. This last component might not be necessary, but the voice on the phone insisted he take it.

Even the Israelis liked the plan, but couldn't resist adding another element. Two masters. Two devils. Two ways to Hell.

Raising his pant leg, he slipped the scope in the strap fastened around his leg, aware of how cold it felt.

A bowl of pecans, still in their shells, caught Jake's eye. He took a hand full and shoved them in his coat pocket. Flexing his hands to chase away the rising stiffness, he replaced the lid on the container. Comfort came with a touch to his chest knowing duct tape secured the wishbone weapon he brought along. He thought of his simple upbringing and how he'd first learned to hunt with such a simple tool. Now the hunt meant something more than knocking a squirrel off a sycamore branch.

He secured the note next to the empty container just as the door swung open. Startled, he faced two workers dressed like himself, a young man and woman, probably in their early twenties maybe younger, he guessed. They laughed seeing him slip on a cap. As they pushed inside he avoided making eye contact and exited, letting the door shut on its own.

~~~

The young man waited for the door to close as he reached for the black haired girl with the pierced tongue. The push of air forced a piece of paper to fly up off the shelf as she stood on tip toes and kissed his neck before latching onto his ear with her teeth.

He laughed, pushing her aside to grab the paper before it floated to the floor and turned it over in his hand. Reading the words, he cut his eyes over to the girl with raised eyebrows.

"What does it say?" She tried to take it from him only to have it lifted higher, out of her reach.

Looking at it again, he read. "It says 'stop me'." His frown made her pause. "Do you want me to stop?"

The breathy laugh sounded soft and inviting. "No way," she said reaching under his jacket to fumble with his zipper.

Tossing the note aside he lifted her onto a stack of boxes and pushed her legs apart. "We better hurry."

~~~

The Speaker of the House waved his security detail off which was no easy task. They usually made some comment about it being their job or it didn't follow protocol. The ritual of leaving them outside in the cold, rain, scorching sun or any other weather outside of their control, amused him. He would remain in his chauffeur driven Mercedes until the protection detail walked in and looked around before posting a guard at the rear and entrance of the establishment he visited. They knew of the threats on the president, thus taking extra care with the speaker. Being driven around Washington pleased him as did having extra care taken on his behalf. By tomorrow this kind of treatment would become routine.

Never a thank you, happy birthday or let me buy you dinner passed the speaker's lips. He sensed their disdain for him which made it all the more enjoyable when he had them stand outside in the rain on a night like tonight.

"I won't be long. Just dinner." He dusted off a few raindrops that blew under the umbrella his protector offered when he got out of the car.

"Yes, sir."

Walking inside the pub the speaker pointed at the bartender who nodded toward the back. "Your usual, Mr. Speaker?"

"Make it a double, Charlie." He smiled. Now a good bartender was an artist worth rewarding and he often did with a generous tip. "Send that little red headed waitress over too, would you? I'm starving." He winked.

The bartender motioned for a waitress as the speaker moved toward the back corner to his usual booth, bathed in a small votive of light.

The booth was empty. Before he scooted across the seat, the speaker glanced around the restaurant to see if anyone familiar sat alone. No one did. The room was in such low light he was unrecognizable. This both annoyed and relieved him. The D.C. public became immune to seeing protection details. This was more of a local place. Tourists caused a great deal more speculation and gawking. With the approaching hurricane only two other tables remained occupied.

The bartender brought his drink and a menu. "I'm sending Susie home, Mr. Speaker. She's scared half out of her mind. Probably close up early. I'll take care of you. The cook is leaving in an hour so you've got time."

The speaker watched the bartender hurry away then flinch as a flash of lightning lit the street, followed by a table rattling rumble.

The man glanced back at the speaker just as he downed the drink in one gulp. Because he was a good customer and often brought high profile people to dine, there wouldn't be a hint of canceling the order. The bartender moved to the door, then nodded at the Secret Service agent standing outside. He knew better than to invite him inside.

The speaker's cell phone vibrated in his inside pocket against his chest. A fleeting memory of Carmen the night before surfaced. He hoped it would be her. One corner of his mouth turned up then straightened when he saw the number.

"Why aren't you here?" he managed to say through clenched teeth.

"The president is on the move and I couldn't get there before streets were blocked off. The ones available were flooded. You should leave."

"The men?"

"Ready. Wait for my call."

"I have a new burner phone." He gave him the number. "Use it if I'm needed."

Satisfied he disconnected as the bartender returned casting an apprehensive eye to the street outside the plate glass windows. "Never mind, Charlie." He slid out and threw two ten dollar bills on the table. "Gotta get those boys," he pointed toward the man standing under the awning outside, "out of this weather."

The two man detail turned the speaker over to the driver who was part of the security team. Horizontal rain competed with the silence inside the Mercedes until it reached the speaker's Brownstone in Georgetown.

Assuring the detail he would not leave his home until the hurricane passed, he let them activate his security alarm. For an extra touch, he handed over the keys to his vehicle so his driver believed he'd stay put. Since he refused to drive himself to any function, they believed him. No visitors were expected.

"This weather is giving me a headache. I'll read over a few papers then I'm going to bed. That little number last night kept me up way past my bedtime," he chuckled at the solemn faced Secret Service agent as he double checked the alarm.

"Yes, sir," he managed to say in a monotone voice that irked the speaker.

He dead bolted the door as they left, noticing they paused long enough to try the door and eye the street both ways. They could be so intrusive at times. Their snub at his choice of after work activities made it all the easier to mistreat them at every possible opportunity.

If security wanted better treatment, they should have gone into another line of work, he reasoned.

The speaker gave himself a glance in the mirror and noticed his crow's feet were a little more pronounced tonight. Frowning, he sniffed at the thought of getting older and moved toward the hall door that led to the garage. From the corner of his eye, he watched the door knob turn on its own then open with the speed of a three toed tree sloth.

The Egyptian took a step inside the foyer and surveyed the rooms he could examine from his position.

The speaker walked into the kitchen as he tossed his London Fog raincoat onto one of the barstools at the breakfast bar. "I need a drink." He opened the cabinet, taking down a bottle of Jack Daniels before reaching for a crystal glass on a cherry wood shelf. "Care to join me?"

On quiet feet, the Egyptian followed him, stepping away from any windows that could reveal his position. "I am Muslim. I do not drink. You know that. Why do you always ask? Is it because you are becoming old and senile? Or do you wish to mock me with your American attitude toward anything Middle Eastern?"

The speaker chugged down his drink and snarled at the dark skinned man lurking in the shadows. He needed to find a way to end their relationship as soon as possible. The promises he made might come back to haunt him.

"No disrespect, Amon." He sat the glass down a little too abruptly causing it to flip over, spilling ice onto the floor. He didn't bother to pick it up, instead threw a dish towel over it. The maid could clean it up tomorrow. By that time he'd have a great many people at his beck and call.

"In this country it's courteous to offer a beverage to a guest." His smile narrowed while he eyed the Egyptian. "Let me change into something more appropriate and we'll be on our way."

~~~

Amon nodded as his gaze followed the speaker from the room. In that moment when lights flickered and wind drove rain horizontally into the windows, he recognized what a blunder he'd made in throwing in with the Speaker of the House. The man was greedy and arrogant; a dangerous combination when dealing with an American politician.

A branch knocked at the kitchen window as his thoughts raced to the warehouse where the four old sailors from the USS Liberty waited for the rescue that would never come. Were there leaks now that the storm had intensified? Did the dampness hurt their aging bones?

Two of them popped nitroglycerin tablets fairly often while the others tried to remain calm and comfort their friends. They spoke in hushed voices of the Wakefield man; wondering where he was and if he were in the same dire predicament. One man, a former Marine, encouraged the other three to be prepared to escape when the opportunity presented itself.

Even though the speaker insisted they be tied up, he could not carry out the order. The containment area was not that large. Where would they go? Providing them a chair and a small table would be more than enough. Amon rebelled and gave each of them a thin blanket. Although extremely hot this time of year, Amon knew that old ones sometimes got cold. It would be a small comfort to old warriors, just like his grandfather who spoke of the Six Day War in 1967.

Their voices carried through the shabby walls meant to contain them. Speculation as to the reason for their capture ran amuck at first. With the sudden appearance of their armed guards bringing food and water twice a day, the old military men began to realize their capture had not been random. Although the guards kept their faces covered with handkerchiefs, the dark skin exhibited on hands and throat remained visible. The tongue of their captors sounded foreign; Middle Eastern. They were intelligent enough to make the connection.

Amon remembered how their rambling turned from 911, to the wars in Afghanistan and Iraq and finally to their forgotten war in 1967. He'd stood at the door listening to their stories of that day so long ago. They knew Israel deceived the U.S., their friend and ally.

That treacherous act nearly drove the world to nuclear war between the Americans and the Russians.

With all the discord going on in Egypt these days and the demonstrations outside the American Embassy, many Americans objected to money going to prop up the fragile Egyptian economy. Unlike America, his people would never give money to a country who openly claimed to hate Egypt. Yet the American politicians continued to believe money could buy loyalty.

Egypt now resembled just another Middle Eastern country that couldn't protect itself from internal strife and discord; radical Islam verses the desire to be free.

The speaker suggested they should shed light on the truth. Egypt's status would rise in the eyes of the world. History implied the Six Day War had been a result of Egypt's aggressive posturing. Many died at the hands of the Israelis. His grandfather escaped only to watch as his comrades were slaughtered.

What would become of this folly? Taking these frail men of a forgotten war against their will, to shame his enemy, seemed fanatical even to him. Killing these Americans and planting evidence to implicate the Israelis, if it worked, would haunt him. The end result of shaming the Israelis and killing the American president might just start another war; one that would level Israel once and for all. Or would it backfire to destroy his country?

~~~

"Ready?" The speaker appeared wearing his slick navy jogging suit. He zipped up the jacket and walked to the window in the living room to check for his security detail.

Although he'd told them to go home he doubted they'd obeyed. A dark sedan across the street appeared to be empty. His eyes went to the row of new condos constructed from old brownstones that had been slotted for demolition. One belonged to the Secret Service to watch over him during times like these; probably a one man operation on a night like this.

"Where did you park, Amon?"

"In your garage." Amon moved to the hall, eyeing the surroundings with contempt. Luxury beyond necessity grated against his upbringing.

"Fool. How are we to leave?" Although his voice sounded calm, there was no mistaking the irritation.

He opened the door that led into the garage. "Your babysitter has already been taken care of, Mr. Speaker. Make sure your home security is as it should be in case anyone checks on you."

"Go ahead. Forgot my raincoat. Be right there."

Amon nodded and disappeared into the garage as the speaker hit the button for the garage door to open.

Jim walked back into the kitchen. He looked around admiring his home before moving to the espresso machine that arrived just yesterday. The review labeled it the best. The speaker demanded nothing less. There hadn't been time to remove it from the box.

Opening a drawer, he moved aside some dish towels until he found the one he'd been saving; the one with his blood on it along with a paper towel he'd wrapped inside the folds. He'd cut himself shaving a few days earlier and used it to blot the mess. He threw it in the island sink as he placed the crumpled paper towel beneath the espresso box. The message written days earlier would reveal being a victim of a conspiracy.

The London Fog raincoat dripped a puddle beneath the barstool as planned. He stepped in the water with his dirty tennis shoes as he threw the jacket over his shoulder. Dragging his feet toward the garage door, then his coat, he created the appearance of a muddy trail on the marble floor.

Thunderous rain bands blew in the open garage as he slipped into Amon's nondescript compact. As the car moved in reverse onto the flooded street, the speaker hoped by morning he would be President of the United States. Timing was everything.

CHAPTER 14

Vice President Warren McCall leaned back in his chair as his wife threw an Indian blanket across his lap. She felt his head again for fever. It was cool to the touch. Better, she thought. Taking the Dr. Pepper from the Secret Service agent as he quickly entered to look for himself at the VP, Dr. McCall added a straw before handing it to her husband.

"He'll live, Terry. Don't fret. I knew he shouldn't have eaten that sushi last night with the Inuit folks who invited him in. But does he listen?" She turned her eyes back to her husband who spent most of the night hanging onto the toilet for dear life. "Lesson learned. Right, Honey?"

The VP frowned as he took a sip of his Dr. Pepper. "Yeah. Yeah. Here I am stuck inside listening to you instead of out there with my Inuit buddies fishing my heart out. They're going to think I'm a wuss."

"You are a wuss, Dear. Now relax and catch up on your reading. Here's the e-reader I bought you for your birthday. *The Old Man and the Sea* is already downloaded," she giggled trying to tuck the blanket around him. "Read this and be glad you can't get into that kind of trouble."

He offered a grumpy "Humph" as his doctor wife left him with the Secret Service agent. "How are things in Washington, Terry? Anything going on I should know about?"

Terry smirked. "Looks like the hurricane will hit pretty close to D.C. The president is speaking to a teacher conference or consortium thing tonight. Prime Minister Levi showed up and is tagging along."

The VP frowned as his brow wrinkled in bewilderment. "Levi? I wasn't informed of any visit?"

"Last minute I think."

Vice President McCall yawned, laying the e-reader on the lamp stand then picked up a western he'd brought along for his fishing trip. "The Israelis don't do last minute. I'd bet my next fishing trip the president has known about this for some time. He should trust me more."

"Yes, sir." The agents knew it was easier to agree. "Can I get you anything, Sir?"

"No thanks, Terry. You're a good man. Oh, turn on the Weather Channel, will ya? I'm hoping everyone in D.C. is as miserable as me."

The agent nodded and did as the vice president requested before leaving the room.

~~~

Realizing Carter walked at her side with a bit more purpose than most of the conference goers, Tessa cocked her head to steal a glimpse of the ex-astronaut. His blond hair, cut close, appeared to be hinting at a touch of gray around his ears. The blue-gray eyes searched their surroundings with a hawk-like determination in hopes of locating her uncle who meant the president harm.

Carter was handsome, maybe too much so. Women found him irresistibly charming. Tessa wasn't proud of the fact that she did as well. The difference between her and the hordes of women who fell for every compliment, lie and exaggeration he fed them was that she found them ridiculous. NASA hadn't liked their heroes to draw that kind of publicity. Managing to make life unbearable by restricting his social activities, Carter left to work for President Buck Austin. Years forced his once celebrity status into oblivion. The public possessed short memories when it came to their astronauts. Without a spacesuit you could count on being invisible. Tonight being invisible worked in their favor.

"Are you staring at me because you've decided I'm way better looking than Hunter, or is there something else you want to tell me?" Carter turned his eyes on Tessa momentarily before slipping his arm through hers, then looking away.

Unsuccessful at trying to pull free of Carter, she realized his grip only tightened. Forcing herself to relax, she teased him with a smile and patted his arm. "What's our story, Theodore Carter Johnson? Are we former friends or lovers?"

Surprised at the coyness, Carter stopped as they entered the ballroom where several hundred tables were draped in white table clothes. He lowered his mouth to her ear and felt a wayward curl touch his lips. "Let's go for lovers. Your friends will probably remember me." He grinned, pulling down her hand into his. "I mean who wouldn't? Maybe you'll find that an interesting option someday." She shot him a disgusted look. "Then again, I'm afraid a mutual friend of ours might just send me straight to hell if I tried anything."

"My uncle catches you being inappropriate he's likely to choose a target besides the president. He's the one you should worry about. He's not a big fan of the government."

"Whatever did you do with that sweet and innocent Grass Valley housewife I met last year?"

"She fell in with a bunch of conspirators who play mind games with innocent people."

Tessa spied her friends several tables from the front. They stood watching their approach with drinks in hand. Shelly, clearly the stronger of the two, eyed them mischievously as if she'd discovered a great secret about her perfect friend. By the time they reached the table, the tarnish to her good girl reputation fell into shambles, without the slightest possibility of an acceptable explanation.

"Ladies, we meet again. I had no idea you were friends with my old flame." He smiled with unabashed elation at seeing them. Without hesitation Carter kissed each of Tessa's friends on the cheek before looking back at her with something like adoration. "Sorry. I stole Tessa away when I saw her wandering around looking for you. We had a little catching up to do." The smile suggested a little more than catching up.

"I'll bet." Shelly spoke as her lips took a sip of a dirty martini. "How is it you're here?"

"Helping out at the Air and Space Museum." He pointed at

Kate. "I thought I saw you there today." He worked a kind of quarterback charm on the women. "Care if we join you?"

"Sure. I want to hear all about your old flame." Shelly shifted her eyes to Tessa as if expecting a great revelation.

Tessa grinned, revealing clenched teeth. Narrowing her eyes at Carter, she addressed her friends. "So everyone have a good day? I never got around to asking." She knew her voice sounded trite.

Too many emotions surged through her veins; Chase's passionate rescue the evening before, being cornered by him in a dark room and now on the arm of the former astronaut. Throw in an uncle bent on killing the president, a hurricane that threatened a blackout and a couple of friends who suspected her of having an affair; it was astonishing that she hadn't collapsed into a blithering idiot. Yet she stood cool as a cucumber, participating in Enigma lies, to protect the president.

Carter slipped an arm around her bare shoulders. "Chilly, Baby Cakes?" He smiled sensing a move to be free from his touch.

Shelly eyed her before taking a sip of her drink. "Baby Cakes?"

"It's a long story, Shelly," Carter laughed. "But…"

"Never mind," Tessa snapped. "He calls everyone that, even the dog."

"You know I got rid of the dog when you left." Again the grin and examining eyes. "You really are a looker in that dress."

Shelly and Kate looked incredulously at their friend over the rim of their glasses.

Tessa felt her embarrassment buckle beneath the anger that threatened to tell the truth. But the approach of two men dressed in uniform choked the words back. She knew them. They'd met a year earlier when she'd been snared into Enigma. Their eyes slid down her body before turning to Carter.

"Hey, buddy!" Carter stuck out his hand to shake the Marine's. "I see you're back on your feet." A year earlier Tessa had managed to topple the man with no more than a broomstick, giving him a concussion in the process. "Tessa, do you remember First Sergeant Cooper? The last time you met…"

Tessa tried a dazzling smile, but the sergeant didn't reciprocate. "Yes, of course." She realized her mistake when he took her outstretched hand in a vice grip response. He looked younger than she remembered. With a nod he released her hand matter-of-fact.

The second man participated in a mission led by Chase at a lab in Knoxville, Tennessee. Forced to tag along brought her into contact with the worst sort of people. His 'awe shucks' grin and twinkling brown eyes was a sharp contrast to his partner. "Tessa. I didn't know you would be here." He took her hand and pulled her close enough to kiss her lightly on the cheek like a familiar friend. "How've you been?"

"Great until I got here," she sniffed as her eyes cut to Carter. "How's the leg?"

He slapped his right leg lightly and laughed. "On a night like this it gives me a little pause."

Crazy as it sounded, Tessa saved him from a Libyan terrorist by pepper spraying the killer. Even so, the soldier still took a bullet in the leg. He glanced at Shelly and did a double take. "Hi. I'm Ken Montgomery."

Shelly sat her drink down and extended her hand. "Ken, I want to be your Barbie."

Ken laughed. "Barbie it is. Who's your friend?"

Kate stepped forward shyly, trying not to make eye contact with Ken's buddy, the Marine. "Kate. So how is it you guys know Tessa?"

Marine First Sergeant Tom Cooper offered his hand to Kate in a friendly shake. "Let us join you for dinner and we'll tell you all about it." Tessa caught the beginning of a cover-up.

It wasn't hard to figure out that Carter arranged baby sitters for her two friends. At least if all hell broke loose they'd be safe. Nothing could protect those men from Shelly and Kate, she thought with amusement. Telling her friends half-baked lies and shimmers of the truth might ruin her already damaged reputation once and for all. Someone needed to catch her up to speed when the evening was over so she didn't trip over some fabricated storyline. Revealing the danger the country faced, with any luck, would stay a secret to the general public.

People took their seats when waiters began placing salads on the table. Friendly noise filled the ballroom over the tinkling of water glasses and silverware. Tessa tried to focus on the nonsense chatter of her friends flirting with the soldiers seated next to them, but like Carter, her eyes took on that danger scan, hoping to locate her uncle before he did anything stupid.

Oblivious to the guests as they started their salads, Tessa noted men at other tables who failed to take the appearance of an academic. Their toned bodies didn't look like teachers who'd feasted on one too many cupcakes in the teacher's lounge. She spotted Zoric across the room, looking sullen and intense, sitting with a group of older teachers who ignored him. She'd never seen him in a suit. It softened him, she realized, and wanted a chance to tell him how handsome he looked if their evening ended on a positive note.

Two tables away sat Dr. Ervin, listening attentively to those around him, but failing to be drawn into the conversation. His eyes, too, scanned the room except for the moment he looked at her and nodded. She realized in that instant the professor was more dangerous than he appeared. Even from her position she could see a shoulder harness bump under his suit coat.

The thought of Chase surfaced. Could he be with the president? Then it occurred to her she should be trying to locate her uncle instead of obsessing over a man who clearly gave little regard to her sense of values.

The night before flooded back into her head as she laid down her fork and took a sip of ice tea. Remembering the pounding rain, the feel of the concrete table beneath her body, clouded her vision of the hundreds of people around her. His dark eyes excavating into her psyche brought back the realization that she'd crossed a line of no return.

Touching her forced a violent reaction at first, but as Chase protected her from harm, the resistance crumbled with what could have been a passionate moment. With a gun exploding in her ear and blood mingling with the puddles on the ground, Tessa knew Chase was not a man to offer romantic dinners or tantalizing words of love. Sickened at her foolish school-girl crush, she tried to refocus without much success.

In the last year each day she said a prayer for him or wondered about his safety. Sometimes he'd haunted her dreams with passion and other times with lethal force. She'd never known a real American hero until the day he saved her from Libyan terrorists. They'd started out as untrusting partners then forged into an awkward partnership. Wondering if their paths would ever cross again, she realized now he would force his will on her for as long as Enigma found her useful.

The disquieting sensation of seeing him again the night before and now here at the conference forced her to acknowledge the danger facing her was not just her uncle making an assassination attempt on the president. Chase murdered the self-respect she held so dear, knowing she may have fallen in love with him.

Tessa would make sure the infatuation boiling inside her never surfaced. She'd given her heart to another man, her husband. Only Robert would remain true to her. Men like the captain preyed on hero worship. He could never love just one woman.

She sighed with resignation.

"What? Did you see something?" Carter leaned in to her ear.

Tessa turned away and glanced around the room. "No. Just nervous," she whispered. "And scared. Very scared."

Carter reached for her hand she let fall in her lap. She lifted her eyes to his and felt surprise at seeing the humor gone from his face. "I'm sorry you got dragged into this again. But you need to concentrate. You just might be able to save you uncle. I saw an old picture of him, but I'm sure he's altered his appearance. Are you with me?" Tessa squeezed his hand. "Okay?"

Tessa nodded. "I'm good."

The meal progressed but neither she nor Carter ate much. Her friends laughed and flirted with the companions placed to distract from the seriousness facing the president. With their attention effectively diverted away from the mayhem lurking in the shadows, Tessa found freedom to scan the crowd. Waiters began pouring coffee and serving dessert when Carter appeared to lift his chin ever so slightly. He resisted touching his earwig.

"Ladies." Carter spoke as he pushed his chair back. He took Tessa's elbow and pulled her up. "Tessa and I are going to get some air before the president speaks."

Shelly waved a dismissive hand without a glance their way. Kate, hanging on every word of her Marine, didn't appear to have heard the announcement.

"What is it, Carter?" Tessa stayed close when they headed toward a side door leading to the service entrance for waiters. Carter took one last glance at the ballroom, looking up towards the closed off balcony with mild concern.

"The president wants to speak to you."

Tessa put on the brakes and spun around in front of her escort. "Excuse me?"

Carter broke concentration as he appeared to drink in the close proximity of the temporary Enigma agent. His mischievous grin turned up at one corner of his mouth as he let his eyes drift around her face then her hair before letting them fall to bare skin above the bodice of her dress.

Landing a soft fist on his chest, Tessa snarled. "Stop it. I hate it when you do that, by the way." She could feel the color rising in her cheeks. "Why?"

"I already told you, Tessa." He moved her forward by spinning her around and taking her hand. "The president wants to talk to you."

"About what?"

"The weather? That dress you're wearing?" He felt her try to squirm out of the hard grasp of his hand. "Your uncle is my guess. Ready?"

They exited the service area into a long hall that appeared to lead outside to the alley. Four Secret Service agents held the double doors open. Even though the rain and wind was deafening it couldn't cover the sudden smell of garbage wafting into the corridor. Tessa remembered that Ronald Reagan had often commented on knowing he'd arrived at a speaking engagement by the smell of the garbage at some obscure rear entrance.

Several other agents carrying umbrellas towered over another man with his head down. He seemed to burst into the hall, shaking his black coat then straightened to his full six foot frame. His eyes took everything in as if he expected something to occur without warning. It appeared almost ironic to see such big men remove the president's coat with gentle care and respect. Although she couldn't hear him speak, Tessa watched President Austin mouth "thank you" as he stepped forward. His eyes lifted, and then zeroed in on her and Carter.

In that suspended moment in time, Tessa realized when their eyes collided; the president was no different than the Enigma agents she'd thrown her fate to. The steel resolve in his walk, the threat in the eyes of undetermined color, reinforced the understanding that here was a man used to getting his own way. There wasn't a lot of gray area with this president.

Unconsciously Tessa eyed his body looking for a pistol bump. She found none. Stories circulated from time to time that the Secret Service removed weapons from his living quarters and his office on more than one occasion. He once admitted in an interview he was just making sure he was ready in case the protection detail needed help.

Rumors of sweeps when the Russian or Chinese Ambassadors planned a visit were common knowledge. Although he respected the Israelis, the Secret Service knew better than to allow him any wiggle room. His nickname among the agents varied from The Lone Ranger to Roy Rodgers, depending on the president's mood.

The Secret Service took him target shooting each week to appease his irritation of not having his guns around. "I'm a Texan for God's sake. It's my birthright." The National Rifle Association loved to quote him.

Carter whispered further gossip into Tessa's ear in hopes of an amused attitude. Each week a new face appeared on the target.

"Sometimes it's a head of state like North Korea or a Somali pirate. The most recent target was the Speaker of the House. Afterwards the agents burned the target. It wouldn't be proper for the president to appear uncooperative with the third most powerful man in the government, despite his despicable behavior toward the men who protected him. The agents resisted taking a shot even after the president encouraged them to vent."

Now the most powerful man in the world moved toward Tessa. Unconsciously she stopped resisting against Carter's grip and slipped her free hand over his arm. He appeared to sense her nervousness, pulling her in closer to his side.

The president stopped abruptly in front of Tessa and Carter, glancing over his shoulder as if signaling a tall, muscular man to come alongside him.

Chase strode up beside the president.

Tessa's eyes, wide with admiration and awe, shifted to Chase. Her mouth felt dry as her lips parted in hopes of speaking something clever, yet respectful. She only managed to clear her throat.

The leader of the free world fist bumped the ex-astronaut on the shoulder. "Good to see you, Carter. I see you managed to get a date on short notice."

"Wouldn't miss it, Sir." His eyes turned to Tessa as if he planned to introduce her.

Chase's lackluster expression revealed nothing of his concern of a possible assassination attempt. He beat Carter to the punch. "Mr. President, this is Tessa Scott." Clearly his attention shot to Carter, then to his temporary agent.

She remembered at that moment how unemotional Chase could sound in times of great conflict and crisis.

Should she offer her hand? Curtsey? Kiss his hand? What? After all it was her uncle that had brought her to this point in time. Maybe she should start with an apology.

As if sensing her discomfort, the president almost smiled as he stuck out his hand. "Scott is it?"

Tessa reached out and let his hand surround hers. She felt a tingling of enthusiasm at being in the presence of greatness. "Yes, sir," came her squeaky response. She cleared her throat again. "Yes, sir."

"The captain tells me you've come on board with Director Clark." It was a declaration, one that couldn't be refused.

Nodding almost child-like, she answered. "Yes, sir. Thank you."

He dropped her hand. "Good job last year at that whole isotope fiasco outside Sacramento. The captain tells me they couldn't have been successful without your help."

Tessa's eyes darted to Chase only to find him staring over her head as if she were invisible. "I didn't realize the captain was given to exaggeration." The sarcastic words crossed her lips before she could stop them. Embarrassed, Tessa quickly put her hand over her mouth as she felt hot coloring move up her neck.

Even though the words forced Chase's robotic stare to shift her way, Tessa wondered if she'd pay for that impudent remark when they were alone. The president chuckled as he hit the back of his hand on the chest of his agent. His attention remained on Tessa.

"Can you shoot, Scott?" The president continued to smile.

"Not very well, Mr. President."

"How about your uncle?"

The question caught her off guard. She found herself hugging

Carter's arm again. She answered only after feeling Carter squeeze her hand and a nod toward the president.

"Yes, sir. I'm afraid he's a very good shot." The hard swallow that stuck in her throat nearly choked her.

"Hmm." The president managed to grunt as he nodded at Chase before moving forward down the long corridor toward a possible rendezvous with death. His gait revealed nothing about his trepidation concerning his safety. Tessa guessed with men like Chase at your side a certain cloak of invincibility could make a person over confident.

Chase ignored her as he brushed by, his attention never leaving the president. Not even Carter's arm that had slipped around her waist deterred him from his appointed task.

"Why didn't the president just stay home tonight?" Tessa quizzed in a whisper as she turned to watch them disappear through doors that eventually would lead to the ballroom. She felt Carter's arm tense as she looked sideways at his profile. Startled to see concern in his usually flirtatious eyes, Tessa patted his hand that rested on her waist.

"The president doesn't like to back down from a fight or a chance to get more votes come next election. Men like the president think they're insulated from mayhem. These kinds of threats aren't new. If he stayed at the White House every time someone got miffed at him, the president would become a prisoner in his own home. This threat escalated."

"Now what?"

"We better look for that uncle of yours. Any ideas?" Carter nodded to some of the Secret Service men that protected the exit. They were all good men, devoted to the president. "Any sense as to how this might play out? Where he would feel the most confident?"

Tessa released his hand as they moved back through the service area. She shook her head, trying to examine the many faces scurrying around the kitchen located behind the staging area for the servers. The sound of silverware dropping, pans hitting stove burners and several chefs screaming about stupidity, created a kind of chaos designed to cover deception.

"My uncle loves to cook." She felt Carter step away.

"Let's split up. Try to look at every single person in here." He pulled out a picture of Jake from a newspaper article from her hometown paper taken ten years earlier. "Has he changed much?"

Tessa gently retrieved the picture then handed it back. "Thinner. Grayer. Not as much hair on top." She touched the top of her hair. "The picture doesn't show the pock marks on his left cheek under his eye, from having acne when he was a kid I guess. He squints out of habit. But if he isn't doing that you'll notice he has one blue eye and one green eye. It's only slightly different."

"Anything else?"

"I look a lot like him. People always thought he was my dad." Tessa looked down, knowing she was selling out someone she loved.

Is this what Enigma did to a person? Had her allegiance shifted from family to protecting a man she never even voted for in the last election?

~~~

"We'll do everything to stop him before he gets too close, Tessa." Carter resisted putting his hand on her shoulder. She might be a temporary Enigma agent, but the hard callousness which would eventually control her reasoning powers remained absent. Her utter hopelessness and vulnerability touched him unexpectedly. Carter offered a slight grin as he lifted her chin with one finger. "You can do this, Kiddo. Not rocket science."

Knowing the reference to his NASA work would please her, he was rewarded with a half-hearted smile. When she nodded bravely and turned to do her search, Carter understood in that moment how she must affect Hunter.

The thought of candy wrapped in poison ivy flashed in his mind. Wanting something like that could get you killed. Although Carter's attraction to Tessa had more to just being female and breathing, he saw something the other agents at Enigma failed to possess. Looking after her in the coming months, if she remained an agent, would fall to Chase. Would the captain put himself in harm's way like a love sick puppy for a naïve woman who would never return his affections? Running interference, keeping the leader off guard, might save his friend from pondering too hard on the possibility of romance.

Watching Tessa carefully scope out the grand kitchen, forced Carter to do the same. Time was of the essence. The slap of metal against porcelain throughout the kitchen registered as brain clutter when he began examining each face. Who looked distracted? Did the slow movement mean an old man? Were there any Middle Eastern waiters giving him too much attention?

Carter looked back to see Tessa standing by a walk-in refrigerator. She reached for the handle as the door swung open and two young people burst from inside, smiling with satisfaction. By the looks of the young woman's clothes and guy's hair they hadn't been getting supplies. They plowed into Tessa unaware that she blocked their path.

"Oh. Sorry, Lady." The young man hiccupped the apology through a mischievous grin. "Better watch where ya stand in this place."

Tessa nodded and caught the door with her toe as the young man threw back a piece of wadded up paper which rolled inside.

~~~

Deep down Tessa imagined Carter asked for her assistance to keep her mind occupied or out of trouble. She wasn't sure which. No one at Enigma could possibly think her capable of making a difference in national security. The isotope fiasco the president mentioned moments earlier was a miracle on her part. Requesting help to locate her uncle made no sense at all. She might as well have a giant fish hook sticking out of her mouth considering the possibility she was now Enigma bait. Once again they were using her as a means to an end. That end would probably result in the death of a man she'd loved her entire life.

The crumpled paper stuck to something in a purple gel. Tessa wrinkled her nose as she pulled it free and smelled the sweet scent of grape jelly. She tried to open the paper without touching the smear. Just as her eyes began to adjust to the dim light, the door swung open, flooding across the words before her.

"Let's go." It was Carter. He watched Tessa pale as her eyes lifted from the paper. Without warning he snatched it from her fingers and read the words *'Stop me'*.

CHAPTER 15

The Secret Service grabbed the two lovers when Carter tipped them off to the contents of the note. A hush fell over the kitchen as everyone watched two of their own being strong armed out the door. The girl started calling the men names like "Nazi pigs" and "Homeland storm troopers." The young man tried to relieve his arm of the vice grip leading him into the laundry area. Once removed, the two were immediately separated for interrogation.

"Are you sure that's your uncle's handwriting, Tessa?" Carter saw that she was shaken. The reality of her uncle's plan paralyzed her with fear. He could see it in her eyes and the way she stood. Her hands twitched and those eyes blinked incessantly. She rubbed her nose to stop a sniff.

Tessa nodded. "Yes," she whispered. She took the note from his hand then pointed to the letters. The Secret Service agent, the one Carter called John, leaned in to see her trace her index finger across the evidence. "The S is printed backwards at first then he corrected it. See?" Tessa turned it around for them. "He's a little dyslexic and constantly struggles with that letter. He did it again here on the p. Backwards then corrected. Letters like d and q were always a little crazy for him too. But he learned to overcome it for the most part. So much so he became a code breaker. He could see things no one else could. That's why he was on the USS Liberty in 1967. It was a last minute switch. He was slotted to go home."

"Let's have a chat with our refrigerator lovers," John said frowning and motioning with his head to follow.

She trailed after the two men as they entered the laundry area. Three other Secret Service agents waited for John's instructions, but he gave none. He moved toward where the young man stood handcuffed to a pipe before looking at Tessa.

"You better take the girl. She'll probably open up to you. Seems like she has a chip on her shoulder."

"Me?" Tessa felt her stomach lurch. Her eyes locked on Carter. She started to shake her head "no" when he pushed her around the corner to where the girl sat handcuffed to a metal table.

She didn't appear to be nearly as rattled as her boyfriend. The frown turned into a snarl as they approached. The knees locked together with feet spread apart gave her the appearance of a ragdoll. The thick black eyeliner had smudged a bit. Tessa wondered if it was due to lovemaking or crying.

Carter nudged Tessa and took a step back as he whispered. "You can do this."

Looking at the girl, the generation gap slapped her in the face. She worked with students all the time. In recent years a growing trend of disrespect and apathy toward teachers became the norm. This girl's narrowed eyes revealed another self-absorbed brat who felt the world owed her something.

The hard swallow in Tessa's throat sounded like a nervous gulp. "Hi. I'm..." Tessa paused knowing she wasn't supposed to give her real name. What had Chase called her a year ago? "I'm Melanie. What's your name?" Sitting on the edge of the table, Tessa tried to smile. Unconsciously she tugged at the bodice of her dress.

"None of your business, Bitch." The response carried a little wayward spit. "I didn't do anything wrong. That moron in there made me go into the fridge with him." She rolled her eyes up to the ceiling then over at the walls. The sound of dryers tumbled rhythmically in the background.

"Are you saying he raped you?" Tessa knew she sounded disgusted.

The girl snickered and eyed Tessa flippantly. "No." For such a short answer the girl let the word slide out like a multiple syllable word. "I'm saying he tricked me into going inside and well," she smirked, "one thing led to another. He's kinda cute, don't ya think? His daddy is rich."

Tessa felt the tension in her shoulders and tried to move them back to appear relaxed. "Rich? How so?"

"He owns a catering business in Bethesda. Jeff works here to make contacts, pass out a few cards to the customers. Thought maybe I'd get on his good side. You never know when a girl could fall in love." The girl eyed Tessa with amusement. "So what's the big deal?"

"The big deal is the note your boyfriend threw on the floor. Did he write it?"

"I don't have to say jack. I know my rights."

Tessa forced a weak smile and looked back to see Carter leave. A moment of panic rose inside her. What was she supposed to do? Clearly the girl was about as intimidated by the interrogation as Tessa would be of a melted stick of butter.

"The note. Was it inside when you got there?"

The girl stared at Tessa with a smug grin. "Go to hell."

Tessa slid off the table and moved toward the girl. "Was the note inside the refrigerator when you entered? I need you to talk to me." A sudden irritation began welling up inside her.

"Make me, you stupid cow."

Before Tessa could stop herself she jammed her six inch black heel into the girl's foot.

Even when the girl screamed and started to rock in the chair to escape, Tessa didn't step back. Tears burst forth from the young woman before she withdrew her heel. Grabbing the young face with one hand, she squeezed.

"Do you know who I am?" Tessa whispered as she heard Carter run back into the room.

"Police?" she sniffed.

Tessa gritted a smile and pinched tighter. "No. I'm a junior high teacher that is sick and tired of self-absorbed brats oblivious to the meaning of respect and appreciation." Her hand continued to tighten. "Do you have any idea how frustrating that is?"

The girl shook her head violently and managed to free herself. "You can't do this to me."

"Tessa!" Carter warned.

She slapped the girl with surprising force. "Of course I can. I'm not the police, the Secret Service or anything else. I'm just an underpaid teacher who wants a little payback."

The girl started to cry and looked to Carter for assistance. Tessa couldn't see him shrug away the young woman's rising fears.

"Now." Tessa forced her voice to soften. She leaned her head in closer. "What did you call me a minute ago?"

"I'm sorry," she screamed.

Tessa felt something inside her snap out of control. What was happening to her? This kind of violence went against everything she believed in. Show kindness and kindness will be returned. Be generous and blessings will follow. Biblical teachings tried to crowd into her psych. She pushed them out. The life of her uncle hung in the balance. Finding him before Enigma or the Secret Service was paramount.

"The note," she snarled. "Don't insult me, give me 'my rights' crap because if you do I'm going to reach in that ugly mouth of yours and rip out that tongue stud. Then I'll ram it up your nose. Are we clear?"

The girl burst into tears again and nodded. Through gulps of air she spoke. "Some old guy was leaving when we walked in." She sniffed several times. "When he shut the door air pushed it up."

"Then what happened?" Tessa kept her body close and threatening.

Snot drizzled down across the girls lips mingled with mascaraed tears. Tessa thought the girl looked like something in a vampire cartoon. She shrugged one shoulder almost shyly before looking up with pleading eyes at Tessa.

"Jeff grabbed it then read it to me. That's all." Her voice sounded a little pathetic now.

Tessa shifted her eyes to Carter who motioned for her to continue. The feeling of absolute power surged through her. The gentle side of her experienced surprise at the unexplored emotional monster brewing inside her. Her heartbeat quickened as she became tipsy with euphoria.

So this is why they do it, she reasoned. *Another kind of drug created a sense of invincibility and strength.* The knowledge that someone at Enigma recognized a thirst for control in her formulated the possibility her virtue was in question. Was it the director or Chase?

"Tell me about the man leaving the refrigerator."

"Donno," she whimpered.

Tessa took a deep breath. "I'm not going to hurt you. Think. What did he look like? Was there anything that stood out? Something different?"

"Well he was old. Older than you or that guy over there." She raised her chin toward Carter.

There was probably an insult in the remark, but she decided to ignore it. "Good. Was he dressed like you?"

"Yes. No. Actually he had on different pants."

The girl wore black pants and a white jacket with a mandarin collar just like the other waiters. "Do you mean jeans?"

"Cargo pants. The kind with pockets on the front and side."

"Build?"

"What?" The girl was starting to regain some control. The rebellion started to surface.

"Short, tall, skinny, fat? Build."

"Taller than you but shorter than that idiot over there that keeps checking out your ass," she quipped.

Tessa turned to look at Carter puckering his lips up in a frown, something Tessa wasn't used to seeing. His eyes met hers as he lifted an eyebrow.

"Who is he anyway? Some dumb Fed?"

"My handler. He's here to make sure I don't lose control. I have a few anger issues. The shrink keeps saying I'll get better," Tessa smiled wickedly as the girl's face paled. "But the shrink isn't here and I've been off my meds for a few days. I'm feeling pretty confident right now." She rolled her head as if loosening up neck muscles. "The hurricane seems to have thrown my emotions into overdrive." A sigh escaped her lips as she nonchalantly continued. "The pants. Did they look empty? Was he stealing?"

"Now that you mention it they were a little bumpy. I don't know. When can I go? Is this about us gettin' it on in the fridge or some old guy?"

"Did he say anything?"

"No. He just looked silly and left."

"Silly?"

"He pulled down a ball cap over his eyes and slithered out, all creepy like. We just laughed at him."

"Did you see him put anything into his pockets?"

"No. Now can I go?" The girl pleaded.

Tessa remembered just a year ago how she'd begged to be released from the clutches of Enigma agents. All requests were denied.

She turned, walking toward Carter who took a few steps back through the door where they could be alone.

"Someone must have left him what he needed for tonight." Carter sounded concerned.

Agent John Elliott, Secret Service joined them and put his hands on his hips. Tessa grew aware of his shoulder holster when his black suit coat pushed back. "This guy says they were in there for a little slap and tickle. Teenagers," he growled with disgust. "Really focused on her not wearing any panties, not much else."

Carter relayed the information Tessa squeezed out of the girl. "They don't know anything else," the agent snapped. "Just a couple of stupid kids. We'll keep them here until the president leaves just to make sure though."

Someone pushed the boy past them and into the room with the girl. Derogatory remarks spewed at the agent. Tessa fought the urge to go back in to make the girl apologize but the agent withdrew as quickly as he'd entered.

"Carter you and your partner split off from us. Head upstairs. I've got the area sealed off but you can go up the exit. My men checked in five minutes ago and said there was no sign of Mr. Wakefield. I told them you were on your way." The Secret Service agent narrowed his eyes as they skimmed over Tessa. "Are you carrying a weapon, Agent Scott?"

"Does it look like she could carry a weapon?" Carter said as he led her out into the long hall where the president entered earlier. "I'm not sure where he thinks you'd put a gun in that dress?" he said flippantly. "I think this exit leads upstairs." The Secret Service agent at the door stepped aside for the two.

"Anything?" Carter asked the bulky agent.

"No. Quiet. No in or out this way. The other guys are at the bottom of the stairs at the far end of the balcony. The door is secured. Here." The agent handed Carter a key. "You'll need this."

Nodding, Carter opened a steel door and turned to see Tessa frozen in place. The anxiousness on her face and the nervous hand movements told him she wasn't quite up to Enigma Intimidation 101.

He extended his hand not realizing his usual boyish grin now morphed into a stern reprimand. "Stop second guessing yourself. You did well in there."

"I'm not cut out for this life."

Releasing her hand Carter pulled out a Beretta from inside his suit coat then nodded toward the stairs. "None of us are. We do what we have to do. Now get your act together in case we run into your uncle. If you're not calm he won't be. Just this once, Tessa, do this for your country and not some misplaced family loyalty. If you want your uncle to stay alive we need you on your game."

"You'll let me talk to him first if…"

The sound of a closing door above them whispered a whoosh.

Slamming their bodies against the cool concrete wall along the steps, their gazes went upward. The lights flickered when a clap of thunder rattled the building. Stimulated senses forced them to creep up to the first landing then on to the top of the stairs. He touched his earwig but there was no immediate response.

Carter tried the door. It was unlocked.

Cracking the door open enough to take a quick look, he saw nothing. Something wasn't right.

"Shouldn't the door be locked?" Tessa whispered.

He nodded without taking his eyes off the empty entrance to the balcony. Motioning for Tessa to follow, they slipped inside.

The thunderous applause of the audience below covered the rage of a hurricane slamming into the D.C. area. A short documentary film on the effects of global warming presented by a National Geographic sponsor sounded epic as the lights dimmed. The deep penetrating voice of a well-known celebrity began narrating the presentation. The music sounded sweeping, laced with ominous warning. Tessa couldn't help but think the background music made for great drama considering they were looking for her uncle who planned an assassination attempt on the president.

Most of the time, the plush carpeted balcony hosted extra seating for conference goers and banquets. Tonight the Secret Service demanded it be closed to protect the president from a shooter. Running lights around the baseboards, although dim, provided enough clear sight for the two Enigma agents.

Stopping, Carter touched his earwig. With a slight nod of his head, he indicated Tessa needed to stay close. A sigh of relief escaped his lips as he moved forward to look over the railing.

"This area was cleared not more than five minutes ago. Someone forgot to lock the door we came through. Screw up. The storm caused a slight delay in answering me. They're at the other end, at the bottom of the stairs. No in or out without their eyes on target."

Tessa tried not to take offense at the use of the word 'target'. Gingerly she looked over the railing. Heights gave her trouble. Feeling her heart pound a little harder, she convinced herself it was nothing like the time Chase grabbed her while she dangled off a bridge.

"Are you alright?" Carter looked around anxiously thinking something had spooked her. "Did you see something?"

Shaking her head Tessa's voice came out in a hoarse whisper. "Seems like I get into trouble where heights and Enigma are concerned."

A mischievous grin appeared on his face. Tessa felt a little comforted by the expression; making the situation more about a rascal ready to make a move on her than pitching forward over the railing because of a stray bullet.

"You certainly got yourself in a lot of trouble a year ago."

Jerking her chin up, she narrowed her eyes. "Really? Is that how you remember it, because I recall that your boss was the cause of everything that went horribly wrong in my life that week?"

Carter continued to smirk as he lowered his weapon and eyed Tessa. "And here you are again, up to your pretty little eyeballs in another conspiracy. Correct me if I'm wrong but you kept saying it was divine intervention that brought you to us."

Swallowing an angry retort, Tessa had to admit it certainly felt that way a year ago. Now she wasn't so sure. God didn't strike her as a practical joker. What in her life would cause God to toy with her sanity again? "That was then. This is now."

Leaning in to whisper, Carter couldn't help but chuckle. "Nice come back. You're such an innocent, Tessa. It's no wonder our captain feels…"

Suddenly he straightened and peered across the vast empty

space over to the darkness on the other side of the balcony. Something moved.

Still annoyed by Carter's lack of empathy, Tessa huffed, following his stare. She saw the shadow too as her body grew paralyzed with fear. Just as she shifted her gaze at Carter, something slammed into his forehead propelling him back against the wall.

CHAPTER 16

The prime minister of Israel waited impatiently with the president in a small room just off the conference hall. The smell of steak and chicken still clung to the air with a hint of smoke from those who requested well done meat. The soft clink of china being cleared, failed to cover the self-serving tone of the Hollywood narrator in the documentary. Speculating that the voice did not match the brain in terms of intelligence, Gilad rolled his eyes upward in apathy. His steely demeanor created a false sense of calm in front of his companion, Samantha Cordova.

Watching her stand prim and proper in her black silk suit, he found the thought of her wearing something black and lacy underneath a welcome distraction. Knowing she brought the Kimber Ultra Carry he'd given her as a gift just this morning for taking such good care of him, he felt confident she would take down any threat against him. A mental note to thank his brother for reconsidering to let Samantha continue to be his escort meant he probably would be in Ben's debt.

Taking a deep breath, he exhaled then glanced at his watch. The sound of fury outside the hotel appeared to be intensifying. Rooms had been reserved in case the hurricane prevented them from leaving after the speech. This could be a hell of a night if things didn't go as planned. It didn't make much difference where he stayed. Chances were no one would be getting any sleep.

The scent of some exotic spice Samantha bathed in earlier, drifted to his senses. Realizing his disappointment of not being able to explore the possible options of another night wrapped in her control, he leaned into her and whispered. "Come back to Israel with me, Dr. Cordova. You and I are good together."

Samantha never flinched as she continued her vigil of surveying the room. The prime minister's bodyguards stood close. There shouldn't have been a need to worry. "You would quickly tire of me, Sir."

The prime minister chuckled lightly. "Perhaps after the first twenty or thirty years, but by that time I will be dead." Her slanted cat eyes turned on him with affection. "Unless I die tonight of course."

"We won't let that happen, sir. Security is tight. Between the Secret Service and Enigma, not even a cockroach could get in. Be a good boy." A seductive smile appeared before she turned her eyes away. "I have plans for you later."

"Hmm," he said between clenched teeth. "Whatever my little brother is paying you I will triple. Think about that."

Sam took a step away. "Yes, sir. I'll do that."

~~~

This effect on men gave Sam an edge others resented. There weren't many women agents at Enigma. Most of them worked in the technology or strategic planning offices. Women instructors, moles and couriers held positions, but the ones capable of being agents often stayed with the CIA or FBI. Career paths were clearer with those agencies. Blurred lines rather than stiff protocol and regulations suited her style. The few women she encountered at Enigma navigated away from her. Then Tessa Scott ruined everything.

Clenching her teeth, the thought of the woman from Grass Valley momentarily blinded her with rage. Without her help a year ago, a serious terrorist threat would have jeopardized the medical community as well as the nation's food supply. Captain Hunter protected her like she was the Holy Grail.

Rejecting the idea the captain held affection for the bumbling idiot nauseated her. The whole team appeared to have fallen for the save-me-I'm-so-helpless façade Tessa displayed. The fact remained, the captain never looked at her the same way he did at that trouble maker from Northern California who stumbled into their lives.

Earlier she'd heard from Director Clark, Tessa had been selected as a temporary agent until this Jake Wakefield mess cleared. The thought occurred to her this could be another distraction that need terminating. Whoever said competition was a good thing didn't understand her vindictive nature.

A movement near the door caught her eye when she realized Chase listened to something on his earwig. With his head down thoughtfully, Sam could tell his concern reached beyond the assassin. Was he thinking of that little twit from Grass Valley?

"Something wrong, Chase?" Sam moved to his side.

He lifted his eyes toward the president. "I'm going to check on Carter."

Sam laid a firm hand on his arm. "He's fine. He's not going to move on Betty Crocker when he's working." She understood Carter only pretended to be interested in Tessa to unnerve Chase.

"I know. Stay close to them." He nodded toward the president and the prime minister. "Just going to have a look around. Thought I heard something."

"I'll come with you."

"I'd feel better with you watching them. Sounds like the Hollywood part is over. The prime minister is up first." Chase eyed Sam. "What's the problem?"

"Why wasn't I consulted on Tessa joining the Enigma team?"

When her frosty glare continued to bore into Chase he spoke through gritted teeth. "It wasn't my decision to bring Tessa in. So get over yourself."

"You mean the director included her over your objections?" she said incredulously as her eyes darted to the prime minister.

"No. The president wanted her. Not me." With an abrupt turn he took his leave. "I'll make it up to you, Sam."

"A girl can only hope," she quipped with an insinuating tone.

~~~

Just as Tessa screamed, a thunderous applause went up, approving of the Global Warming presentation. The master of ceremonies announced everyone would be receiving a complimentary copy of the film. She rushed to Carter's side, panic making her breath come in short bursts.

"No. No. No." Tessa cried out as she nearly fell over a folding chair he'd knocked over as he propelled backwards. "Don't be dead. Don't be dead." Her words sounded hopeless even to her ears.

Unconscious, he failed to respond to Tessa's hands touching his chest and face like an anxious child searching for clues. Something warm and wet covered her fingers when she tried to slip them underneath his head. The dim light covered only his torso, leaving his head in darkness. The flood of tears burst forth as she laid her fingers on his juggler to reassure herself he lived. Closing her eyes, a strangled prayer escaped her lips in hopes that God would save him. So lost in her hysterical grief, she failed to notice the approach of a dark shadow.

A bony clasp took her by the shoulder. She whirled around, falling back against Carter to stare up at a man dressed in a white jacket. As he leaned down, extending his hand, Tessa tried to crawl away.

"Get up," he demanded in a familiar gruff voice. "He's not dead." His voice came out like a growl as he waited for her to trust his extended hand.

"You tried to kill us, Uncle Jake," she sobbed pushing his hand away. Staggering to her feet, Tessa brought her fists up to her heart.

Jake moved the Enigma agent with his foot enough to see the gun lying beneath him. Reaching for it, he then checked to see if it was ready. Satisfied he stuck it in the waist of his pants.

"I would never hurt you, Tessa. God Almighty, child, I'd think you'd know that by now." He nodded down at Carter who started to moan. As Tessa tried to drop to his side, Jake cut her off. "He'll be okay. We need to move. There's not much time. I'm going to need your help."

She pointed a quivering finger at the middle of his chest as she tried to stop her wobbly knees from swaying. "Help you? You're trying to kill the president and now my friend is unconscious thanks to you," she barked over another round of applause.

"And you're going to help me," he snapped. "I know who you're working for and they are no better than me." He grabbed her arm, jerking her to his chest. "They're killers, spies and glory hounds that do the president's dirty work. I'm disappointed in you, Tessie," he said as he started to drag her after him, fingers digging into her upper arm. "I'm going to get my buddies back and if that means killing two birds with one stone, I'm doin' it. You hear me?"

"Two? Who else?" Tessa stumbled after him. Maybe if she went willingly there would be time to talk him out of this crazy nonsense.

"Gilad Levi."

"Are you insane? His people will kill both of us. Don't do this, Uncle Jake. I beg you. Let me help you get them back. But not this way." Tessa laid her trembling hand on her uncle's chest. "Please. Think of Dad and Mom. What will they say? Jake, please."

He shook his head violently. "Too late."

Pulling flex ties from inside his white jacket, she took a step back, but couldn't out maneuver the old man. The strength in his jerk caught Tessa off guard. Before she could scream a warning to the people below Jake pushed a red bandana, he retrieved from another pocket, into her mouth.

Desperate to stop the madness, Tessa shook her head and tried to speak. He forced her to follow him. Only the night would be his judge. He apparently wasn't going to let things like family get in the way of retribution.

Jake reached down and lifted his hunting rifle from the darkness on the floor. Habit forced him to double check the readiness of his weapon. Tessa wondered in that instant how he managed to slip it in without setting off alarms.

The moan that penetrated Tessa's gag drew his eyes to her briefly causing a wave of sadness to engulf his eyes. Nothing would ever erase the terror she'd witness tonight. Would hate replace her love for him? Sacrifice verses regret would be his burden if he survived this night.

Holding the rifle against his body with one arm he reached out, cupping Tessa's chin in his leathery hand. A weak smile, begging for forgiveness crossed his mouth momentarily. "I love you little girl. Always have. I'm sorry you got caught in this. A man's gotta do what's right. Someday you'll understand."

Confusion leapt to Tessa's eyes pooled with tears when he

grabbed her by the right arm. A year earlier, Chase saved her as she slipped off a bridge. She'd dislocated her shoulder in the process and suffered periodically with pain as a result of the captain's quick fix. Even before Jake yanked, she knew what was coming; the jolt of white hot pain followed by blackness that would overtake her. A fleeting question of how Jake knew this weakness entered her mind when he gave it a jerk.

~~~

Kneeling down next to his friend, Chase felt for a pulse. His eyes never stopped scanning the immediate area, looking for the two people who held the key to tonight's impending disaster. Even as Carter regained consciousness, Chase alerted the others of the situation. Without giving the order he knew security would shift into overdrive.

Carter moaned as his eyes fluttered open. Placing a hand on his forehead, he moaned. "You're not going to kiss me are you?" Blinking away the fog, he tried to sit up with Chase's assistance. "Sorry, I thought you were Tessa." Even injured and in dire circumstances Carter made jokes.

"You're bleeding." Chase said turning his friend's head. "Guess your head isn't as hard as I thought. What happened to Tessa?" Chase looked over his shoulder then transitioned to a hunched position, not wanting to become the next target.

"I had to fight her off me, Buddy. Sorry." Lifting a pecan smeared with blood off the floor, he frowned. His eyes narrowed when he looked around for his Beretta then Tessa. The big picture started to come into focus. "I was shot with a nut?"

"He's a country boy. Slingshot is my guess."

"He could've put my eye out," he said incredulously.

"He also could have shot it out." Chase frowned. "But he didn't. The question is why?"

"It was dark. Maybe he was afraid he'd hit Tessa."

"Did you see anything? Anyone?"

"No." Anger began building inside Carter knowing he'd been outsmarted by a Tennessee hillbilly. He touched the back of his head feeling a trickle of blood. A throbbing had already begun, but he pushed it aside to concentrate. "I think I remember hearing a man's voice. Southern. Must've been Wakefield. Crying. Yeah. I heard someone crying."

"Then he's got Tessa. We need to find her before guns start blazing and she gets caught in the crossfire."

Thundering applause rose up from below as the prime minister took the podium. Moments earlier both he and the president took the stage together, shook hands and pretended to make a joke which resulted in everyone laughing. When the president motioned for Gilad to go first more welcoming applause followed.

Chase could hear Gilad begin to speak, enunciating his words with care so everyone could understand his thoughts on the friendship his country shared with the United States. The prime minister was well aware how his deep, hypnotic voice affected an audience. Unlike his brother, Gilad loved the spotlight.

A crash at the far end of the balcony drove down the agents instinctively. Their bodies, already tense, froze mere seconds as they scanned the area. Moving with stealth precision both men rose just enough to focus their attention on the possibilities of what lay ahead. The dim light prohibited a swift forward assault. As they neared the source of the commotion, the movement of a metal chair tipping over, followed by a groan, forced Chase to level his weapon at the figure awkwardly trying to stand.

"Get up!" Chase ordered when he saw the surprised suspect stumble back against the wall. Without another word he rushed forward and lowered his gun. "Tessa," he managed to say as he pulled her to a standing position. Yanking the rag out of her mouth, Chase worked to free her hands.

She rubbed her wrists before pushing the dangling curls away from her face. When Carter hobbled up to join them she couldn't resist giving him a hug. "You're alive!" Her hand gently touched his forehead before turning back to Chase. "When Carter fell, I saw blood and thought he'd been shot."

"We think your uncle used a slingshot. Carter found a pecan on the floor. When he fell he busted his head open. Where's your uncle now?" Chase couldn't mask the impatience he felt.

"He tried to dislocate my arm, but I managed to jerk free."

Chase remembered causing the original injury a year earlier. Unconsciously he reached out and touched her bare shoulder. The warmth of her silky skin created a memory he'd retrieve later when there would be time to savor the experience. "Are you hurt?"

~~~

Even though his voice sounded gruff and unforgiving, he genuinely cared about her well-being. Her hand instinctively went to rest on his. Noting its roughness forced her to lift her eyes to find him eyeing her with intense scrutiny. She felt the color begin to rise up her neck then onto her face as his hand slid dangerously down her arm, as if exploring for injuries. Did he notice the quick intake of breath she took? Could he see her heart beating through the pale skin shrouded slightly in darkness?

Pushing his hand aside, she cleared her throat. "Except for the fact that was the first time my uncle ever raised a hand to me, I'm fine. I don't know how he found out about my arm, but he knew, Chase. He tried to dislocate it so I'd be out of commission. I never told anyone about the accident, not even my husband. Even he thinks I fell off a chair or something stupid."

"Is he armed?"

"Yes. A rifle was hidden in that dark spot below the railing."

Having no idea that the mention of her husband pulled Chase back to reality, she watched as turmoil brewed in his eyes. It wasn't his style to chase after married women. The flirtation confused her earlier considering how many women found him desirable. There was no way of knowing he fantasied about her lying in his arms or that the pain in his chest resulted from his perilous fascination he held for her.

Scowling, Chase snapped, "The gun he took from Carter?"

Tessa smiled weakly as she shifted her eyes to the wounded agent. Turning, Tessa reached down to the floor and lifted the Beretta her uncle took earlier. "When he tried to stop me I managed to pull the gun out of his waistband. He saw you coming so there wasn't time to…"

Chase grabbed for the gun which she pulled away quicker than he'd imagined possible. His glare made Tessa pucker her lips rebelliously. "You're going to hurt yourself."

"Why, because I'm a woman?" Tessa found his attitude a little high and mighty for her taste.

"Because you don't know what you're doing," Carter groaned

as he turned to see more agents and paramedics enter the balcony. "Besides it's my gun."

"Not anymore," Tessa smarted. She liked having the upper hand on Carter for a change. "I'm not sure you need a gun by the way your eyes are crossed." She cringed as Chase moved toward her. "Trust me. I know all about this gun." His frown confessed an impatience Tessa knew would be dangerous to tease.

With one swift movement Chase relieved her of the Beretta. "No doubt something you memorized from the handbook at the gun range you've been sneaking off to for the last year."

She couldn't hide her surprise.

"There isn't anything you haven't done for the last year that Enigma doesn't know about, Tessa. I'm well aware that you're comfortable using this handgun, but not in a situation like this. You're not ready."

A paramedic pushed Carter into a chair to begin his examination. "We've got to find your uncle. What did he say?"

The rapid eye blink started in spite of trying to hide her true feelings.

"Don't lie to me, Tessa." Chase pushed his face into hers knowing the effect of his intimidation. "I'd hate for you to see me kill him, so if he has the slightest chance of surviving you'd better stop covering for him. Remember what he just did to you. Does that sound like the man you grew up with?"

Tessa watched other agents combing the area for clues, taking orders through their earwigs. The scene felt like it'd gone into slow motion as her eyes turned to Carter, clearly dazed by his fall.

When she looked back at Chase she realized he resembled an apocalyptic hero out to wreak havoc on those that would do the earth harm. A fleeting thought occurred to her that perhaps video designers had the captain pose for their promotional advertisements.

Squaring her shoulders, Tessa admitted the captain was right. Jake was not the uncle she loved so long ago. "He plans to kill the Israeli Prime Minister too." She nodded with her head to an area behind Chase. "He disappeared into the darkness that way."

Even as Chase turned to head the direction indicated, Tessa rushed to his side. With disapproval, he turned to scowl at her. "Don't even think you're leaving me behind. I could be the one thing that stops this madness and you know it."

"Okay," he nodded. "Just do as I say so you don't get your head shot off." He gave orders for the Secret Service to move in closer to protect the president.

"I've done this before, Chase. I know how things work." She didn't mean to sound cross.

"As I remember it, you weren't good at taking orders." His voice was low as he raised his gun and stepped in front of her. "I'm hearing that no one came down the other exit or staircase." He continued to whisper as they made their way around the balcony.

"We've completed the entire loop." Tessa stood at the end of the balcony closest to the stage where the president now spoke. She looked behind her. "Is there a dumbwaiter? Wouldn't there have to be a way to get food up here when it was used for banquets?"

Chase lowered his gun. Moving to an alcove shrouded in darkness, he ran his hand along the upholstered wall. A small knob that blended with the fabric met his fingers. With a quick jerk, the door swung open with a creak as he raised his weapon, ready to eliminate any threat.

"Empty," he exhaled as Tessa stepped forward sniffing the air. "What is it?"

"Cherry pipe tobacco. My uncle's favorite. I used to love to sniff his shoulder when he hugged me. He used to say that was the reason he couldn't give up smoking." There remained a heavy sadness in her voice Chase noticed that seemed to force her to clear her throat to keep emotions in check. If Chase saw so much as one wet trail on her face he'd banish her to a safer place. Focusing on her words helped him avoid the pain in his chest. "He took this down, maybe returned it so we wouldn't suspect anything. I think he's trying to get out of here."

~~~

Chase mumbled something in cyber space as his eyes bore into his temporary agent. "I know it's hard, Tess, and I'll do my best to keep him alive." It was difficult for him to feel empathy for a killer even if Wakefield meant something to Tessa. Just like always her eyes touched a spot inside him he believed to be dead and withered.

A nod of understanding and a slight smile forced a heavy sigh through her lips. "He's down there. Maybe you should move the president off the stage."

The orders were given. Chase knew the president would not budge in the middle of his speech.

"Chase, how would he get a weapon pass security?"

"I've been wondering the same thing. Someone is helping him."

"Are we looking for more than one shooter?"

Chase shrugged as he motioned for Tessa toward the dumbwaiter. "Looks that way. Or maybe there's just an inside man." He nodded at the dumbwaiter. "I'm too big to get in this." He swung the door open as wide as it would go. "I need you to take it down now. Agents are on the way so they'll help you out."

"How will that help," she asked even as she moved closer to the dark space that would carry her down.

"Tell me the first thing you see, how you feel, does your legs cramp?" He looked down at her bare legs and couldn't repress a wolfish grin. "I can help with any cramps."

"I just bet you can," she frowned not wanting to admit the thought occurred to her. "This is embarrassing." She groaned as she let him lift her up into the enclosure.

Scooting back then pulling her legs up, careful to keep her knees together, she became aware of Chase's smoldering examination of her body. She turned sideways and pulled up her knees so the door would shut. "I don't know how he could walk after this. He has some arthritis in his knees. This would be painful for him even after a few seconds."

"We're done under estimating your uncle."

Tessa reached for the door. "Someone will be waiting to get me out of here?"

He touched his earwig. "Just pretend you're Jake. I'll head that way." After shutting the door he pushed the button for her to descend.

Starting down the stairs, Chase held his gun down at his side. Five seconds. It shouldn't take long. At the bottom of the steps he made a turn to find the back entry to the food service area where several agents were already waiting.

Twenty seconds.

A chime sounded just as Chase entered the small service area.

Thirty seconds.

"How long should it take?" The other agents shrugged and let Chase push closer.

Another minute and a half ticked by.

"Open it," he ordered as he rushed up.

The two agents blocked his view as one pulled open the door. When they stepped aside, Chase could clearly see the dumbwaiter.

It was empty.

CHAPTER 17

The wind rocked the small sedan as it came to a halt in front of the partially boarded up building. It looked like it may have been a garage in another life for city vehicles. The speaker sat motionless for a few minutes as did Amon, waiting for an impossible pause in the onslaught of wind and rain. With the car still running, Amon inched closer to the entrance. The metal door swung open, revealing a short man cringing in the wind. He appeared to force himself between it and the door frame as if it were giant jaws ready to snap shut.

The speaker tried to get out of the car only to have the door knock him back into the front seat. Amon struggled as well, but managed to pull himself around to the passenger side of the vehicle. Another man joined him from inside the building and pried the door back open so Amon could pull the speaker to shaky legs.

It was no surprise the speaker allowed Amon to cover him with his own raincoat or that he leaned into the younger, stronger body for protection. The speaker had grown accustomed to being pampered and shielded from the ugliness of the world. Why would this be any different?

Debris swirled around them like frantic dancers of destruction. With every step, the wind pushed them back two. Amon felt the pelting of something sharp against his face and heard the speaker yelp as they managed to shove him inside the building. Taking a deep breath of relief, Amon motioned for one of his men to pull the door shut. He sat aside his instinct to shake the water from his ebony hair at the sight of blood trickling down the speaker's face.

"You are hurt." Amon turned to one of the men who had assisted moments before. He nodded back toward the rear of the room and the assistant scurried off. "Let me look. I was a nurse in Cairo during Arab Spring." He gently touched the cut over the speaker's left eye causing him to flinch.

"This is your fault," the speaker complained. "You should've driven me closer." He threw off Amon's coat to the oil stained floor, but kept his own on with a shiver.

Amon withdrew his hands and frowned. "It is not deep. I will let you clean it. No stitches, I think."

"You think!" he barked. "Since you're the nurse, you clean it."

"I am not one of your mindless interns that perform upon command, Mr. Speaker." His voice was cool and calm considering the weather outside. "You'll do it yourself if it is done."

One of his men returned with a first aid kit. Amon nodded toward the speaker. It was tossed so quickly the speaker missed. The sound of the small kit clattering to the floor created a wicked smile on Amon's face. "I hope you are better at strategy than you are at receiving first aid."

When Amon pivoted to walk away the speaker retrieved the plastic box then hurled it at the Egyptian. As it caught the back of his neck, Amon stopped shortly and looked over his shoulder at the speaker. His men looked down and stepped back as Amon causally walked up to his co-conspirator. The speaker realized too late, he'd pushed his luck too far.

Standing close enough to the speaker he could smell the liquor on the politician's breath. He felt disgusted. With a swiftness that surprised the politician, Amon grabbed him by the throat using one hand and began to squeeze. The speaker pawed at the hand wildly, resulting in a tighter grip.

"Listen to me old man. I do not like you and you clearly do not respect me. Let's get through this night without killing each other." Amon released the speaker and slid his hand down the lapel of the London Fog raincoat. His voice took on a softer tone. "You should get out of this. You will catch a cold. The next president of the United States needs to appear fit for duty when the time comes."

The speaker masked his fear by stepping back and jerking off his coat before throwing it to the concrete floor. "Watch yourself, Amon." His voice sounded garbled as he rubbed his throat.

"Your advice, as always, is invaluable, Mr. Speaker." He turned to walk away. "Clean yourself up. It is past time for prayers."

~~~

Covering her nose, Tessa hoped to avoid breathing in the faint smell of stale food. Her stomach ached. The tension disagreed with her digestive system. Squirming, she felt the dumb waiter bounce gently as if it'd caught on something. The thought of being stuck in such a confined space with her knees practically under her chin compelled Tessa to spread out her arms and push against the side. Something gave way under her finger tips, causing the door to fly open.

For a moment she wondered if she'd reached the bottom floor, but saw a walkway lined with what looked to be electrical service for the hotel. Several light bulbs dangled precariously, glowing with a faded voltage.

When she reached out to grab the handle her awkward position toppled her out. Bracing the fall with her right hand drove a sharp pain up her weak shoulder. Her uncle hadn't dislocated it, but yanked hard enough to make it tender. Struggling to get up, she heard the dumb waiter door slam like a tennis ball against wood. At the sound of its descent, Tessa rose and stared at a shadow holding a rifle.

His silence comforted her knowing Jake was thinking. She used to ask him as a small child why he was such a quiet man. He would gather her up in his arms and give her a piece of peppermint from his pocket before saying he was thinking about how to make the world a better place. Could he have been devising this night's rendezvous with death even back then?

"Uncle Jake?" No reply. "Uncle Jake, I'll do whatever you want. Just don't," she swallowed hard as she took a timid step forward as she rubbed her shoulder. "Just don't hurt me. Okay, Uncle Jake?"

A slow movement into the light revealed a man she hardly

recognized. Gone was the uncle who took her hunting, wore a crown at her tea parties and read to her when he filled in as a babysitter so her parents could have a date night. The lines around his eyes and mouth had deepened. His thinning gray hair looked white in the eco-friendly light. The funny colored eyes she'd once loved to stare into were now rimmed in dark circles and puffy skin.

"You'll help me get my friends back?" It was a question that sounded like an order.

"Yes. Just, please don't shoot the…"

"No! You help me. No questions." A threatening step forward caused Tessa to freeze.

"Okay. Just tell me what the plan is so I know how to help."

"First tell me who those men were I saw with you. The dark one first. The one in the picture."

"He's Serbian. He works for the government, just like the man you took down."

"And the last one? The big one who helped you."

"The captain. He's in charge. He asked for my help."

Jake narrowed his eyes to focus better. "Who are they? FBI?"

Reaching out to him Tessa shook her head. "Homeland is all I know, Uncle Jake." Lying to her uncle wasn't easy. He knew her as well as anyone. "It's a secret agency that works for the president."

The sound of applause could be heard again drifting upward. She guessed they were over the stage.

"Do you work for them?"

"Yes, as of last night. It's temporary. It's a long story, Uncle Jake. Robert knows nothing about this. I'll explain later. But now we need to go to the captain and explain before you get killed."

He shook his stubborn head, inching forward. "I've got a job to do, Tessie. I can't let my friends down." His voice took on urgency. "How can you help me?"

"Do you even know who did this or where they are being held?

"Not yet, but" a grin started to appear on his lips, "I hog tied the one they sent to make sure I did my job." A sniffle laugh escaped him as he looked over the metal railing where more applause drifted upwards.

"Why did you tie him up?" Tessa hoped he was having second

thoughts about shooting the president. "Can't he tell you where the men are? You could've brought him to us to help."

"Doesn't speak much English and I kinda knocked him out with a broken pot I found behind a dumpster about two blocks away. I figured there was more than one of them watching me. Where you see one cockroach there's lots more hiding."

"Where is he now, Uncle Jake?"

"The weather was looking ugly by the time he came to. Since he couldn't tell me anything I could understand, I gagged him. After that I helped him get in the dumpster to ride out the storm. Didn't figure on it getting this bad though. He may have flown that puppy down to Pennsylvania Avenue and straight into the White House." A chuckle escaped him as he took another step closer. He almost sounded carefree.

Between security cameras and the Secret Service, chances of them getting out were slim to none. If she could usher him from the building maybe he'd survive. "Let's go get him. Maybe I can understand him. Your hearing isn't what it used to be. Do you know how to get us out of this area? They'll be looking for me any minute."

Jake nodded and reached out to touch Tessa's arm. "Sorry I tried to hurt you. Levi said…"

"Gilad Levi? He told you about my arm? How did he know?"

He shrugged. "Doesn't matter. He's a shifty SOB, I'll tell ya that. Those Israelis haven't changed one bit."

Tessa could see that this line of communication would only get him agitated. "Okay." She could now lay a hand on the arm that cradled the rifle. "How do we get to a lower level?" Forcing a weak smile Tessa watched her uncle tilt his head and adore her with his eyes. "I love you, Uncle Jake. Let's get out of here."

A rattling of metal against hurried footsteps jerked the two back to reality as their eyes peered into the darkness.

"Uncle Jake?" Tessa watched as her uncle smiled lovingly at her. "Ready?"

He nodded.

~~~

Chase wished the metal didn't echo. He could hear voices as

he lifted Carter's Beretta to a readied position. Hearing a woman's scream accelerated his cautious approach as he topped the narrow stairs.

Outlined in dim light he saw Tessa bending over a body on the floor. "Tessa." He rushed forward as she jumped up. Trembling with fear, her eyes went to the man convulsing on the floor.

"He's having a seizure!" Tessa pushed the hand down that carried his weapon. "Do something!"

Foam poured out of the old man's mouth as Tessa fell back to her knees to restrain him. "Make sure he doesn't hit his head. I'll get help." Chase took several steps and turned away as he touched his earwig to speak. "Get the paramedics up here." He gave the location. "Looks like a seizure. Yes. Agent Scott is here too. Move it."

Pivoting on his heels, he found Tessa standing less than two feet from him. She looked pained. Those blue eyes that made him feel like he was drowning were batting with a nervous anticipation. Never a good sign.

"I'm sorry," she whispered.

The moment he underestimated the situation, Chase looked down to see that Jake's body was gone. "What the…"

Before he could finish the sentence something slammed into the back of his knees, pitching him forward. He rolled to his back in time to see the butt of a rifle make contact with his nose. The pain forced him flat on the floor. Blood ran over his lips as he tried unsuccessfully to rally. Tessa fell down beside him. In that fleeting moment when she brought her lips to his ear, he felt the pain in his chest that came with her touch.

"I quit."

CHAPTER 18

Staggering to his feet Chase wiped his nose against the sleeve of his suit jacket. Someone tried to take a look at his injury, but he shoved them off so hard the paramedic staggered backwards. Blinking back the sharp pain under his eyes, he tried mentally to clear the cobwebs. His forehead felt like it collided with a hammer. After discovering his earwig was missing, he searched on the floor. Hoping he'd see it in the proximity of Carter's gun dropped during the scuffle, the captain realized that too was gone.

Pulling back his shoulders, Chase reached inside his jacket and pulled out his own weapon. The image of the old man jamming the butt of his rifle into his face forced him to admit the woman tricked him yet again.

Standing still for only seconds, he recalled Tessa's soft hair touching his cheek as she relieved him of his earwig. He remembered how she ran her fingers along his bloody cheekbone before shouting at her uncle to stop.

Stop what, he wondered. He looked around him as Secret Service agents began looking for signs of the two. Tessa threw an arm across him and nearly landed in his lap. Squinting his eyes, Chase visualized the old man, foam around his mouth with the butt of his gun ready to land another blow. She'd protected him from further attack. Maybe she knew if he rallied the old man's neck would be snapped like a twig. Either way Chase needed to get to her before the Secret Service.

"Stop," he shouted. He looked around at the men speaking to

others throughout the building with annoyed expressions. They knew the woman worked for Enigma. "She's listening to you. Everything you say lets her know where you are so shut the hell up!" He stormed into the darkness. "Get the president off the stage now!"

~~~

Tessa watched her uncle wipe the remaining foam from his face as he peered out through a small crack between the door frame and door. Luckily she'd picked up some Alka Seltzer in the hotel store. Developing an upset stomach earlier in the evening, Tessa knew it would only get worse before the night ended. With the sound of footsteps, she forced her uncle to pop one in his mouth. Seconds later, fizzy foam poured from his lips.

Tricking Chase would be her undoing. He hated insubordination, especially from her. Putting the moves on her meant nothing more than enjoying the bare skin exposed in a rather revealing dress. How many times had she seen him turn the charm on and off? Whatever innocent charade she'd try now would be wasted. He wasn't anything like her husband Robert, who could be manipulated with a little remorse.

The image of the two men in her life almost made her laugh out loud. Robert's picture would probably be next the word predictable in the dictionary, whereas Chase's would be looming next to lethal. Robert obeyed the letter of the law, like the professional lawyer he strived to be. Chase used the law to break others, sometimes with his bare hands.

Robert believed her to be plagued with indecision and clumsiness, which he said could be endearing at times. The man who dragged her into an alley and forced himself on her believed Tessa to be a dangerous manipulator who couldn't be trusted. His intentions felt wild and brutish when he'd crushed her against his chest the night before. Promises of protection through gritted teeth would now turn to revenge. Robert was safe. Captain Hunter resembled quicksand.

Tessa listened to dead silence on the earwig. "We need to move, Uncle Jake."

With the help of the earwig Tessa knew people were on the

move with the president. She touched the door as Jake stepped aside to check his rifle. Leaving a smear of blood she'd taken from Chase's face she made a small arrow pointing down and out the hall. She pushed Jake back when several men rushed by toward the stage door. Secret Service.

How many were left to guard the exterior door? Two more? Three? She knew enough to understand they didn't abandon their post without orders. The door would still be covered by more armed Secret Service waiting for her or the president.

Leaving traces of blood on her escape route was a last second decision. Would Chase be able to follow? She feared the vulnerability she now faced. Would Chase kill her too, in order to take down her uncle?

Unexpectedly she recognized Chase's voice, causing her hand to touch her ear. He'd secured another earwig. Imagining him ripping it out of someone else's ear made her flinch. Now she realized his warning drove the guards forward for extra protection. That meant more agents outside protecting the door. At first she thought a dog was growling before the hair started to stand on the back of her neck.

"Tessa, if you're listening to me, I'm coming for you. And when I catch you, and I will catch you, I'm going to teach you a lesson you'll never forget." There was a pause. "Provided you survive long enough to remember it."

The lights flickered. The roar of the storm sounded like an angry giant pounding on the exterior. The smells from the kitchen mingled with the sickening sweet smell of rotting garbage as the exit door sucked open. Gingerly the two slipped out into the corridor. If they could get to the kitchen they might find a way out.

The wind sounded like a roar as it forced itself into a space which acted like a wind tunnel. Even though they were at the opposite end, blowing rain reached in like sharp icy fingers. Jake nearly lost his balance as he moved out onto the wet floor near the kitchen doors.

Tessa cringed for only a second as rain blew in to sting her bare skin above her breasts. Her eyes were drawn to something red washing into the corridor. Blood.

In the time it took to touch her earwig she knew the large lumps sprawled across the loading dock were bodies, not trash bags blown from containment areas.

"Agents down!" She screamed. "Repeat! Agents down. Do not bring the president into the exit corridor! Chase! Somebody! Listen to me!"

There was a moment in time which would later haunt her in the middle of the night. The nightmare began to unfold. Although it occurred at warp speed, Tessa would experience it in slow motion over and over again until she jerked awake drenched in sweat with a pounding heart.

Jake swung around toward the door bringing up his rifle. He'd seen the bodies too. The stage doors opened vehemently with agents coming through two deep before Tessa spied the president. She stole a glance back at the exit as masked men with some kind of automatic weapon burst in and stopped short for a couple of seconds. Their bodies hunched with anticipation in what would follow. Weapons lowered toward them.

Without hesitation, Jake shot one in the chest, sprawling him in front of two others who tripped and fell. Their guns discharged into the overhead lights, leaving the corridor in darkness. Only the light from the exit sign remained. The escape route, now bathed in a pool of pale light revealed a floor glistening with a mixture of rain and blood.

The invaders hunched low like shadowy monsters wearing ski masks. With determination, Tessa swung around toward the president and his protection detail. They pushed him back toward the door when the lights went out. Their weapons raised, the brave men who protected the president tried to neutralize the threat.

"Uncle Jake, get down," she screamed as she fell to the floor and tried to crawl toward the Secret Service. Earlier she'd relieved Chase of the Beretta then rammed the barrel of weapon into the top of her bodice. The butt of the gun rubbed her chin as she scampered toward what she believed to be safety. Her knees ached. The crazy thought of losing one of her new shoes made her look back toward the fire fight unfolding.

Jake continued to fire his rifle as the Secret Service came alongside him. She wasn't sure why they didn't kill him. Maybe the fact that he fired at the greater threat kept him alive. She knew he had to be close to empty. Did he have more ammo? Could he reload under such dire circumstances?

She watched two more attackers fall but just as many Secret Service fell. One dropped across her legs smashing her flat. With elbows pressed into the concrete, Tessa managed to pull free of the dead weight on her calves. Something wet and sticky running down into her half on shoes created a gag reflex. She felt a bullet whiz by her ear, forcing her head down so hard she nearly knocked herself unconscious against the floor.

Tears gushed out of her eyes from the sudden jolt of pain. She looked up to see the president hunched down behind John Elliott, the point man for the Secret Service. He'd been the one who forced her to interrogate the girl. He walked backwards, gun drawn, pushing the president back against his will. The wall stopped them. John's gun was drawn with other men to stand and block a fatal shot.

As she tried to crawl again she heard John's agitated command. "Stay down."

Was he talking to her or the president? Her eyes lifted to John just as she watched his gun fly up and out of his hand. The same instant his hand fell to his neck as an explosion of blood flew back on the president. He tumbled forward, leaving the president exposed.

Something clicked inside Tessa. She saw chaos in the stock market, battle lines drawn for war, NORAD open missile silos, and her children crying. She scrambled up with the grace of a three legged gazelle.

"Mr. President!" She jumped in front of him, grabbing him by the shoulders. His eyes went wide with surprise as he put his hands around her waist. She tried to pull him down to the floor, but he resisted as his eyes watched the unfolding mayhem. The tug of his hands nearly pushed Tessa aside. She could feel him draw her near as if it were her who needed protecting. "I'm sorry, Mr. President."

Reaching inside his jacket she found an exposed spot on his neck. Between her index finger and thumb Tessa grabbed some skin around his juggler and pinched viciously.

President Austin looked down at her in bewilderment and pain as she released him. He jerked back hitting his head against the wall. This gave Tessa enough time to knock him off balance and force him down. A bullet ricocheted off the wall just as they hit the floor. As awkward as it felt, Tessa flipped over and found that she had straddled the president's lap.

A fleeting press release appeared in her head: *"The president was found dead with an unknown female sitting in his lap. Speculation is that…"*

Tessa pushed the report from her head.

"Chase. Chase," was all she could manage to yell as another Secret Service agent fell.

With horror Tessa watched one of the attackers take his gun and slam it into her uncle's head as he tried to reload.

Jake waved the others back saying: "Take care of the president." He fell through the swinging doors of the kitchen as another masked man rammed the barrel of his gun into the old man's gut.

The smell of gun powder, sweat and something else repulsed her as the attackers stepped in over her uncle.

The agents backed toward the president, eyeing her as she covered his body. She rolled off with a clumsy attempt to stand as she reached down for him. Would they shoot her too? "He's safe," she declared staggering while trying to pull the president to his feet.

Thirty seconds. That's all it had taken to nearly destroy the leader of the free world. Tessa knew, as did the agents, it would start again as soon as the attackers reloaded and sucked in some courage. She guessed they were surprised at the appearance of the Secret Service coming through the doors.

She wasn't sure if it was a flash of lightning or the timid attempt of a street lamp to reactivate outside that drew her eyes to the kitchen doors swinging open. Without hesitation her arms flew out in front of the president as she deliberately fell against him. She pulled her gun from her dress and released the safety as she shouted to the remaining agents.

She managed to cry out. "Behind you."

~~~

The protection detail pushed Gilad to the floor when gun fire broke out. Screams shattered the open space of the ballroom. Sounds of toppled chairs and breaking water glasses clattered to a carpeted floor as the hurricane slammed into the windows outside.

The crashing of exploded glass showering down on the guests who chose to watch the unfolding storm from the lobby could not be heard over the panic of educators trying to find an escape. The hum of electricity powering hotel systems ceased as chandeliers quivered above tables. Their glass pendants danced to a dangerous melody, as a warning smell of burning wire began to drift throughout the room. A few candles flipped over catching a dried flower arrangement on fire. Several quick thinking teachers smothered it out with their suit coats.

"Get off me," Gilad demanded as he physically shoved Micah aside with a grunt. "Give me a gun." It was an order that Micah understood and quickly jumped to his feet. When Gilad waved him away the giant of a bodyguard positioned himself in front of the prime minister. "Did you hear me?" he quipped. Micah fished in his pocket for a small caliber revolver and handed it to his boss. "Sam."

Samantha already helped alleviate the darkness by turning on the flashlights brought along for such an emergency. She now checked her weapons, one in a shoulder harness and another strapped to her hip. Running a hand down her leg, it was obvious to the prime minister's men she carried more than two equalizers. Nodding to Micah, she knew it was pointless to insist on protecting his boss.

"Stay here, Sir." Sam was all business now. Her eyes narrowed, wide lips thinned and her movements grew quick. She looked back at Micah. "Get him out of here. Go through the front if you must, but not the way the president left. I don't know who is out there but…"

Gilad frowned and pushed forward. "I know."

Sam eyed him incredulously. "Mr. Prime Minister? What have you not told us?"

"One man is Mrs. Scott's uncle. The others are Egyptians or someone connected to them. They weren't supposed to get this far."

"You knew they were coming?" Sam stepped forward in a threatening manner only to be shoved aside like a toy by Micah. "What have you done?"

"I have an informant at the Egyptian Embassy. Someone is trying to stop Israel from admitting their sins against the USS

Liberty that we bombed in 1967. They want to force a crack in the relationship between our two countries. It was under control until…"

"Until what?" she snapped then clenched her teeth together.

"I've said enough." He nodded at his men. "We're going in too."

"Like hell you are," she hissed as she pivoted toward Ari, another one of Gilad's giants. Eyeing him she considered a swift kick to his groin, but the sneer on his face revealed he prepared for such an assault. "Get out of my way, Ari." She pointed her gun at his groin then arched her eyebrow. "You can come with me but your boss stays. Understood?"

Ari looked at the prime minister then to Micah. "Keep him restrained. I'm going with the woman." Micah nodded and extended his arm as Gilad attempted to shove past. A series of colorful adjectives and threats followed, but Sam and Ari left the room with two other Mossad in tow.

The shooting stopped just as they came to the exit door of the corridor. Evaluation of the situation was impossible without a window. A great deal of chatter flooded into Sam's earwig until she pulled it out and shoved it into the pocket of her jacket. Focusing in chaos was her specialty. Stretching her neck upward then rolling her shoulders back, she exhaled slowly then inhaled the same way.

The image of Chase's face flashed momentarily in her mind's eye but she quickly buried it. There was no way to know if he made it to the president. The sound of Tessa's call for help earlier, then for Chase, meant the president stood in the crosshairs. Agents were down.

"Ready?" Sam looked up at Ari who nodded his blond head.

The door swung open and the corridor detonated with flashes of gunfire.

CHAPTER 19

Vice President Warren McCall sat in a wooden chaise overlooking the water from his deck. The weather, according to the Alaskans, had been warm compared to other years. In his opinion this was as close to perfect as you could get. Washington D.C. in the summer could be sweltering. The mountains rose up in the distance with such majesty that the VP started humming *God Bless America*. He'd laid the western novel down and now forced himself to sip the white soda his wife brought him earlier. They'd run out of Dr. Pepper, his favorite.

"I'm the Vice President of the United States. I should be able to get what I want to drink."

"You're being a baby, Warren. What do you think your Inuit buddies would think of all the whining? I'll tell you what they'd think. The vice president sounds like a spoiled little girl. You wouldn't be able to handle a rocking boat or cold icy water that splashed on you. Shut up and drink," his wife demanded as she took his pulse. "You want to go fishing then let me treat you. You have food poisoning. It's not like you can get two rooms away from a toilet."

The VP groaned feeling his bowels pinch. He frowned. "Some vacation this is turning out to be. Can you at least send one of the boys across to the mainland to get my Dr. Pepper? I promise I'll be a good patient after that. No fussing..."

"Whining, Warren. It's whining." She withdrew her fingers from his wrist and offered a soft smile. He'd waited a year for this trip. Knowing how hard he worked in D.C. made her feel almost sorry for him. "Okay. One of the staff is taking the boat across to pick up supplies. I'll add some Dr. Pepper to the order. Do you think you can wait a couple of hours or do I need to medicate you?" This time she laughed and drew a chuckle from her husband.

"I'm sorry to be such a bother, Peggy." He reached for her hand then kissed her knuckles.

She bent and kissed him on top of his head.

"Mrs. McCall, the boat is getting ready to push off. Anything else you need?" It was Terry, the vice president's Secret Service agent. "Do you want to go into town? I'll watch Mr. McCall like a hawk."

She looked down at her husband who shooed her away. "Go. The sea air will do you good. I know how you like poking around in all those little foo-foo shops for knick-knacks. Just don't forget my Dr. Pepper," he warned good-naturedly.

Terry stood aside. "I'll get your agent, Mrs. McCall."

She thanked him and said she'd be down at the boat dock in a few minutes in time for the departure. A change of clothes and a light jacket before heading off delayed the trip another fifteen minutes, but no one appeared to mind as she was helped aboard the fifty-six foot yacht. Turning to look up at the deck, she shaded her eyes, trepidation toying at the recesses of her mind. The vice president stood against the railing waving like a school boy. It reminded her again of why she loved him.

It would be the last time she saw him.

~~~

Amon walked into the holding area where the old men from the USS Liberty waited. They were all seated around a wobbly folding table. A deck of cards appeared to be in use as he looked in on the former warriors. Mildew and dirt mixed with the scent of rain dripping from the overhead windows. Their loud voices stopped once aware of him. He wasn't sure if their voices rose because of the storm or if their hearing failed. Two wore hearing aids. He guessed the other two probably should, but were too proud to cave into old age.

Their glares intensified when he did not speak readily. One

man rose and threw his cards down. "Are you going to tell us why we're here?"

Amon's smile became cynical. He approached the table causing the other three to stand and move away. "It is for your own protection."

"Protection from what?" The one they called Simon snapped. "Who are you?"

"That is of no consequence."

"Like hell it isn't. We're American citizens. By your accent I'd say you aren't from around here."

He pulled out a chair and sat down. "You are correct. I represent the country of Egypt. I have come to talk to you about the bombing of the USS Liberty in 1967."

A stout looking man with snow white hair and glasses banged his fist on the table. "Get in line."

"And you are?" Amon smiled, not in the least bit intimidated by the old man's posturing. "Another sailor from the ship, no doubt."

"No. I'm a United States Marine."

"My sincere apologies. Then you would be Mike Strafford. I suppose your ability to speak Russian on that fateful day did you no good at all." The old marine remained quiet. "But your friend Jake had skills in Russian and Hebrew. He heard what was happening to my people a few miles away in Arish, did he not? A problem for Israel."

The old marine folded his arms across his chest as if he were looking over the deck of a ship. "You cannot question me like this. We can give you our name, rank and serial number. No more."

Amon burst into laughter. When he regained composer, he rubbed his eyes. "Americans are so dramatic. I love it." He stood and pushed the chair under the lip of the table. His British accent thickened. "I admire your allegiance to a country that swept the whole affair under the rug. Your President Johnson and his advisors did not wish to lose Israel as a friend since the Russians were funneling money to us. They sacrificed the honor of brave American men to keep the Israelis happy. Even after Israel admitted bombing your ship they claimed it was a case of mistaken identity."

"Our colors were flying." Simon pointed an arthritic finger as if it were a loaded gun. "Every man was a witness to that. They mowed us down like we were rabid dogs. The only reason they stopped the slaughter was because they heard the radio broadcast of the 6th Fleet saying help was on the way."

"Yes. Some would say God works in mysterious ways." Amon eyed the group carefully.

"Why are you holding us?" Amon raised a questioning eyebrow as to the identity of the new voice. "Carl Robbins." He appeared to stand at attention for a few seconds after saying his own name. Pretending to stare in the distance for a few seconds, he then refocused on his captor.

"You were to testify before a hearing in a few days concerning the USS Liberty. I merely wanted to make sure you had your stories straight before speaking to a group of men and women who really aren't all that interested in what happened over forty years ago. With terrorism, unemployment, immigration reform and insurance issues, I wanted to make sure you were heard, my friends."

"Let's get something straight. We aren't your friends." Simon's lip snarled then quivered. It had been a long time since he'd had to stand up to anyone.

Amon nodded in acceptance. "Perhaps you are correct. The Israelis will probably just claim," he tried to think of the words, "sour grapes, I think you say. They paid some money years ago to make it go away and yet it never has. Thanks to you and other survivors, the issue has now come back like the hurricane that rages outside." The men looked at each other for guidance. "I want to hear your stories. Nothing more." He turned to see two of his men enter with trays of food. "It is not much; soup, some sandwiches and cookies. The cookies are stale as is the bread but the soup is hot. The bottled water will do, I hope. Please sit and eat. Then we will talk."

He watched the old men sit down reluctantly and eye the food placed before them. It wasn't until he left that he heard them begin to eat and murmur amongst themselves.

~~~

"I'm going to die today," Tessa thought with some hysteria. *"I*

better do something to make it count so my kids will be proud of me."

The agents were already leveling their weapons to shoot when the attackers burst through the swinging doors of the kitchen. The rapid spit of bullets to darkness made flashes of light explode like fireworks. She wasn't sure of anything except the smell of gun powder and the president trying to relieve her of the Beretta. Somehow she managed to keep a tight grip as her elbow unconsciously jabbed his gut to prod him toward a door she believed to be a safe room. Several hours earlier she'd come through those doors to meet the leader of the free world.

An agent fell, but fired again to topple an attacker. Cartridges being expelled from weapons were silent as they hit the floor. Between the roar of the storm and automatic gun fire Tessa couldn't even hear that she was screaming. The corridor suddenly looked like strobes making a death dance as two more agents fell while reloading.

Covering her head with one arm, she pushed the president toward the door. Something zinged past her forehead then her arm, causing her to lose her footing. Having hooked her arm through the president's she felt herself being dragged down.

"Stand up," she ordered before realizing the president had been shot and was falling.

Looking toward the attackers she became aware they had stopped firing. The agents were alive but injured. One tried to rally and was rewarded with a shot to the head. Heavy breathing, groans of pain from both sides of the law, now mixed with the thunderous sounds of the hurricane coming through the outside doors.

Twisting to fall against the president, Tessa could feel blood sticking to her back. Was he dead? All she knew was that the masked attacker moving toward her pointed his weapon as she lifted the Beretta with a shaky hand.

Squeezing her eyes shut for a split second to clear the watery vision of fear, Tessa began speaking: "Though I walk through the valley of the shadow of death, I will fear no evil..."The Beretta shook so badly that when she pulled the trigger the bullet hit the floor between the attacker's legs. The gun flew back out of her hand. She tried to recover it unsuccessfully.

She watched him look down at the stray shot, then at her, as he outstretched his arm to finish her. "And why will you fear no evil?" he asked in sarcasm.

Tessa offered a weak smile then pointed behind him and his two men. "Because he is going to kill you."

Whirling around, the attackers saw the shadow of a large man as he unloaded his weapon into them. The attackers dropped before knowing they were on the abyss of hell. Chase charged the kitchen, but jumped back when three more men slammed into the door, knocking him off balance.

Sam and Ari shoved open the door to see Tessa covering the president from further injury.

"Grab him, Ari." Sam ordered.

He handed Tessa his Uzi before bending down and lifting the president into his huge arms. She watched Sam rush past her. The sound of gunfire exploded into her ear yet again as she saw an attacker fall against Chase. He shoved him aside as the remaining two limped toward the door only to be mowed down with Chase and Sam firing at their legs.

The sound of silence above the storm sounded like angels singing to Tessa as she watched Chase and Sam exchange words, then check the last two bodies. They were trying to crawl away when Sam grabbed one by the foot and twisted. A scream split the momentary calm. She imagined the female agent smiling at the reaction. The captain pulled the last man to his feet by his hair then slammed him against the wall.

"Who sent you?" The man whimpered with pain. Chase jerked the mask off his face. "Name." He shook his head in confusion just as Chase shot him in the foot. "A name or so help me the next one takes off your other foot."

Tessa edged her way up the wall, clinging to it like a lifeline as Ari burst back through the door and relieved her of the weapons in each hand. As she stumbled forward without taking her eyes off of Chase and Sam, she remembered her uncle who had fallen in the door.

Zoric appeared at her elbow with gun drawn. His grip around her waist did not feel friendly. Looking at the fallen around her, she searched for her uncle. The smell of death hung heavy in the rain blowing violently through the open dock doors. The angry moan of wind sounded like a death rattle.

Another gunshot from Chase's gun made her flinch then grab at Zoric's suit coat.

"You don't have any more feet to shoot so I'm going to start working my way up." Chase's determined voice frightened Tessa as she watched him ram his gun into the attacker's crotch. She wondered how the man could keep holding back.

"Okay. Okay." The man shouted. "I didn't know where we were going; just that it was a big party where big wigs would be. I was told it was a robbery."

Chase jabbed the barrel of his gun harder into the man's body. "Try again," he spoke through gritted teeth as he pushed his own bloody face into the attacker.

Within a few seconds the man couldn't stop talking as snot mixed with salty tears which now ran across his lips. "Sam, finish this," he ordered. Turning he saw that police and other agents flooded the hall. The wounded agents were being looked after and the dead covered respectfully. Blood made the floor sticky.

But the one he sought with his half swollen eyes stood next to Zoric. Chase could not stop himself as he raised his gun and stormed toward her. She watched him with what little courage she possessed, but still tried to pull free of Zoric's hold. Backing away, Zoric released her to Chase's vice-like grip on her forearm. The jerk of her sore arm caused Tessa to yelp as Chase dragged her away from Zoric and tossed her against the concrete wall.

His broken nose and swollen eyes made his once rugged face look like a monster. Blood smeared down his cheek and down the front of a once white shirt making Tessa comprehend the pain she'd inflicted on him. She tried to step forward only to be pushed back with such violence it knocked the wind out of her. Her hand went to her chest as she tried to slide away from the man who once swore to protect her.

When he reared back to slap her, Zoric caught him around the chest, pulling him back.

"Enough." Zoric saw the fear spring into Tessa's eyes as she cowered against the possibility of feeling Chase's wrath.

She lunged forward toward the kitchen where she'd seen her uncle fall. From the corner of her eye Tessa knew both men reached for her. But it was Sam who caught her by the hair jerking her to the floor. Her back slammed so hard she wondered if something hadn't broken. Her tail bone would definitely never be the same.

Sam kneeled down on one knee. She ran her gun up the middle of Tessa's chest and neck until it rested beneath her chin. "We meet again, Betty Crocker. I see you're headed for the kitchen where you belong." Sam cooed with a vicious smirk.

Trying to wiggle away only made Sam spring to her feet and step on Tessa's bad arm. When she cried out, Sam smiled over at Chase who waved her off. Frowning, the female agent joined others who began questioning one of the surviving attackers.

The captain glared at her through what looked like slits for eyes. His jaw tightened and released several times as he looked at the mayhem around him. She couldn't help but wonder if he were trying to estimate how many witnesses he'd need to silence after he killed her.

Rolling to her hip, Tessa made an ungraceful attempt to stand. Chase watched her like a hungry lion. He made no attempt to assist her painful rise. Another agent offered his hand until Chase cleared his throat and jerked his head in a motion to leave. The anger in his ridged stance warned Tessa she'd have to tread lightly. Too many lies had passed between them in the last year. Why would he believe her now?

She put her hand timidly on the kitchen door and grimaced as she tried to open it.

"Where the hell do you think you're going?" Chase said cutting her off. "You're going to pay for what you did to the president. If I ever find that worthless uncle of yours I'm…"

Tessa straightened. "Find him? He was just inside this door. Those men knocked him down when he was protecting the president." She barreled into him without much affect. "Get out of my way," she demanded half-heartedly. He didn't budge but even so, she could see into the kitchen. "Where did they take him? Is he okay?"

"I don't know. Maybe he had another seizure." The unforgiving voice of the captain gave Tessa pause as she looked up at him.

"He was right here," she said forcefully pointing down at the floor. "Ask one of the agents."

Chase grabbed her by the arm and shook her before throwing

her back against Zoric who approached cautiously. "Who should I ask? That one? Because he didn't make it. How about Charlie over there? Wait. No, he's dead too." He pointed at the others. Some would live but they were in shock or badly injured. "I think you better come up with a better story."

"Or what? You'll shoot me in the foot?" She shook her fist at him. "I was trying to protect the president, not kill him, you idiot." This seemed to push him to the edge as his jaw began to flex. He stepped toward her.

Tessa cringed as she tried to turn into Zoric who only stepped away from her toxic presence.

"Captain Hunter?" It was Ari, one of the prime minister's men. "The president is asking for Mrs. Scott."

Chase grabbed her by the forearm and dragged her after him. She tripped once and nearly fell to the floor. He pulled her up with such force, she wondered if falling hadn't been a better option. "You're hurting me," she yelled, trying to land a fist on his chest with her free hand.

When Chase opened the door to the safe room he was stunned to see the president covered in so much blood. He was awake and talking to the prime minister who was the color of paste. John Elliott, his bodyguard, could barely breathe as his eyes looked up at Chase.

Tessa pried Chase's grip from her arm and fell down next to the president. Taking his hand, she bent closer and tried to fake a smile. She felt Chase grab her shoulder when the president started to speak.

"Gilad?"

"Yes, old friend."

"If that big brute doesn't turn Mrs. Scott loose, I want you to shoot him."

CHAPTER 20

The large hand slid over Tessa's bare shoulder and squeezed long enough for her to know Captain Hunter could jerk her to her feet if he chose. For good measure, she pushed his hand off, as if it were a brown recluse spider before turning back to the president. She was aware of men speaking into cyber space to obtain help for the injured, especially for the man who lay beneath her fingertips.

The building quaked against the ferocious storm. The roar of winds screamed through weaknesses in the exterior and broken windows. Even though they were protected against flying glass and rain they all knew the guests in the rest of the hotel had not been so lucky.

Chase peeled away the president's shirt after kneeling across from Tessa. He started to gingerly relieve him of the bullet proof vest. Someone had already managed to take his jacket. Blood still flowed down his neck to his shoulder. The president tried to look over at the wound, but released a sigh when his strength failed him.

"Mrs. Scott," the president whispered hoarsely.

Tessa leaned in after pushing her fallen locks behind her ears. Her hands quivered as she took his right hand that reached toward her. It felt clammy. Blood began to dry between his fingers. His grip now reminded her of her small daughter's instead of the powerful, almost painful, handshake he'd used with her earlier in the evening.

"Yes, Mr. President." Tessa tried to smile without letting her eyes reveal the tears she forced back.

"You pinched me," he declared wrinkling his forehead.

"You wouldn't let me protect you, Sir. And you tried to take my gun."

"Hmm. Well I guess," he swallowed then licked his dry lips. "I guess I owe you my life. Thank you." Tessa took the bottle of water being handed to her from one of the Secret Service.

"Take a sip." He shook his head no. "Please, Mr. President. We have a long evening ahead of us and we really need you to take orders." She stole a glance at Chase who eyed her cautiously before slipping his arm under the president and raising him just enough for him to take some water.

"I'm tired," he sighed. "Everyone stop looking at me like," he coughed, "like I'm dying."

"Rest, Mr. President. We'll get you to a hospital soon." Chase laid him back down as if he were a newborn.

"Did you get those guys?" His eyes shut in fatigue. "Who were they?"

Chase replaced the once white linen napkins from the open wound with new ones. "Most of them. Jake Wakefield got away." His eyes cut to Tessa as his bottom lip stuck out in disgust. "We don't know who they were."

"No." The president tried to move his head as he opened his eyes. "Wakefield."

"What about him, sir?"

"Fought for me." His eyes squinted in pain. "Protected us."

"You must be mistaken, Mr. President." Chase leaned back on his heels. "He was here to kill you."

"No. Help." He looked over at John Elliott who seemed to be fading. "Ask John."

Chase reached out and laid a hand on John's leg. "Is this true?"

John nodded. "If he hadn't been there we'd all be dead. Took us by surprise." He started to slip away into unconsciousness. "Saw them drag him inside the kitchen. Another way out. Injured too." Then he was gone into darkness.

The captain jerked his head around to stare at Tessa who had poured water on another napkin and began cleaning the president's face. Silent tears were streaking her eyeliner and her nose started to run. "He's unconscious."

Tessa felt herself being pulled up by strange hands as Chase stepped over the president and let others see to his immediate needs. He led Tessa to the side, but she couldn't take her eyes off the president. When someone blocked her line of sight, she surveyed the room. She spotted Ari and Micah hovering around the prime minister as he paced. There was a mixture of fear and revenge in his eyes as he spoke on a cell phone. All the adrenaline coursing through her veins minutes earlier now evaporated. Just as she wondered if her knees were capable of holding her up, Tessa felt Chase's arm around her waist. His touch comforted her as much as it had terrified her in the corridor.

~~~

"Easy, Tess," he whispered as he led her to a toppled metal chair which he managed to upright with his foot. Easing her down she leaned back only to feel the cold jolt through her skin. Chase laid his hand against her shoulders and rubbed up and down before removing his suit coat. Wrapping it around her bare skin, he could still smell the lotion she must have rubbed into her neck and arms before coming to the banquet. Although it now mixed with the smell of gunpowder, he felt his body stir, imagining how he might eventually explore her body.

Chase squatted down next to her and looked up into her face which she turned away with a haughty disposition. She jerked her chin up in a show of false bravery. He placed his hand on her thigh, noting it was now caked with the president's blood. Moving her leg away she reached to knock his hand away from touching her. He grabbed her hand tightly with one hand, then pulled her legs toward him with the other.

Even though she tried to pull free and pry his hand off with her free fingers, he held tight. In fear more than frustration, she took a swing at him and connected to his jaw with her fist. He closed his eyes and swallowed, feeling his face begin to throb again.

Sucking in her breath she imagined the pain he must be feeling. "Chase," she whispered with remorse. His jacket slid away as her arms went around his neck. His face pressed against her throat as his hands slipped around her waist. The moment lasted only a split second as he gently pushed her away. Timidly she touched his face with her fingertips before reaching to her cheek to wipe away the trails of black mascara. Shaking her head, Tessa surveyed Chase's terribly swollen face.

"I didn't know Jake planned to hit you. That wasn't supposed to happen. Honest."

Pouring some water on napkins he wiped the blood from her upper thighs. The deliberate downward motion rubbed warmth not only into her legs but parts of him. His thoughts rushed toward the alley the night before with Tessa's legs wrapped around him. The ebb of passion appeared to awaken in her and duty prevented him from taking advantage of the moment. He exhaled.

"Honest? You and I have some real trust issues." He fought the urge to push the blond curls away from her cheeks that stuck to the black eyeliner. "We're going to have to work on that."

Tessa did the little girl nod as a sign of fear and surrender. "I know. I know. Just how much trouble am I in, Chase?" Her eyes searched his or at least what she could see of them. She so wanted to comfort him. It was way too crowded for any of that.

Chase patted her leg and felt her bruised fingers entwine with his. "According to the president you're some kind of hero. I doubt he'd let Enigma take disciplinary action."

"I was afraid you were going to kill me," she choked. "You hurt me." The sound of betrayal claimed her voice.

His eyes dropped to their hands and rubbed his thumb across her knuckles. "Something I'll regret for the rest of my life, I'm sure." Chase tried to sound amused as he smiled unconvincingly. "I need you to stop lying to me." His hand began to squeeze.

"Okay."

"When I say 'stop lying' that means always tell me the truth," he warned.

"What if it's a life or death situation and..." she saw his mouth tighten. "I will. Promise."

"Tessa, so help me the next time you pull one of your tricks I'll turn you across my knee." He inhaled deeply again. "I..." he stopped, thinking hard of what to reveal about his attraction. "I care about my team. You are part of that for now. I can't have you deviating from the plan. I don't care if it's the Lord Almighty telling you what to do. I'm the one who gives orders and you're the one who follows them. I can make your life miserable if you refuse to comply. I can wreck your life with the push of a button. You have got to learn to trust us. There is no other option for you now."

"Am I going to jail?" She tried unsuccessfully to remove her hand from his and leaned her face closer to his.

He reached up to touch her face with his free hand and thought better of it. "No. But I can't promise your uncle won't. He's in some serious trouble."

"But he can explain. He had help."

Chase pulled his coat back around her shoulders. "From who?"

"Me." It was the voice of Gilad Levi, the Prime Minister of Israel.

~~~

The vice president felt better after munching on some saltine crackers and cheese. Terry found another Dr. Pepper in the back of the refrigerator. They shared the small meal on the deck overlooking the blue water. The two men got along better than most people Terry had been responsible for protecting. He actually liked the vice president and his wife. Some Secret Service agents had not been so lucky over the years. There were stories of agents being treated poorly or spoken to like servants. But both the president and vice president appreciated their protection details and never failed to praise their service.

Mrs. McCall had once made the agents come in out of the rain while they posted outside their Maine home. Another time she'd brought them earmuffs and scarves with hot chocolate every hour. She spoiled them. Last Christmas she'd given a party in honor of their protection detail along with other staff members. They made life bearable for the vice president. All the children and spouses received generous gifts because of their sacrifice. She never missed a birthday, anniversary or graduation concerning the families of those that served. The proceeds from the two books she'd written went to a scholarship fund for those children of agents who'd died in the line of duty.

Terry stood and stretched as he spotted the returning yacht. "You better look chipper if you're thinking of fishing tomorrow."

"I'm lots better. I feel like I could eat a horse."

"Don't let those animal activists hear you say that if you ever plan to run for president." Terry grinned at the vice president as another agent rushed out with a phone. "What is it?"

The agent looked over at the vice president groaning as he pushed himself out of the chaise and meandered toward the railing to watch the yacht. He could see the vice president's wife come on deck as the vice president waved to her.

Terry clicked off and tossed the phone back to the second agent. He grabbed the vice president by the arm and tugged. "You need to come inside, Sir."

"Why? What's wrong?"

"The president has been shot." He tried to pull him, but the vice president was so stunned he froze.

"Peggy," he whispered as both the men looked out to see the yacht idle the engines and begin its arrival.

"Mr. Vice President, we need…"

Before he could finish the order an explosion rocked the air, forcing both men down onto the floor of the deck. Immediately, two more agents were at their side dragging them to safety.

Jumping to his feet Terry assisted the vice president only to feel him stagger backwards. Everyone watched the debris flutter down like an animated cartoon to where the yacht sailed seconds earlier. It was gone.

~~~

Amon turned slowly to eye the Speaker of the House. Sitting in a folding chair with a cup of coffee in hand, the congressman's eyes took in his surroundings with contempt. The sneer he wore each time one of Amon's men entered the room spoke volumes. Something told him even when Jim Gault became president nothing would change between Israel and the United States.

Too many Americans like the "kick ass" attitude the tiny nation demonstrated to the world. In their minds it was the land of Jesus, and you couldn't turn your back on Jesus. The evangelical right seemed to think of the Egyptians as the people who drove Moses across the Red Sea only to have it collapse on the Pharaoh's army. The liberal left saw it as political suicide to vote against

Israel. A great many wealthy Israelis contributed to their campaigns.

Although relations eroded with the last president, the current administration appeared to be on good terms with the prime minister. He wondered if it had something to do with the prime minister's brother being a leading security advisor to the president. Or perhaps the current political climate with Egypt was seen by many Americans as toxic.

Why send money for the military when the Pentagon had cut back on supporting their own troops around the world? Money that went for better education and health care for Egypt's poor was viewed as outrageous considering the state of affairs with American students. Shoring up infrastructure between Alexandria and Lake Nasser when thousands of bridges in the U.S. needed to be replaced became fodder for conservative talk show hosts each night.

The fact that several Egyptians were involved in bringing down the Twin Towers on 9/11 stuck in American craws. Riots, protests and the beatings of Coptic Christians in the streets of Cairo left Americans resenting any involvement with a people that couldn't appreciate democracy. Voting the Muslim Brotherhood into power then changing their minds a year later, brought Egypt to the brink of ruin once again. Tourism, the life blood of Egypt, had all but dried up. No longer safe to travel to the Pyramids of Giza or float the Nile to view the civilization that had given the world so much kept Americans home.

Sometimes Amon felt ashamed of his country's inability to cooperate and make progress. Centuries taught them to be corrupt and honor strength through force to achieve success and control. The money, like the tourists, would soon dry up if Americans chose to put pressure on politicians in Washington.

This act of madness was another act of terrorism fashioned by the third most powerful man in the United States. No good would come of it. Was it too late to change course, or should he see it through and hope the speaker spoke the truth in his promises to protect Egypt?

"Why are you staring at me, Amon? Are you thinking about changing the plan?"

Amon poured a cup of hot water and began dunking a tea bag

slowly into the liquid. He looked at the blue shark on the side of the cup and thought how poetic the words of "bite me" sounded for this particular situation.

"Why would you imagine such a thing, Mr. Speaker?" Amon turned to face the speaker. The cut on his face now looked invisible with the bandage. "Is it because you cannot trust a Muslim or an Egyptian?"

The speaker sat his cup down a little too quickly, spilling the dark liquid across the metal table. "It's because you show more respect to those old men than you do to me. They're trouble makers."

Amon let a slow smile spread across his face as he took a sip of the tea. "I show them respect because they have been victims of the Israelis just like my people." He sat the cup down gingerly on the small makeshift counter constructed of old lumber and two sawhorses. "They were once American warriors. Those warriors were forgotten and dishonored."

"Why do you care about a ship everyone has forgotten except for them and now you?" The speaker stood and pretended to do a casual stretch of unconcern.

Amon thought of his grandfather who survived the El Arish slaughter by hiding. He never forgave himself for living when his fellow soldiers perished. "It is time the truth be told. That is all. And you? Why do you care? It was your idea to start the hearings, suggesting war crimes had been committed against Americans. All investigations were silenced. Even the men aboard that ship were bullied into silenced."

"It was their duty to take orders." The speaker's arrogance showed no sympathy. "They remained silent because they thought the truth would come out. Some believed the whole ordeal was being dealt with expeditiously. But as time marched on memories began to fade, recollections of the events became confused. Even politicians that helped cover it up got old and died." The speaker smiled and threw his hands in the air. "I'm just doing my patriotic duty, Amon."

"So why kill the president? He appears to be a reasonable man."

"He's one of those conservative-Christian-types that think Jesus is still walking around Jerusalem. His wife is a devout

Catholic and sponsors several charities connected to Israel."

Amon lifted his cup to his lips and took another sip as he became aware of the storm intensifying. The building seemed to be shaking. "Again. That is not uncommon for Christians to have great affection for Israel. It is in America's DNA. You haven't answered my question. Why kill the president?"

Jim narrowed his eyes and gritted his teeth. "The truth is I don't like him. He's a self-righteous, pompous ass that walks around Washington like he's John Wayne. Everyone just smiles when he slurs his speech or uses the wrong word like he's some kind of beloved cowboy. He makes everyone believe he can change the world in four years; tough on crime, smack down terrorists with a heavy fist, better education for the poor, shoot to kill drug dealers or at least no second chances. The reforms in the tax code and banking will be our undoing."

Amon started to chuckle as he sat his cup down.

"What's so funny?" The speaker had worked himself up into frenzy.

"You are a jealous, petty man who can't get over that he didn't choose you to be his vice president." Amon was aware the speaker had been in the running for the position.

Choosing Warren McCall for his experience as an ambassador and a two term senator made sense. He was an outdoorsman who advocated for cleaner fuels while courting oil and coal companies to lead the revolution to energy independence. In one of his speeches he called them the new Sons of Liberty. Throwing their support behind Buck Austin and Warren McCall was a no brainer.

"I would've been a better leader than John Wayne or Jeremiah Johnson." He rolled his neck to loosen up.

Amon took a sheet of paper from one of his men that entered cautiously. He read it twice. "I guess we will see, Mr. Speaker. You may get your chance. The president has been shot."

"And the vice president?" The speaker sounded breathless with excitement.

"Yes. It appears that there has been an accident concerning the fishing boat." Amon slowly lifted his eyes to meet the speakers. "Would you like for me to begin calling you Mr. President?"

Jim laughed robustly. "Let's not get ahead of ourselves, Amon." He walked over to the Egyptian and slapped him on the back.

"What a night, Amon? What a night."

CHAPTER 21

Hurrying to the loading dock with another Secret Service agent, Chase hoped he'd be able to retrieve the president's blood stored in the trunk of the Beast. The water now flowed like a raging river and swirled around the windows of the limo. Even if Chase made it out to the vehicle and managed to open the trunk the contents would be contaminated instantly. They probably already were. The option of airlifting the president to Walter Reed Hospital wasn't an option in this storm. He left the agent at the door for security as he made his way back to the kitchen. Other agents huddled around a prep table, going over the second escape route of the shooters.

The kitchen staff had all told similar stories about men with guns bursting through the door, threatening bodily harm and shooting the place up to make a point. They were ordered on the floor with the threat of death. With light extinguished there was little else they could tell them. Most of them cowered on the floor, praying help would be on the way. When gunfire erupted again, yellow muzzle flashes were all anyone remembered. No one saw Jake Wakefield leave with the remaining attackers. There appeared to be no way of knowing if he walked out on his own accord or needed help.

The question now was why did they take him? Clearly he had not attempted to shoot the president as everyone had believed he intended to do. Chase looked around the kitchen with only his eyes and flashlight.

What was missing in this picture?

He followed a trail of blood until it ended at a small service door. The only way to enter was if someone opened the door. That probably led the attackers to use the loading dock doors.

The two captured weren't armatures or Egyptian. It was a reasonable assumption they were freelancers, ex-military bad boys that couldn't follow the rules and got discharged. Another possibility could be paramilitary groups that hated a centralized government and wanted to intimidate any administration that threatened their lawless life styles. Anarchy became their mantra.

People willing to pay these kinds of agitators gave them confirmation their objective was sanctified by their philosophies of destruction. In Chase's mind it was just another name for Taliban; renegades wanting all the power and doing whatever it took to obtain it.

The question still remained, where were the Egyptians in all of this?

Opening the service door he saw what he thought might be blood, but the blowing rain, darkness and wind made closer inspection futile; too many contaminants in an alley. By the time a forensic team gathered evidence the hurricane would have carried vital information up the eastern seaboard. The water now swirled to the top of the step and it would soon be pushing under the door.

He saw something starting to float where the water began lapping over the edge. He picked it up with curious fascination before shoving it in his back pocket. Pulling his shirt tail out from his pants he let it drape to hide the bulge the object formed on his buttocks. Chase jerked the door shut against the storm and turned the deadbolt as he watched Zoric dragging a couple in their late teens to join the other servers.

"Found her and another kid cuffed in the laundry area. Only one way in or out." Zoric tried to contain his satanic grin when he looked from the girl to his boss. "She's scared someone named Melanie is going to blame her for this." Chase looked a little confused at first then remembered the code name he'd given Tessa a year earlier. "I think our little girl scout in there with the president has morphed into an Enigma agent."

Chase frowned as his hand went to touch his nose then left eye. His head felt like a hammer pounding inside. "Any word on Carter?"

"Probably a concussion, but he's with the president. Looks like a mash unit in there. The director is being patched through as soon as tech support can get a good connection." The two men fanned their flashlights across the floor and moved toward the safe room for the president. "The paramedics that tagged along tonight seem to have President Austin stabilized for now." He nodded as they opened the door to see the president still on the floor. "There's more, Chase." The captain stopped shortly and looked down at his partner. "The vice president's wife has been killed. He should've been on the boat instead of her. Freak luck, if you can call it that."

"Has the situation been secured?" The tone in Chase's voice sounded more concerned than irritated. "We need to make sure the Secret Service has Speaker Gault under lock and key. If anything happens to the president and the VP then he'll have to step up to bat."

A Secret Service agent brought Chase a tablet. Vernon's face appeared. "Boss, the director is here with me. I'm turning it over to him. Connections are tricky tonight so keep it short and sweet."

Nodding to his tech man Director Clark appeared on screen. "Chase, it's not good news. The speaker's detail tucked him in tonight and left one guy across the street on watch. That agent was found dead about ten minutes ago. Agents managed to get inside the speaker's house and found a bloody rag in the sink. Muddy tracks and a note were left behind. Looks like the speaker slipped one over on whoever grabbed him. The lab can do an analysis of the mud, foot prints and so on, but with the storm flooding so many streets, any evidence that matches up will be washed away and moved to another area. The blood matches what we have on record for the speaker. The only unknown fingerprints found were upstairs in the bedroom."

"Have you identified those?"

"Nothing in the system. Agents said a woman visited him a couple of times. The speaker bragged to them that she was a hand full, if you get my drift."

Tessa timidly pushed up alongside Chase and cleared her throat. "I might be able to help with that."

The director frowned and rubbed his eyes. "Why am I not surprised? Mrs. Scott, I would ask you how you could possibly know such information, but I have reason to believe you'd just give me some lame excuse like divine intervention." Tessa nodded in agreement but remained silent. Then suddenly the director yelled. "So who is it? I don't have all day."

"I don't know her name," she jumped. "But there was a flight attendant the other day that came on pretty strong to the speaker when I flew in." Her voice cracked so she tried clearing her throat once, but no more words came out until she coughed. "The speaker sat next to me. Complained he wasn't used to flying back with the peasants."

"That sounds about right," the director quipped. Tessa gave him a quick description and mentioned he'd given the flight attendant a card. She suggested Dr. Ervin may have been more observant than her. "His orders were eyes on you, no one else. Your description will have to do."

"The paramedics on scene say the president has lost too much blood." Chase failed to hide his uneasiness. "He'll never make it to morning if he doesn't get a transfusion. The blood in the Beast is contaminated or least we think so. The car is mostly under water."

"I'm having Vernon patch Dr. Kelley in to assess the situation. She's the best. Stand by."

The screen began looking like fuzzy snow as Vernon tried to work his magic on the other end. Chase observed Tessa staring at the president as she hugged the suit coat around her shoulders. The six inch heels were gone now and she appeared to be flexing her toes as if they were cold against the tiled floor. Two hours ago she looked like a goddess in that dress. The obstinate tilt of her head and temper she turned on like a faucet had vanished. The blond curls she tried to tame into remaining on top of her head now fell down around her bare shoulders. The soiled dress, although splattered with blood, still evoked a sexiness Chase found disturbing. The little pout on her lips drove him a little crazy as he let his mind drift back to holding her in his arms the night before.

This madness must stop, he reasoned. The ache over his heart punched him without warning, making him flinch, but he covered the reaction by shifting his weight and touching the found object in his back pocket.

Lowering his head slightly, he could watch Zoric move next to Tessa and mumble something in her ear. She nodded without looking up at the dark Serbian. A year ago Tessa would have tried to escape any close proximity to the ghoulish agent. Now as Zoric gently placed his long fingers on the back of her neck and drew her closer to his moving lips, Tessa remained unaffected with downcast eyes, listening. He ended with what looked like a gentle kiss on her ear before turning away to attend to other matters. Chase realized that even though some people have angels guarding them, others may have demons. Tessa had both.

He wondered if Zoric tried to make amends. Tessa's optimistic attitude and wholesomeness became the catalyst for Zoric's resurgence into the art world. Something about her gave the assassin focus on calmer, less lethal pursuits. His work transformed from the nightmarish Salvador Dali to romantic Mary Cassatt.

Chase extended his arm toward his newest agent until he could touch her shoulder with his fingertips. She turned her eyes on him and offered a smile of forgiveness. He could do nothing but return the gesture.

~~~

Tessa edged toward him as someone tried to push by her and kneel by the president. Taking a deep breath she only shrugged, not trusting herself to speak. A cell phone started ringing from somewhere inside the safe room and all eyes fell on her small clutch someone retrieved earlier, then dropped it on the floor during the chaos. She tried to fetch it, but in two strides Chase had it opened and the phone pulled out. He looked at the caller ID then handed it to Tessa. As he clicked the answer slide he also hit speaker.

"Careful," he warned posturing for another confrontation.

Tessa looked at the number. "Robert?"

"Honey, are you alright? It's all over the news the president has been shot and maybe the vice president too."

"The city is on lock down for the hurricane. We can't get much news. I'm at the hotel so not to worry. We lost power but you know Shelly and Kate, just another opportunity to party then exaggerate the truth later on." Her eyes locked with Chase's, or at least what she could see of them. Empty of emotion, she understood his warning.

"Having fun?" Her husband sounded so cheerful. "Kids have been on a terror just so you'll feel sorry for me. You might put a bug in Homeland Security's ear while you're there and tell them we need a little help out here with our kids." A chuckle followed.

Tessa's mood soured. "Don't compare our children to terrorists, Robert."

Robert didn't pick up on her tone. "Okay. Okay. Better go. Gotta get the grass mowed, but I'm worn out. Do you remember the name of the mowing service the neighbors across the street used last summer?"

"No. Go ask them."

"Then I would have to listen to Brad go on and on about his golf game. No thanks. I'll just wait until you get home."

Watching Chase's eyes narrow and his nostrils flare with impatience meant trouble. His jaw began to tightened and release, not a good sign. "I have to go, Robert."

Robert sighed dramatically. "Okay. Love you and miss you. Try not to let those two chronologically challenged friends of yours get you into trouble."

"Never. Kiss the kids for me." Tessa clicked off realizing instantly she'd not told her husband 'I love you.' She handed the phone back to Chase. Without taking her eyes from his, Tessa realized in that instant Chase didn't approve of her husband. Was that going to be a problem?

"Is he always such an ass?" His words came slow as he took the phone.

Her stern look of warning forced him to look away as his tablet came back to life. She came alongside him as a picture of a woman appeared.

"Dr. Kelley," Chase spoke with respect. "Looks like we took you from a party. You look stunning as usual."

"A rascal to the end, Captain Hunter." Dr. Kelley grinned as her eyebrow arched in some kind of mischief. "What the hell happened to you? You look terrible."

Tessa could see her face easily. She was older than Chase; maybe fifty but her smile and pale skin gave her a youthful glow. A gust of wind probably wouldn't move her short blond hair. She looked more like a rock star than the president's physician. The grin hinted at a history between the two.

"Mary Pat," Chase started, letting his familiarity slip through. "We're in a mess." He turned the tablet around to show her the president. When she ordered him to go in closer he obeyed. "Paramedics say he needs blood now. Do you know his blood type?"

"Yes. A lot of good that will do you without a donor. By the looks of everyone there, the president isn't the only one who could use a pint of good blood. I've looked over the records of the agents who are able to still put one step in front of the other. None of them match, not even your team."

"I do," Tessa said moving closer to Chase. The doctor shifted her eyes to Tessa and did a quick visual examination. "Dr. Kelley, I'm a universal donor. I can give the transfusion." Tessa's voice sounded urgent knowing time was running out.

"Who is this, Captain?" The doctor wrinkled her forehead.

"Tessa Scott. I'm not sure she's in your system. New."

Mary Pat smirked. "I bet Agent Cordova is extremely pleased about that." Slipping on some small black frame glasses the doctor began typing on another hand held computer as she spoke. "Sorry. I don't see her in any database. Of course, with your people they never really appear unless the president orders it." Her eyes shifted to Tessa again. "Blood type? Scott is it?"

"O Negative. I'll do whatever you want."

"Most people don't know their blood type, Ms. Scott. How is it you do?"

Tessa noted the tone of skepticism. "I've had three kids. My blood could be a problem to an unborn child. We also had a blood drive at my church two months ago. The Red Cross said I needed to make a point of giving often because of my blood type. The very next day I was called to the hospital to give blood to an injured child. So…"

Dr. Kelley held up her hand. "Good enough, Scott." She pulled the glasses down and started typing again.

Chase looked from Tessa to the on screen doctor. "Mary Pat, can she do it without red tape and an act of congress?"

The doctor wrinkled her button nose and shrugged as she tilted the glasses to the top of her head. "I don't see we have a choice." She smiled down at something on her hand held. "Ah. There she is.

O Negative. The Red Cross keeps pretty good track of their special people." Her eyes went to Tessa and winked. "Now listen to me. Get one of those paramedics over here and the two of you listen to what I've got to say. There's a good chance we'll be cut off before this is finished so I'm counting on that big brain of yours to remember what I'm going to tell you. That way if I lose the connection you guys can carry on until I arrive or reconnect."

"Thanks, Doc. You're still the prettiest one on the president's staff."

Dr. Kelley clicked her tongue in mock contempt. "So you say. Remember you still owe me dinner. I aim to collect when this is over since I now know you're in town. Listen up. We've got a lot to do."

~~~

Amon stood in the center of the largest room staring at the metal door as it flew open. His man tried unsuccessfully to hold on to it as three men ducked inside. Two he recognized. They were men the speaker had enlisted to shoot the president. Apparently they met with resistance considering only two returned. He could only speculate as to the identification of the third man.

It took two men to pull the door shut as water pooled behind them. Besides the sound of wind, water came like arrows through the high windows, pinging off rusted metal pieces forgotten by the previous occupants. The flatbed trailer at the side rested on flat tires.

Amon wondered at the red, white and blue banners draped on the sides with the words *Let Freedom Ring, Happy July 4th*. There were other hints the building was a storage facility for parades and festivals: a dunking booth, popcorn stand, another enclosed trailer with food advertisements on the side. The speaker must have known the building would not be visited again for another year if all of this was for their Independence Day celebration. He felt a kind of amusement at the thought they were holding old warriors in a place that smelled of honor and freedom.

Amon watched as the two hired thugs turned to brush the water from their clothes. The third man stood with head bowed, shivering. "Who is this?"

"Jake Wakefield, the fifth USS Liberty man on your list." The square jawed man had a smoker's voice. His shaved head showed hints of a brown crown. A four o'clock shadow appeared on his face.

Amon knew of Wakefield, had even spoken to him on the phone. The picture he'd seen did not match this disheveled man.

The second man was taller, thinner than, and not nearly as muscular, as Square Jaw. There were colorful tattoos visible on his neck and hands. If someone at the hotel noticed the man he could be a liability.

Amon walked over to Jake and extended his hand. "Mr. Wakefield, it is a pleasure to finally meet you."

Jake lifted his eyes to examine Amon's face then spat on the floor rather than shake his hand.

A smile spread across the Egyptian's face as he dropped his hand. "Very well." Amon noticed the old man's upper ear had been grazed by a bullet and he'd taken a round through his right arm. "Tell me, Sir; are you on any blood thinners?"

"Why? You wanna stick me and watch me bleed to death?" In spite of his confrontational tone Amon did not take offense. He proceeded to answer the questions. "No. I'm fit as a fiddle or at least I was 'till these yahoos shot me."

Square Jaw gave the old man a shove to the floor then a kick to the hip. A painful moan escaped Jake's mouth as he grabbed the elbow he landed on.

"Do anything like that again and I'll have to reprimand you," Amon said coldly to the captor.

"I don't answer to you," he came back sarcastically.

Amon's eyes went to his own man still standing at the door. "Pity. You would be a lot better off if you did."

Square Jaw snickered, running his hand across his hard face then the top of his head. "Well I certainly don't take orders from any Arabs. Right, Mick?"

Skinny Tattoo Man nodded as his eyes started a scan of the room.

Amon sighed and shrugged helplessly. "Again, you'd be better off if you did." He nodded to his man at the door. Stepping aside to assist Jake, two shots popped from a silencer, dropping both men with gunshots to the back of the head.

Jake jerked his head around at the man guarding the door to see him lower his weapon and straighten into an almost attention stance. Dumbfounded at the turn of events, Jake let Amon pull him to his feet and felt him dust the grime from his clothes.

"Not to worry, Mr. Wakefield. We will attend to your wounds. They do not look serious, but this is a dirty warehouse and I don't want you getting an infection. Since you aren't on blood thinners I'm assuming your heart is in good shape and I don't need to secure medication for you in that regard." Amon began maneuvering him to a small side room as he looked over his shoulder at the door man. "Get someone to help you take out the garbage."

Another Egyptian saw to Jake's medical needs as Amon brewed coffee for his newest captive. After Jake drank the black liquid he stood on his own accord, although a little wobbly as his old knees made an arthritic pop. Two more Egyptians entered the room and escorted him away. He sloshed through pools of water that poured down from a leaky ceiling. The smell of mildew reached his nose as he noticed a rat scurry into darker areas of the building.

A ribbon of flickering light formed beneath a door that his guards unlocked. They stood back for him to enter but did not offer any words or threats. Jake watched them as he stepped inside the room flooded with candle light.

"Look who's here." A chorus of old familiar voices bounced off the walls. "Is that really you?"

Jake found himself surrounded by his shipmates from the USS Liberty. "Hell of a mess, huh guys?"

They smiled and patted his shoulder, careful to avoid his injuries. They all spoke at once, asking questions and retelling how they came to be prisoners.

Something moved in the corner of darkness causing Jake to stiffen. He spread out his hands as if by doing so would protect his mates. "Who's there?" he demanded.

The man stepped out into the dim light sporting a bandage over his left eye and a bruise on his cheek. In a shaky voice he spoke. "I'm Jim Gault, the Speaker of the House. I'm afraid we're in a lot of trouble."

CHAPTER 22

The crew of the USS Liberty formed an arc to look at the Speaker of the House. He took two steps forward hinting at a limp to his left leg. Dropping his hand down to touch it did nothing to alleviate the pain. Pointing at a chair one of the men quickly pulled it out and helped the speaker sit down with a thud. He offered a weak smile.

"I'm..." the speaker began.

"I know who you are, Mr. Speaker," Jake mumbled somewhat confused. He looked at his mates. "Why is he here?" His eyes settled on the speaker who appeared to be a little out of sorts, maybe even a little confused.

Mike Strafford nodded toward the politician. "He's the one that got the ball rollin' for our hearing. It appears the Israelis aren't too keen on that. Hired those fellas out there to stop us."

Jake glanced at his friends then sat down to look eye to eye with the speaker. "Who are they?"

"Egyptians. They're pretending to care about you so if we're found you'll say you were treated well."

Jake adjusted his hip to lift off the hard chair. A throbbing began making its way down his leg where he'd taken the kick. "No. I meant who do they represent? Muslim Brotherhood, Al-Qaeda, who?"

The speaker shook his head. "I thought they represented a group that wanted a smooth transition to a new government since the Muslim Brotherhood were forced out. When I started this whole process they reached out to me."

Jake adjusted his arm where he'd been nicked by a bullet. His ear stung with the tightness of the bandage. Noticing that the speaker began to tap the table with his index finger displayed an impatient irritation.

"So who are they if they aren't a terrorist group?"

The speaker touched his face and frowned deeply. "I now believe them to be an off shoot of the Islamic Liberation Organization." He waited as if wanting them to pummel him with questions, but they remained quiet, taking Jake's stoic lead. "You will appreciate this." He edged closer as if he were letting them in on a big secret. His voice became a whisper causing the men to cock their ears or bend down closer. "After the Six Day War in 1967 the ILO formed. They were an off shoot of the Muslim Brotherhood. Their main goal was to overthrow Arab regimes that practice a loose form of Islam. They believed those regimes should be forcibly ousted."

"Never heard of them," Mike Strafford snapped as if he were being lied to. "You fellas?" He looked around at the shaking heads of his friends. Only Jake remained glued to the speaker's tale.

"Why is that important?" Jake asked matter-of-factly.

"They attacked a military academy in 1974 killing eleven. They hoped the attack would bring about a mass uprising, much like the recent Arab Spring. The then President Sadat managed to capture and execute many of the members. The only other time our government has heard from them is when they kidnapped a group of Soviet students on holiday in Giza. Since they were Soviets we didn't get involved. That event appeared to cause them to go underground."

"So why now? Why here?" Jake cocked his head as his eyes narrowed in disbelief.

"The CIA believed that the group decided to change tactics and become more involved in governmental positions. They were absorbed into many factions of Egyptian politics. Slowly over the last three decades they've managed to infiltrate the highest positions of government in hopes of putting someone into power that would bring their dream of an Islamic state to reality."

Mike Strafford pulled out a chair and sat down next to the speaker. "They had their chance with the Brotherhood. Tough nuts is what I say." The others nodded in agreement.

"They wanted the Brotherhood to fail. In their opinion the Brotherhood had begun a watered down approach to Islam and Israel. They're ready to take over as soon as elections are held."

"I can't see why taking us would benefit them." Jake heard Carl Robbins speak as if confused.

Jake bit his lip then spit a trickle of blood to the floor from a loose tooth he'd sustained in his kidnapping. "I know why. The Israelis admit to what they've done and the president comes clean on the cover up as well. Everybody gets a pat on the back, smiles and hugs to the Israelis for admitting they're a snake in the grass. We get our medals and recognition. In two weeks all is good with the world."

The speaker leaned back in his chair and eyed the old warrior with caution. "Exactly. Egypt wants the Americans to be outraged and unforgiving. Kill the president and blame the Israelis, and Egypt keeps their funding and their standing goes up in the world. Poor Egypt."

"Kill the president!" Carl thundered. "That's insane."

Jake watched his friends begin a confused chatter before turning his eyes back to the speaker. He was struck by the smug look of victory on the politician's face. "Settle down, boys. Nobody going to kill the president."

The speaker looked pained as he spoke. "Before they started hitting me I heard one of them tell the leader the president had been shot."

Except for Jake, the news sent the men into a frantic discussion of what would become of the country and them. "Now boys, being shot isn't the same as being dead."

"I hope you're right, Mr. Wakefield." The speaker shook his head in despair.

Jake stood to ease the pain in his hip. He bore a thin smile as he looked down at the speaker. "How'd you know my name was Wakefield?"

~~~

A hushed silence filled the hotel kitchen as agents stood guard on all exit doors. Only the sound of a hurricane beating against the building made any kind of impression of danger lurking outside. Darkness broke in pools of random light given off by flashlights or small candles taken from the banquet room. The two metal tables that had been used as food prep islands now looked like hospital gurneys as a man and woman lay atop them. The kitchen staff had been ushered to the banquet hall. Earlier, paramedics set about sterilizing the stainless steel tables before gingerly lifting the president to its surface.

President Austin had been unconscious for over thirty minutes when he came to, looking startled and confused. He whispered John Elliott's name and was reassured that his agent was being looked after. Chase stepped forward and bent over the bare chested president, examining the wound on his neck. Dr. Kelley had warned removing the bullet could be disastrous. Leaving it in place could cause enough pressure to stop the bleeding. If he made it to the hospital, a full work up could be done to determine if the bullet should be removed or left as a souvenir. The bullet that hit his lower arm had been a quick fix and required no more attention since it passed straight through.

"Mr. President, we're going to be giving you a transfusion soon. Are you up for that?" Chase's voice, although made of steel, sounded low and comforting even to the most powerful man in the world.

He nodded and licked his lips. "How?" The weakness in his voice alarmed the paramedic and made a sign to get started.

Tessa lay on the table next to him. They were practically shoulder to shoulder with a tube running between her arm and his. The pressure cuff on her arm hurt but she knew necessity demanded it to be there so her blood would flow. She gently touched the president's hand with her cool fingers causing his head to turn slightly.

"Mrs. Scott." There was no surprise in his voice. "Are you a member of my political party?"

Tessa squeezed his hand. "I am today, Mr. President."

The president tried to smile before slipping into unconsciousness.

Staring at the ceiling bathed in shadows that appeared to move like giant ghosts, her thoughts flew to home, her kids and even Robert. She wondered about the new neighbors, the grass being mowed and whether or not she paid the electric bill before leaving.

Was she thirsty or hungry? Did she eat her dinner with the dashing Carter Johnson playing footsie with her under the table? The vague memory of pinching his leg as hard as she could merely encouraged him to lean in to her and try to nibble her earlobe.

Were her friends Shelly and Kate still with their soldier dates? Did they wonder where she was? Would Carter tell them they had a romantic tryst in her suite?

How much blood could she give without dying? Would they drain her like government vampires? Did her uncle lie bleeding in some rain swollen ally, dying from a combination of a gunshot wound and drowning?

Tessa felt a feathery touch on her face as tangled curls were moved aside by a calloused index finger of Chase. A year ago she would have flinched at his touch. Now she could do nothing but crave his warmth. One corner of his mouth turned up in a grin as he pulled a stool to her side. Before he sat down he checked her vitals then laid his hand gently on her cheek.

"You look like a raccoon." Tessa hated seeing that black circles formed under his eyes.

He smiled. "How's my girl?" Sitting unevenly on the stool made him look as if he'd do battle at any minute.

"A little scared of needles, but I guess I'll make it." Tessa didn't realize she was batting her eyes again.

Chase chuckled as he rubbed a spot on his chest. He took a white tablecloth from Zoric who nodded to Tessa. "I'm going to put this over you, Tessa, so you don't get chilled."

She smiled at him, enjoying the way he accidently touched her with a sensual kindness.

"Needles, huh?" Tessa made a pouting mouth at his sarcastic comment. "You're hunted down by two hit men, a favorite uncle threatens to kill the president, you get caught in the cross fire meant to kill the president and in the process you save him not once, but looks like a second time." The grin faded. "And I guess the fact that I nearly knocked you senseless was unnerving as well." His voice hinted at remorse.

Tessa extended her hand and opened her palm. "Chase," she whispered. He snatched her hand as if it were a lifeline and squeezed. She pulled his hand and laid it over her heart. "So sorry.

Forgive me. I'll make it up to you."

Chase slid off the stool and leaned down over Tessa, bringing his face inches from hers. His lips came close to touching hers. With lips trembling, she dared not speak in fear of losing control. In the last year she'd grown stronger, fighting the impulse to cave at the slightest sign of danger. The experiences a year earlier somehow cloaked her in a thin veil of bravery she knew could easily be shattered. Her training into the world of national security left a lot to be desired.

"I never meant to trick you, Chase."

"There is something you can do to get back in my good graces." Chase squeezed her hand then touched her hair.

Tessa nodded, trying to avoid looking at his wide expressive mouth forming a half smile like a hungry wolf. "Anything."

"It has to do with Spider Man house shoes and flannel pjs." His chuckle made Tessa's smile widen until she too laughed low and soft like lovers do.

"I'm saving that one for when I steal the launch codes, Chase," she spoke good naturedly.

This brought a laugh from deep in his throat as he stood up straight and tall only to bend back down when he'd finished. "So I guess that's a 'no'."

"Get me those launch codes and we'll talk," she teased.

The awareness that Chase once again was but a breath away made her heart flutter. She calculated that in this position it would be dangerous to the president if she tried to resist a kiss. Was that his intention or was that her fantasy?

It's my patriotic duty to just lay helpless and submit to Chase's will for the sake of the president. Tessa felt her eyes begin to close as her lips parted in anticipation.

"Chase," snapped Samantha Cordova tartly as she bumped against the table.

As if in slow motion, Chase stood to his six foot one height and looked down at his agent with sour disregard. "Yes, Sam?" He waited for her to speak. She appeared to have been running, since her breathing grew ragged and her face carried a reddish flush. "What is it?"

She handed Chase a small laptop and spun it around. "Dr. Kelley again. Wants an update."

Chase glared at his agent before taking the computer. Dr. Kelley's image was already waiting for him. "Doctor."

"How's our boy, Captain?"

"Not sure." He looked at the paramedic who gave a thumbs up. "Optimistic. Looks like you've changed clothes." The doctor now wore scrubs and appeared to be slipping on a raincoat. "You're not thinking of going out in this?"

Dr. Kelley nodded quickly. "The hospital is twenty minutes on a good day. I need to get started so I can be there when the president arrives. Emergency radio said in the next hour the eye of the storm will be over us. I'm going to start out if I can."

"Too risky. Stay put until the calm. I'll have the director send a car. He'll know how to get you there in one piece."

The doctor smiled mischievously. "Ahh, Captain Hunter, you do care."

"If only you weren't married." Chase spoke with stoic seriousness.

"Say the word and I'll give the old boy an injection," she said with sexy intent.

From somewhere behind the doctor, Chase heard a powerful male voice. "I heard that Mary Pat."

Chase chuckled. "Give Tom my best. And don't go out until you hear from Enigma."

Dr. Kelley saluted with flippant disregard before signing off.

Chase shoved the computer back at Sam who caught it precariously. He didn't need to say anything. The irritation was evident. She pivoted on her feet and left.

"Old girlfriend?" Tessa said as Chase turned to check on the president. He went over the upgrade in condition before speaking. His eyes made sure the saline drip was replaced as he moved to Tessa's side.

"Worked with her a time or two in Iraq when I was a Ranger. Back then I was a medic. She saved a lot of lives. Worked tirelessly without complaint, unless she couldn't get supplies or meds for the wounded. Then you'd better duck. Patched me up more than once after I joined Delta Force. The woman was a miracle worker. Got to know her family after she was assigned to the president. Good people."

Tessa remained silent, listening to the rhythm of his voice;

how it deepened at times then became flat and unemotional. She watched how his mouth moved when he spoke with the bottom lip sometimes protruding slightly as if thinking before he released a word. The quiet tone he now used masked a dangerous situation surrounding them, yet she felt comforted listening to reminisces about Iraq and Dr. Kelley.

She followed him with her eyes as he left her side. He walked about the room checking on a few agents who were wounded, but refused to leave their post. Occasionally, Chase laid a hand on a shoulder or checked an abrasion, adding a few words and a nod before moving on to another matter. After every quick exam his eyes drifted back to her and she rewarded him with a smile or an "okay" sign.

"Almost done," he declared opening a bottle of water. "I think we may have gotten a little over three pints of blood."

He began removing the tube from her arm as the paramedic did the same for the president. Pulling the table away from the president another paramedic was able to bandage Tessa's arm as Chase slipped an arm underneath her back to lift her to a sitting position.

When Tessa squeezed her eyes shut and braced her hands down on the table he tightened his hold around her shoulders. "Careful. You're going to be pretty woozy for a while. Drink this." Holding the bottle of water up to her lips he watched her drink, trying not to notice that a few drops dripped from her mouth to her chin. "Drink it all, Baby," he whispered.

Her eyes cut to him as she paused then removed the water from her chin that had already begun to fall on her upper chest. She shook her head. "Enough."

"You got any more of that saline solution?" he quizzed the paramedic. He nodded and looked at Tessa holding her head. "Get a line in her," he ordered roughly.

Tessa snatched the bottle from Chase. "Okay. I'll drink it. No more needles."

A devilish smirk formed on his wide mouth. "Nice to know you have a weakness." Chase retrieved several more bottles of water before helping Tessa off the table. "Want me to carry you to a chair or can you walk?"

Tessa saw Samantha enter the room and frown at Chase's arm

around her. "I can walk." Flexing her shoulder in stubbornness, Chase dropped his hand to her elbow. Letting herself be ushered to a folding chair someone had brought for her, Tessa decided to make eye contact with Agent Samantha Cordova. She didn't want any trouble with her.

The two women's brief encounter a year earlier forced Tessa into service with Enigma. A complicated relationship began to form with Chase at her side that brought out the worst in Samantha. The woman, used to getting her own way about almost everything, soon realized she was being ignored by the one man she desired.

On one level, Tessa wanted to reassure Sam once this nightmare concluded she would fade back into the woodwork. However, the catty side of her enjoyed making the most beautiful woman in the world panic.

Tessa fidgeted, feeling the sore tail bone Sam had given her when she'd thrown her to the floor. In that moment of weakness and pain, Tessa watched as a snide grin formed on the agent's full lips. She guessed Sam was remembering the act with satisfaction.

Sam took a couple of leisurely steps her way and stopped. Looming her five foot ten inch frame over the injured and now weakened Tessa caused a smile to spread across her lips. Chase stepped away to check on the president. She was forced to look up at Sam. The attempt at intimidation was evident in the agent's eyes.

"Comfortable? Can I get you some barbwire to sit on?" She kept her voice low and threatening.

Tessa smiled sweetly. "Yes, please. Since you ate yours for breakfast I wondered if you had any left."

The smirk faded from Sam's face as she pushed out her lips in a moment of thought. "You might fool the rest of these guys with that southern good girl crap, but I've got your number, Betty Crocker. Better watch yourself."

Continuing to smile, her knees trembled as the woman glared down at her with lethal contemplation. "Oh I've got him to do that." She nodded toward Chase who chose that moment to look their way. "But thanks anyway, Sam. I'll be sure to let Chase know of your offer."

With a deep throated growl of irritation, Sam moved away as

Chase came back with another bottle of water. He took the first empty one from her fingers. "You girls getting acquainted," he asked drily, knowing full well Sam never played nice when it came to other women.

Taking a swig of water, Tessa nodded. "Thought we'd have lunch when this is all over. Of course she said I had to buy."

His laugh caused several to turn and look their way. Trying to choke it back due to the seriousness of the situation, Chase shook his head. "You always manage to make me laugh."

Pretending to have a new idea, Tessa gasped. "I know. I can be the agent that gets everyone in a good mood when things go wrong. I can do an internet search of national security jokes and tuck them into your mission portfolios. I've even got some NSA pickup lines. We can requisition some gag gifts as prizes for the funniest mishap on the job. What'a ya say?"

Chase shook his head trying to smother his laugh. "I think Carter is the only clown we need at Enigma. By the way he says you couldn't keep your hands off him. Any truth to that?" His smile narrowed and an eyebrow arched slightly as if accusing her of something.

"All true." She watched Chase's smile disappear. "If I hadn't kept moving his hands and pinching him I'm afraid I might not have made it to the balcony so I could give my uncle a clear shot at his thick head."

Carter walked up frowning and rubbing the back of his head. "I know you're playing hard to get. You just haven't realized I'm a real catch." His eyes were on Tessa, but he managed to elbow Chase good naturedly. He turned his eyes to his boss. "Just got word. The big birds are ready to go. Calm as a cucumber outside. Be on the roof in fifteen. We better get him ready. Ben is coming to join us. Wants a come-to-Jesus-talk with the prime minister."

With a few snaps of his fingers people started hustling. Making preparations to move the president up fifteen floors by stairs needed more hands to help. Some of the agents could shoot if necessary but many of them couldn't lift more than a weapon at this point. Chase sent Zoric out into the ballroom for volunteers and returned with twenty young men that looked like they were in good shape.

Two of them were his own men, First Sergeant Cooper and

Lieutenant Montgomery. They looked relieved to be joining the action instead of babysitting Tessa's friends. Their clothes looked in disarray with the lieutenant's shirttail hanging out and a smear of lipstick on Cooper's chin. Chase eyed them with a harsh examination. Making a quick adjustment to the shirts and removable of lipstick on their cheeks from Tessa's friends, both men stood at attention as if waiting for inspection.

"At ease, men, you're not under orders tonight, but I do need your help."

Both men took charge of the volunteers sending them in relay teams up the stairs to hand off the president as he was carried up toward the roof. Flashlights were duct taped to the stairway railing to offer minimum light for the transport. Agents spread out along the way to make sure no threat against the president occurred. Several paramedics tagged along. One carried a saline bag attached to the leader of the free world as he made his ascent. The other kept a close vigil on any change he noticed in the president. The decision to send the president's agent, John Elliott, on the helicopter became necessary for his survival.

Bringing up the rear, Chase, Zoric and Samantha followed, making sure no surprises transpired. They hoped an uneventful transport of the president to the hospital where Dr. Kelley and her team waited would move at a steady pace. Carter stayed behind to secure the area along with the Mossad. Tessa remained in the kitchen alone, sipping water, as she promised to do.

The kitchen became void of noise. Even the wind outside abandoned its onslaught against the exterior doors. The room became stale and oppressive with heat. Smells of burnt food left in hot skillets wafted lightly in the once chaotic space filled with Secret Service and Enigma agents. Only one candle remained, flickering timid threads of light around its small container. Soon it would be extinguished too and darkness would swallow the space where Tessa sat nursing a third bottle of water.

The dizziness disappeared as Tessa stretched her legs. She removed Chase's jacket he'd wrapped around her shoulders for the second time. The temperature seemed to be rising. Looking down at her once beautiful black dress, she sighed, knowing her husband would never see her in it. What would he think of all this intrigue? He would probably never know how close the country came to falling into economic chaos or that evil stalked the streets of Washington D.C. with her uncle leading the way. Hopefully Robert would never realize the role she played in the mayhem.

She tried to stand in slow motion and found that the room did not sway. With determination, Tessa moved to the trash can and dropped her empty bottle before reaching for a fourth bottle of spring water from the counter. It was warm to the touch. She tried to loosen the cap, but her hands remained a little weak and shaky. Running some hot water over the lid made her next attempt successful.

Two swallows and Tessa moved toward the door where evidence of more light existed. Pushing the door open she found the corridor empty. Red exit lights made eerie streaks on the wall, blending with the trails of blood that looked like a Pollock painting.

Queasiness overtook her stomach, forcing another quick drink of water. It was at that moment she knew the desperate need for air. Staggering toward the loading dock doors, she jerked one open to see two Secret Service agents. She held up a hand when one stepped to assist her, but withdrew when she rushed to the edge and began throwing up.

Someone cleared his throat before handing her a handkerchief. Nodding a thank you, Tessa wiped her mouth and face, then took another swig of water to rinse out her mouth. She was too embarrassed to look at the agents. The fact that they took several steps away to give her privacy, made their presence less intrusive. From the corner of her eye she noticed they looked into the darkness without saying a word.

Tessa began to breathe easier and managed to sip her water. She extended her hand out to let the rain dripping off the roof run across her fingers before smearing it on her face. Leaning against the end wall, she decided life would continue. The pinging of leftover water made music against something plastic in the alley. Occasional flashes of street lights played with the darkness as a gentle breeze moved against her exposed skin. The horrible storm had somehow erased the smell of garbage and replaced it with a sweet smell of freshness. It reminded her of the spring rains in Franklin, Tennessee where she grew up with her uncle always nearby.

The agents directed the beams of their flashlights out at the Beast. The president's half a million dollar ride made them shake their heads, seeing the trash that washed up on the trunk and hood during the flash flood. The water now receded to a six inch nuisance. Tessa thought she heard the two men speculate if the car would still run after the abuse of the storm. There was also talk of the decoy Beast parked in what was supposed to be a secure location.

She tuned them out, choosing to focus on the sounds of dripping and the realization her strength ebbed closer to normal. Closing her eyes, she bent one knee to rest her foot against the concrete wall. Someone had found her a pair of tennis shoes in the laundry area; abandoned by a forgetful tourist and ended up with the dirty sheets and towels. Even though they were a half size too big it was better than going barefoot or wearing six inch heels.

The doors to the corridor flew open startling the agents who immediately pulled their weapons. Two men stormed out with halos of light behind them. Their angry voices were combative. One of the agents stepped forward as a large man stood in the doorway blocking the agents' entrance.

"Leave," demanded Director Benjamin Clark to the Secret Service agents. "Now."

The second man looked at the giant behind him and jerked his head toward the inside so that he moved as well. "Ari, you can stand inside. There is nothing here to threaten me unless it's a wet rat. Now be gone. I'm sick of all this suffocating attention," Prime Minister Levi barked.

Ari nodded politely and stepped aside for the two agents who appeared to have forgotten Tessa standing in the shadows. They pulled the door partially shut but left enough room to barrel through if a hint of danger occurred.

Tessa pushed herself farther into the corner. Why hadn't she just made herself known when they started ordering people around? Jumbled thoughts pressed into her brain; *Should I clear my throat or maybe fake a puking episode to gain sympathy?* If she suddenly appeared would Ari the Giant swoop out and break her in half? Before she could determine a solution, the men began to argue.

"What have you done, Gilad?" Ben fumed.

"I have done nothing but protect the interests of Israel. Something you do not seem to find important. What would our father say?" Gilad sounded as if he liked to play the 'father' card.

Imagining a glow of temper flashing like strobes across the director's face, Tessa held her breath. "Our father wanted justice for those Egyptians who were murdered in the desert in 1967. He wanted Israel to take responsibility for what they'd done. But not like this, Gilad. You have endangered my president. I will never forgive you for that."

To Tessa's horror she watched the director pull a gun from inside his suit coat as the Prime Minister of Israel took a shocked step backwards.

CHAPTER 23

Two Egyptians dragged Speaker Jim Gault out of the containment area where the USS Liberty men were held. He tried to force their hands off his arms, but only managed to get a slap upside the back of the head for his efforts. His yelp echoed in the hollow halls. Once the door was slammed shut and bolted the speaker jerked free of his captors. Storming off to where he knew Amon would be waiting, his temper began to flare.

"Look at me," he yelled. "Your thugs apparently don't know who I am."

Amon examined the speaker's face with amused eyes. "Nor do they care, Mr. Speaker. You are an American dog they would just as soon extinguish as keep alive. Do not taunt them."

"They work for you; therefore you're responsible for their actions. Don't think I will forget this uncivilized treatment. It's absolutely barbaric."

"Yet you had no trouble ordering the president and vice president killed." Amon smiled child-like before pushing out his lips in a pout. He watched the speaker admire himself in a spider cracked mirror hanging haphazardly over the makeshift coffee center. "Besides, we both know they are not my men."

The speaker whirled around angrily. "So you say. Whoever they work for feels confident enough in letting you lead them. When this is over you'd better make them pay for getting out of hand when they roughed me up."

Amon chuckled. "I'm afraid your injuries are my fault. I

merely told them to make them look realistic." He moved to a chair where he rested his hands. "Did the old warriors believe you were a victim?"

"They did until Wakefield got there. He's suspicious and untrusting. Looks like he was cut from a piece of rawhide. I don't like him. Why did you choose him to kill the president anyway?"

"It was the logical choice. He has harassed the Israelis for years about justice. President after president has suffered his rant about revenge and accountability. He even started a Facebook page just to keep the dialogue going. I'm sure looking back, he will reevaluate that decision."

The speaker jerked a chair out and flopped down, nearly toppling it. "The men who went after the president, where are they? I knew that old hayseed wouldn't go through with it. Good thing we saw him leave the Israeli Embassy."

Amon sighed with a nonchalant shrug. "Those men are all dead, it seems. Except for the ones that brought back our last hostage, of course."

The speaker looked stunned. "Then where are the ones who brought back Wakefield?"

"I had them shot." Amon smiled with great pleasure. "They were disrespectful. I have a low threshold for such things." His warning came cool and calm.

A visibly shaken speaker opened his mouth, but words failed him. After fidgeting under the amused stare of Amon, the speaker leaned on the table and ran both hands over his face. Puffing out a disgusted grunt, the speaker gained some composure. "If you're trying to intimidate me, you'd better think twice. I left a little insurance behind at my condo in case you started to get ideas of your own." Amon's smile began to fade. "You killed one of my Secret Service agents, broke into my house."

"What stupid thing have you done, Mr. Speaker?" Amon's voice began as a low sign of concern.

"As long as I get through this as we planned, you will be safe. I will protect you."

"Somehow I find that hard to believe. You have nothing to fear from me." Amon arched an eyebrow. "Besides, Egypt has everything to gain from this little fiasco. With you as president, I'm sure you'll do everything in your power to make sure the

Israelis are blamed for the assassinations. Your country will be outraged. Whether it can be proved or not, the seeds of deception will be planted. Not even the winds of a hurricane, like the one that surrounds us could remove the conspiracy of betrayal." Amon propped his hands on the table and leaned in toward the speaker. The anger in his black eyes could no longer be masked. "And you are a fool if you think I, too, have not taken precautions to protect myself and Egypt. A man who would betray his own country..." Amon frowned. "Hamiiha Haramiiha."

The speaker snorted. "Speak English."

"'Its protector is its thief.' Meaning you are like the fox guarding a henhouse."

"'God helps those who help themselves.' Benjamin Franklin," the speaker sneered.

"I doubt God has anything to do with your plans, Mr. Speaker."

The speaker paused, pushing out his thin lips. "Any more news on the president or vice president?"

Amon shook his head. "There is a break in the storm now. I suspect we'll be able to make connections again shortly. The last thing I heard was that the vice president's boat exploded with him and his detail aboard. All the information is being kept pretty quiet. I'm not sure the public is aware of anything except an accident. As for the president, my source said he had sustained several injuries that were not survivable."

Jumping to his feet he yelled, "You said he was dead."

"Yes, well perhaps I jumped to conclusions with that report. It's unlikely he could survive with such an onslaught of firepower."

"Maybe if you hadn't gotten trigger happy with the men I hired, we'd have a better idea of his condition."

Amon nodded. "I apologize, Mr. Speaker. You, of course, are correct as always." The look of humbleness crossed his face as his eyes looked downward in surrender. "Now, if you'll excuse me I will check on my helpers to see if they have been able to pick up any news on the radio." Just as he bowed his head respectfully, he heard a disgruntled "humph" from the speaker which nearly caused him to stop. Knowing the politician couldn't see his face, Amon smirked as he strode from the room.

Once he'd retreated a safe distance from the speaker, Amon slipped into the room where several other Egyptians sat smoking and sipping on bottles of water. They jumped to attention as he waved them to relax. He reached into the pocket of his jacket with the utmost care. Pulling out his phone, Amon hit stop then replay on the recorder.

"'Maybe if you hadn't gotten trigger happy with the men I hired to kill the President we'd have a better idea of his condition.'" Followed by his own voice: "'I apologize, Mr. Speaker...'" Amon smiled with satisfaction, knowing he just gave the speaker enough rope to hang himself if this event went sideways.

Amon clicked off knowing that the admission of guilt from the third most powerful man in the United States would also secure Egypt's billion and half in yearly aid. He chuckled loud enough to draw the confused glances of the other four men in the room. Reassuring them with quiet words, he directed them to begin the search for more news on the world outside their building.

~~~

Tessa sucked in her breath as her hands flew to her heart. Gilad Levi remained reserved at the gun his brother held. Her heart began a rapid beat and breathing became difficult in that split second. She felt faint at the possibility before her. If Director Benjamin Clark killed the prime minister another layer of chaos would ensue.

The prime minister turned his head slightly to look over his shoulder. Tessa realized in that moment the gun was pointed into the darkness where she stood, not at the director's brother.

"Step out where I can see you." The director's gun waved to the side before redirecting the weapon toward her once more. The stream of light from a security light over the door created the shadow of a huge gun barrel.

Moving forward with her hands lifted, she was careful not to make a threatening move. As the eerie light flickered over the scene, she watched the director lower his weapon. A scowl spread across his face as his chin raised enough to show displeasure. She remained silent; fearing something inappropriate or stupid would spill from her lips. Waiting for a reprimand, her eyes darted between the two men in nervous anticipation.

Before she knew what was happening, the prime minister grabbed her arm, pulling her forward gingerly. He offered a patient smile then slipped his arm around her shoulders. They slumped at his touch.

"You are trembling." Gilad's voice showed genuine concern. "Why is she even out here, Benjamin? She's in no shape to be moving about on her own accord. Have you no regard for your agents?" His accusing tone brought Ari outside and quickly evaluated the situation. "My dear," he said pulling her around to face him. "Ari will take you inside. Whatever you need he'll see to it." He nodded to his protector.

Tessa looked up into the shadowy face of the leader of Israel with new eyes. "You put my uncle up to this, didn't you?" She removed his hand on her upper arm. "You told him about my arm. That's why he tried to disable me so quickly."

Benjamin stepped up beside Tessa. "What are you saying, Mrs. Scott? That my brother somehow knew of your accident a year ago and gave that information to your uncle in case he needed it to subdue you?"

A shiver ran up her spine as Gilad began to frown at her with irritation. "Yes. Your brother," Tessa looked away from the prime minister's penetrating glare, "also had his men bring my uncle's rifle so he could make good on his threat to kill the president. The only thing is he never wanted any part of that. He only wants Israel to confess their sins. Apparently both of you are well aware that there is a great deal to be accountable for concerning the USS Liberty. Was it you who sent pictures of me and Agent Zoric to him? How about breaking into my hotel room? Was that also your people?"

"Gilad?" Benjamin now pulled Tessa out of Ari's reach and placed himself between the giant protector and his unwilling agent. "How did you know about Mrs. Scott's injury? Have you been snooping in my business or do I have a spy?"

Gilad exhaled deeply. "We *explore* one another's activities all the time. Do not show such indignation with me. Have you not done the same with Israel? It was not so difficult to find out about your little Grass Valley housewife a year ago. There were alerts worldwide about isotope terrorism. We merely followed a trail that eventually led back to Mrs. Scott which led to her uncle." His eyes turned to Tessa. "In spite of his repeated threats over the years, I must say I like the old guy. He promised to take me squirrel hunting when this is all over."

"I think that's code for 'accidents happen.'" Tessa mumbled under her breath. "I can't imagine him ever doing anything you ask. He hates Israel for what they did to him and the crew of the Liberty. You destroyed their ability to move on with their lives when your country lied about not knowing it was an American vessel. They can't even trust their own government thanks to Israel."

"All of that is true. I came this week for the hearings and to put this to rest once and for all. The Israelis involved with that clandestine affair also wish to move on, if that is even possible. Our father suffered greatly in the years that followed. He never forgot what duty forced him to do."

Tessa felt a little dizzy and staggered before grabbing Ben's arm. "Why now? These threats and promises of a hearing have gone on for years. Nothing ever came of it. Yet a few weeks ago everything started falling into place. I don't understand. What am I missing?"

"We uncovered a plot to kill the president." Gilad moved toward the door and Ben led Tessa in the same direction. Once inside Gilad pointed at a toppled chair and it was immediately brought to Tessa. Ben eased her down then stood with his hand resting on the back, which made a squeaking sound.

"We forwarded the information through appropriate channels for your agencies to begin the search for whoever was involved," Gilad continued.

"And?" Tessa asked quietly, caught up in the knowledge her uncle was somehow part of the conspiracy.

Gilad shrugged. "Nothing. The trail went cold almost as soon as it surfaced. It wasn't until," he paused letting his eyes shift to his brother, "we received a tip about four weeks ago that someone in your government was financing the whole assassination attempt."

Tessa looked up at the director. "That's about the same time I got the grant to come to D.C. Was that your doing, Director

Clark?" Although she'd put in for the grant six months earlier she'd been told her eligibility for such a large amount of money and sponsorship most likely would be bestowed upon someone at the local junior college.

The director's voice sounded frosty. "We always had plans for you, Mrs. Scott. This just expedited the inevitable. We believe your uncle is under duress because his fellow Liberty mates have been kidnapped. Like the others, he thought this time, some acknowledgement of the bombing would be finally labeled a war crime and hold Israel responsible. He's worked tirelessly for many years to see this come to pass."

"He was concerned when he knew I would be here for the conference."

Gilad took a chair that Ari pushed toward him. "Yes. Like us, someone else has been looking into ways to foster your uncle's support. You are the weakest link, my dear."

Tessa bristled at the insinuation. "Maybe that's true. Did you know that he also planned to kill you if he got a chance?"

Gilad smiled then chuckled. "He said as much. Ari and Micah nearly dropped him to the floor." His laughter boomed looking over at the sour expressions on the faces of his protection detail. He rolled his eyes toward Ari and Micah. "Apparently, lacking a sense of humor is part of their job description." The two Mossad agents continued to stare into space as if the prime minister spoke of someone else. "Together, your uncle and I devised a plan to draw out whoever was behind all this."

"You should've kept me in the loop, Gilad," Ben said hotly. "Maybe all of this could have been avoided. I should arrest you right now and throw your sorry..." He stopped, seeing that Ari and Micah's attention had shifted to him and their body language indicated they were annoyed. "The hurricane has a few hours to go before we can resolve this." Ben looked out the open doors and noticed hints the onslaught was about to begin again. His phone pinged and he looked at the message. "Thankfully the president has made it to Walter Reed Hospital. His physician had a team standing by."

~~~

A relieved sigh escaped Ben's mouth as his stiff shoulders twisted slightly toward relaxing. He couldn't help noticing as he looked back down at Tessa that her eyes shut momentarily as if in prayer, but quickly opened again. He laid his hand on her shoulder and squeezed.

A fleeting thought of gratitude entered his mind, knowing that at least one person on his team had the ear of God. The woman continued to bewilder him as to her entrance into all their lives at Enigma. Both naive and annoying, the woman made allies and enemies wherever she went. He couldn't decide if she was part angel or demon.

The effect on his people had been significant. She'd given the shy computer genius, Vernon Kemp, the courage to talk to women. The ghoulish artist skilled at torture and interrogation now painted stories of beauty and strength. Samantha became less sure of herself and more out of control, becoming a dangerous agent who demanded closer monitoring. Even playboy Carter Johnson; the guy who never met a mirror he didn't like and could easily be distracted by a long pair of legs, had become more focused and less abrasive. There hadn't been any sexual harassment complaints in quite a while.

The director of Enigma wasn't sure if all the changes had anything to do with the Grass Valley woman. Most of those events could be explained one way or another.

The biggest change had been in his team leader, Captain Hunter. Whatever ongoing relationship brewed between them was speculation at this point. The man everyone looked to in a crisis had always been quick to pull the trigger. Charging into dangerous situations compelled other men to follow him without question. He'd become cynical and bitter over the terror he'd witnessed.

Escaping China after his missionary parents were killed by the Red Guard, losing his sister to a drug overdose, then his grandmother in the Twin Towers, created a calloused and hardened fighter on the battlefield. The strain had begun eating away at any humanity left in him when Tessa stumbled haphazardly into his life.

Even before he could see his face, Ben knew the approaching shadow belonged to the captain. He walked with purpose, all the while looking cautiously to any open doorways shrouded in candlelight or fading flashlights.

Feeling Tessa's shoulder pull back beneath his hand in some kind of bravery, the director felt her begin to stand awkwardly. By putting his hand on her elbow she stood with enough grace to hide the weakness she probably experienced after giving the president her blood. He stole a look at her face as the captain came into their light. Her blue eyes appeared to spark before a blush started up her neck.

Smiling at her clumsy attempt at strength, Chase stopped in front of the group. "The president regained consciousness as he got on the bird, Tessa. Wanted you to know he was in your debt."

Tessa cocked her head, relieved at the news. "He's going to be okay, isn't he?"

"I think so. Thanks to you. I don't know what we would've done without you here tonight," Chase bragged. "As always, you're amazing."

Ari cleared his throat to get their attention. "Do you two want to be alone or can we get on with the business at hand?"

Hero worship gleamed in her eyes, Ben noticed. She needed to manage that a little better.

Turning back to the prime minister as the smile vanished, Tessa blurted out. "Who are you working with, Mr. Prime Minister? I doubt it's the United States government. And who has my uncle?" Her knees began to weaken as he answered.

CHAPTER 24

Chase cut his eyes to the director. "Did you know the Egyptians were negotiating with Israel, Ben?"

Ben shook his head. "Not until earlier tonight, after the president was shot." He nodded toward his brother. "He told me then. Those men you killed in the alley last night were former secret police. Of course the Egyptian Embassy is denying any knowledge of them or why they would be here." His harsh glare refocused on his brother. "But now we know that isn't true. Right, Mr. Prime Minister?" The tone came across as condescending. "There's someone on the inside of the embassy feeding you information. When the two henchmen didn't return with Jake Wakefield the other night it was soon discovered they'd been eliminated."

"Yes. I was contacted and sent my own people out to find him. It wasn't that difficult. He was sloppy. He spent the night at the Israeli Embassy as my guest."

Tessa blurted an angry retort. "There's no way my uncle would stay with you on his own accord. You kidnapped him and implied I was working with the government against everything he stood for. That must have been when you filled in the blanks about my connection with Enigma and the injuries I sustained a year ago. No wonder he didn't trust me." She could feel her heart rate escalate and her face turning red. "You made me look like I was betraying him."

Gilad took a deep breath. "Israel needs closure on this USS

Liberty matter. Someone in my confidence could see that in order for the United States to continue their generous aid package several things needed to occur. Our relationship with your country has been rocky until President Austin took office. There had been a great deal of damage to our reputation."

Shifting his weight to one leg, Chase folded his arms across his chest before speaking. "You suspected Americans weren't happy with giving money to a nation like Egypt. It wouldn't be too difficult in raising Israel's status, even if it meant admitting to some pretty powerful mistakes."

Gilad nodded before looking to his brother. "Unlike you, my brother, I want what is best for Israel. This president, unlike the last one, has a soft spot for the land of his Jesus. Admitting to our transgressions will not sit well at first, but with the honoring of those men left from the Liberty and me standing by the president's side, I believe a new kind of respect will emerge for my nation."

Tessa's bewildered expression could not be masked. She looked to the director, hoping he'd fill in the blanks so she wouldn't sound foolish.

"I find it hard to believe the Egyptian government would try and kill the president and vice president. Who is behind this?" The director's voice, although even toned, came through gritted teeth as he glared at his brother. "When this gets out, Americans will insist on funding being withdrawn from Egypt and you know it."

"That's what I thought," Gilad confessed. "However, I think I've been played. My source is either feeding me wrong information or he's playing both sides to see which one comes out on top."

"There's another option," Ben snapped. "Israel really is behind the assassination attempts. You make it look like Egypt has blood on its hands."

Gilad's face reddened. "Israel is the best friend you have in the Middle East. Why would we do such a thing?"

"You probably wanted to threaten rather than injure. That way Egypt could easily be implicated especially since you have someone on the inside. The Liberty hearings move forward, all is forgiven, no crimes against humanity for Israel because everyone is so outraged over the president being shot."

"You listen to me, Benjamin. We had nothing to do with this.

After all, I was the one who let your Secret Service know about the threat. I'm sure the CIA has already followed up on all that information."

Tessa's head was moving back and forth as if watching a tennis match. She rubbed an oncoming headache as their voices escalated. "Stop it," she snapped as her hand pressed against her forehead. Her voice softened as she looked up at the two brothers. "Please."

Chase reached to slip an arm around her waist. "Come on. I'll get you some water. You need to get hydrated." Ari blocked his path. He looked up into the giant's face and snarled. "Get out of my way."

Ari smirked, comfortable with his intimidation factor. He stepped aside and let them pass. He then went back to standing at attention near the prime minister.

After walking into an empty kitchen where only one candle still burned, he located another bottle of water. Before handing it to her he twisted the cap off. She took a quick sip only to have him force another one. When he reached for the bottle to repeat the action Tessa stepped away, jerking the bottle out of his reach.

"Stop it. I'm not a child and I know what to do. You just have to force your will on me, don't you?"

She wasn't aware that her voice cracked or that her eyelids were batting rapidly. The next big gulp choked her, forcing a spew of water down her chest and up her nose. The coughing started as embarrassment washed over her.

Chase leaned against a counter. Watching with apathy, he tried to hide the amusement playing at the corners of his black eyes. "If you didn't want the water you should have just said so," he offered off-handedly. "Spitting at me is a little undignified, don't you think?"

Frowning, she pulled off several paper towels to pat her chest and face. "Very funny."

This time when she lifted the bottle to her lips for short sips she eyed Chase with caution. She couldn't see much of his face, only the white of his teeth and the creases around his eyes.

He must think I'm a bumbling idiot, she thought with regret. She sat the empty bottle down and heard it roll off the table to the floor. *I am a bumbling idiot. What have I gotten myself into?*

"Feeling better? I probably can find some aspirin or…"

"I'm good. Thanks." Tessa diverted her eyes to the floor and pretended to search for the plastic bottle with the toe of her shoe.

Both stood in silence for several minutes before Chase pushed off the counter and came to stand in front of her. "We need to talk about your uncle, Tessa."

She cocked her head and eyed him with what looked like a reprimand waiting to explode. As her chin dropped, her lips pursed to be argumentative.

"Did Jake actually say he was working with the Israelis?" Chase spoke in a whisper as if he didn't want others to hear their conversation.

"Implied more than anything. He did, however, say the Israelis brought in his gun. I think he was planning on taking a shot at the prime minister too. But when he saw those men storm in at the same time the president came through those doors…" Tessa caught her breath as if choking on the flashback. She filled him in on the man in the dumpster too.

Chase waited for her to finish, allowing time to caress her face with his eyes. The rapid blinking stopped and her breathing was trying to catch up with her recovery. The paleness of her skin appeared to be returning to that peaches and cream complexion he found so tempting to touch. In spite of her disheveled appearance the flickering candle light failed to hide Tessa's wholesome kind of beauty.

It was almost a reflex now to jerk her chin up in stubbornness when she thought Chase was questioning her truthfulness or loyalty. "At this point, I have to believe my uncle planned to take out the president." The tone in her voice sounded hopeless. "He wanted to save his friends from the USS Liberty. He didn't want them to die another kind of death by deception. It weighed on him. Coming here for the hearings…" She swallowed hard. "This was to be closure for those men. Finally someone wanted to listen to their story. My uncle was a hero on that day. He saved lives and never received his Medal of Honor because it would bring too much attention to a botched attack on an American vessel."

Chase nodded in agreement. "Let's find him, Tess." He lowered his head enough to force her to look up. "The truth, good or bad should be told for the sake of those men. They're heroes and

Israel needs to come clean about the whole affair."

~~~

Aware how close Chase had come to her made the warmth in the room intensify. Her eyes focused on the way his lips moved when he spoke, the deep throaty sound of his voice and the way his chest rose and fell as he breathed. His ethnic heritage made him appear darker in candle light. The scent of gunpowder and sweat reached her nose, making her nostrils flare. He unconsciously raised a finger and rubbed a spot over his heart like she'd seen him do many times.

The black tie had been removed and his exposed throat was visible from two open buttons. Tessa let her eyes slide down to his neck then back up to his black hair. She noticed the scar near his ear and wanted desperately to touch it, feel it throb beneath her fingertips. A need to press her lips against the spot flooded her senses. Did the memory of that scar haunt him when he looked in the mirror?

"Tessa, I want," Chase stepped so close his body nearly touched hers. This time she didn't retreat in panic at his obvious desire to have her. He stared at her mouth creating a heady sensation to rise deep inside her. Words failed as they stared into the other's eyes, trying to make sense of the confused passion rising up between them when...

"Captain?" It was Samantha Cordova. Her eyes went to him then Tessa before leveling a dangerous glare back at what she perceived as the competition. She lifted a cell phone. "It's Tessa's husband." She emphasized 'husband' as she handed him the phone. "Nice looking," she cooed. "Athletic too I bet. He's called several times."

Chase stepped back before tossing the phone to Tessa. She nearly dropped it as her face began to redden with embarrassment. "Yes, Robert?" Her voice sounded anxious even as she watched the captain leave the room, but not before he nodded for Sam to remain.

"Hi, Honey. Just checking in. Is the storm still pounding you guys?"

The activated speaker made her nervous. Tessa met Sam's

eyes boldly and refused to look away in intimidation. "The eye passed over about an hour ago. It's starting to look ugly again. Any news?"

"The Weather Channel says another few hours then just some bands of rain. By morning you should be in the clear. All the major network channels are covering the president's assassination. No word on if he'll make it or how it happened. I guess they've got the vice president in a safe place. Reports there say he might be dead. Donno. What a mess," he moaned. "Tessa?"

She noted a voice tone change. "Yes."

"I want you to know how much I love you." Robert's voice sounded warm and familiar, safe and comforting.

Tessa's eyes shifted to Sam who arched an eyebrow in amusement. "I love you too, Robert. I absolutely do," she insisted as a feeling of guilt washed over her.

"I mean I really do, Sweetheart. Knowing you're there in a hurricane, the government is going crazy, not knowing about the president…"

"I'm okay, Robert. Really."

"Reports say people are dancing in the streets in Gaza. Embassies are on lockdown all over the world. Americans are advised to be careful and have an escape plan if they're abroad. I talked to our financial advisor a bit ago."

Tessa switched the phone to the other ear. "Why?"

"Thought this would affect our nest egg investments. The stock market will be closed for a few days so nothing will happen." He sighed. "I'd feel better if you were home."

"The kids okay?" Tessa wondered if he'd just had enough being a single parent.

"Yeah. They're in bed. Heather needed three bedtime stories tonight. I left work early and took them swimming for a few hours then fed them that fettuccine you left us. That stuff is coma food. No arguments about bedtime. It was delicious, by the way."

"Oh, Robert. I'm sorry."

"For what?"

"Being so…"

"Wonderful? I'm the luckiest man in the world."

Tessa closed her eyes and turned her back on Sam who had begun to smirk. "I better go, Robert. My battery is almost gone. I'll try to call you tomorrow if electricity is restored."

They clicked off and Sam grabbed the phone to see how much charge was left. She tossed it back after realizing the phone wouldn't last long. "That was touching. Does your husband know about your little flirtatious attempts at seducing the captain?" Samantha's voice had gone to the pit bull growl she used to alarm Tessa.

"I'm not flirting and if you weren't so obviously in love with him you wouldn't let your jealous insecurities show," Tessa bristled.

"You better take care of that husband of yours or someone might just turn his head enough to get a little action on the side." Sam watched Tessa's frown deepen. "From what I hear he has an eye for the ladies."

Tessa tried to push past her. "And how would you know that?"

"Remember that little piece of Irish trash that was supposed to be protecting your family a year ago while you were tramping through the woods with our captain?"

"How could I forget? She was a terrorist that couldn't make up her mind what side to be on."

"According to her, your Robert put the moves on her there at the end. Seems the two of you had a tiff before separating for vacation. He wanted a consolation prize for being with the kids."

Tessa didn't believe her, but it grated on her nonetheless. "You're not only insecure you're a liar, Sam." She felt a hand on her arm just before being jerked around to have Sam push her face into hers.

"Stay away from Chase or so help me I'll make it my mission to screw with your happy little life. You got that?" She pushed Tessa away and stormed out of the room.

When this is over, I'm so out of here and done with these crazy people, Tessa proclaimed silently to herself. *I want my dull, boring life back, including Robert. It beats having Satan's spawn up in my face all the time*

CHAPTER 25

Before slipping out of the kitchen to find a restroom, Tessa grabbed Chase's jacket. The revealing dress kept her tugging at the bodice. Since her bladder felt like it would explode any minute, covering most of her body made her feel presentable. She nodded to one of the wounded Secret Service agents that sported a bloody bandage around his head. Whispering "restroom," he nodded, pointing her toward the back of the room where the interrogation of the girl with the piercings took place.

The restroom, bathed in darkness, created a slight hesitation in her. Glancing back toward the entrance she relaxed. The spill of bright light given off by an LCD fusion lantern sitting on the floor gave her confidence to move forward. Her long shadow grew like some kind of ominous guard. Going into a dark room, in a strange place, gave her an uncomfortable foreboding, but her bladder insisted she take the risk.

Heat from the washers and driers still filled the room. She once again pulled off Chase's jacket and draped it over her arm, careful not to lose the cell phone she'd shoved inside the pocket.

Slipping into the restroom, Tessa made quick about the business she'd come to do. After washing her hands, she splashed some tepid water over her face. She tried to see herself in the mirror. Even though she'd removed one shoe and left it to prop the door open, the small restroom was too dark to estimate the damage to her appearance. The dangerous thought of how Chase had devoured her with his eyes before dinner sprang up again.

Probably why he took off when Sam came in to give me my phone. I look like a reject from a carnival freak show. The assessment arose after lifting her chin and bringing her face closer to the mirror. Dabbing her hair with some water she managed to twist it up into a bun. At least it would be cooler, she reasoned.

She bent down and retrieved her shoe, propping the door open with her hip. Remembering that she'd hung the jacket on the back of the door, Tessa let it begin to shut. Just for a second the darkness began to overwhelm her. She snatched the door handle and threw it open to find a flashlight shining in her face.

Throwing her free arm up over her eyes blocked enough brightness to realize something loomed in front of her, solid and tall. She smelled perspiration and spearmint as a gritty hand covered a scream she tried to release. The sound of the flashlight clicking off sent shock waves of anticipation throughout her body. Hands jerked her body around as she tried to squirm free. His free arm went around her neck so tight it forced her body to stop struggling. Tessa's heart hammered, causing breathing to become labored.

"Stop squirming. You're going to get me out of here. Understand?" When she didn't respond he tightened his hold around her neck. "Do you understand?"

Tessa nodded as tears rolled down her cheeks.

"There's a car in the parking garage." His voice sounded like he had marbles in his mouth.

She nodded. His breath made her nauseous when his mouth touched her ear.

Warily his arm came off her neck. Just as he took a small step back, Tessa sunk her teeth into his fingers. Whirling around, she forced her knee up into his groin. A surprise howl escaped his mouth but he managed to grab her by the hair. He caught the bun of her hair, yanking her to his side. Stumbling forward in a bent over position, he couldn't prevent her from slapping at him. A muffled scream for help failed as his fist swung and missed her. Dodging him forced Tessa to fall to the floor. Stunned, she crawled forward, but the stranger cut her off. Reaching down he grabbed her arm and snapped her to a standing position like one of her daughter's stuffed animals. The strength in his hold left no doubt he would kill her if she continued on this preposterous attempt at resistance. The sound of hurried footsteps reached their ears.

The intruder reopened the restroom door and dragged her back inside before locking the door. He shoved her against the sink so hard it felt like it would crack against her lower back. Slamming into her, she became immobile as he once more covered her mouth with his large hand. There was no room to wiggle free, but she continued to try, only to be rammed harder against the porcelain sink. With each breath, she felt the sickening realization that his chest crushed against hers.

Voices called inside. Was it her name? Using his free hand he grasped her neck and squeezed. "Not a word."

This time Tessa couldn't even nod her surrender.

The voices faded.

Her entire body quivered with terror as the attacker jerked her forward then threw open the door. "Put that coat on. Now," he demanded.

Although her hands trembled, she did as he ordered, feeling the cold chill of possible death if she didn't comply. "Please. I'll do as you ask, just don't kill me. I have three little…"

"Shut up." His face came so close Tessa felt rough whiskers rub against her chin.

Tessa gulped back tears, determined to be brave.

He reached into his pocket and pulled out some kind of thin fabric which Tessa recognized as discarded pantyhose. It smelled of detergent and bleach. Somehow comforted by the realization the thing he was tying around her mouth was clean helped her gain some composure. Trying to shake her head free, Tessa sniffed.

"Please. Don't gag me. I won't scream."

The attacker sniggered. "Yeah, right." He once again pinned her against the door frame until she allowed him to finish the gag. Next he took out what felt like thin twine and tied her hands together in front of her. "Be a good girl," he mocked as he shoved an FBI hat on her head. "Now I'm going to make some noise so you can walk me out."

He pulled out the flashlight from his vest pocket and turned it on before sticking it between his teeth. Pinning Tessa between his back and the concrete wall, he pulled out a string of firecrackers followed by several round items about the size of a quarter. He stepped forward before turning and handing them to Tessa. When she didn't raise her tied hands to take them his hand grabbed her by the neck and shook.

"You better be a little more cooperative if you want to live. I know who you are," he snarled.

Tessa's eyes blinked with rapid nervousness as she tried to stop the silent tears pouring from her eyes.

"You're the one who got the old man to flip on us. Now here I am left with nothing but a few firecrackers and you to get me out of here. Wonder what the old guy would think about that? Guess we'll see."

Tessa realized the menacing man knew where her uncle was taken. Maybe she had a chance at saving him from an unreasonable death. Sucking up her courage, she sniffed one last time and nodded in compliance, as if she were ready.

"Okay. Good girl," he soothed. "We're going to make a little noise and a whole lot of smoke." He heard her moan through the gag. "Worried something will catch fire?"

Jerking her in front of his body, he felt her stumble, so he yanked again to show his displeasure. "If I don't get back soon your uncle is going to be kicking chunks with the devil himself. No funny stuff. Hear me?" Feeling her nod he slipped on his own hat.

~~~

It sounded like gunfire; rapid and loud followed by an ear splitting explosion. Everyone hunkered down, waiting only seconds before guns pulled and heart beats steadied. Chase squatted down next to Zoric and Sam. They looked like panthers ready to strike. Carter, who had been napping in the corner, jolted upright at the commotion. The screams of the people in the ballroom didn't concern him at this point. The noise came from the rear where all the action from earlier in the evening took place. The crowd most likely heard the booms and feared the worst. Was it the hurricane or more attacks? He hoped Dr. Ervin would take charge of the chaos and offer some reassurance once information could be passed along.

The immediate problem was the smoke coming under the door. He heard coughing, gagging and overwrought voices as their door swung open. Several agents stumbled in covering their mouths with one hand, a gun dangling at their side with the other. Chase, along with his agents and several FBI agents, helped the Secret Service men inside. Slamming the door, he realized Tessa, Ben and the prime minister remained outside the safe room.

"What the hell happened?" Chase pushed against the door with his hand as if that might stop another attack. "Where are the others?"

Micah, the giant guard who kept close to Gilad rushed forward and shoved Chase aside. "Move," he demanded.

"Micah, stop and think a minute. You don't know what's out there. Ari is at the prime minister's side. The size of that guy would block anything that might hurt your boss." Micah was the less intimidating of the two guards. "Cool head." He could feel his own heart beating. "Stop. Listen. Then we go. Okay?" Speaking with a calm voice stopped the Mossad agent. "Okay?"

Micah took his hand from the doorknob as his answer, but his expression of murder did not change.

"Now, what happened out there?" His attention turned to the government agents.

"Hell if I know, Chase. Two guys came out of the laundry room wearing FBI hats; one had on a sport coat, one tall, another kind of short. The short one didn't seem to fit since he wasn't wearing a suit."

"What did he look like?"

The Secret Service agent shook his head. "There was just enough light to see that he wasn't wearing a suit. Didn't have time to pay much attention to the other one."

Another agent coughed before speaking up. "Looked like some kind of military vest, maybe camo. He seemed to be leading the other guy who carried a container. You know, like a plastic butter bowl or what you put in the fridge with your leftovers."

The Secret Service agent banged his hand down on the table. "Just as I yelled to stop he lit something."

"Like what?" Chase asked.

"Not sure. A lighter maybe. He put it inside the bowl then slung it our way."

Chase jerked the door open, rushing out into the corridor with Micah at his heels. The Israeli quickly pushed past him with no fear, gun drawn and yelling in a booming voice for his boss.

Knowing Micah would look after the three men at the end of the hall, he ducked into the kitchen where he'd last seen Tessa. He didn't call out, thinking the intruders might still be inside.

Sam and Zoric appeared immediately at his side.

"I left her here, Chase," Sam said matter-of-factly as her eyes scanned where she pointed a flashlight.

They spread out for a quick search with no results.

Joining Micah in the corridor, the Enigma agents watched him pull Ari up off of the two men he protected. Ari had knocked both men down and easily covered their bodies with his. He did not apologize for the hard fall or nearly suffocating the prime minister. Even though Gilad fumed with loud exaggerated protest, Ari took it in stride and dusted the debris from the man's suit and straightened the crooked tie.

"Thank you, Ari. Micah." The prime minister tried to calm himself. He'd survived several assassination attempts, but this one came close.

Carter and the other agents joined them. "Looks like firecrackers, cherry bomb-like things and some smoke bombs." He handed the semi-melted bowl to Chase. "Just trying to escape. Guess they were hiding in the john."

"The woman who gave the president blood went in there to use the restroom." It was the Secret Service agent with the bandaged head.

Without asking Sam rushed to check out the space and returned shaking her head solemnly. "She's gone."

Ben grumbled. "They stepped right over us. I couldn't move because Goliath had me pinned."

"You're welcome, Director Clark," Ari said with the patience of a Buddhist monk. "I assure you it wasn't my intent to save your life, but your brother's."

"I have no doubt," the director said flatly as he stepped up next to Chase. "Get some of your people out there. The water has subsided so they would be able to make it a ways. My guess is they're going to try and get a vehicle."

Chase nodded toward several men to search. "If that's so then it would have to be a parking garage. Anything on the ground would be useless."

Sam took a deep breath. "There may be another way." All

eyes turned to her. "I gave Tessa her phone back." Chase's face wore a mixture of anger and relief. "There isn't much juice left on it. If she left it on, we can track her." Sam clenched her teeth so hard her jaw muscles started to flex.

"Get Vernon on it. Maybe we can still find them before it's too late." He watched his two soldiers who babysat Tessa's friends, turn and head for the safe room. They were capable men who would return when Vernon had the news he wanted. His eyes then turned on Sam who stood statue still waiting for the reprimand that would reduce most people into tears. "Anything else, Sam?"

"No." She frowned as her eyebrow arched in stubbornness. "Chase, if I thought Betty Crocker had been in danger, I wouldn't have left her alone to, once again, get us all in so much trouble."

Chase glared menacingly at her as he pushed past her grim face.

~~~

The man forced her to get in the car then pushed Tessa down into the floorboard of the backseat. He didn't bother to blindfold her. His reckless driving made her already queasy stomach ache. Pinched into the car so tightly that there was little room to roll around, only her head moved back against the seat when he swerved or skidded around a curve. She was able to see the flashing red of what she guessed to be stoplights. Rain still pelted the car and she could hear the wind tossing flying debris against the windshield.

She tried to remove the phone from her pocket. Even though her hands were tied, Tessa managed to wiggle the phone from Chase's coat pocket. A cramp nearly paralyzed her shoulder. Waiting for the pain to subside, she tried to feel which end of the phone had the on button. Just as she thought she'd laid a finger on the correct button the car lurched to a stop then accelerated. The phone flew out of her hand.

Minutes later she was frantic to feel the car swerve, then jam on the brakes.

CHAPTER 26

By the time Tessa was shoved into the grimy building, there wasn't a dry thread on her. The hat blown from her head revealed the knot of hair had collapsed like pieces of twisted rope around her quivering shoulders. Covering half of her face, she felt too frightened and exhausted to try and move it. With eyes on the floor, Tessa hoped the submissive stance would spare her further roughness from her captor.

She heard voices as generator driven lights lit the expansive room. The smell of oil and mildew made her eyes water. A gag rose up in her throat at the pungent odor of coffee and boiled cabbage. It grew stronger as her captor grabbed her arm and yanked her after him. He stopped and waited for the owners of the voices to greet them. Trying to understand their words left her confused as she realized the words were not English.

The chatter stopped when she heard the dangerous click of an automatic weapon. A little over a year ago she didn't know the difference between the snap of an unlocking car door and the lethal intent of a Glock being readied. Jerking her arm free, Tessa side stepped her kidnapper in case… She didn't know in case of what, just that she needed to not be too close.

"What do we have here?" It was Amon, speaking in a pleasant voice, trying to force his British accent to sound welcoming.

Continuing to hang her head, she took a step back as Amon approached. He reached out and lifted her head by cupping her chin in a firm grip. "Look at me." His voice revealed patience.

She refused until he squeezed her chin so hard her eyes darted up to meet his familiar brown eyes. Startled by the knowledge they'd met before caused the Egyptian to smile. "Yes it is I. We meet again, Mrs. Scott." Amon motioned for one of his men to hand him something. He turned back to face her with a pair of garden shears held up in front of her face.

Tessa eyes crossed as she eyed the rusty blades. A whimper escaped her mouth as her whole body began to tremble. He lowered the shears, slipping it under the twine around her hands and snipped several times to set her free. After handing the tool back to his man, Amon gently turned her around and untied the gag.

"There. That's better." Looking over his shoulder he gave one of the men an order in his native tongue. "Get her something to dry off with. See if there are any more blankets." He turned back hearing her teeth chatter. "You are freezing." His eyes moved to her captor in a surprisingly angry glare. Grabbing Tessa's hands he pulled them up to show him the bruises. "Was this necessary?"

He rubbed his private parts and snarled. "She nearly made it impossible for me to ever have kids."

"A gift to the world, no doubt," Amon offered with amusement. His eyes turned back to her. "I'm going to need some information from you, Mrs. Scott. But first I'll make you some tea. Or would you rather have coffee?" She tried to shrug indifference, but it looked more like shivering. "Very well. I have coffee made. Let's try that first." He took her arm gently and led her to a hall before pointing into one of the small rooms for her kidnapper to wait. "Someone wants to see you in there. Keep your voices down. I do not want Mrs. Scott to be frightened further. Do you understand?"

The kidnapper's quick steps followed a retort. "I don't take orders from you."

Amon froze, leveling a deadly glare at Tessa's captor. "The last man that said that to me decided he was wrong."

"Yeah?" The man smirked as he flipped off Amon.

"Yes." He whispered. "Dead wrong."

Tessa couldn't help but notice her captor paused only a few seconds, weighing the implications of Amon's final warning. Then he disappeared into another room.

She wanted to jerk away from Amon's touch, remembering the evil way he'd looked at her several nights earlier on the roof of the W Hotel. Was his warning meant to redirect her uncle from his appointed fate, or prevent her from danger? He failed to press upon her the consequences of getting involved. Unsure of what else she could have done besides telling Zoric of the meeting and the missing picture, Tessa wondered if at any time she could have changed the outcome of this moment by refusing to cooperate with Enigma.

What if she had just let her uncle do what he set out to do? Would the president be dead? Did those Secret Service agents have to be wounded or die? Maybe Carter wouldn't be suffering from his head injury if she had just stayed home in her beautiful Victorian house in Grass Valley.

Now was not the time for regret or to conduct self-examination. These men tried to kill the president of the most powerful nation on Earth. Ending her life for being rebellious or stubborn would be carried out in the blink of an eye. This man, whoever he was, pretended to be a gentleman, but she was not confused as to the reality of her situation. Her safety was only as good as the information he desired.

He took on the role of kind stranger. Tessa allowed Amon to help her sit down in a wobbly folding chair. She cringed at the coolness of the metal when it touched the back of her exposed legs. Sucking in her breath caused the Egyptian to call to someone. He smiled at her as a Middle Eastern man appeared with a ripped beach towel, sporting the picture of a cartoon character. Nodding to her without making eye contact, he extended the gift to her. Her eyes went to Amon.

"It is all right, Mrs. Scott." He removed Chase's wet jacket, replacing it with the towel. Wrapping it around Tessa's shoulders, his hands felt as if they lingered a little too long before he lifted her rope-like hair over the top. "We mean you no harm."

With the grace of having refreshments at an upscale tea room in London, Amon handed her a chipped cup of coffee. She held it between her fingers, loving the way the warmth began to spread through her hands. Never sure whether she really liked coffee or the way it made her feel externally, had always been a point to ponder when she'd been in college. Now it had become such a habit that Tessa always held the cup until the brew cooled too much to drink. Staring down into the black liquid she wondered if it was safe to drink.

As if reading her mind he spoke. "I used bottled water to brew the coffee." He pulled out a chair to sit across from her. Their knees touched. "It has been cooking for over an hour, maybe longer. I'm afraid it may be too strong. In my part of the world we like our tea and coffee very strong. I find that Americans like their coffee full of sugar and milk. Do you think that also reflects the American lifestyle, Mrs. Scott?" She continued to stare down into the liquid as her shivering stopped.

Amon remained quiet for a few minutes, waiting for Tessa to sip the coffee. When the cup began to tremble he removed it from her fingers. "I'll put this over here until you're ready. Feeling better?"

Seduced by his calm, reassuring voice Tessa lifted her eyes to meet his, but lowered them again to stare at her hands.

"Yes. Thank you." Her voice sounded small even to her. The storm started slamming against the upper windows, rattling the threat of violence if any attempt at escape occurred.

"Now, Mrs. Scott," Amon spoke with a voice turned toward seriousness. When Tessa jerked her head up to meet his eyes, he paused before continuing. "Your blue eyes are startling. Has anyone ever told you that, Mrs. Scott?" Silence. He smiled before pulling his chair closer. "They remind me of the desert sky along the Nile River."

"So you're Egyptian," she whispered.

"I never said that." His English accent was perfect. "I merely compared you to a place I've been many times. Now we must talk. The one who brought you here is a very bad man." He pointed to her wrist. "I realize that must sound rather redundant at this point. However, he was sent to finish a job tonight that your uncle failed to complete."

Tessa squeezed her hands together to keep from gripping the side of the chair in frustration. "Where is he?"

"Not to worry. He is being cared for and you will see him soon. But I need some information first, Mrs. Scott." Amon eyed her to check the level of cooperation. "Did the president die of his injuries this evening?"

Tessa shook her head. "He was alive when they helicoptered him to the hospital. His wounds were very serious. He lost a lot of blood."

"I see. And what of the vice president, Mrs. Scott? Is he dead?"

"They kept talking about an explosion on his boat. I wasn't even supposed to be listening. They treated me like it was my fault the president got shot." Her eyes watered, but she refused to cry.

"Because of your uncle?"

She nodded as her eyes began that nervous batting that revealed way too much about her temperament. "I tried to stop him. It wasn't his fault he couldn't go through with the assassination. Please don't hurt him. He's a good man, a brave man. All he wants is to get his Liberty friends and be left in peace."

"Yes, well I'm afraid that is going to be difficult." He patted her knee with a smooth hand like a patient father only to have her jerk away from his touch. With his hand suspended in midair, he smiled at the response. "I apologize. I should not have touched you. You are lovely and I..." He stood then walked to the coffeemaker before emptying the grounds into the trash that once had been a five-gallon popcorn can. "And what of the Israeli prime minister? Was he injured in the assassination attempt?"

Tessa dropped her eyes to her hands. "I watched him fall as your thug and I escaped. I don't know if he was hurt. We only had firecrackers." She tried to look sideways to examine her surroundings.

Amon smiled. "That probably is a good thing. We wouldn't want Israel to get the wrong idea about all of this."

"I want to see my uncle." Tessa raised her head and forced her voice to sound strong.

"Did the prime minister say anything about who might be behind this terrible attempt on your president's life?"

"I want to see my uncle now," Tessa's voice gained more strength.

"Answer my question, Mrs. Scott and then we'll see about your uncle."

"The prime minister said someone at the Egyptian Embassy was feeding him information."

"Interesting. Did he say who?"

"No. Just that he thought he'd been lied to and wasn't very happy about it." Tessa stood with the grace of a baby learning to stand. Her tail bone hurt where Sam had thrown her to the floor and she still felt weak from giving blood to the president. But she wasn't going to give that bit of information away.

"I see." Amon appeared to weigh the information. "Are you working for the government, Mrs. Scott?"

Tessa snorted a hateful reply. "Of course, I am. Between teaching school, three kids and a husband who is rarely home to help out; I do a little undercover work for the president. I get a little bored if I don't keep busy. The extra money comes in handy for the jacked up gas prices. Oh, by the way, thanks for all the crap going on in Egypt and everywhere else in the Middle East so Americans can just keep paying those high fuel bills. I can't tell you how that has impacted our way of life. Great move on your part."

"Did you know that when you are angry your eyes turn a kind of violet color? You are quite enchanting, Mrs. Scott. Most American women I've met have not impressed me." Standing, he took a step toward her. She stepped behind the chair to form a barrier. "Why is it that you are not intimidated by me?"

"I'm a junior high teacher in a public school. Not much scares me." Her retort sounded flippant and disrespectful considering she was lying. "Take me to my uncle or I'm leaving."

Amon burst out laughing and motioned for her to follow him. "Since I cannot allow a beautiful and courageous woman to exit into such dangerous weather, I will grant your request."

Following, she eyed every dim space along the way. Quiet voices of men came from the room where her captor disappeared. Another room held men in western style clothing, but were obviously Middle Eastern by the language they spoke. Deciding she was being led to a more confined space, the thought arose that this new captor had others ideas about how to make her submit. Inwardly, she trembled, and knew that her resurging strength would not last long if he attacked her.

Surprised when he stopped and unlocked a metal door, she watched as he pushed it open for her to enter. "We will talk again later. I will have someone bring a fresh pot of tea since the coffee did not please you."

Tessa eased by him and backed into the room, never taking her eyes from his. The closing of the door sounded terrifying. She almost called out to him when a voice forced her to whirl around.

"Tessa? Is that you?"

Recognizing the voice, she choked out his name. "Uncle Jake?" The next thing she knew the man of her childhood was holding her in his arms, his tears mixing with her own.

~~~

The storm roared to life again as Enigma agents discussed a rescue of Tessa. The flashlights dimmed and the candles flickered out one by one. The humid heat in the corridor and kitchen formed beads of sweat on brows that dripped into eyes and down necks. Voices were low and intense.

Even Samantha Cordova, usually calm and collected, looked pensive. Zoric listened with bowed head and offered no comment. The veins pulsing on his neck spoke volumes. Although he struggled to concentrate, Carter listened, careful to keep a vigilant eye on Chase. He might need to be the cool head in the storm brewing inside the man he respected.

Unaware that the edge of calmness in his voice mimicked the eye of a hurricane, Chase asked questions about the new information Director Clark obtained from his brother concerning the Egyptians. His body, stiff and tall, looked to be at attention except for his hand that held a melting ice pack against his nose.

"Zoric did any new information come out of those two Sam and I shot?" Chase switched the ice to the other eye to see his agent better.

The Serbian shook his head as he snarled. "They weren't giving anything up, and to be honest, I wasn't allowed to be persuasive. Those FBI guys were in the way."

The director narrowed his eyes. "I'll take care of them if you want another crack at them." Ben was reminded once again when a smile spread across the Serbian's face, that in another life, blood would be dripping from his agent's exposed fangs. "Very well. Let's do it. Any volunteers to assist?"

Sam started for the door. "I will."

Chase stopped her. "My job. This won't take long. Get what and who we need to head out when the storm lets up." He locked eyes with her. "This isn't your fault, Sam. We both know that Tessa attracts trouble like a heat seeking missile." With a disgusted sigh he continued. "I'm not sure bringing her into Enigma is the right thing. I know we talked about this but…"

"I have a few suggestions as what to do with her." Sam's voice edged with hatred as she turned away to follow his orders.

The two FBI agents shifted their weight as the Enigma men approached. They only thing they really knew about Enigma were inflamed descriptions of how they approached interrogations. Both men waited outside the prisoner holding area until Director Clark lured the FBI agents into following him to help with another task. They appeared to be aware of the power the director possessed. It was common knowledge he not only was the brother of the Prime Minister of Israel, but the ear and confidence of the president.

~~~

Chase stared straight ahead, careful not to make eye contact with the FBI. Besides, his thoughts tumbled toward Tessa. The person who took her may have already disposed of her body. A loud swallow, followed by an intake of breath formed when the image of her lying in some rain swollen street, injured or dead, came to his mind eye. A fire of rage flamed deep inside him.

She was an innocent, an example of why he did the job that others could not. He promised her protection and knew he'd failed, just like he'd failed to protect his sister so long ago. Why did the ones that touched him so deeply have to die?

Dear God, if you're there, let me save her, he prayed for the first time in years.

CHAPTER 27

Amon joined Speaker Gault and his hired man in what had become the coffee room. Rain dripped in the corner onto an overturned metal bucket. The soft ping was rhythmic and peaceful compared to the howling wind outside. Windows at the top of the room rattled. The Egyptian wondered if they would shatter and rain down upon them. The speaker appeared not to notice. It occurred to him that this politician considered the weather his to control, not fear.

"What did the woman have to say, Amon?" The speaker frowned at the coffee in his Styrofoam cup before sitting it down on the soiled make-shift table.

"The president was barely alive when he was taken to the hospital." Amon's eyes fell on a cockroach making its way toward the abandoned coffee cup. He hoped it would seek refuge inside before the speaker lifted it to his narrow lips for a final sip. "Rumors on the radio are that he is already gone." He shrugged while continuing to lie. "Vice President McCall has been confirmed dead."

The speaker's wide smile, followed by a hand through his tinted hair, caused him to square his shoulders. "Excellent." He faked a pouty frown. "I mean. Dear God in Heaven. What will we do now that our fearless leader is gone?" He eyed Amon's guarded expression. "Change of heart, Amon? Those old guys in there get to you?" A sneer appeared. "Perhaps you're feeling a little protective of our new prisoner. My friend here," he nodded toward the brute who managed to escape with Tessa, "tells me you were quite hospitable when she arrived."

Amon's eyebrow arched in contempt.

"You do understand they all have to die?" The speaker's voice grew slow and deliberate.

"And what of us, Mr. Speaker?" Amon's snarl of disapproval continued. "Now that you're down to one man, how are you going to manage to eliminate the rest of us?" The smirk thinned on the speaker's face. "My seven to your one. Not very good odds."

The speaker looked over at his thug for reassurance. Satisfied that the mercenary could barely contain his rage, knowing two of his buddies were ordered killed by Amon, the politician continued. "I need you, Amon. Killing you was never part of the plan. Remember you are the one who will rescue and return me to the FBI so I can begin my transition to rule."

"You mean govern, don't you, Mr. Speaker?"

A sarcastic chuckle escaped the speaker's lips along with the rehearsed speech. "You got a tip about my whereabouts. Egypt will be praised for their assistance in saving me. Together we will mourn the deaths of our beloved president and his inept vice president."

"And you will not forget Egypt when it comes time to continue your financial support?"

"We've been over this before." He waved a dismissive hand as he reached for the cup of coffee. "Jake Wakefield will be blamed for his interference. From what you've already told me the Israelis entertained him last night shortly after your men ended up missing. The connection now is solid. They were behind the attack. Since we sent in my people to *assist* Wakefield in accomplishing this, no Egyptian can be connected. They're all dead now so the trail is clean." His eyes darted to the one remaining hired gun standing in the room. "You, of course, will receive the entire fee for your continued silence and cooperation."

"Fine with me," the thug added. "Give me my money and I'm headed for Mexico."

The speaker had already informed his last man of the account in Mexico City. It would be a simple procedure to access the money. Mexico was full of independent contractors if his mercenary turned into a liability later on.

"And, yes," the speaker looked smugly at the Egyptian. "Your country will receive the grateful financial support of the United States. Take the money and continue killing each other for all I care."

"My country is in transition. Do not mock us."

"I wouldn't think of it, Amon. With a little prodding from me you'll also get the Israeli money. Americans will turn on them once their involvement is established. It's good for you and good for me." The speaker took a deep breath as if he tired of the whole topic.

Amon nodded, still skeptical of the speaker's trustworthiness. "Would you like to return to the Liberty crew to fill their heads with more of your dribble?"

"I suppose. Maybe Mrs. Scott will be more forthcoming with me than you. Don't wait too long. It's getting a little crowded in there. Do you think you could bring in a few more chairs? Someone is always standing. Now that the woman is there, I'll be expected to surrender any chance at resting. Those old goats are probably tripping over themselves for her."

"As you wish, Mr. Speaker." He took his foot and shoved a chair at him. "Carry this one. We wouldn't want them to know your true colors are far from red, white and blue."

~~~

Tessa felt warm in spite of the damp clothes. Seeing her uncle safe and sound went a long way at raising her spirits. The men who served on the USS Liberty in 1967 now stood before her with concern etched on their lined faces. Each introduced himself as if in roll call before an admiral. She shook each extended hand and let her uncle explain where he was on the ship the day it was attacked by Israel. Two of the men cracked a joke about her uncle being just a pretty Marine stuck on board to be the eye candy.

Tessa knew better. Her uncle had been on board because he spoke Russian, Hebrew and a little Arabic. He had been slotted to return to Germany after serving at a listening post in Iceland for six months. To make sure the Russians weren't getting involved in the Middle East, Jake ended up in the thick of it. All the other interpreters were unavailable or already on their way home.

"It is such an honor to finally meet all of you." Her hand unconsciously lay across her heart.

She asked about their well-being and was assured the Egyptian took good care of them. Although they didn't trust him, his concern for them appeared to be genuine. He'd even secured their luggage so any medication schedule could be easily maintained. The food had been greasy and cold but palatable. Several cots were set up for the men to take turns using as beds while the rest sat at the table. Mostly they were bored.

They caught her up to speed about the Speaker of the House being held prisoner and appeared to have been roughed up.

Tessa saw the look of skepticism cross her uncle's face. "What are you thinking?"

"Why rough up your most valuable hostage? How did he know who I was? I never told him and no one sure as hell told him in this room. The speaker said he heard those Egyptians say the president wasn't going to make it too."

"He might not." She looked bewildered.

"Those Egyptians can understand English better than they speak it. When they talk to each other you can bet it's not in any language the speaker can understand. Somebody is talking to him. My bet is on our smooth talker who made you coffee." Jake pulled out a chair for his niece and tucked the towel tightly around her shoulders. "We can't trust the speaker."

"We've got to protect him, Uncle Jake. If the VP is dead and the president dies he's the next president. No one knows where the speaker is. They already think the worst. Someone took out one of his bodyguards."

"We've got to get out of here," Jake tried to sound confident. "We'll take him with us."

Just then the door opened and the speaker was shoved in so violently he stumbled across the floor, only to fall against the table. A chair was tossed in after him before the door slammed shut with the sound of a bolt being thrown.

The speaker's breath grew labored as he tried to speak. "They're a bunch of murderous savages." His eyes turned to Tessa who stared back with terror. "Are you all right?" He moved with great effort to her side before laying a hand on her shoulder. As she flinched away, he appeared to be offended at her rebuff. "Did they hurt you?"

Tessa shook her head.

The speaker began peppering her with questions about who she was and how she came to be a hostage. His concern made Tessa a little less leery of his possible involvement. The room began to spin when she tried to stand. With quick action, Jake caught his niece and guided her to one of the cots. "You better lie down, Tessie. You've lost a lot of blood."

"Blood?" The speaker watched as the old Marine lowered her onto the bare army cot. "She's bleeding? I thought he didn't hurt her?"

"She gave the president a transfusion. Hopefully it was enough to save his life." Jake removed the towel. Goosebumps immediately appeared across her pale shoulders. One of the other crew members took off his windbreaker and tossed it to Jake for his niece.

A dark cloud appeared to have crossed the speaker's face. "A transfusion?"

"My niece is a universal donor."

"But," the speaker's voice cracked with irritation. "That man just told me he was dead."

Tessa burst into tears as she covered her face. "No. It can't be. He was doing better when he reached the hospital." Jake tried to get her to lie down. "Something must have gone wrong."

"Tessa, calm down. You're getting yourself all worked up. They're probably just trying to scare the speaker."

The speaker frowned at the possibility. "Indeed," he whispered. "I'm going to have to negotiate our way out of here."

Tessa started to lie down then jerked back up. "No. I may have already done that." She grabbed her uncle's hand and smiled before looking at the others. "They can find us."

The speaker straightened as did the other crewmen.

"Good lord, how?" One of the crewmen clapped his hand against his upper thigh smiling as he moved closer.

"My phone. I had it in the pocket of that wet suit jacket I carried in. It fell out during the trip here. I tried to turn it on. I thought I had when that troglodyte dragged me out of the car. If I turned it on then they're tracking me. There wasn't much battery life left so I don't know how much information they'll be able to get. But if I know our tech guy he'll find me. All of us." The tears were gone now as she jumped to unsteady feet.

Jake slipped his arm around her and kissed her on the temple. His eyes went to the speaker who was a contrast to the happy faces of the Liberty crew. The scowl across his pinched face and pooched lips made him look almost cartoon-like.

"Problem, Mr. Speaker?" Jake asked, noting how the politician backed toward the door.

"You just had to butt in didn't you, Mrs. Scott?"

Confused, Tessa looked up at her uncle's face that had gone stone cold. "Excuse me?"

"Now I'm going to have to make sure none of you make it out of here alive." The speaker used his fist to bang on the door that immediately opened. Two Egyptians and the man who'd taken Tessa loomed in the doorway. "I appreciate your sacrifice of saving me. I'll make sure all of you become heroes to the American public."

Jake jerked his chin up and gritted his teeth as his friends stood at attention to the best of their ability. "We've been heroes since June 8, 1967. Something you'll never understand or could ever be."

"Humph. Being a hero is for saps, Mr. Wakefield." The speaker exited the room. The slam of the door echoed like thunder.

~~~

The Enigma Team jammed into one of the SUVs belonging to the Secret Service. It accommodated the five of them easily. The two soldiers assigned to babysit Tessa's friends had passed them off to Dr. Ervin and climbed in the back of the SUV to add support. Director Clark rode in another vehicle with the two FBI agents he'd tricked into leaving their prisoners alone with Zoric. Several Secret Service agents, who could still handle their weapons, were also in attendance.

Reinforcements were spread a little thin on a night like this. Jake Wakefield and the rest of the crew of the Liberty were not, nor had they ever been, a priority. The search for the Speaker of the House now took on a new level of importance considering there had been an assassination attempt on both the president and vice president. Every able-bodied agent from multiple departments was on the job to find the speaker alive.

Enigma wanted something different. They wanted revenge. The other men who joined them were willing to help because they had failed at protecting the president. They weren't in the best of shape having suffered injuries during the first attack. A promise of retribution stoked the fires of revenge as they headed out into the hours before dawn. If they could find Tessa, and maybe even Jake Wakefield, a grateful president might just forgive their shortcomings.

"Talk to me, Vernon." Chase spoke with a calm that others sometimes thought unnerving. He was the calm before the storm. Speaking into cyber space to his tech genius, he remained focused. "Anything?"

"I'd say you're less than a mile away now. The signal died there. I'll send you the coordinates."

"Then she could be anywhere from that point."

The storm dumped an enormous amount of water onto the streets. Some places were impassable, making the two vehicles move about like roller coaster cars. One of the men in the very back of the car complained of car sickness. Chase met the soldier's eyes with a glare into the rear view mirror. The silence that followed indicated he'd been appropriately reprimanded and would keep further comments concerning his stomach to himself.

"You're right there, Boss." Vernon's voice snapped.

Chase put his finger to his ear as if by doing so would lower the volume. "I see nothing, Vern."

"The signal is old. Maybe it died before it stopped for good. What do you see?"

"I'm at a stoplight. Flashing."

"Already tried pulling up traffic cams. The only ones working are the ones near the White House and Capitol Hill. Can't help you there." Chase knew Vernon liked Tessa. She was one of the few females who managed to loosen his shy tongue. "Poor Mrs. Scott. She's probably one scared lady. Wonder how she managed to get her phone out?"

Chase knew the young techie was thinking out loud. "Probably slipped it in my suit coat I loaned her."

"Suit coat?" Vernon's voice had taken on a slow interested

tone then silence. Chase knew better than to ask why. When the tech took on the air of cyber god, he had learned to just stand back and be amazed. "I think I might just have found her, Boss."

"Vernon, if you have, I'm promoting you to my new best friend."

"Good." It was Carter Johnson. "Because I'm tired of the job."

Zoric turned his eyes back at the ex-astronaut in the backseat. "Second fiddle would be a promotion for you, Carter." He winked at Sam who wore a sour expression.

"Let's have it, Vern. It'll be light soon. They may try to move before then."

"The suit you wore tonight, was it the one designed for special occasions for you to wear with the president or other dignitaries?" His voice sounded almost robotic as the faint click of computer keys provided background noise. Before Chase could verify, Vernon gave him more news. "Your suit coat has an optic thread in the lapel so that if ever you're taken hostage, lost, or…"

"I know what it's for, Vernon. I just didn't know it was in that suit. Just tell me where she is." He didn't want to sound impatient. Vernon loved showing how much smarter he was than everyone else, but time was of the essence.

"Right. Turn at the next corner, go three blocks. Looks like it might be a warehouse or passed-its-prime area of old businesses. I'll see what else I can find out. Be careful. Not in the best neighborhood."

"Who the hell is going to be out on a night like this?" Chase growled.

The trip took longer than expected due to flooded streets and debris blocking their way. By the time the SUVs neared the expected target, thirty more minutes passed.

They pulled to a curb and killed their lights. Surrounded by dilapidated buildings, the team waited and watched before pulling into a parking lot. Several dumpsters overflowing with discarded construction materials provided cover for the vehicles as they waited.

Leaving their cars could jeopardize the team's safety. They didn't know what they were up against. Chase wasn't about to lose any Enigma members. It occurred to him that if he hadn't involved Tessa again, she wouldn't be in this trouble. Any other time he would have justified the danger he'd put his people in by saying it was for the good of the country. Now that didn't ring so true for him.

What was it about the woman that caused him to second guess everything he knew to be solid and predictable? His life was complicated enough without the accident-prone housewife mucking up the already turbulent waters of national security. Was this some kind of sick joke God chose to play on him?

"Vern, can you zero in on an exact location?"

A moment of silence passed before Chase's ear piece crackled to life. "Looks like you're on top of it, Boss."

Chase wanted to get a closer look, but at what? Everything looked the same. No strange cars parked about. No people. No visible lights.

A sudden flash of lightning flickered twice revealing another dumpster across the street. Sitting between it and the wall of the building was a car.

"There." It was Zoric.

"I see it." Chase unbuckled his seatbelt.

The sounds of making ready took on an ominous feel. He spoke only a couple of words to prepare the second car. In five minutes they edged out of their SUV.

Wind and rain now was not much more than a summer storm. Occasional flashes of lightning hinted more pockets of intense downpours could occur any minute, driving the Enigma team and the security force to take positions across the street. They tensed when a light appeared in a small window near the front door.

The door of the old cinder block building swung open, letting a pool of light spill out momentarily, and then disappeared as the door shoved closed. The team watched as a man rushed to the car by the dumpster. He hunched over and pulled his collar up close to his neck as if doing so would keep him dry. As his hand touched the car door handle an arm circled his neck like a vice. Jerked back into the recesses of darkness in the ally, he struggled to free himself. The sound of someone else getting into the car and the smashing of the overhead light drove him to try and twist free. He stopped fidgeting when a large man jammed a pistol in his gut.

"How many inside?" Chase pushed his face within inches of the man who stood a head shorter than him. He mumbled something shaking his head. This time he repeated the question in Egyptian Arabic. One of the Secret Service men had easily subdued the Egyptian around the neck and now rammed a knee in his buttocks. Before a yelp could escape Chase covered his mouth with his hand. At the same time he freed him, Chase slammed him against the wall of the building.

Zoric came alongside of Chase and held out the phone. "Coming to get this?" The man's eyes widened and tried squirming again. The switch blade Zoric always carried came out and opened with swift intent in front of the Egyptian's face. "How many?" He didn't bother to speak in Arabic.

When he tried to kick Chase and push free, Zoric sliced his ear. His scream dissipated in the rumble of thunder as the Serbian landed a blow upside his head. The final move was jabbing the point of his knife on the edge of the Egyptian's throat, paralyzing him with fear.

The captain stepped forward again and leaned in. "How many?" This time the Egyptian acknowledged the Arabic and held up nine fingers before speaking. "Give us the lay out?"

The Egyptian nodded which caused Zoric to withdraw his knife. But just as he did the man spit in Zoric's face and tried to knee him in the crotch. Chase landed a blow to the man's jaw, dropping him to the ground.

"Do it." Chase looked at Zoric then motioned for the others to come with him to wait.

Director Benjamin Clark frowned as he shook his head. "I'm staying. Get these Feds away from here so they won't have to cover anything up."

One Secret Service man spit on the ground. "Carve him into a jack-o-lantern for all I care, Zoric. I didn't see a thing."

The FBI agent was a little more squeamish and moved ahead of Chase. "This is illegal, you know that, right?"

Chase sniffed at the agent's distaste for the truth in this matter. "That's kinda what we do, Agent Martin." Chase moved toward the door in case it reopened with another Egyptian. "If you don't want to get your hands dirty, now is the time to go back to the car."

The agent came in behind Chase as he thought he heard a desperate scream behind him. "Just don't like the sight of blood, that's all. After tonight I want you guys to fade back into the shadows where you belong. Your ghoul back there takes too much delight in his job."

Turning his head slightly to look at the FBI agent, Chase grinned. "He's good at what he does. He got those guys back at the hotel to roll in two minutes. You'd been screwin' with them for several hours with nothing."

The agent took a deep breath. "Like I said, when this is over stay away from the FBI."

He wasn't sure if he should tell the agent, but now that he'd assisted in this rescue, Director Clark would not hesitate to blackmail him into being an inside source. The director was shameless like that. The two Secret Service Agents would be brought in too.

Zoric and the director joined them. "Good news. The speaker is in there. Nine people, if you count the speaker." He wiped his knife on his arm before folding it closed and inserting it back into a pocket.

"We need to proceed with caution, Chase." It was the director. "We can't risk the speaker's life."

"What about other hostages?" Chase watched the door for danger.

Zoric checked his gun. "He said a bunch of old men and a woman."

"Sam and Carter took the other agents to check the back." The director nodded to the darkness. "Cooper and Montgomery are going to cover us when we go in. They'll catch anyone who tries to leave. Said they owe Mrs. Scott."

The sky opened up and torrents of rain washed over them. "Did he give the layout of the building?"

The director frowned at Zoric. "He wasn't able to speak by the time I asked that question."

Chase's eyes shifted to his partner.

With a shrug Zoric smiled, almost with glee. "My hand slipped. Sorry."

He nodded toward the door. "Let's do this."

CHAPTER 28

If needed, silencers would muffle the first sounds of gunfire when they went through the door. Discovering an empty room with one overhead light flickering toward failure, Chase quickly took it out. Luck was on their side. Just as the bulb crashed, lightning rattled the windows, followed by a long rolling rumble of thunder.

Wondering in that split second if Tessa was praying again, made him question his lack of faith. She believed God protected her at every turn. It irritated him to think she just might be right in thinking such nonsense. He'd given that up long ago when his parents died in China trying to save the masses. Where was God when they needed them? How about his sister when she died all alone from a drug overdose? What about the men he watched perish in Afghanistan? Didn't God listen to them cry out?

The image of Tessa sitting in some room with a gag shoved in her mouth made him want to grin. He would save her this time, realizing she'd probably say: "Well, it's about time. I thought I was going to have to do this all by myself."

Either way, he knew she would be scared. That part of her would never change. Never exposed to the terror of the world until they met, forced her into a dangerous pact with Enigma a year earlier. As she evolved into an extraordinary woman, Chase grew smitten with her spunk and tenacity. That's all he thought it was until she disappeared from his life. That familiar pain in his chest returned as soon as he laid eyes on her several days ago. Maybe if he just...

"Something's not right, Chase." He recognized Sam's soft whisper in his earwig. "The backdoor is ajar and there's a lot of nervous activity going on inside. Advise."

"We're inside. I can hear the ruckus. Count to ten and proceed with caution."

Enigma spread out toward the corridor where men moved back and forth between rooms. They appeared to be dragging out men, bound and struggling to stay standing on unsteady feet. The captors hurried while yelling at their prisoners who tried to jerk away, only to be slapped or shoved into a wall.

One of the prisoners fell to the floor and looked up, making eye contact with Chase who nodded a sign of "everything was about to explode into action." When the jailor reached down to grab the USS Liberty survivor by the collar, the American turned his head and bit the captor's hand as hard as his jaw would allow. Just as he yelled out and started to drop his other fist on the old sailor, Chase pulled the trigger, sending him back two steps then down.

Other Egyptians poured out into the corridor, some using a hostage as their shield. Before they could get any shots off they were either shot from behind by Sam and Carter's team or by Chase's. Three threw up their hands in surrender yelling for mercy. The smell of gunpowder hung in the air. A series of coughs from the hostages broke the sudden silence as Enigma started checking the wounded.

"Who are you?" coughed one of the hostages as he staggered forward and stuck out his hand.

Chase switched his Glock to his other hand and grabbed the old man's and smiled at the vice-like grip. "Secret Service and FBI, Sir."

No point in telling him about Enigma. They never took credit for anything connected to national security. Living in the shadows gave them certain autonomy; no questions asked and no restrictions on solutions.

The other men slowly pulled themselves together and pushed toward Chase.

"The Speaker of the House. Is he still here?" Chase scanned the area.

Carter moved up behind the old warriors and shook his head

that he hadn't seen the speaker.

Another man nodded to Chase. "He's gone. Took Jake Wakefield and his niece too."

"Who did?" Chase felt Director Clark at his elbow.

"Another one of them." He pointed at the wounded captors. "Except that Amon fella took pains to make us comfortable."

"Oh, shut up, Mel!" It was Mike Strafford. "He was in charge. He left us here at the mercy of these guys. They were just about to kill us."

Zoric came out of one of the rooms. "They were packing up, my friend. Looks like they were getting ready to burn the place down. Gasoline all over the floor. A few packed boxes of supplies. Guess they didn't want it to look like anyone had been staying here."

"Do you know who this Amon in charge was?" Chase looked back at the old warriors.

"No. But he was a heck of a lot nicer than the speaker. That guy is a snake."

"What do you mean?" Chase didn't like where this new information was headed.

"He was in on it."

They all took turns telling their small bits of information which started to piece together like a puzzle.

"Do you have any idea where they took Jake and Mrs. Scott?" It was the director.

"No. But by the time they left, we thought the Egyptian in charge was trying to make a call to someone he claimed would give them sanctuary."

The feeling of doom fell over the director as he remembered the prime minister's phone ringing periodically. His brother would look at the caller I.D. then ignore. Was his brother telling him the truth about not being involved? "Did he say who?"

"Sorry."

Chase touched his ear as Montgomery began to speak. "Saw some activity a few minutes ago. A car pulled out from another garage about 60 meters west. Cooper and I took one of the cars and followed, lights off. Stopped at another building. Looks like maybe three. Advise."

"Get a closer look. Speaker Jim Gault may be a hostage."

"Sir, it didn't look to me like anybody was being held against their will."

Chase paused with a sense of bewilderment. Three. That meant the possibility that Jake and Tessa had been moved somewhere else or they were still here, or maybe dead.

"Captain, this place is wired to blow. Plastic explosives up high on the beams. See." Sam pointed up. "We can't reach them in time. The building comes down, the gas burns and all that is left will be vapors. Probably be detonated by a cell phone."

"Get everyone out except the Egyptians. Bring them to me."

She nodded and disappeared.

Sam shoved one of the Egyptians toward Chase as the others began filing out the building.

"Thanks, Sam. Now get the hell out of here." Chase eyed the Egyptians with a stern frown.

"I'd like to stay, Captain." Sam's eyes turned on the Egyptians who made the mistake of eyeing her with lust. Her next words were in Egyptian Arabic. "I would like to tie these dogs to a pillar before it blows."

Chase raised his chin in stubbornness without taking his eyes from the nervous men before him. "Very well." He too, spoke in their language. "Any gas left in those cans?"

"Nearly 4 liters."

He smiled satanically. "Pour it over their miserable heads."

Director Clark walked up and clasped his team leader on the shoulder. "Hurry it up. We don't know how much time we have."

"We have more time than these girls." Chase watched Sam throw gas on the Egyptians. They tried to back away until he lifted his gun.

"I wouldn't start moving around. My gun might go off and spark a bar-b-que."

They stopped fidgeting.

"The old man and the woman. Where are they?" Chase felt the director pull away and move with the FBI to escort the Liberty crew toward safety. Carter hung back and Zoric held an Uzi at the Egyptians' backs.

Nothing.

Chase nodded at Sam who threw the gas can off to the side. She walked to an abandoned tool bench and lifted a butane torch.

The self-igniter needed to be connected to the end and Sam made it a point to attach it with a slow, methodical style as she smiled wickedly over at the Egyptians. With little effort, she had a flame going in seconds before moving like a tiger stalking its prey.

"Where did they take the woman?" Chase felt almost amused as the men stared at the flame Sam carried like a bouquet of flowers. "You've got five seconds or you're left here to roast."

"Where is your humanity?" One of the men was visibly shaken.

Chase shook his head as his lips thinned. "Not one of my strong suits. The woman. Then I'll get you out of here. One. Two. Three. Four."

The Egyptians all started talking at once. Two were begging so loudly tears ran down their face.

"Five."

One of the men jumped forward. "There's a room below. We took them there. They would be buried and forgotten soon enough."

"If you're lying to me I will kill all your family and make you watch. Then I will lock your worthless ass in a cell with a film rolling for eternity how I killed them. Do you understand?" The man nodded his head so fast Chase thought it might pop off. "Is he telling the truth?" The others also agreed. "Take them out. This one goes with me."

"Yes. Yes. I show you. Then we leave."

Sam pointed the flaming torch toward freedom as the two remaining men awkwardly skittered toward the door Carter swung open and held against the wind. Just as they started through Carter stepped back. The wind caught the door and slammed it into the Egyptians, knocking them to the ground. They crab-crawled away as Sam leaned over them with narrowed eyes.

"Have I told you today how sexy you are with a blow torch in your hand?" Carter put his shoulder into the door and opened it again. "Something about a woman and fire."

Sam gritted her teeth as the two Egyptians cautiously stood. "You really know how to turn a girl's head." Her bark could be heard above the dying wind. "I almost set them on fire you idiot." The gas covered men were now shaking in terror as a returning FBI agent motioned them to follow him.

Carter smiled at his partner. "I love it when you get excited. You know we could be making our own fire every day of the week." The door closed behind them as they entered the darkness. "You're not fooling me with the hard to get routine."

She whirled around as the light of the torch went out. He crashed into her chest. "I am never going to be with you, Carter, so shut the hell up."

"Guess you prefer the older guys." Carter's face was close enough for Sam to read the sour expression. "Since Tessa may join us from time to time you'll have to abandon your Chase Hunter quest."

Shoving against Carter's chest didn't move him, only caused his smirk to reappear. "But hey. That's good for me."

Storming off into the dark, she tried to catch up with the FBI agent who took her prisoners.

Carter turned back to go inside. He wasn't going to leave Chase and Zoric on their own if they needed an extra pair of hands.

~~~

Chase headed toward the end of the room where trucks once parked for service. Now it was empty except for a flatbed truck used in parades. The floor, smeared with a wet mixture of oil spills, rain and now gasoline, felt slippery.

The hostage got a shove if he slowed. Zoric brought up the rear.

Holding his hand out for Carter to stop at the door, Chase wanted someone to be at the top of the stairs to escort them to safety if things went sideways. He nodded and held up a flashlight as he propped the door open.

"Down there." It was the Egyptian. "Now can I go?" Zoric jammed his Uzi into the man's kidney. A groan of pain echoed down the steps. A shove started him forward into the darkness.

Chase pulled a small flashlight from the FBI jacket he'd secured from the car. The beam was dim but when shaken, offered enough light to allow safe passage. The smell of dampness and gasoline assaulted their noses as they reached the bottom of the steps.

A sound in the corner drew their attention. The beam of light jerked in that direction. Bound and gagged on the floor, lay Jake. His eyes were wide open until the light forced them shut. He squirmed violently as if that would somehow make a difference. They did not rush to assist.

No sign of Tessa. The first thought in Chase's head was his prisoner lied.

The Egyptian shivered at the cold and nodded for them to move forward as his eyes started to scan the recesses of darkness. The moment Chase wondered why his prisoner appeared uneasy; the sound of someone else in the room caught his attention.

In the instant they stepped forward, their feet hit something slick. The Egyptian prisoner fell face down at Zoric's feet, tripping him up so that he staggered toward the bound man on the floor.

"Tess…" Before Chase could finish her name a large metal container smashed into his face causing his flashlight to fly into the air. He staggered backwards as someone shined the light into his bruised and battered face. "Damn it! Get that out of my face!" He demanded knowing that Tessa had taken his light.

In the next second he felt arms around him in a grateful embrace. Chase didn't have time to savor the feeling of her hair beneath his chin or the heaving of her breasts against his body. With one hand he touched his ear wig and with the other he managed to encircle the woman that continued to excite and mystify him.

"Got'em. On our way."

Tessa released him and ran back to her uncle who Zoric managed to free with his knife. The Egyptian prisoner started up the steps at a run when Chase reached him in two steps and grabbed his ankle with a jerk. He fell down against the step with a thud.

"Not so fast." Chase pulled him back down the steps on his stomach. The hostage tried to grasp at anything to stop the pain as he was dragged down to the floor. "I'm not finished with you."

Zoric helped Jake stand, but knew right away, that something was wrong.

"I think I got a couple of busted ribs, boys." Jake sounded almost nonchalant. "I'm pretty sure they broke my arm." He nodded at Tessa. "They were getting a little rough with her. I wasn't going to stand for it." She put her arm around him to assist with his walking.

"Oh, Uncle Jake. They could've killed you."

Zoric slung his Uzi and helped Tessa with Jake's weight.

Chase grabbed the prisoner by the collar and jerked him to his feet, although he slipped in the solution Tessa had spilled on the floor. He finally managed to stand and tried not to look at Jake.

"That's the fella that wanted to take advantage of Tessa." Jake spit out the words as he tried unsuccessfully to lunge forward only to be held back by Zoric and Tessa.

Chase tensed as he shook the prisoner then kicked him in the butt so hard he sprawled head first into the wall.

With a groan he turned around and faced the light shining in his face.

"What did he do, Tessa?" When she didn't answer, Chase's eyes shifted to her with such deadly intent, she shuddered with fear. "Tessa," he demanded.

"He tried to touch me. When I kicked him..."

"He knocked her down." Jake tried to pull free only to be pulled back by Zoric.

"Let's go. Those explosives are wired to blow by remote." Chase nodded toward the stairs. The prisoner pushed off the wall and stepped forward. "Not you."

He panicked. "I did what you asked. You can't leave me here."

"Watch me." Chase started up the stairs and felt the man hurry forward. With one swift swing he turned his gun to hit him upside the head, sending the man staggering down to the floor.

"I can tell you who gave the orders. I know who hired us. They intend to do your government harm," he begged. "I can help you find them before they continue the killing."

Chase paused half way up the steps. "First tell me who planned this?"

"Your government man." He edged back up the steps; both hands gripped the hand rail for support. "And someone more powerful."

"Who?" Chase let the Egyptian walk up a few more steps.

"When I get out. The explosives will go off soon. We must hurry."

Chase nodded then shoved him up the steps before catching up with the other three.

Carter yelled. "Let's go." He waved as a flash of lightning lit up the night behind him.

In that instant the Egyptian darted for the side of the room and grabbed one of the guns taken off the dead mercenaries earlier in the evening. He aimed it at the three and laughed. In the next instant he pulled the trigger and Jake fell. Tessa's scream smothered beneath the rumble of thunder that shook the building. His weight pulled her to the floor.

Zoric swung his Uzi around, but not before the Egyptian fired three more shots into Chase's chest. The team leader dropped to his knees as Zoric turned and emptied his weapon into the Egyptian. The Serbian started to reach for Chase, but was waved off.

"Get her out!" He panted like a man that had run a race. "Now. I'll take care of Jake."

Tessa jumped to her feet. "No. I won't leave you. Zoric do something." She reached for Chase who put his hand on his heart. The last bolt of lightning had snuffed out any electricity available for the building. He looked at his hand to check for blood but fell to a sitting position without determining how long he had to live.

~~~

Dropping his weapon Zoric jerked her around to face him then threw her over his shoulder like a sack of flour. She tried to escape but he began to run for the door where Carter kept yelling "Hurry."

Just as Zoric ran through the door Carter took a step inside. He knew he had to try and reach Chase. Another bolt of lightning hit the building, sending sparks through the windows. They fell to the floor and ignited the gasoline sending up a wall of fire. Throwing up an arm against the sudden flash of light, he felt a hand grab him by the collar and pull him backwards. It was Sam.

"Are you crazy? You can't go get him!" Sam yelled over the rumble of thunder. He started in again and she wrapped her arms around him in desperation. "No. Carter, it's too late. I can't lose you too." He pushed free and turned to see the main floor ablaze. Sam hooked her arm through his and pulled with all the force she could muster. "This is going to blow. Pull yourself together."

Carter nodded and started to run with his hand tightly on Sam's arm. The rain started dumping on them as they reached the director and the others who made it out safely.

~~~

Tessa eased off Zoric's shoulder and started forward only to be slammed down to the ground when an explosion made everyone duck and cover. She staggered back to her feet and into Zoric's embrace as tears flooded down her face. Her screams fell silent above the sound of breaking class and finally another explosion that caved in the front part of the building.

Watching the destruction swallow the Enigma team leader, Director Clark's face twisted in rage. The others came up to stand as helpless onlookers. It wasn't a feeling they were accustomed to. Somewhere in the distance a siren faded in and out as the thunder storms rolled over the burning building.

Only Tessa openly wept. Her body convulsed with grief for an uncle who had always been a part of her life and a heart that burst for a love that would never be discovered.

CHAPTER 29

The three men stood silent, waiting for the sound of cleansing. When the explosion rattled the door, the Speaker of the House smiled before exhaling. He nodded toward the door for his mercenary to lead them out as he pocketed the cell phone which sent the signal to detonate the explosives.

Amon shook his head in disgust as the speaker showed no remorse for leaving American citizens to either be burned to a crisp or smashed to unrecognizable pieces by fallen beams, bricks and concrete that rained down upon them. The thought of his own men being left behind would haunt him forever. He should have known the speaker wouldn't let anyone survive the tale of deception.

"And Americans call us monsters." Amon's voice sounded bewildered. "You should never have told the old warriors you were working with us. They could have escaped."

"What's done is done." The speaker pulled his collar up closer to his face.

He'd taken the windbreaker from Tessa when Amon's men took her away. Running a finger over her bare shoulder, the speaker regretted for a moment having to destroy such a lovely creature. Then she'd spit on him like a rabid dog and hurled insults that reflected poorly on his mother.

When he insisted the man holding her take advantage of the situation, she refocused her attention on getting free. It only managed to inflame an already interested jailor. Her uncle succeeded in jerking free and landing a few punches only to receive a beating of his own. Seeing Wakefield shoved down the stairs gave him a feeling of dusting his hands of a dirty problem. Unfortunately Amon intervened on Mrs. Scott's behalf and ordered the men to return to their duties after securing their prisoners.

"I want nothing more to do with this." Amon pushed past both the speaker and his mercenary and got behind the wheel of the car. "All hell is going to come down on my people if there is a connection. You didn't follow the plan and now I am vulnerable."

The speaker fastened his seatbelt as his man shut the car door and got in the backseat. He sighed. "Things change. You can still be the hero in this. Drop my friend off at Union Station."

Amon shifted his eyes to the rearview mirror to look at the dangerous man in the backseat. His words were of no comfort. "I can find my way to the airport. My plane doesn't leave for Mexico City until late afternoon."

The Egyptian continued to stare into the mirror and thought his passenger resembled Satan. A nod to him was given before he started the car. "And how could this possibly be good for me?"

The car moved out and accelerated. "Simple. Drop me off a block from the FBI and I'll walk in."

"And be picked up on all the cameras? No thank you."

"Then you pick a spot and my friend will leave me his burner phone. I'll call in. When I'm picked up, I'll tell them the kidnapper wore a Star of David. That will get them buzzing. Ditch the car and go wherever you planned to go in the first place. Egypt will still be in the clear and I'll still make good on my promise to continue funding your corrupt government."

"And the evidence?"

"Exploded or incinerated. If help was on the way they were too late. Maybe we managed to take a few of those Secret Service bozos out if they made it inside."

Amon frowned over at the speaker as he sped through a blinking red light. "Those 'bozos' laid down their life for you every day."

"Don't get all touchy feely, Amon. If I remember right, you had one of them killed across the street from my house."

~~~

The flames engulfed what was left of the warehouse. The rain did little to quench its thirst for destruction. The wind fanned flames to an adjoining building as first responders began arriving. Distant rumbles of thunder went unnoticed as the Enigma team stood looking into the darkness. Tessa let Zoric pull her body against his and circled her waist as if he were afraid she'd escape and head toward the flames. They all stood with an almost robotic stance.

The Liberty crew shook their head in disbelief, knowing one of their own perished in hopes of saving them. Their shoulders slumped and they found they needed to lean on each other for support.

Even the surviving Egyptians looked on in horror. The realization they might have ended up on the bottom of a concrete pile if the Americans had not arrived, brought home they had been duped. They also knew that the rest of their days would now be spent in some place called Guantanamo.

Smoke swirled toward the survivors as search lights flooded the exterior of the wreckage. The smell of a burnt disaster made several of the team cover their faces, but their bodies stayed ridged with anticipation.

Director Clark jumped forward as his hand went to his ear.

Enigma eyes turned to him in confusion.

The director's eyes squinted as he stepped forward again. This time several others touched their earwigs.

Tessa felt Zoric push her aside as he ran forward. Then the others started toward the flames.

She ran after them, not knowing the sudden emergency, but only that she must follow.

Figures appeared like ghostly aberrations, staggering through the smoke. A man cradled another body in his arms. His uneven steps continued from around the side of a wall that looked like an accordion fan. Tessa recognized the spot where she'd been dragged from a car. Her legs picked up speed and without knowing why, she started screaming his name.

"Chase! Chase!"

He carried her uncle like a baby even though he was wounded. He managed to clear the danger area by the time Enigma reached him. Tessa's uncle was taken from Chase's arms and she somehow knew paramedics would look after him. Zoric tried to grab his friend but Chase reached out to Tessa.

"Chase." She caught him in her arms as he fell to the ground pulling her down with him. His chest, covered in blood, spoke of no tomorrows. "Oh Chase. Open your eyes. Open your eyes." The nightmare she'd dreamed each night unfolded into reality.

With great effort he opened his badly swollen eyes. His twisted nose and soot covered face exposed blood trickling at the corner of his mouth. Lifting his hand his fingers touched Tessa's face.

"Closer."

"Don't you dare leave me, Chase. Don't you dare. Do you hear me?"

"I need to tell you how I..." he licked his lips. "I feel." He closed his eyes.

In the first hint of morning's rays, Tessa thought his lips appeared blue. "You've got to live." She bent down and whispered a promise into his ear. His dark eyes opened as his hand fell to his side. "I..."

Zoric pulled her back so paramedics could reach him. Grim faced, they took his battered body to a waiting ambulance. "We'll go to the hospital as soon as we finish up here, Tessa. Your uncle was badly hurt, but alive."

"How did they survive?" Tessa let Zoric hold her as she laid her head on his shoulder.

Sam and Carter walked up.

"They must have made it out the back where we came in." Sam pointed into the chaos. "Looks like they hid behind some concrete barriers stacked a few feet from the door. Probably saved them." Sam nodded toward the fire. "How's Chase?"

Zoric didn't answer, not really knowing how badly his friend was hurt. He chose to lock eyes with her instead. She turned and strode away with Carter at her heels.

Director Clark fell into giving orders to his team, FBI and Secret Service that had assisted. The Liberty crew went to the hospital for observation while measures were taken to secure the prisoners.

Agent Martin of the FBI put out a notice that the Speaker of the House might make an appearance. He was to be filled in on the condition of the president immediately as well as the vice president. Questioning of the prisoners and Speaker Gault, if he showed up, would take place as soon as possible. They wanted to know who was involved before more mayhem ensued. The quicker they rounded up the terrorists the sooner Wall Street, NATO and NORAD could go back to a boring existence. Knowing now of the speaker's involvement, they wanted to keep their plans close to the vest.

~~~

Montgomery and Cooper watched from their parked car as the dark sedan let out a tall, muscular man at Union Station. Cooper got out and followed.

The next stop was near the capital building. Speaker Jim Gault got out then bent down to say something to the driver. After slamming the door he flipped off whoever drove away before punching in some numbers on the cell phone. The soldier watched him lift a phone to his ear, then look up at the sky streaked with morning light. His tapping foot displayed impatience, not fear.

Montgomery pulled away from his location, determined to find the third man in the car. He'd driven only a mile when an explosion caught his attention. Hitting the brakes he saw the sedan in front of the Smithsonian's American History Museum. Pulling his weapon, he ran to the dark sedan engulfed with flames. He didn't wait. No one could have survived. He backed toward his car at the sound of more sirens. He did not want to be caught in this precarious position. If he was caught on camera he would have some explaining to do.

~~~

Ari drove through the empty streets of Washington D.C. after returning the prime minister to the Israeli Embassy. He had switched cars three times before applying a dark sticky film to the windshield and side windows of the white rental car. The black ski mask barely fit his large head. The leather gloves were hot as was the black turtleneck tee shirt that covered his chest.

He'd covered the plates with a car dealer's decal. For good

measure he fixed a bumper sticker to both sides on the car. One read *If it can't be grown it has to be mined.* The second had a coiled snake and the slogan *Don't Tread on Me.* He didn't really understand the significance nor did he care. With the added touch of an American flag on the back window and some cartoon character kneeling at the Jesus cross, Ari felt confident that if any cameras were still working, the farce would be enough to conceal his identity.

The car pulled into the underground parking lot of the Air and Space Museum. There was a great deal of standing water preventing him from going down. Ari came to a stop and let the car idle. The passenger door swung open and a man jumped inside panting. With a quick look into the rearview mirror, Ari backed out of the garage as if he'd taken a wrong turn.

"Are you Ari?"

Ari turned his covered head toward his passenger. "Do not speak to me."

"You think you are better than me because you are Israeli?"

The acceleration of the car suddenly stopped, throwing the passenger forward against the dashboard. "I am better because you are Egyptian, Amon. Keep your mouth shut and do what I tell you. I thought throwing you into the Potomac River was a much better idea than this. But I suppose holding you under in the Jordon River will be just as good. Imagine dying in the land of the Israelis, Amon."

Amon fastened his seatbelt and stared out the windshield for the rest of the trip.

~~~

"You are insane bringing that Egyptian here." David handed the prime minister a cup of coffee. He was the only person who could survive such an insult.

The prime minister shrugged. "What is the saying? 'Keep your friends close and your enemies closer?' I am but following that advice. Besides we are guaranteed he gets out of the country this way. He flies home on our aircraft, then we smuggle him across the border. Simple."

"Nothing is simple about this. Amon was playing both sides.

When it blew up in his face he tucked his yellow tail and claimed to be trying to get us information." David snorted in disgust.

"Yes. That is regrettable. We were not able to protect the president after all. Jake Wakefield tried but failed. At least the Liberty crew survived."

"And they will get their fifteen minutes of fame shaming Israel for what we did decades ago."

Gilad Levi took a gulp of coffee and smiled. "Very true. But the real story is who tried to kill the president. The news media will salivate over that one for weeks. No one cares about these Liberty men. It will be a ninety second flash in the pan on the news networks and then back to the hunt for the vice president's wife murderer. That's a much more interesting story. Americans love drama." The prime minister frowned. "I rather liked her. She was a good woman. Her killer needs to be punished."

"When?" David refilled the prime minister's cup.

"Soon."

"And Amon?"

"I owed him a debt."

David leaned against the buffet and looked up at the ceiling before rubbing his eyes in frustration. "Yes. But he will continue to taunt you about his sister and the child she bore you. If she had not died in childbirth do you think she would have given you the baby?"

Gilad waved him off. "We shall never know. As long as I have breath, my son will be protected. Amon's days are numbered."

~~~

Tessa looked in on her uncle. Doctors said he would make a full recovery. His shoulder sustained a serious gunshot wound. The broken arm would enable him to predict the weather in the future. He slept soundly as she placed a kiss on his forehead, satisfied he would heal.

The Director of Enigma wanted her to hold off on contacting her parents about the events landing him in the hospital. Dr. Wu suggested she needed time to process a story to feed everyone before running into press and friends. The director agreed and delivered a severe warning to Tessa if she did not comply. He had already made sure her two friends from home were being fed a line of misinformation concerning her whereabouts to keep them satisfied as to her whereabouts.

Tessa's husband was not as easily swayed. With numerous frantic calls and threats to go to the police, the director stood by while she called home to reassure him she was more than okay.

"Chase was awake earlier, Mrs. Scott." Dr. Wu walked her toward his room. His calm demeanor reminded her of a thoughtful Buddhist monk. It was only the pistol bump under his loose Asian style jacket that kept her from running down the hall like a silly school girl. "Do not stay long. You have a lot to do at Enigma. I will wait outside the room until you have finished. I too, must speak to the captain."

Nodding, she pushed the door open to Chase's room. Propped up against several pillows he appeared to be sleeping. Except for a sheet half draped across his abdomen he was bare chested. There was a bandage over his nose and left eye. A saline drip was attached to his arm and for the first time, Tessa could easily see the tattoo on his right arm. She needed to remember to ask him what the Chinese characters meant, but decided she'd copy them and find out for herself.

She couldn't help but watch him. He was beautiful; dark skin, taunt muscles and angular features that spoke of his Cherokee heritage. Although his black hair was cut short, she wondered what it would feel like beneath her fingertips. Would it be as coarse as his manner or would it be soft like the way he sometimes looked at her?

The dim lights drew her to stand next to him. The realization Chase was alive and would live to fight another day made her hand fly to her throat to stop a sob. Looking down at his chest she reached out to touch several long scars, then stopped. There were no fresh gunshot wounds. Why had he been covered in blood? She started to snatch her hand back when Chase reached out and grabbed her wrist and jerked her forward.

Tessa caught her breath as he forced her closer. "Where are your wounds?" She was pulled over his chest now.

Chase cleared his throat. His voice was hoarse. "Disappointed?" Even having been close to death did not seem to vanquish that wolfish grin that now played at the corners of his mouth.

"You were covered in blood. I saw that man shoot you more than once." There was no keeping the confusion from her voice. He released her wrist forcing her cool hands against his skin.

~~~

He sucked in his breath at her touch. "Damn, woman. Your hands are like ice." When she started to step away he took her hand and gently tugged her back. "I had on a bullet proof vest." He chuckled. "Did you think I was some kind of superhero?" Tessa's eyes began a rapid blink indicating she was slipping into panic mode. "Your uncle was bleeding badly. Anyway, those shots hurt like hell. Took the wind right out of me. I planned to get your uncle and follow you out. The lightning had other plans. I went out the back and took cover. Some debris hit us knocking me out. When I rallied I... Well you know the rest."

There was no sense in stating the obvious. Besides, the way Tessa was looking at him made his chest hurt in a different way. Those blue eyes of hers swallowed any attempt at hiding his feelings. He met her gaze and dared touch her tosseled hair. She needed a shower and some clean clothes. Someone had given her an oversized FBI jacket and she'd zipped it to the top. In his head Chase somehow remembered how she'd looked in the black dress. He imagined her a goddess, toying with any self-respect at hiding his feelings.

"Thank you for saving Uncle Jake," she whispered laying her hand on top of his.

Chase could feel his body stirring and knew he was going to make an ass out of himself if he didn't take charge of the situation. "I'm not sure I want that old hillbilly in my debt." Tessa started to smile. "You on the other hand made me a promise, as I remember."

Tessa stood up so straight it looked like a broom stick had been shoved down her back. Her lips parted, but words froze on her tongue. Chase could feel her hand trying to free itself so he tightened his grip.

"Promise?"

Chase arched an eyebrow and narrowed his almond shaped

eyes. "When you thought I was dying. You bent down and said…"

"I know what I said," she stuttered. "I'm not sure what you heard but…"

Chase rolled his eyes upward in disbelief, feeling her fingers trying to slip away. "Let me think." He dropped his amused look back to her. "Something about if I'd just stay alive you would…"

Dr. Wu walked in the room. "Mrs. Scott, there's a car waiting for you. The director wants you back at Enigma." His eyes went to Chase's hand holding Tessa's. She managed to jerk away and hurried to the door. Dr. Wu stared at the rosy blush creeping up her face. The doctor watched her leave the room before turning his eyes back to Chase. "Problem?"

Chase burst out laughing causing a confused look to appear on the doctor's face. "You might say that. A problem I have every intention of solving."

CHAPTER 30

President Buck Austin smiled when his wife kissed him on the cheek. He was pale, but his heart beat strong. He finally told the Secret Service if his wife didn't stop fussing over him he was going to insist they remove her. When she leveled a dangerous glare at them, they held up their hands and admitted he was safer with her at his bedside.

The team of doctors led by Dr. Kelley had successfully removed one bullet, but decided the one near his neck would have to stay. He admitted the thought of a souvenir of his ordeal made him feel not only invincible, but lucky as hell. Although weak, his spirits were high and his temperament normal. His children were kept home from school just in case the threat against the first family was ongoing and not allowed at Walter Reed Hospital.

When Vice President McCall arrived at the president's bedside, Mrs. Austin hugged him and started crying. She and Peggy were friends. They shared a partnership with their husbands that few women could understand or accept. At least they had each other in times of loneliness and fear. Now her friend was gone. She tried to comfort the vice president, knowing that it was useless. It wasn't until the Prime Minister of Israel appeared that Mrs. Austin took her leave.

The three leaders remained silent as the Secret Service left them alone. The sound of the machines monitoring the president's vital signs and distant sirens on the street below filled the room. Gilad put his hand on the vice president's back and shook his head.

A loss for words was new to him. The vice president nodded a grateful acceptance of the gesture before turning to the president.

"Is it true Jim Gault was behind all of this?"

The president nodded then shifted his eyes to Gilad to continue the story. "My informant told me weeks ago about someone in your government making a power play. I immediately informed the president. The investigation indicated the crew of the USS Liberty might be involved."

"The Liberty? Wasn't that the ship you guys tried to sink in '67?" The vice president's tone was far from friendly.

"Yes. But these men were being set up. Israel was to be made the scapegoat as well. The speaker threw in with an Egyptian terrorist group everyone thought dead years ago. He promised if they'd help him become president then he'd make sure Egypt never lost any of the gravy money you send them every year. With Israel looking like the culprits in the assassination attempts, our funding would be cut off. The USS Liberty hearings set the stage to expose Israel of our shameful behavior in 1967. The president and I decided to go forward with the hearings, admit wrong doing once and for all."

The president fidgeted and tried to push himself up. Gilad reached down and raised the bed for him. "Those men will get their medals. The hell with the hearings. We're doing it this week before Gilad goes back to Israel."

"But Mr. President..." Gilad started.

"I've decided." His snappy tone made the prime minister smile. "You must be feeling better considering your temper is showing."

"Now what about that snake in congress?" The snarl on the president's face was evidence he wanted to get down to business.

"Do you plan to use the Liberty crew as witnesses?" It was the vice president.

The president shook his head. "They've suffered enough and so has this great country. Gault doesn't even know they're still alive."

Gilad cleared his throat. "We don't have much time, Buck." He lapsed into being familiar. He sounded almost friendly. "What do you want to do?"

The president looked at his vice president and saw a mixture of suffering, loss and fury. "Give the 'go ahead,' Gilad. Don't screw it up."

The prime minister nodded and took out his phone. "Your NSA still trying to tap into my cell?"

"Humph." The president took the glass of water his vice president handed him. "You're paranoid, Gilad."

Gilad punched one button on his phone. "I'm Israeli. Being paranoid is in our DNA. That's why we've survived." Lifting the cell phone to his ear, he spoke into the mouth piece. "Do it."

~~~

Jim Gault surveyed the destruction left by the hurricane as a new Secret Service agent drove him home. Several side streets were completely closed off because of debris left by flooding. The smell of sewage and garbage couldn't be escaped as they sped through the D.C. area. He gave the driver several curt directives on how to drive and the best way to get him safely home.

He was anxious to get a hot shower. The FBI made it a point to bring the speaker a plate of hot food and coffee after he'd arrived at their headquarters. With a smug smile, he remembered the treatment he'd received; like a lost prince now found. *Do you need anything, Mr. Speaker? Are you hurt, Mr. Speaker? This chair is more comfortable. Let me do that for you, sir.*

The head of the Secret Service was present during his brief questioning. He finally complained he was just too tired to continue and wanted to return home for a few hours of rest. They complied without objection. Why would they? The blame game was in full swing and he preferred to just let them duke it out in private.

The speaker spoke harshly to Corbin Watts, head of the Secret Service about his incompetence to protect him and the president, not to mention the vice president's lovely wife, Peggy. He was going to demand an investigation ASAP. In the meantime he'd better be thinking about what kind of career move would be appropriate. He suggested dog catcher.

Now he was nearly back where he started twenty four hours ago. Things didn't go as planned, but at least the media would be trying to get his story. That could be a good thing if he played his cards right.

"Who is that outside my door?" The speaker leaned forward as the car pulled to the curb. "Another new guy?"

"Yes, Sir."

"Good. Hopefully these agents won't be the screw ups the last ones were." The driver nodded grimly. "I'll need the car around four this afternoon. Swing back then. In the meantime stay across the street."

"I think we should post at your back door and front, Sir. You've had a close call." The agent was firm.

"Yes, I have, thanks to your inept agency. That will be fine," he snorted, opening the door as another agent appeared to escort him up the steps of his Brownstone. "Park the car then stand at the backdoor."

"Thank you. I'll only be a minute." The driver pulled away from the curb and disappeared into a garage across the street.

"Mr. Speaker, you have a guest inside."

The speaker froze thinking of several possibilities, none of which gave him comfort. "Who?"

"The young woman you met several times earlier in the week. We checked her out and she was on your list of approved visitors. Would you prefer I removed her?" The agent opened the door with ease.

The speaker frowned and breezed in before shutting the door with his foot in the agent's face. He threw the FBI raincoat on the foyer chair as the grandfather clock in the living room struck eleven.

What a morning, he thought as his eyes looked around his home. *I should be in the White House, not this house painted white.* He heard light footsteps on the stairs as his eyes darted up with nervous anticipation.

"Carmen." His eyes slid down her body remembering how flawless her body had been beneath his fingertips. She was dressed in her flight attendant uniform. It reminded him of the first night they spent together. They made a game of removing every stitch until she'd done the same to him. "Carmen," he sighed as his hand went out and touched her short bouncy hair that seemed to shine even in the dim light.

"Jimmy, I was worried. I heard you had been kidnapped. Are

you all right?" She leaned in to kiss him tenderly on the mouth and made it a point to press her breasts against him. "Let me make you a drink before I leave. I have a flight to catch soon."

"Yes, that would be just what the doctor ordered. And I'm fine. I'll tell you all about it when you come back."

Carmen kissed him again and moved into the kitchen. "Go in there and sit down. You know how I love to serve you." She smiled with wickedness.

The speaker removed the zipped up jacket of his sweat suit he'd worn since the day before. He sniffed it and frowned as he sat down and put one leg up on the sofa. The decision to throw it away would rid him of evidence connected to the failed plan. He didn't like to fail. And he certainly didn't like to be reminded of it.

"Here you go." Carmen brought him a glass of ice and a bottle of bourbon. "It's so sticky outside I thought you might like to chill this a bit." He nodded as she began to pour. "Aren't you joining me?"

She laughed lightly. "Another time. The airline frowns on us drinking before a shift." She stretched out her hand with the drink.

The speaker took it and held it in midair as Carmen leaned over and ran her fingers through his tinted hair. "Drink up, Jimmy." She reached up and unbuttoned the first few buttons on her blouse then paused. That was all the encouragement the speaker needed to take a large gulp. One more button and one more gulp. Then he drained the glass.

Carmen smiled again, but the sweet, coy expression vanished. In its place appeared a cold hard sneer. "Thank you, Mr. Speaker."

The speaker realized something was wrong. His heart beat faster and his left arm had a burning pain. He tried to speak and reached for Carmen to help him, but she took a step back. His terrified eyes began searching the room for help.

Nonchalantly she buttoned her blouse as she walked to a mirror hanging on a wall over an oriental chest. She fussed with her hair then pulled at her uniform to make it perfect. Turning back around when she heard a sound like a croak come from the speaker, she moved to his side like a spoiled feline.

"Oh, I'm sorry, Mr. Speaker. I guess I should explain. I'm not just a flight attendant." A look of both bewilderment and realization flooded the speaker's eyes. "You see I work for

Mossad. It wasn't a good idea to screw with the Israelis." She patted him on top of the head. "Or with me." She lifted his other leg onto the couch. "Just relax. This won't take long. The longer you fight it, the longer you'll suffer. You know, like how you made those Liberty men suffer." His eyes went wide. "And the president, of course. He isn't real happy with you right now." Carmen walked out into the foyer and picked up her umbrella. She waved to him and smiled. "I'd like to say it's been a pleasure, but frankly, Mr. Speaker you're really a lousy lover."

Carmen walked casually down the steps where a Secret Service agent waited. "Everything okay in there?"

"Sleeping like a baby." She smiled and looked up at the parting clouds. "It's going to get hot again."

The agent nodded. "Want me to call a cab for you?"

"I think I'll walk for a while. There's always a few cabs a couple of blocks away. If not I'll take the bus. I heard the subway is down."

He handed her a card. "If you need anything let me know." The agent smiled. "My boss sends his regards."

Carmen looked down at the card then winked at the agent. "Hmm," she purred. "I appreciate that. I'll pass it along to my boss."

CHAPTER 31

Two days later Tessa waved to her friends pulling away from the curb in a cab. They were skeptical at first about her being near the president during the fire fight. It wasn't until Montgomery and Cooper verified her involvement they started acting like she was some kind of celebrity. The full story would never be revealed to them. The two military men continued to show up at every opportunity to keep the two women off balance giving them their undivided attention. Flowers, dinner and other romantic gestures kept the two women from asking too many questions. The two soldiers stood with Tessa as the women waved goodbye.

"You know they expect you to continue to be in their lives, right?" Tessa walked toward the entrance of the W Hotel where her things had been moved.

Montgomery grinned and elbowed his friend. "They were a nice diversion. I think we can swing that, Tessa."

Cooper remained quiet as he opened the door for her. She wasn't sure if he had ever forgiven her for landing him in the hospital a year earlier. He continued to be polite, although he rarely made eye contact. Tessa nodded a thank you as she entered.

As of yet there were no cameras or media blitz around her. No one knew that she had given the president a life-saving transfusion. The president's advisors were still trying to put the best possible spin on the tragic events. Careful not to reveal too much information, world markets remained steady after Wall Street opened again. The confidence of the American people in their government remained unchanged, and the president's approval rating sored.

Tessa wanted nothing to do with being the center of attention. She felt as if her life had already taken an unexpected turn since the president personally asked her to join Enigma. She wasn't sure why they wanted her or if it was just a gesture of thanks. Standing in the shadows, while others took the credit for the good, bad, and ugly of national security, appeared to be easier than having the press and congress scrutinize everything you did.

The temptation to accept grew stronger than the consequences of continuing to live an uneventful life. A few days ago she thought "boring" sounded better than national security. The president made her an offer that would be difficult to refuse.

Captain Hunter's two dedicated soldiers walked Tessa to her suite and did a security check. Leaving her in the care of a uniformed officer outside the door, felt like overkill. She was to meet with Director Clark over brunch and discuss the future. Her uncle's release scheduled for later in the day meant a trip to the hospital in order to take him to his hotel. The other USS Liberty crew members waited for him there while they recuperated from their ordeal. In the meantime Tessa curled up on her sofa to read the papers and catch up on the latest news.

She tried to feel guilty at making calls to Robert when she knew he couldn't answer the phone. Having been gone for nearly a week, he would be at his wits end taking care of the house and kids. Thankfully, she'd hired a sitter before the trip to fill in when necessary.

Now what would she do about the children? They were everything to her. Not even the president could take that connection away from her. She'd stand her ground on the issue of being an attentive mom. If her babies weren't taken care of then Enigma would be looking for a new agent.

All her fears were addressed later with her new boss. The director of Enigma was cordial and reassured Tessa anything she needed would be at her disposal. There was a very grateful president in her debt.

"I would think that a woman of faith, like yourself, would believe that all would be planned out for you." He sounded a little flippant.

Tessa smiled sweetly and retorted quickly. "I just wasn't sure how God was going to handle you, Director Clark." She took pleasure in watching his fake smile fade. "To change the subject," she paused and leaned in closer, "has there been an autopsy on Speaker Gault?"

The director swallowed his bite of sausage and nodded. "Massive heart attack, it seems." He looked at the rest of the sausage with concern and laid his fork down.

Tessa met his narrowing eyes as he chewed. "All good things come to those who wait."

"Amen, Sister." He surprised Tessa with a sudden chuckle as he dabbed his mouth. "I've taken the liberty of contacting your parents about your uncle and his improved condition. They are pleased you'll be here when your uncle receives the Medal of Honor. It's been a long time coming."

Taking a sip of sweet tea she continued. "No hearings?"

"President Austin wants this to be done since it was the springboard for all that has happened. My brother needs to get back to Israel. Rather than stay he's made a video to be played at the presentation."

"And has there been any information as to Amon's whereabouts?" Tessa waved the waiter off when he tried to refill her glass.

The director forked some eggs into his mouth, chewed and swallowed before answering. "No. Nothing. I have my suspicions, but my brother has refused to receive me at the embassy. He even refused to see Samantha Cordova. Strange since he has become quite fond of her."

"Do you think he knows where Amon is hiding?" Tessa leaned back in her chair and pushed the food around the plate with her fork. She'd barely touched the quiche and salad.

"My brother is capable of many things, Tessa. He may have had dealings with the Egyptians, but he would never do anything to harm the president. Of that I'm sure." He took a sip of his coffee. "He leaves within the hour for the airport."

"I thought he would have stayed for Peggy McCall's funeral."

"The Israeli Ambassador will represent the country. Pressing matters demands my brother back home. Hamas is making threats against Israel again. Gaza is a never ending headache for Israel."

"I would like to have spoken with him again and apologize for my rude behavior the other night."

The director smiled like a patient father. "No need. He took it as some of your spunk showing. I smoothed any misconceptions he may have had. But I will pass your concern and regrets along. You never know, Tessa, there may be another time when the two of you will meet."

Tessa rubbed her arms with a shiver. "Knowing how dangerous your brother can be I might have to pass."

"Indeed."

The director informed Tessa that Secret Service were on their way to her Grass Valley home to pick up Robert and the children for the ceremony the following day. Arrangements were made for them to fly out later in the day.

Tessa panicked. "Good Lord. He will freak when those guys show up."

"Yes. I suspect he will. Perhaps this would be a good time for you to contact him." The director looked at his watch before motioning for the check. "There's a three hour time difference. He hasn't left for work yet." He signed the check and handed it to the waiter. "We've already discussed how your husband is still to be kept in the dark about your connection with Enigma."

Tessa nodded as she took out her phone. "He's never going to let me quit my job at school, Director Clark. He's going to be concerned about the care of our children. He's been made a partner at his firm and works a lot of hours. I'm expected to be…"

"I'm well aware of the demands your husband puts on you, Tessa." He leveled a glare at her. "I will handle all that. You need only to be the sweet, innocent wife and mother he believes you to be." A tempered smile reached his lips at seeing Tessa's eyes widen. "Trust me when I say, your husband will be happy for you to take on new responsibilities by the time I'm finished stroking his ego."

She bristled at his insinuation. "You make him out to be self-absorbed. Nothing could be further from the truth."

"We will see, Tessa. As I said, let me handle Robert. You have nothing to worry about concerning your family. It is the wish of the president that you remain with us and be happy with whatever it takes. Just sit back and let things fall into place."

"But I…"

The director held up his hand to stop her from speaking. "The clock is ticking, Tessa." He touched his ear. "The Secret Service is at your home. Call him." The director stood and walked away without another glance back at her.

~~~

"Yes, Robert, I know they're Secret Service. You're coming to Washington today. I'll give you a list of what the children need. I'll pick up the rest here. It's just for a couple of days." Tessa walked onto the elevator and rolled her eyes up at the ceiling then to the corners and every other spot around her looking for a camera. Was this her life now? Paranoia?

"Yes. Uncle Jake is finally getting his Medal of Honor. I want the children here to witness it. Mom and Dad can't come. Uncle Jake asked the president if you could attend and he gladly granted his request."

She listened patiently as the doors of the elevator opened and she made her way to her suite. A police officer stepped aside as he opened the door for her. His presence meant Amon was still on the run. She nodded a thank you and strolled inside, laying her purse down on the foyer table. Robert sounded excited at the prospects of meeting the president.

"Robert, you need to get busy. Your plane leaves in a few hours. The Secret Service will get you to the airport in Sacramento. I'll see you at dinner. No. I have plenty of room here. Love you too."

Just as she clicked off, her cell phone rang. The new Enigma phone she'd been assigned looked very much like the old one. Chase's picture appeared then faded as he hung up. In seconds a text appeared.

"Will see your tomorrow at the White House ceremony."

Tessa tossed the phone on the sofa. How could he anger her even with a text? She resisted calling him back. The thought of him being conscious enough to remember the promise she'd made in a moment of weakness still managed to turn her face crimson. Why had she done such a thing? For a short time the only idea she could think about was life without the captain. She would have done anything to save him, to give him a reason to live.

Well, he'd lived and remembered her desperate attempt to revive him. The humiliation of that weakness would no doubt plague her the rest of her days.

She knew he'd been released from the hospital, but didn't ask where he'd gone. The members of the team had not contacted her. Only Dr. Wu had checked in on her, making sure she wasn't suffering from post-traumatic stress or some willy-nilly breakdown. He'd come to her suite, ordered some muffins and made tea. He'd stayed for about an hour talking about nothing in particular. Tessa wondered if she gave him any insight to her feelings about Chase by participating in his off the cuff conversation.

To avoid thinking about the captain and his well-being, Tessa focused on her family and realized how much she missed them. Maybe they could take a few extra days to sightsee Washington. They might have to get cheaper accommodations, but it would be worth having the children see so many wonderful things.

But ultimately her thoughts wandered back to Chase. She picked up her phone and stared at it for several minutes, battling a voice inside to be careful. With the press of one button, the phone began to ring.

"Hello." The masculine voice was warm and confident.

~~~

Chase arrived early at the White House. He told himself it was because he needed to be working. But the truth was he was anxious to see Tessa. She'd not returned to his hospital room after he'd teased her about the promise. It still brought a grin to his mouth when he thought about how anxious she'd been for his welfare. He was careful not to bring it up again when she'd called the previous day.

For the first time since they'd met they just talked, about the weather, politics and even the possibility of aliens and Area 51. Their conversation lasted ninety two minutes. It had been friendly, but not personal. Stretching out on the bed, he tried to imagine what she was doing when her soft voice came over the phone. Enigma was never mentioned or her future role there. They treaded on dangerous ground when it came to their relationship. Keep it simple, he thought. But Chase knew he was kidding himself. He wanted complicated, not simple.

He turned to Carter and Sam. "They're here. We'll let the Secret Service escort them up. The president is in his office waiting."

"Should he be up?" Sam looked around the area where guests had begun to arrive.

"Dr. Kelley tried to stop him, but he wanted to give the American public the impression he was good as new."

"Is he?" It was Carter. He too was doing the visual scan.

Chase shrugged. "Here come the Scotts." He nodded at Tessa's family coming through the doors. "I don't want Mr. Scott to take notice of any of us." His eyes went to Sam. "Especially you, Sam. He's not lightly to forget you."

Sam moved out of the immediate view of anyone but the team.

The Scotts entered the White House with wide eyes and excited voices. The boys had grown tall over the last year and looked a great deal like their father. Sean Patrick, although only twelve showed signs of being ready for a growth spurt. His brother Daniel wasn't as husky as he'd been a year earlier. He too would be tall.

Chase's eyes went to the little girl holding Tessa's hand. She bounced happily and asked her mother question after question, which Tessa answered patiently. Her reddish brown hair was much curlier than Tessa's and hung down almost to her waist. Her rosy cheeks and pouty mouth created a carbon copy of her mother. She swished her new taffeta dress around to make the blues waver as she walked. Chase felt his heart lurch again. Was his chest hurting because of the bruises the gunshots left or because a second female had just branded his soul?

Robert was smiling so big Chase wondered if his face would crack. He talked a little too loud to his boys, explaining about the building of the White House and how it once had been set on fire by the British. They listened attentively to him although their eyes strayed to other areas around them. Sean Patrick spotted Chase and stared without smiling. He could feel the young eyes begin an evaluation of him standing in the shadows. He did not step away to avoid scrutiny.

"Mom, who's that?" Sean Patrick stepped from his father who had moved away to inspect a painting and pulled Daniel after him. Tessa straightened and followed the direction where her son nodded.

"Sweetie, I don't know everyone here." With a timid smile Tessa reached out and laid a hand on his shoulder. When did he get so strong, she wondered?

"I will find out!" Heather dropped her mother's hand and ran to Chase, her taffeta dress swishing as she giggled.

"Heather. Stop." But it was too late. Heather ran so fast she couldn't stop herself and crashed into Chase's legs. Robert turned around briefly, but continued talking to his second child.

Tessa walked up to the captain feeling a nervous kind of dread wash over her. Sean Patrick stepped up beside her and reached for his sister's hand which she jerked away.

"Bub wants to know who you are." Heather had always called her oldest brother Bub for brother. "Who are you?"

This time Sean Patrick grabbed her hand and jerked her back. "Sorry, Sir. She's little."

"Am not." Heather tried to twist her hand free, but gave up when Sean Patrick tightened his grip.

Tessa looked up at Chase's face, pleased that the swelling was nearly gone. Even though he wore sunglasses, traces of his black eyes, turned yellow, could still be seen. A narrow white bandage striped across his nose. In a clean suit and tie, Chase looked like any other Secret Service or FBI agent.

"I'm so sorry, agent. They're very curious."

Chase smiled and squatted down eye level for Heather. "I'm Agent Adams." He needed to remember that name in case it ever came up again. "And you are?"

"I'm Heather. This is my bubber. I mean brother!" She pointed to him.

Chase smiled when he saw how embarrassed the young man was at his sister's description. He took her small hand in his and shook it. "Nice to meet you, Miss Heather." He then extended his hand to Sean Patrick and was surprised at his grip. "So what do you think of the White House so far?"

Heather smiled. "Cute place."

Chase laughed and stood up to meet the anxious eyes of Tessa.

She was dressed in a navy suit. The typical unruly hair had been pulled back in a neck ponytail. Unable to resist a full body scan with his eyes behind sunglasses was now possible. Finally he locked onto the area below her ear where he wished he could taste. "Mrs. Scott, nice to see you."

Before she could respond, Heather started pulling on her mother's hand. "Does he carry a gun, Mommy? Sean Patrick says people who work in the White House carry guns."

"It's not nice to interrupt, Heather. The agent was speaking."

Heather pushed out her lip and looked up at Chase. "Sorry, Agent Adams."

Chase had the over powering urge to scoop up the little girl and team up against her mother and brother. "So what have you been doing since your mommy has been gone?"

"I watched some movies."

Sean Patrick squirmed and pulled his sister to his side with a "shush."

Tessa caught the signal and felt her alarm bells go off. "What kind of movies, Heather? Disney?"

Heather shook her curls and smiled her biggest smile. "I'm not sure. I didn't understand most of them. I think about trucks."

"Okay, Heather. Time to go." Sean Patrick tried to pull her away.

"Hold on," Tessa snapped at her son and freed her daughter of his grasp. "Trucks?"

She smiled up at her mother, then Chase. "Yes. I know 'cause they kept saying 'mother truckers. Mother truckers. Mother truckers.'" Sean Patrick slipped his hand over his sister's mouth.

Tessa sucked in her breath with exasperation and glared at her son. Chase started laughing so loud that other members of his team turned to have a look. "Does your father know you watched those kinds of movies?"

Sean Patrick gave her a sheepish look that put guilt squarely on Robert's shoulders.

"We'll talk about this later, Sean. Your father is waving for us. Take your sister." The boy started to open his mouth, but started walking backwards, when his mother growled. "Now, young man."

Tessa turned her eyes back on Chase who clearly found the whole scene amusing. "I'm going to kill him," she said under her breath.

Chase leaned forward and whispered. "I'd be happy to do that for you, Tessa."

When Tessa stepped back and met his covered eyes, she realized the truth in his words. A cold revelation of what Chase was capable of dawned on her. She might have a bad case of hero worship for the captain, but she must never forget that killing for him was no big deal. It was a means to an end. Robert would always be in danger if she didn't keep her feelings in check.

His head turned in the direction of her family. "Nice kids."

She saw the rest of the team come up behind him. "What now?"

"Training." He reached behind him and grabbed Sam by the arm and pulled her a little forward. "Sam, I promised you I'd make things up to you. You're in charge of Tessa's training."

The look of panic paled Tessa.

Sam made a witch-like chuckle deep in her throat. "Thank you, Chase. You won't be sorry."

"No. I refuse." Tessa started to turn away, but felt Sam grab her arm and jerked.

"You somehow think there's free will in Enigma, Cupcake." Sam's voice sounded like she'd gargled gravel. "Lesson number one. No free will."

CHAPTER 32

It would be too late by the time the press core realized the mistake. A cameraman with ties to questionable groups in the Middle East let Amon assume his identity after giving the Israelis the slip. That in itself was a feat worth retelling to sympathetic jihadists if you lived long enough to brag about the event. The thought occurred to him, the escape may have been orchestrated by the Israelis, hoping to shoot him in the process then claiming the success to the American people. The Israelis almost never screwed up a prisoner transfer. But he really didn't have time to ponder the implications.

If he could make it to the press conference and confront the Medal of Honor winners, they would vouch for his innocence. To be captured before that time meant being under lock and key with the FBI. Things happened in captivity. His story needed to get out. There was still time to discredit Gilad Levi and Israel.

Amon looked enough like the cameraman when he pulled a Redskins baseball cap down low over his forehead that no one gave him a second glance. Even though security was extremely tight, he looked familiar and appeared to know where he was going. Even one of the reporters called out to him and made a joke about backing the wrong football team. Amon flipped him off and grinned. It was a normal thing to do.

This could be a dangerous folly, Amon knew. There wasn't time to plan. All Amon wanted to do was tell the truth. The Israelis obviously hadn't finished with him. The thought of serving his enemy sickened him. If he got to the president in time, then his life would mean something. Posing as a cameraman, he might be able to finish what he started.

Inside his hollow camera he carried a small can of pepper mace. Walking through the front doors, he saw Tessa Scott and her family. He'd been allowed to read the paper at the Israeli Embassy so seeing her alive and well was not a shock. After all, this whole ceremony was to honor the very men he'd held prisoner. He also knew Jim Gault was dead and probably at the hands of his own government.

The children started playing tag and laughing, causing the distraction he needed to breeze in and past her family. He couldn't resist cocking his head at Tessa, having been smitten with her blue eyes and blond hair. She showed courage during the ordeal and admired her contempt for the Speaker of the House.

Unaware that Tessa saw his reflection in a mirror long enough for her to turn and stare after him, he walked by her husband who chatted with a congressman from Tennessee.

In those split seconds, Tessa grabbed her children by their collars and shoved them at two of the burly men checking bags and purses of guests. The boys stopped their mischief as large hands took a firm hold. Startled, Heather held onto her big brother, Sean Patrick.

"Get them down," she screamed so loud her voice echoed.

In that second, she was aware of two things; her eyes darted to the shadows where Chase drew his gun and moved forward like a lunging panther.

"Amon." Her voice was astonishingly loud as it echoed in such a grand foyer.

The second thing was the Egyptian turning and grabbing her husband around the neck with his arm. After dropping the camera, he rammed something into Robert's back. It was unclear as to what the object might be, but Tessa imagined the worst.

Robert's eyes bulged when the knowledge of what had occurred hit him. He reached up and grabbed the arm, as if doing so would free him. He made a choking sound.

"Let him go, Amon." It was Chase. His gun was raised with both hands. Other Enigma agents, Secret Service and FBI now were on the scene, guns drawn. Chase stole a glance over at Tessa and saw the children ushered outside.

"I want to speak to the president. Now." Amon looked around him for shooters. They would soon realize he was armed only with pepper mace. "Get him or I'll kill this man."

Desperate words spilled from her lips. "No. Amon. Please," she begged. Later she would realize that Robert looked at her in confusion, trying to piece together those seconds of knowledge that didn't make sense.

Robert tried to jerk free and managed to open about a foot of space. The big man with a gun pulled the trigger and his attacker collapsed to the floor. Staggering toward Tessa, she ran to gather him in her arms. He panted and looked over his shoulder at agents bending down over the dead man.

Still clinging to Tessa, Robert watched as the agent who saved him approached. "Are you all right, Mr. Scott?" Chase tried to sound concerned.

Robert swallowed and nodded. "Yeah. I guess so. Thanks, man. I don't know how I can ever repay you."

Tessa felt Chase's eyes shift to her even though they were still masked by sunglasses. "I'll think of something." To reassure him, Chase patted him on the arm. "I'll have someone take you in another way so the kids won't see this. You better get them. They probably heard the shot."

"Thank you," Tessa whispered. "I owe you." That probably wasn't something she should've admitted considering the promises were stacking up. Chase merely nodded and walked away.

~~~

By the time the Scott family returned home two days later, Tessa was ready to settle down to a normal life again. The anticipation of problems with Robert asking too many questions about how she'd known it was Amon in the White House was explained by telling him his picture had been everywhere in the paper and on the news. It wasn't a lie, just misdirected truth.

Getting his picture taken with the president and lunching with the first family had Robert strutting like a peacock. He planned to frame the pictures and hang them in his office. Knowing a Medal of Honor winner and being a part of the revelation of the truth concerning the USS Liberty made Robert extremely proud. The media buzz concerning the appearance of Amon got him interviewed, but for some reason never aired.

To Tessa's surprise, Robert eagerly embraced the job offer Benjamin Clark presented to her. The director told Robert she would be working on her Ph.D. in geopolitical studies at Sacramento Science and Technology. Her position as a liaison on special projects for the State Department involved some travel, but the director assured Robert there would be help for him at home when needed. The idea that the president took an interest in his wife's educational skills was presented as a result of her uncle's introduction. One thing led to another and Robert said she'd be crazy not to jump at the chance. He remained clueless as to her roll in saving the president's life.

"I saw your salary, Tessa." Robert hugged her, worried she might refuse. "Think of all we could do with that money. Better than the pittance the public school pays you."

"I don't teach for the money, Robert. I teach because I love children and learning."

Robert snorted. "Spoken like a bleeding heart. Take the job. You deserve it."

Tessa sighed. "What about the kids? Who will take care of them when we both are unable to be here?"

Robert dropped their bags in the living room. "I've got that covered. Our new neighbor is nothing short of amazing. The kids love her. I checked her out. She used to be a preschool teacher and is now retired."

Tessa took a peek at her garden out the kitchen window. "I don't know, Robert."

The doorbell rang and excited children stampeded to the door, throwing it open. Tessa and Robert moved to join them and were greeted by a sixty-something woman with red hair streaked heavily with gray. Her delighted laughter filled the Scott home as the children talked all at once trying to tell about their trip. It was obvious how interested she was in their stories. She held a casserole dish between potholders.

"Martha, so good to see you." Robert could smell something delicious. "This is Tessa, definitely my better half. Meet Martha." Robert reached for the potholders and sniffed.

The two women eyed each other with reserve. Martha nodded

and continued to hold a smile. "I've been hearing a lot about you." She followed Robert to the kitchen with Tessa on her heels. "My husband is bringing the salad and bread."

"What about dessert, Miss Martha?" Heather's bird-like voice made the neighbor laugh. "Not tonight, little one. But I'll make some cupcakes tomorrow just for you." Heather started dancing around like a ballerina.

Robert grabbed some plates as he removed the foil from the top of the lasagna. "Finally get to meet the man of the house, huh? It's about time. I think the neighbors were starting to talk about the two of us."

Robert's grin made Martha blush as she waved him off. "Go on."

It was then Tessa noticed the soft accent. "Irish?"

Martha met Tessa's suspicious eyes with her own that sparkled with mischief. "That I am. Married my husband when I was a girl. Not much of the accent left but sometimes I just can't help it." The doorbell rang again. "That would be my better half." She patted Robert on the shoulder and headed to the door. "Come on with ya." She motioned for the whole family to follow her.

When Martha opened the door for her husband to enter, Tessa staggered backwards and covered her mouth to keep the gasp of surprise from escaping.

"Hello, neighbors. I'm Francis Ervin, Martha's husband. Am I in time for dinner?"

Tessa started laughing and realized Benjamin Clark had been correct. She would want for nothing concerning her family. It was hard to resist hugging the professor's neck as he winked at her before carrying the rest of their dinner to the kitchen.

It was late when the Ervins started home. While Robert shooed the children off to bed, Tessa walked across the yard with her new neighbors. Martha took the first step toward reassurance. "It will all be all right, Tessa. Your children are so precious and well behaved. It would give me great joy to help out whenever you need me."

Francis had disappeared into their house, then reappeared holding a small package.

"Thank you, Martha. I'm glad someone like you has moved into my friend's house. It's time we make new memories." She took Martha's hands and squeezed. "This is all too much for me to comprehend." She looked at the professor and pointed a finger. "And you. You're a rascal. Why didn't you tell me?"

Francis handed her the small package. "Orders. The director wasn't sure how things would play out or if you'd fight him on joining us at Enigma. I'm glad we'll be working together, Tessa."

"Was it a lie about you working on a book about the USS Liberty?"

"No. I'm going to meet with all those men who were kidnapped to talk about their stories. Your uncle said they needed a few weeks to absorb everything."

Tessa looked down at the package, but it was so dark outside she couldn't read the return address. "What's this?"

Martha patted her forearm. "It came for you yesterday. I think it's from a mutual friend. Good night, Dear."

Tessa turned off the lights before heading upstairs. After checking on the children and finding them asleep, she went to her bedroom. Closing the door, she laid the package on the dresser. Robert came out of the bathroom bare chested in his boxer shorts.

"I think I'll take a quick shower too." Tessa yawned, feeling the weight of the trip crash down on her. True to her words, the shower took only a few minutes. Teeth brushed and floral scented lotion rubbed into her skin, she entered the bedroom. The only light in the room was the small lamp on Robert's nightstand. He pulled off the black rimmed glasses he'd started wearing and laid them aside to stare at his wife.

"What a trip, huh?" He eyed Tessa moving across the room in her white tee shirt and shorts. It was obvious her body still had a few damp places. "What's in the package?"

Tessa held it up. There was no return address. She pried the end off then carefully reached inside. Something soft touched her fingertips before she pulled out the contents.

"What is it?" Robert started to yawn as she carried the contents to bed.

"Spiderman socks." Tessa sat down on the bed. She fingered them, loving the softness. Without hesitation, Tessa began pulling them on her feet. She extended her legs to give them a look. She smiled, remembering the night she followed a dangerous man into a dark room and the mention of Spiderman socks.

Robert turned out the light. "Didn't know you were a Spiderman fan." He felt Tessa straddle him and run her hands down his chest. He reached out to touch her smooth skin.

Tessa leaned in and whispered. She moaned as his hands caressed her. "I'm going to imagine that you're my hero tonight. No more talking."

ABOUT THE AUTHOR

Tierney has been in education for over thirty years. She recently stopped teaching World Geography for a nearby college to pursue her writing career. Creating a workshop for beginning writers, speaking at schools and serving as an officer in the writing group Sleuths' Ink, are some of the things she does when not writing. With the creation of *Winds of Deception,* Tierney is now working with one of the crew members of USS Liberty in hopes of obtaining the Medal of Honor for him.

Besides serving as a Solar System Ambassador for NASA's Jet Propulsion Lab and attending Space Camp for Educators, Tierney has traveled across the world. From the Great Wall of China to floating the Okavango Delta of Botswana, Africa, she ties her unique experiences into other writing projects such as the action thriller novel, *An Unlikely Hero,* the first in the Enigma Series. *Rooftop Angels* the third in the Enigma series. Living on a Native American reservation and in a mining town for many years fuels the kind of characters she never tires of creating.

Along with teaching and writing, Tierney enjoys family, gardening, reading and music. Other pursuits involve learning Hebrew in hopes of incorporating the knowledge in future volumes of the Enigma Series. She likes to research and sometimes that has involved learning new skills, such as being certified with various weapons.

She has settled in the beautiful Ozarks, but there's never a dull moment in Tierney's life. And that is just the way she likes it.

SNEAK PEEK INTO VOL. III

Find out what happens next in Rooftop Angels. Read the first few pages to see if Tessa and Chase can create a little more chaos.

PROLOGUE

Her husband must have forgotten to activate the security system again when he'd taken the kids to their evening activities. Tessa noticed the lack of blinking lights on the master panel when she'd entered the house through the garage. The well-lit laundry room showed no signs of disturbance, not that you could tell with the mounds of dirty towels, soiled football jerseys and lopsided white shirts that needed a once over with a steam iron.

The door swung open into the kitchen filled with a darkness that felt like mud, heavy and unwanted on the bottom of your best shoes. Even the nightlight next to the stove offered no help. With an awkward search for the light switch, she fumbled with her bag of groceries then dropped her briefcase to the floor. When Tessa found the wall switch and flipped it on she stood with a familiar paralyzing fear she might not be alone. Just like always, she stood still for a few seconds surveying the surroundings.

Robert called her a spook; afraid of her own shadow, of everything and everyone. A week didn't go by without him telling her she needed to lighten up. No matter what, he promised to protect her. But her husband didn't know the secrets she carried.

With the groceries placed on the island, Tessa's eyes went to the night light laying precariously on the edge of the counter, the globe smashed. She pulled open a drawer and slipped a butcher knife out then dropped her hand to her side. The open style kitchen spilled light into the dining room and family area. Timers on table lamps missed their appointed time that should have flooded the room with light.

Knowing she needed to stop and return to the garage to wait for Robert and the kids made much more sense than going inside. What if... Tessa didn't want to think about her family coming home to danger. She swallowed hard as her feet took baby steps. That's when she noticed the time flashing on the microwave. Could there have been a power surge? Tessa smiled, relieved that now there appeared to be a logical explanation for the timers and maybe even the security system failure. That didn't explain the smashed night light, however.

The heavy exhale filled the dining room as she entered with more confidence and bent down to retrieve the timer from the wall socket to reset it. Tessa's body tensed as she touched the timer lying upside down on the wood floors. She'd laid the knife down on the dining room table only a second ago. Now her fingers fumbled nervously in search of it.

As Tessa pulled back her shoulders her eyes once more searched the depths of darkness in her home. Then she saw him. He was near the double windows. An attempt to close the shutters still left a ribbon of light to slip through revealing his large form not more than ten feet from her.

His silence spoke danger before he vaulted toward Tessa. A scream shattered the silent darkness as she tried to back away only to fall against a chair that hadn't been pushed completely under the table. She grabbed it and pulled it out in time to block the intruder's advance then swung the butcher knife at his head. He blocked it with an arm that felt like solid steel. Even though he managed to knock it from her grasp, Tessa felt the fabric rip. The split second she needed to escape forced her toward the stairs.

Inside her night stand rested a loaded revolver. If she could make it there, she'd kill him. Tessa had no qualms about protecting herself or her family. She knew the staircase even in darkness. The knowledge gave her an edge on the danger that stalked her up the staircase.

The beat of her terrified heart grew louder in her ears than the sinister laugh that trailed after her. She felt his hand grab her foot, bringing her down hard onto her knees. The intruder was taken aback when Tessa rotated on her hip and kicked him so hard in the jaw that he fell back against the railing. With a grunt, she scrambled up to the landing and raced to her bedroom.

As she entered, she nervously pushed in the lock button on the door knob. Without waiting to see if her efforts to slam it shut were successful, she rushed to her night stand. She yanked out the drawer as the man kicked open the door. Her hands searched for the holster she'd Velcroed to the upper inside of the drawer.

The sound of his heavy breathing revealed he'd stopped at the door. She wobbled as she pivoted to turn and leveled the revolver at his chest.

"So help me I'll use this." The moonlight spilled through the open windows across her weapon.

The man was easily seen now. He was over six foot. The dark ski mask hid any features she could remember to report later. His body looked muscular covered in black clothing. She could hear his heavy breathing as if he were winded. With a disturbing calmness the man appeared to be considering her threat as he looked around the room then back at the weapon. The moonlight touched his demonic smile that showed itself in the opening of the ski mask. One cautious step forward drew an immediate reaction.

Tessa pulled the trigger, not once but six times. Only clicks. She looked down with horror at her weapon then to the intruder who reached in his pants pocket and took out bullets. He extended his hand to her as if offering a gift before letting them fall through his fingers to the floor. Something resembling amusement escaped his throat.

Without hesitation, Tessa hurled the gun at his head making contact. He stumbled sideways enough for her to charge toward the door in hopes of escape. With an angry howl, the man grabbed her around the waist and dragged her toward the center of the room. He stopped several times when Tessa nearly broke free. Each time his grip grew stronger until he shoved her against a bedpost.

A swift kick to his shin only managed to be rewarded with another shake as he pushed his face in hers. "Stop!" he demanded.

Something snapped inside her brain from autopilot to DEFCON 4. This would not end well if she didn't fight for her life. His size told of brute strength. How would she ever escape? With her fingers, Tessa tried to reach for his eye holes only to feel her hands captured by the man as he pinned her between his body and the edge of the bed. Feeling his rock hard body, the realization her strength was no match for his washed over her when he jerked her into his arms.

The intruder took one hand and touched her long hair before sliding it down her face. She cringed as his fingers, smelling of tobacco and beer, rubbed across her trembling lips. Opening her mouth slightly as if to speak, the man's eyes focused on her tongue. Cocking his head, as if preparing to hear begging or protest, he slipped a finger inside. The unexpected crunch of her teeth sunk deep into his skin. He growled and released her in one step. Once again, the thought of escape surged through quivering limbs as he picked her up with a labored grunt. The bed groaned as her back smacked against the mattress. Tears of panic threatened to blind any hope of escape when she rolled to her knees and scrambled away.

"Stop!" he demanded again.

Vice grip holds with rough hands locked around her ankles before jerking her legs flat against the covers. The springs creaked as she felt him climb onto the bed then swing a leg over her prone body. Before he could apply his weight, Tessa flipped over to her back causing him to almost pause in midair. A sinister smile appeared in the mouth opening of his ski mask. His clothes were intact but there was no mistake of his body wanting her. The pressure against her left no doubt where he was headed. With fierceness, he grabbed her face and forced her to look at him. When she closed her eyes he shook her head.

"Look at me!" He growled like a dog.

Tessa did as she was told. His eyes were black as the night and most likely his soul. Would she need to remember that? He smelled of perspiration now. Maybe if she could get him to touch something besides her the sweat might have traces of DNA. What she did know was that his breath reeked. The black clothes appeared mismatched and void of any significant details. Even the smile revealed crooked teeth, a sign he'd not been given the best of dental care. He sat up and reached down to unbutton her blouse.

"Easy," is all he said. When the last button came loose, he spread open the cotton fabric and eyed her. Just as he extended his hand to touch her neck and begin its descent down her chest, she doubled her fist and landed a blow on his ear.

Stunned, he shook his head and grabbed the side of his head. The growl started again deep in his throat. He pulled back his fist to return the favor when she swallowed her pride then held up her hands in surrender.

"I'm sorry. I'm sorry," she quivered. "Please. Don't hurt me. I'll do whatever you want. Just don't hurt me."

The man stopped as Tessa lifted her hands up over her head to rest on the pillows. Eyeing her, he pushed himself down against her again.

"See. I'll be good. I promise. Just don't hurt me," she begged in small helpless sniffs.

The man leaned forward and captured each of Tessa's hands in his as his chest lowered.

Tessa ran her tongue on the outside of her lips then pretended to bite them. Desire sprang to his eyes. Although forced, her voice became a husky whisper. "Slow. Please." Tessa nodded as he leaned closed to enjoy a first taste. "Yes."

His grip loosened as he began to feel the firmness of Tessa's mouth against his. Caught up in the moment he didn't feel Tessa raise her knees throwing him off balance or notice that her hands jerked down, throwing him into the headboard. Tessa flipped him off her so easily he fell off the bed into the corner of the nightstand, clipping his head on the way to the floor.

Tessa reached for the flashlight on the opposite nightstand and jumped off the bed. She circled around to where the man moaned and struggled to get to his feet. Turning on the light she stuck the beam in his face, blinding him. He raised an arm up to block the light as he staggered to a stand. Tessa swung the foot-long flashlight at his head, but his reflexes were still better than most. He knocked it across the floor.

"Honey, we're home." Her husband Robert and the kids had arrived back from evening activities.

Both Tessa and the intruder looked at the door then at each other.

Pointing at the open window she shoved gently at his chest. "You better go." Her voice turned matter-of-fact. The intruder paused a little too long. "Go. Now. Before it's too late." She walked to the window and held back the sheer curtain.

He turned and bolted toward her. Pushing out the screen with utmost care, he took a moment to look back at her one last time and smiled.

Tessa rushed to flip the light on. The bullets were scattered near the door. She took her foot and pushed them under the dresser as she lifted the gun from the floor. With a nervous jerk, she opened her underwear drawer of the dresser and shoved the gun in the back. The jewelry box, her father had made her on the sixteenth birthday sat perfectly on top. Pulling the drawers out, Tessa dumped the contents across the floor.

"Honey?"

Tessa heard Robert at the top of the stairs. A final look at the staging before she licked her fingers then rubbed them under her eyes to make a trail of eyeliner. Another drop of spit placed on her cheek and she was set to go. When she flung open the door and ran to her husband with a breathless cry of helplessness, Tessa wondered if God might be frowning at her. "Oh, Robert!"

He pushed her at arm's length noticing the muddled appearance. "What is it?" His tone now revealed concern.

"A burglar!" Tessa tried to catch her breath as she felt Robert pull her back in his arms.

"Are you hurt?" He pushed her back again looking at her blouse.

Tessa shook her head. "No. I was changing in the bathroom when I heard him. I locked myself inside. When I heard you come in I rushed out to warn you. I guess it scared him off. He went out the window. Oh, Robert." Tessa fell against his chest once more to touch up her face with a quick lick on two fingers, then streaked them under her eyes.

"What about the alarm? Didn't it go off?" He watched his two boys and little daughter scamper up the stairs to stop suddenly at seeing their shaken mother.

"It was off when I got home. I guess you forgot again," Tessa lied. If God wasn't frowning he would be now, she reasoned.

Robert looked visibly afraid. "I could have sworn I activated that when we left. I'm so sorry, Tessa. This is my fault." He pulled out his cell phone and dialed 911.

The children hugged their mother, patting her like she did them when they were hurt.

"The police are on their way, Tessa." He kissed her before walking toward the bedroom to take a look around.

313

~~~

The man easily hopped over the fence into the neighbor's yard. He crouched for a minute to make sure no one saw him. Dressed in black, it was doubtful, but he was a cautious man. With the fake teeth removed and shoved inside his jacket, the man proceeded to move to the back door of the modern style house, so unlike the one he'd just invaded.

He already knew where the spare key was hidden. The old couple who lived here were predictable; under the doormat, like so many other people in the neighborhood. The woman next door had been different. It had taken him thirty minutes to find it. The security system needed to be updated so he merely pulled the outside wires to disconnect it. Rather than pay a few dollars more a month to get a wireless system they were left vulnerable to someone like him.

The red rotating light of a police car pulled into the drive of the house where he'd just escaped. A smile spread across his face remembering the blue of the woman's eyes, the firmness of her lips and the bite of her teeth. He stuck his wounded finger into his mouth to suck the oozing blood. His body still stirred at remembering how she felt beneath him. If only her husband had not come home...

He peeked through the door panel into a dark kitchen as he turned the key in the lock. Someone was home. Lights filled a distant living room and the sound of the television caught his ear as he moved with the skill of a cat burglar. They started talking with excitement as the two figures appeared and moved to answer the front door. He couldn't understand what they were saying, but he imagined it had to do with the police car next door.

The doorbell rang just as he moved toward the refrigerator. He leaned against it, hoping whoever it was would not want to come in. Too many unexpected surprises in one night for his liking. Not only was he hungry but his body craved a very cold shower.

It was the police. They asked the usual questions; had they seen anyone, heard anything, did they lock their doors, etc. He imagined the officer handing them a card with his information and number in case they thought of something. The door clicked shut and the sound of a dead bolt being thrown made him wonder if the couple might be afraid.

The television became silent and he heard footsteps move toward the kitchen. They spoke in soft voices until they entered the kitchen, flipping on the lights.

They didn't see him at first. But both saw him by the refrigerator at the same time. The man trembled just slightly and the woman gasped as her hand flew to her throat. All three stood looking at each other in silence.

The woman stepped toward him and reached for his ski mask. She was far from gentle as she snatched it off. After tossing it onto the table she shook a crooked finger. "What in goodness name have you done?" Hands dropped to a narrow waist.

He ran his hand across his face before opening the freezer door. He took out a package of frozen peas and laid it across his face where Tessa had managed to make contact.

"Did you hurt Tessa?" she demanded in an Irish accent that always seemed to thicken when irritated. "And what about those babies. Were they home?"

"Do you have any ice cream, Martha?" He looked back in the freezer with unconcern.

"Answer me, Chase Hunter or I'll flog you here and now!"

The old man pulled out a chair and sat down. "You better give us a full account or she will make your life miserable, Chase."

Pulling out the vanilla ice cream Chase frowned as his eyes scanned the label. "Is this all you got?" He tossed the peas back inside before shutting the door. Martha handed him a spoon before walking to the china cabinet to get him a bowl. Before she could complete the task he'd already opened the container and began eating from the box.

"I didn't hurt her. The kids and What's-His-Face were gone or at least until the end of the training session." Chase leaned against the counter and scraped the last bite of ice cream from the bottom of the box. He licked the spoon and met Martha's angry eyes with his. "She's fine. This time she shot me." A half-hearted chuckle slipped out as a drip of ice cream slid down his chin. "Samantha did a heck of a job breaking her in. I guess we're done with that part of the training." He smiled with the spoon clenched between his teeth. "It was just getting interesting too."

Martha grabbed a damp dish towel and snapped it against

Chase's leg making him yelp. "What the hell?"

"Watch your mouth in this house, young man or I'll shoot you myself."

Chase winked at her husband. "Yes, ma'am."

The old man, Francis, pointed a finger at the Enigma team leader. "I've seen how you look at Tessa. She's a happily married woman, Chase. Don't mess that up."

Chase didn't like being told what to do or how to live his life. "I've gotta go. It's getting late." He tossed the empty ice cream box in the trash can and laid the spoon in the sink. He leaned over and kissed the woman on the cheek. "Care if I shower and change before I hit the road. The police might be at the entrance to this happy little subdivision. I don't want to fit any description Tessa gave."

They both nodded and waved him away.

When Chase left the room Francis turned to his wife. "I don't like where this is headed.